Praise for ...

THE MEDICI BOY

"On the basis of Donatello's great statue of David, and against the background of the witchhunt against gay men in 15th-century Florence, John L'Heureux has built a gripping story of love, genius, and betrayal."

JM Coetzee, Booker Prize and Nobel Prize for Literature,
Elizabeth Costello, Waiting for the Barbarians, Disgrace.

A novel bursting with love—collegial, artistic and erotic. John L'Heureux brings to life the bliss and treachery of the Italian Renaissance through prose as passionate as his characters. Deeply enjoyable, THE MEDICI BOY soars like an operatic aria, before breaking our hearts.

David Henry Hwang, playwright, M. Butterfly, Chinglish.

"Intensely appealing, viscerally gripping, and unfailingly human in its characters, L'Heureux's most recent novel beckons with the undeniable promise of great writing to all lovers of historical literary fiction that easily manages to transcend its time parameters."

Booklist, Starred Review

TIGHT WHITE COLLAR

"Close to the bone . . . a moving vision of the torments of spiritual solitude."

The New Republic

THE CLANG BIRDS

"A delicious, rollicking novel."

San Francisco Chronicle

"John L'Heureux has written an exceedingly funny and intelligent novel that is certain to scrape like heavy sandpaper against a good many thin skins."

New York Times Book Review

FAMILY AFFAIRS

"Witty, vital, and perspicacious."

New York Times Book Review

"L'Heureux sits, stodgy as old Chekhov, observing real human beings and putting them on paper, pore by pore. He's a wise writer, with a wisdom as old as the hills."

John Gardner

JESSICA FAYER

"Chilling, cutting alarming offbeat, haunting, strangely touching . . . one of John L'Heureux's finest novels."

The Boston Globe

"A beautifully crafted and deeply moving work."

Joyce Carol Oates

DESIRES

"John L'Heureux's vision is eerie and unmistakably his own. These are oblique, ironic moral fables and they are written in a spare, elegant and witty prose."

The New York Times Book Review

A WOMAN RUN MAD

"L'Heureux is elegant, cunning, and wickedly funny. The reader will feel played with, but it's that kind of novel, a psycho-philosophic thriller— and more."

Washington Post Book World

"One of the most intense reading experiences I've had in recent memory. A WOMAN RUN MAD was impossible to put down."

New York Times Book Review

AN HONORABLE PROFESSION

"Brilliant and complex. Mr. L'Heureux is a deeply ambitious novelist, one who isn't afraid of dealing with dark themes and what it means to *be fully human, especially in the frightening and ecstatic world we create behind the darkened bedroom walls."*

New York Times Book Review

COMEDIANS

"Mr. L'Heureux's stories work on several levels at once: the serious and comic, the realistic and fantastic, the personal and allegorical. They are not stories you have read before, you will want to read a number of them more than once."

Washington Times

"COMEDIANS is a treasure . . . L'Heureux's prose is fascinating and elegantly powerful. It's a strange, witty, sexy book that's both wonderful and impossible . . . impossible to put down."

Cleveland Plain Dealer

THE SHRINE AT ALTAMIRA

"John L'Heureux's fine new novel may not just disturb you but haunt you. Prepare yourself for an ending that's the obverse of catharsis and that also leaves the reader with no hiding place. In plain, unornamented language L'Heureux is writing about sin and redemption."

San Francisco Examiner

"L'Heureux's most ambitious novel . . . Readers will marvel that he has somehow conspired to redeem the unforgivable."

Los Angeles Times Book Review

THE HANDMAID OF DESIRE

"Wickedly entertaining"

New York Times Book Review

"A subtle literary joke that reflects the unique intelligence of a deeply thoughtful, intensely serious man."

Washington Post

HAVING EVERYTHING

"A master of understated, ominous moments in a marriage in which not asking the question can be more disastrous than asking. Sharp, moving, poignant."

Washington Post Book World

"HAVING EVERYTHING is an unforgettable exploration of what it means to become fully human."

Seattle Times

THE MIRACLE

"L'Heureux seems to be standing on the shoulders of giants."

San Francisco Chronicle

"Admirable . . . delicately nuanced . . . L'Heureux has created in THE MIRACLE a set of characters who feel fiercely authentic, not least in their contradictions."

New York Times Book Review

Winner of the gold medal in the Commonwealth Club of California's book awards, 2002.

PRAISE FOR JOHN L'HEUREUX

"A writer who picks up his readers by the scruff of the neck and won't let go."

Chicago Tribune

"A deeply ambitious novelist, one who isn't afraid of dealing with dark themes and what it means to be fully human, especially in the frightening and ecstatic world we create behind the darkened bedroom walls."

New York Times Book Review

"L'Heureux's efforts to weave myth, extremity, and a religious note into modern urban and suburban settings are high risk. The result is powerful and original."

The Los Angeles Times

The Medici Boy

by
John L'Heureux

ASTOR
+BLUE
EDITIONS

THE MEDICI BOY
Astor + Blue Editions

Astor + Blue Editions,
New York, NY 10003
www.astorandblue.com

Publisher's Cataloging-In-Publication Data

L'Huereux, John. THE MEDICI BOY—1st ed.

ISBN: 978-1-938231-50-6 (hard cover)
ISBN: 978-1-938231-49-0 (epdf)
ISBN: 978-1-938231-48-3 (epub)

1. Historical Literary Novel—Fiction 2. Fiction 3. Inspired by the creation of the David by Donatello—Fiction 4. Love Story The illicit love affair between the genius Donatello and his model—Fiction 5. Homo-erotic Love—Fiction 6. 15th century, Italy 7. Florence (Italy) Title

Includes an Afterword by the Author © 2013, bibliography

Book Design: Bookmasters
Jacket Cover Design: Danielle Fiorella

Other Books by John L'Heureux

The author wishes to thank the John Simon Guggenheim Memorial foundation for the generous grant that allowed him to spend a year in Florence researching background for *THE MEDICI BOY* . . . and he particularly thanks André Bernard for his moral support during the writing of this book.

For Joan
only and always

THE MEDICI BOY

1400–1420

CHAPTER 1

I<small>T IS RIGHT</small> and just to confess at the very start that it W<small>AS</small> fornication that took me out of the Order of Friars Minor and set me on the path of sin. I am an old man—perhaps sixty-seven—and make this confession at leisure and in detail since, imprisoned in this monastery, I have nothing left but time. And, to speak truly, I write this for pleasure as well. Having long left behind me the possibilities of lusting and loving, I find satisfaction in watching my quill move across the page. There is no waste; I use the reverse side of paper that has already been ruined by false starts, ink stains, the wanton mistakes of inattentive copyists. On the finer side of this confession, blotted, you will find Holy Scripture, a nice irony. I have myself served as copyist—and do yet—and I know it is easy to err, even in the service of God.

The unwanted son of a rich merchant and his Dalmatian slave girl, I was taken in by a dyer of wool and consigned as a boy to the Fratelli of Saint Francis where I proved a failure as a monk. Later I failed as a painter and still later as a sculptor. From birth I have been a creature of lust and misadventure and I have continued on in the usual way of men who have come to nothing. Thus I have no claim to your attention. I can make none. I presume to write this only because of my long association with two men: the *cattivo* Agnolo Mattei who is burning now in hell, God have mercy, and Donato di Niccolò di Betto Bardi, my master, whom the whole world reveres today as Donatello, the greatest sculptor of our time.

I was born—perhaps—in the year 1400, a time of great portents that the world was ending. It rained blood in Orvieto, there was a plague of frogs in Pisa, in Florence fire was seen in the sky for three nights sequent. It is said that in Paris a two-headed baby was born speaking Latin and Greek, but that of course was harmless folly, and in any case the world continued on as wise and foolish as it had always been. No worker in dyes knows the date of his birth, though everyone remembers the turn of one hundred years, and it is certain many unwanted sons were born in 1400 and so perhaps was I.

My mother, Miryam, was a Dalmatian slave in the house of a rich merchant of Prato, and when it was clear that he had made her pregnant, he married her off—with a persuasive dowry of forty florins and a chest of bed linen—to a wool dyer in the Via dei Tintori. Thus was I born, officially legitimate, to Matteo Franchi and his new wife, Miryam, who two days after my birth died of the Black Pest.

The *pestis atra*, the Black Pest, has marked the most important moments of my life. It was the Black Pest that carried off my mother two days after my birth and it was the Black Pest that released me for a time from the Rule of Father Saint Francis and I used to think—but no longer—that in the end the Black Pest would see me off, swollen and foul smelling, to the silence that never ends. But I cannot repent its ill favors since it was the Black Pest that brought me, hastened on by my sins, to the *bottega* of my lord Donatello.

In TRUTH, I was lucky from the start. Begotten on a slave girl by a rich merchant of Prato, I was—for a goodly fee—born in the house of Matteo Franchi and was greedily sucking at my mother's breast when, with no warning, she came all red with fever. Black buboes appeared beneath her arm and in her groin—they took me from her nipple then—and before the third day of my birthing, she lay dead. I should have died with her but I did not. It was the will of God. I was put to nurse—for a small fee—until Matteo, the dyer of wool, was assured he could keep my mother's dowry. After that, in secret, he placed me on the steps of the foundling hospital with a note and a basket of swaddling cloths and left me there until a year later when the merchant inquired about my well-being. By this time Matteo had found a mistress with a liking for children, and since this Spinetta could not bear children of her own, they took me back. Soon after my return she became pregnant—who knows the mysterious workings of God?—and within ten years she had popped out four babies, all of them sons. Matteo married her after the second.

I grew up playing in the colored muck of the Tintori where the dyers boiled their wool in huge round vats, turning the cloth with long paddles, until the indigo and woad made the raw wool blue, and the dyers' hands burned and their arms took on the colors of the dye: indigo here, and in other vats the red of tomatoes and the deeper red of blood, violet and purple, green and onyx.

At seven, I was of an age to help with the dyeing but I was not tall enough or strong enough to control the long heavy paddle used to stir the vats. It was for this reason that the accident occurred. It was a midsummer day and the sun had long been hot on my back and the weight of the paddle moving among the woolen cloths became too much for me. I lost the paddle in the boiling vat. It was the second time this had happened and the dyer, a little drunk and in much anger, cried out upon me and struck me smartly on the head with his closed fist. I fell from the stirring platform and for a time lost sense of who and where I was, and when I returned to myself I had a great ache in my head. My leg was tingling strangely and I flailed about with my arms and for a while I could not speak. It seemed no great matter, but it was the start of the spells that would return now and again through all my life. These spells were from the devil, the dyer said, and he spoke more truly than he knew.

I was the oldest of the dyer's boys when, two years later, the merchant who begat me on my mother took notice of me. It was again a summer day, I remember, heavy with the hot stink of the dyes and the dead stink of the privies, the sun glinting on the river in the distance, and the hammering of the carpenter who was repairing a breached vat. I knew by then that the merchant was my natural father.

"Who is that one?" he asked.

I was standing on the platform at the boiling vat, pushing the heavy load of wool with my long stick as the madder turned the gray cloth red and the boiling water sloshed at my hands and arms.

"Luca," the dyer said. "He is the oldest. And he's strong and fair." He seemed to forget he beat me soundly whenever he was drunk.

"Is he mine?"

"Sir," he said. "He is like a son to us."

"Can he read? Does he know his numbers?"

I looked up from the vat of boiling wool and said loudly, "I would like to read. I would like to know my numbers."

The merchant laughed at my impudence and said, "Send him to the Friars," and almost as an afterthought, he said, "I'll pay." He looked around, as if this were his family and he was pleased with it.

"How many do you have?" he asked.

"Three," Spinetta said. She was heavy with child. "And now a fourth."

"And Luca," the dyer said. He did not mention that I sometimes had spells. "He is our favorite."

But the merchant wasn't interested or deceived. "The Friars," he said again.

* * *

So it was that I became a student in the Order of Friars Minor. The merchant, I discovered later, would have taken me into his own house, but his wife would not tolerate the idea that the son of a slave girl should be brought up as one of her own. But I was well-favored because of my mother, and my rich father looked kindly on me and did for me what he thought best. To atone for his sin he gave over my life to God.

I was sent to the Brothers of Saint Francis where I could learn to read and write and do numbers and where, in time, I could embrace a life of poverty, chastity, and obedience. Thus freed from all worldly desires, I would atone for his sins and, as it might happen, a great many of my own.

CHAPTER 2

MY WORLDLY DESIRES were simple at the start since there is nothing more simple than reading and numbers. I loved reading the sweet, unbelievable stories of Saint Francis's *Fioretti* and later, with my plodding Latin, I struggled through the *Confessiones* of Saint Augustine and the *Cur Deus Homo?* of Saint Anselm of Canterbury and I developed a certain facility with the abacus. The merchant, who was himself a student of painting, paid for me to be instructed in that art, or rather in the art of drawing with a stylus. Study was great joy to me and work in the fields was a necessary evil since it took me from my books. I learned silence and I learned to love it. But it was drawing that I enjoyed most, especially when it was found I had some skill at it. I was praised, reluctantly, by Father Gerardo, our superior. And then at age twelve I discovered purity of mind and body just in time to lose them.

Attenzione! What men and women do in bed was nothing new to me. Anyone who has grown up in a dyer's cottage with two rooms and five children and a neighborhood latrine knows all the mysteries of the body by the time he is six. By nature and inclination dogs copulate and geese copulate and the dyer and his wife copulate, and do it again and again as their mortal essence spurts from them and they reproduce, and in a brief time grow tired of it all. That was no surprise. What surprised me was desire. This desire was a hard ache in the groin: it was relentless, stinging, a fire in my mind and body. By merely taking thought, sometimes with no thought at all, I would go hard, even at prayer, especially at prayer, and I would kneel straight up, my back stiff, my head bowed, and—engorged and erect—I eased myself against the prie-dieu. I firmed my mind with determination not to spill my seed, not in chapel, not at prayer, and mostly I succeeded. But at night on my straw pallet there was no escape. My hands were quick and deft beneath the covers and I spilled my seed with ease but—I was twelve—with a relief that was only momentary. Once more and yet again, and then at last sleep.

Confession was no help. I told my sins—the kind and number and the frequency—and my confessor shook his head and said again and again that I must promise to be pure with the purity of the angels. I must try. Purity is all. I promised and I tried, but angels are pure spirits unencumbered by this thing between my legs that had a passion and a will of its own, and I was not pure spirit.

This was my life, then, from age twelve to fifteen. Prayer and study and work in the fields all day, and my hands on my engorged *cazzo* in the night. My spells had ceased for a time. No more tingling of the leg, the great pain in my head, the flailing arms. I had grown out of spells and into private sin.

Father Gerardo, our superior, decided I should spend more time drawing. It would occupy my mind, he said, and my hands as well, and thus keep me from sin. This was not a matter of my ability. It was a matter of obedience. And who could tell? Perhaps one day I would paint, he said. Perhaps one day I would study with a master painter and thus bring great credit to our friary in Prato. And so I was assigned to make two murals in the refectory in imitation of those great paintings by Niccolò Gerini in the church of San Piero Forelli. The first was to be his *pietà*—that is, our Lord risen from the tomb with our Lady beside him—and the second, on the opposite wall, Saint Francis with the stigmata. In preparation I sketched a copy of the *pietà* on an oaken panel in a one-to-twenty proportion—a simple mathematical equation—and was surprised that my little copy actually resembled the original. Father Gerardo was more surprised than I and said he had great hopes for the painting and great hopes for my hands. Then I sketched the *pietà* in charcoal on the refectory wall, but after it was well advanced and I had painted in the faces and the hands, Father Gerardo assigned the other postulants to complete the work. He feared lest I commit the sin of pride in considering the painting my own. And so too I proceeded with the mural of Saint Francis receiving the stigmata, except that crouching at Saint Francis's feet where Niccolò Gerini had painted in his patron, I sketched a likeness of the merchant who begat me and turned me over to the Friars. In this way no matter how many postulants completed it, I had made the painting my own. When the merchant saw the mural he recognized himself at once and, flattered, said, "The boy has gifts. Send him to Arrigo di Niccolò. He will teach him much." He added, knowing the friars, "I'll pay." Father Gerardo nodded and smiled but I was not sent to study with Arrigo—*causa superbiae* again—lest I become proud. It was God's will.

By the end of my postulancy year the murals were done—higgledy-piggledy in finish and design—and though I had escaped the sin of pride, I remained unchaste. Despite my prayers, despite fasting and nightly chastisement with the cord and the *catena*, I continued to commit the lonely sin. I told our Father Gerardo I had failed, that I was not meant to be a Brother of Saint Francis. But Father had boundless hope for human nature and great joy in prayer and he said that with God's help and the help of the Virgin Mother I would change and become chaste, because this was God's will and perhaps his mysterious way of keeping me humble.

In this way I became a novice in the Order of Friars Minor.

As novices we lived the true life of the friar. We prayed. We meditated on poverty and chastity and obedience. We learned the rule of Father Saint Francis, and what it means to be a servant of the poor. Chastity and obedience we took for granted, but poverty was the essence of our lives. When it was my turn, I begged from house to house—bread or a coin or whatever charity was offered—for Francis believed that the greatest poverty is to beg for one's bread. "Poverty is having nothing and desiring nothing," he liked to say. "Thus we enjoy all things in the freedom of not possessing them." This was a paradox I found hard to understand at the time and impossible to understand now that I am a prisoner of the Fratelli. But it was all I knew. And I knew it was God's will.

At the end of that year, though still unchaste, I was admitted as a Brother to the Order of Friars Minor, promising for the next three years to live as a monk who is pledged to God by temporary vows until he is admitted to solemn vows: that is, I was offered but not yet accepted.

CHAPTER 3

As the youngest of the new Brothers I was sent on trial to care for the aged and dying at our tiny mission house on the river. The Brothers of Saint Francis always dwell among the poor—they are our mission and our reason for being—and the poor live chock-a-block in mean and dirty streets where the gutter is very often the privy and where grueling labor wears down the body and the soul. Our mission house stood in the poorest section of Prato, near the fulling mill on the Bisenzio River. It was a small house for a small group of Brethren, seven old and dying monks, with myself and Brother Isaac to minister to them. Brother Isaac was nearly eighty. In his late years he had suffered flashes in his brain and then had lost much of his speech, but he continued to cook well and in any case our food was simple.

He prepared the meals and I served them. Father Alfonso, our priest, though he was one of the dying seven, still managed to say Mass and hear confessions and to lead the morning prayers.

It was my office to look after the Brothers. I dressed the ones who could still get out of bed, I fed them and washed them and helped them to the privy. Some were not able to get up, and for them I brought the basin and emptied it each morning and night. The old are a race unto themselves. Their bowels are second only to God and the privy second only to chapel. Indeed, they would sooner miss the chapel than the privy. Our privy was a model of good order, always clean, always efficient. It was built on an ell extending just beyond the riverbank so that, after the office of Prime and before the office of Terce, the Brethren shat into a branch of the gently flowing river. It is true that further downstream the dyers washed their wool but by that time the shit had dissipated and no offense was offered. This green river, the very life of the city, has always been hard used. Once the Brethren were settled for the morning, it was my task to go to market for the fish and game. I bargained with the peasant women over baskets of leeks and beans, with fishmongers for tench or carp or eels, with farmers for cheese and milk and eggs. I bought bread from the baker and meat pies when he had them and, on feast days, a cooked roast pig with a Mary apple in its mouth. Each afternoon I begged for alms. These tasks, plus obligatory prayer, made up my day and, to some extent, controlled my thoughts and desires. But at night, on my cot, I remained Fratello Luca of the busy hands.

Prato is not like Florence. The first business of Florence is money and, after that, rich cloth and fine sculpture, whereas the sole business of Prato is wool. Prato is a merchant city of little houses with foul alleys between them and the noise and smells of a slum ghetto, with not enough air and sunlight and too much of the muck that comes from living close and working hard. There are canals with fulling mills and dyeing sheds leaning into them and the stench of the dyes and sulfur and alum, but there are gardens everywhere and in spring they perfumed the air. The streets are often too narrow for a cart to make its way, and it is easier to get to market on foot than in a cart, which was well for me since our little mission house possessed no cart and no horse or donkey to pull it.

Cutting down back alleys and over canals, I had found a short-cut to market that took me through the tiny *campos* of the decaying Gualdimare quarter directly to the market square. In fact, that is not quite true. This route was not so quick but it was more pleasant since it followed the river where the children played along the banks, and took me past a world of kitchen gardens and backyard privies, and through the Camposino San Paolo where twice—my heart racing at the sight of her—I had seen the whore, Maria Sabina, drawing water at the well. The trip to market was my favorite duty.

It was May, a hot morning after a long spell of rain, and the air smelled freshly of green things growing, of primrose, lavender, tansy, and mint. Telling my beads, my mind wandering, I had passed the river and the kitchen gardens and was crossing through the Cam-posino San Paolo—not everything that happens is the will of God—when I heard a voice and stopped to listen.

"*Eh, Fratello mio!*" It was the low voice of Maria Sabina calling me. I had thought of her often, had summoned her image in the night as I lay on my cot, and now here she was, calling me in her low soft voice. I looked at her. A thin red scar ran from her brow to the corner of her mouth, but she was full-bodied and beautiful nonetheless.

"Signora," I said, and nodded. "Signorina."

She was leaning against the well-head in the Camposino, her black hair loose about her shoulders, and her hands folded modestly at her waist. She was smiling at me. A dirty white cat lay curled up next to the well and two speckled chickens were scratching at the sand near her feet. The scent of mint, thick and honeyed, hung in the air.

"I've seen you passing here before," she said, and paused. I stood still, unable to move. I considered whether the reason I took this shortcut so often was the hope that one day she would stop me and say, "*Eh, fratello mio!*" If so, I was inviting sin. And it is true that at this moment I wanted to lie down with her, there, in the center of the Camposino next to the well. "You are much too pretty to be a Friar," she said. "Yes?"

I could think of no reply and I knew I should leave at once but I stayed there, trapped by my desire. I had never lain with a woman.

"You should come with me." She tipped her head to the right, toward the outside staircase that led up to the second floor. She came close and stood before me. "Don't you talk? I think you would like to talk to me." She looked at my face closely. "You are very handsome, very fair." She put three fingers lightly on my chest. "And you are well made." She let her fingers drift from my chest an inch or two down toward my waist. "Come with me," she said.

"I have no money," I said. "The money I have is for market."

"Come with me," she said, taking my hand.

I followed her up the staircase to a little gallery with three doors. All three had been left ajar, and she turned to smile at me as she pushed open the middle one.

Inside it was dark, with a low ceiling and only one tiny window covered with a wooden shutter. Two narrow cots stood end to end beneath the sloping roof and there was a small table with stools for sitting. I could smell the stale scent of frying oil.

I pointed to the two cots, questioning, and she said, "My sister. She is at the market." She slipped a wooden peg through the latch of the door. "Now," she said, "we are alone, my little Brother, and I will make you very happy."

In seconds she had removed her surcoat and her gown and then her kirtle underdress. She stood there, gloriously naked, her arms open and extended toward me. I was slow about this new business. My scapular lay on the floor already but I was still fumbling with my cowl and hood. I stared at her. She seemed to shimmer in the dim light. Her breasts and her belly and the dark smudge of hair between her legs. She came to me and placed the back of her hand against my thigh. She moved her fingers lightly on the cloth, feeling for my *cazzo*.

It pulsed hard against the gentle pressure and she took her hand away. "Good," she said. She smiled and kissed me softly on the lips. She helped me lift the tunic over my head and then the undertunic and then she laughed. She had not imagined Friars wore undershorts. She tugged at the cord around my waist. It loosened and my undershorts fell away. "*Eccolo, che bello!*" she said. She put her hand around my *cazzo* and led me to her bed.

She lay down on the narrow cot—it was of feathers, not straw— and pulled me to her. And then, suddenly, it was as if I had always known what to do. I felt that I had entered another world where there was no sin, where everything was natural and right. I lay beside her and caressed her breasts. I let my hand explore her body, the tender spot at the base of her throat and the tiny line beneath her breasts and all the hidden places I wanted to seek out for my hands and my tongue. I gave myself up to her, easy, unashamed, and before it was too late, I entered her and expelled my seed.

The entire world went white. I thought I must be having one of my spells. When I came back to myself, I looked at her and she was smiling. There were no mysteries for her in what the body can achieve but she seemed pleased nonetheless. She arched her back, tossed her hair from side to side, and stretched, languorous, satisfied.

And so I had congress with a woman and it was good. This could not be sin. This was just us, a man of seventeen and a woman not much older, lying together because it was good to pleasure one another. How could this be sin? Suddenly I saw the waste and folly of all those years spilling my seed in secret, my hands hot, my body frustrate with desire. How perfectly we fit together and how easily. Only God could have found such a seamless way to join man and woman together, to reconcile Adam and Eve, if only for these few moments of perfect union. How could anyone ever have thought this sinful? I lay there praising God.

"Now let me," she said, "*fratello mio.*"

"Luca," I said.

"Luca *mio*," she said.

She pushed me over on my back, and I felt the gentle weight of her great breasts as she leaned across me to trace the lines of my face. "You are too beautiful to live," she said, and with her forefinger touched my brow softly, moving from the line of my hair to my eyebrows and then to the sockets below, her fingertips upon my eyelids, barely touching me but filling me again with desire. I took her hand and moved it down between my legs, but she said no, not yet, and returned to my face, the swell of my cheekbones and the straight line of my nose and then my lips. "Like silk," she said, "like a baby's lips." She caressed them with her finger and caressed them again with her tongue. And once more I took her hand and said, "Let me do this to you, let me touch you like this, I want to touch you."

"Later," she said. "This is for you to remember."

"I can't," I said. "I can't wait," and I had her again, this time— with her assistance—slowly, patiently, prolonging the gentle agony of penetration.

We rested, wet now from our efforts, lying side by side. "Now me," I said, but no, she was not done, and this time she caressed my arms and shoulders, my legs and my privy parts, the swell of my buttocks and the small lump of my navel, and again it was good. "*Now* me," I said, and she said yes, and I began to explore the endless mysteries of a woman's body and the special points of hers, the sweet and tender pink about the nipple, the fineness of the skin within the thigh, and the low mound of Venus, the soft hair, the tender rippling flesh that stands guard there. We made love once again, exhausted now but de- termined, and her flesh was like fire. In the end, it was time to leave.

"Why me?" I asked as I said goodbye.

She smiled, and adjusted my cowl and hood, and kissed me softly.

"It must have been the will of God," she said. "Besides, you are very fair."

The bells began to ring for the Angelus as I was about to leave the Camposino. I stopped where I was and made the sign of the cross. "The angel of the Lord declared unto Mary. And she was conceived by the Holy Ghost." I was in a kind of daze, my mind reeling, but I said the Magnificat and the final Ave and blessed myself. Numb still, I watched while the white cat sat up, scratched beneath its chin, and settled down for another nap.

I leaned against the wall to void my bladder and, from old habit, said the Gloria to keep my mind away from sin.

CHAPTER 4

FATHER ALFONSO LISTENED to me, running his beads through his parched fingers, nodding now and then, but listening. He was an old man dying of some withering disease that had left him little more than a bag of bones held together by his leathery yellow skin. He gave off a vinegary smell that was not unpleasing. His eyes were clouded—he could scarcely see—but he listened with care to what I said. He leaned on one elbow and supported his bald head with the palm of his hand as I knelt on the floor by his side.

"I have been unkind and impatient and negligent in my prayers, Father," I said. "I have eaten an oatcake out of the time of meals. And I have been hard in my heart against one of the older Brothers."

"Yes."

"For no good reason."

"There is never a good reason to be hard of heart."

"I kick against the goad, Father. I have not been a devoted Brother of Saint Francis."

He said nothing.

In the silence the sharp smell of the oil lamp pricked at my nose. Outside in the dark the birds had begun their night murmuring. It was the hour after supper when we were allowed to read the lives of the saints or, if we were so inclined, the works of the Latin Fathers.

"What is it you want to confess, Brother Luca?" He knew me well.

He had grown tired of waiting and now there was no way but to say it straight out. "I have had carnal knowledge of a woman, Father," I said, "Three times." I paused, awaiting his response. When he said nothing, I was emboldened to speak honestly. "But I cannot see it is a sin. How can it be a sin when it is what we were made for? Here," I made a gesture. "Why did God give us this and fit us so perfectly to a woman and not intend for us to use it? How can this be?"

Other priests—almost any other priest—would have struck me for such defiance of God's law. Father Alfonso only shook his head and I was made more bold by his silence.

"It is not like touching myself. To lie naked with a woman is to have nothing—as Father Saint Francis preached we should—and to give everything." I had thought this through carefully. "It is a going out of myself. I do not see how it can be a sin."

"Oh, little Brother, what can I say to you? Children who grow up with no one to love them are often confused in this way. You reach out. You are hungry for love. And you confuse it with the movements of the flesh. It is not love. It is lust. It seems natural and therefore right, because it is so easy but, as we know well, the descent to Avernus is always easy . . ."

"But is it not better than spilling seed alone? In the dark? Shamefully?"

"Listen to me now and remember what you are. You are a Brother of Saint Francis. You have a vow of chastity that prohibits carnal acts of any kind, alone or with others. You cannot choose one kind of death over another and say this is a lesser death."

"But this is not death at all."

"Fornication is a sin. For every moment of pleasure there will be an eternity of pain in the fires of hell. Think on God's punishment. Beg for His mercy."

In the silence I could hear one of the Brothers cough. He was very old and his lungs had dried out, so that he spoke with a rasp and his cough was hard. Everyone around me was dying and I wanted to live. I lowered my head further and thought of hell. And then I thought of Maria Sabina. There was a humming in my brain and my heart beat faster. My voice, when I spoke, seemed to come from somewhere outside of me.

"I cannot ask for absolution, Father."

"Then I cannot give it."

I continued to kneel by his side, quiet, numb.

"I will pray for you," he said. He placed his dry hand on my brow.

Alone in my cell I knelt down and prayed. I trembled at the thought of what I had done. I had committed a mortal sin and I had refused to ask for absolution. These were grounds for dismissal from the Order of Saint Francis, of course, and they were grounds for eternal damnation as well. I prayed to understand what I must do next. I should go back and ask for his forgiveness, and then for God's forgiveness, but I could not. I had made a break and was determined to be free.

I got up and sat at my little writing table. I would hammer this out of my brain.

Adam and Eve were driven from the garden because they ate the forbidden fruit, and only afterward were they told to go and multiply. They were enjoined—by God Himself—to go forth and make love. Surely even the schoolmen would agree to this: from the beginning it was God's will that we should come together in this way, and so he had blessed it with physical pleasure and crowned it with a sense of giving. The seed is not spent. It is poured into this sacred vessel, to become or not become a child, as God sees fit.

I reviewed my arguments and returned to Father Alfonso. He was asleep but, saint that he was, he sat up in his cot and pointed to the floor next to him. "You've come to confess," he said. "You are a good Brother of Saint Francis." But he listened impatiently as I talked of Adam and Eve and God's command. "It is fornication!" he said, exasperated. "Your self-deception is worse than the sin itself." He said a good deal more but I was only half listening until I heard him say, "You must leave the Order of Saint Francis and consign yourself to misery while you live, and suffer the pains of hell when you die." He raised his hand and made the sign of the cross. "In the name of the Father and the Son and the Holy Ghost. Amen. May you find God's mercy."

That night, willful and still determined, I did not confess my sins. I returned to my cell and in the quiet and the dark I reckoned with my conscience. He must be right, of course, he was a priest and old and wise. I would be damned, an outcast while I lived and a soul in hell forever after. What could I do? I was an ignorant monk, reviled as a bastard from my birth, beaten and starved by the dyer and his wife, offered up to God by my natural father, friendless, without a family, and damned by my sins of desire. By lust. Because it could not be love, I acknowledged that, and so it must be lust. I tried to imagine myself in hell, in the second circle Dante reserves for the lustful—the pain of fire, the eternal flames—but in truth I could not imagine God damning me forever. Not me. Not really. I was not important enough to bother with. And what had I done that was so bad? And yet . . .

In the morning I went early to Father Alfonso and confessed my sins and received absolution. I had held it a light thing to be a Brother of Saint Francis and to live as a servant of the servants of God. But now that I might have to leave the Order, I saw that this mission house was my home. Father Alonso was my father and the dying Brothers were my family. I did not want to leave. I told myself it was fear of sin that sent me off to confession, but deep inside I knew it was something other. It was fear itself.

I knelt by Father Alfonso and told my sins. I promised to sever relations with that woman, to avoid every occasion of meeting her, and to sin no more. But inside I was angry: I had been brought to the edge of freedom and I had turned back. But then Father Alfonso pronounced the words of absolution and suddenly I found myself in tears. I was forgiven. I was born new and clean. I was a child of God once more.

CHAPTER 5

IT WAS LATE summer—September 8th—and the annual city fair was in its third day. Each year at this time Prato celebrates the greatest of its sacred relics, the *cintura della Madonna*, the sash worn by the Mother of God herself. The main square—the Piazza San Giovanni—becomes host to cloth merchants from all over the world who come to this fair to honor Mary and to show their wares, to sell, and to make sharp bargains. The Church of San Giovanni dominates the piazza that bears its name. Its stone porticoes extend in three sides around the piazza to make a great open market in the center and to provide shelter beneath its arches for makeshift booths where cloth is displayed on trestles. Here is wool and linen and fine damask and, close in to the church, the rich gold and red and green brocades of the master weavers of Florence. At fair time Prato empties itself into the square. Work in the fields is suspended and throngs of children push their way among the red robes of city officials and the dun cloaks of fieldworkers and the rags of the poor who have come for meat pies and shallot tarts and herbs fried in batter and whatever they can cadge from the rich or the unwary. Merchants wearing turbans and bloused trousers of Constantinople bargain with Jews from Florence and with rough Norsemen who grow their yellow hair down to their shoulders.

Housewives and burghers and slaves mingle in the street. And, as Saint Augustine reminds us, death stalks silently among them all.

Three months had passed since my promise to sever relations with Maria Sabina, to avoid the occasion of sin, and to remain a child of God. I had tried to keep my promise and I had nearly succeeded. I prayed for purity. I kept myself free from the private sin, mostly. I took care to go to market each morning by the direct route and thus avoid any possibility of running into Maria Sabina. To speak truth, however, on two occasions I did pass through the Camposino San Paolo, leaving a chance encounter with her a matter for God to decide.

Indeed, on the first occasion I lingered there a while hoping Maria Sabina would see me and come out and invite me in, and when she did not, I went quickly up the stairs and, trembling in my knees, I knocked on the door. Her sister opened it—smiling at my eager guilt—and said Maria Sabina had gone to market and did I want to wait? The sister, Alessandra, was my age or perhaps younger and made me feel a fool, so I went on my way, a monk disgraced. In truth I would gladly have spent time with Alessandra, for she was young and slender and, I thought, eager to please. I would have welcomed the chance to try out my new skills on her. I could not get her from my mind and that afternoon on the way home, wantonly and without reason I spilled my seed behind a bush and that night I confessed both sins. It was an economical confession, two for one, and I knew myself a hypocrite.

On the second occasion I resolved merely to pass through the Camposino and if Maria Sabina was not there, I would keep on going—fast—to market; if she was there, I would just talk with her, briefly, and wish her good morning, and go away. She was there standing by the well and we went at once, without a word, to her little room above the stairs. She asked her sister Alessandra to leave us for a while and I was sorry to see her go, she was so lovely in herself. Maria Sabina and I made love, once, and then a second time. This was months ago, in July, and I had been chaste since that day.

Now it was September and I was on my way to market on this third day of the Madonna's feast. It was hot already at the eighth hour of the morning. The smell of sweetbriar mingled with the scent of grapes fermenting and the acrid smell of newly pressed oil was in the air. Everything was ripening. Even the weeds that sprang up along the gutters were in flower. The kitchen gardens were thick with late lettuce and beans and leeks. There were pots of sage and parsley set out upon the windowsills and stairways.

In the trees the birds were chirping. There were no other sounds, not even the barking of dogs. Everyone was at the fair.

I was crossing through the tiny Camposino San Paolo just as Alessandra descended the stairs. She was shorter than Maria Sabina and slighter of form, but she had the same kind of dark beauty and her eyes were a deep green. I had not noticed this before. "The handsome friar," she said, and laughed. "Sabina will be glad to see you. She's not feeling well enough to go to the fair." She went off across the Camposino as I stared after her with desire. When she was out of sight, I went up the stairs.

Maria Sabina lay propped up on one elbow, looking at me as I peeped in the door. "Alessandra says you're not well," I said.

"I'm hot," she said, "I have a fever," and indeed her face was warm to my touch. I brought some cool water from a jug and gave her to drink and then I mopped her brow with a wet cloth. "That's better," she said. "I feel better." I sat on the floor by her side, looking at her, stiff with desire. I stroked her hair and lay my palm along her cheek and in a while I kissed her softly and then not so softly. She opened to me and we made love, with some haste this time and with less pleasure than before, and though I was eager for more I could see that she was exhausted, ill. Her flesh was on fire.

"Are you all right?" I asked and she nodded vaguely. I got her more water. I soothed her brow again. But despite my desire and despite her good will, in the end she said, "Go. I feel much better now. But you must go."

I WOULD BE late to the market. The best fish would be gone and the olive bread and at best I would be late with the stuffs for dinner. Brother Isaac was patient about everything except tardiness. I would have to bring him his favorite treat, oat cakes of two kinds, sweetened and unsweetened. He would not be deceived by this but he would be more forgiving.

Even from a distance I could hear piping and the sounds of lute and tambour. Tumblers and acrobats were at their work, and jugglers who kept several apples in the air at once and sometimes even knives. There was a tiny monkey on a leash with a begging cup in hand and a silk turban on its head. Players were crying out news of their performance at the inn: the tale of Adam's fall and the true history of King Herod and the comedy of Noah and his Wife. The players always interested me. They are lechers, it is true, but men of wit and talent nonetheless. The fair was at its height and the smell and din of the crowd were overpowering. I wanted only to purchase the stuffs for dinner and be on my way.

I had bought hot game pies and loaves of twopenny bread and a mess of comfits so that Brother Isaac would have only small preparation for dinner when suddenly a trumpet blast rose from the crowd in the square. Three more blasts followed, and from just beneath the church steps a loud cry went up, shouts of pleasure mixed with curses and obscenities. Bets had just been placed. I turned, expecting to see a game of hazard, and found instead the cruelest of Prato's festival sports: a live cat had been nailed to a post and three men, their heads shaved and their hands tied behind their backs, were competing to crush the life out of her by butting her with their naked heads. The cat was terrified and, maddened by pain, she clawed furiously against their blows. Blood coursed down their heads as they took their turns, laughing boldly, while the cat shrieked in terror and the crowd shouted encouragement and abuse. But the cat could not seem to die and the men would not give over. There was laughter and spilled blood and the screams of the crucified animal. Finally someone crushed the cat's chest and silenced it forever. He was declared winner and he was marching about in triumph now, his fist raised above his head, spreading the ripe stink of fear as he proclaimed his victory. Money exchanged hands. The cat hung dead on the pole, a bloody rag. The crowd receded.

I had always hated this sport. I prefer cockfighting or bear baiting, sport where men can at least pretend it is the animals and not they themselves that are by nature vicious.

I was about to leave the piazza when at the foot of the church stairs I caught sight of Spinetta, the dyer's wife, crouched in the beggar's posture, a beautiful child of two or three beside her with a wooden begging bowl in hand. Spinetta saw me just as I saw her. She rose and hurried to me at once.

"You've bought so many things," she said, pointing to my heavy sack, "and we have nothing."

I made a little bow. "You let her watch this?" I asked and indicated the bloody mess in the square.

"Him, not her. He is a boy. He likes it, for the fun. But you, you are so big now and so handsome, Luca, and you always were my favorite, you know that, even with all my boys, you were the first we had and my favorite." Spinetta spoke like this when she wanted money. She had come to the friary often enough to beg food and charity, and the Brothers always gave her something, knowing that Matteo had gambled away his money once again, or drunk it up in cheap wine, and the children had to eat. "My Luca," she said, "how we loved you." I sometimes thought she had come to believe it. But of course what she had loved was the money that used to come from my natural father, the merchant, when I was still a child and, now that I was grown, went instead to the Friars. She remembered the money and the old days of the merchant's visits and I too remembered them well. They had made me feel wanted, but they earned me extra beatings from Matteo and a short ration of food from Spinetta. And when I lay awake nights, hungry or beaten or both, I would think of them as the dyer and the dyer's wife. I could never bring myself to call them Father or Mother. I would have a real father one day, I was resolved on it, if only in heaven. Not this Matteo. Not this Spinetta. So I had thought then, innocent and still believing. "And such beautiful hair you have." Spinetta touched the reddish brown ruff surrounding my tonsure. "Look at this one's hair," she said. "He is my angel, my Agnolo." And I found myself surprised because I could see she loved him.

"His hair is beautiful," I said. It was nearly white, the color of new corn silk, and it fell in curls about the child's face.

"You thought he was a girl," she said. "It helps with the begging. See? A boy." She lifted his shift to expose his genitals. The child looked at me, defiant.

"He's a fine boy." I bent down and said to him, "You're a fine boy, Agnolo. And you're a good boy." He gave me a wide false smile and a hard judgmental look. "I must go," I said, "I'm late with the Brothers' dinner."

"And nothing for the boy? Some little thing?"

"It is not my money. It is begged money. I cannot . . ." Nonetheless I put a few small coins into Agnolo's bowl.

Spinetta kissed me on each cheek and on the mouth. "Come," she said to the child, "Come on. We don't want to lose our place." And she pushed her way through the crowd to the center of the church steps.

I wiped her kiss from my mouth with the back of my hand.

I shouldered my sack and left the fair in a wild confusion of feelings. My loins ached and my flesh was rubbed raw and I was dizzy with the smell of sex, but the dead cat and the cold staring eyes of the beautiful child, Agnolo, came back to me, and back again, with Spinetta's whine for money, and the sweat and din of the crowd. I was feverous, I could tell, and I was late for Brother Isaac who did not care about fevers, and I felt myself a monster of hypocrisy and sin.

＊ ＊ ＊

I LAY ON my cot with someone bending at my side. It was Father Alfonso. His face was distorted and there was a roaring in my brain— one of my spells, I thought—and I could barely understand what he was saying. "I will pray for you," he said, and left. Then there was a long silence and I was falling, falling, into what seemed a lake of fire. I was dying of thirst but there was nothing to drink and there was no one to ask for water. Father Alfonso returned and bent over me once more. He placed his dry hand on my brow and pulled it away at once. "You are burning up," he said, "You have a fever," and the way he said it made me think this was no ordinary fever. Then he put something cool on my forehead and for a moment the burning ceased and I drifted off to sleep.

When I awoke, it was deep night and, dizzy and disoriented, I prayed to the Blessed Virgin that I might understand the vow of chastity, and desire it, and live with the purity of the angels. My hot hand wandered from the attitude of prayer and sought my private parts and lingered there. And suddenly I stopped and pulled my hand away. Even in my fever, I knew that something was wrong. There was a lump in my groin. No, it could not be, it could not possibly be that. I probed, tentative, with a single finger. It was a lump, without question. I pulled my hand away and said, No, and I said it aloud. And then, as if that might have changed something, I slipped my hand back to my groin and felt it once again, a swelling the size of a small egg, hard and resistant, a dread reminder that death rubs shoulders with us everywhere we go, and at that moment I realized what had happened.

I had brought home to the friary the *pestis atra*, the Black Pest.

CHAPTER 6

"Men ate lunch with their friends . . . and dinner with their ancestors in paradise." Giovanni Boccaccio wrote that in 1348, more than a hundred years ago. Since then the *pestis atra* has come and gone many times, but in its horror it is always the same. Giovanni survived that first fatal wave of death and in his *Decameron* he described those three years of the pestilence in aweful detail.

It all began when twelve Genovese galleys sailing from the east brought their corruption to the ports of Sicily. Some say rats carried the infection, some say cats or fleas, but everyone agrees it began with these ships and these sailors tainted by the markets and brothels of Athens and Constantinople and Porec. In their clothes and in their touch, even in their very breath, they carried an invisible poison. Sickness clung to their bones. To inhale the same air was to invite death.

From Sicily the pestilence spread in all directions. From Sicily to Corsica and Sardinia. From Sicily to Valencia and Barcelona, and to all Iberia. From Sicily to Pisa and Florence, to Orvieto and Prato. It was a blaze from the barbarian east that swept all Europe and the lands to the north and west, until nearly half the population of the world lay dead. Some say fewer, but it is not so. There had been warning signs, of course. Earthquakes had shaken Naples and Padua and Venice. Months of rain had destroyed the crops all over Italy. Wine had soured in the casks. People dying of hunger were forced to eat grass and weeds as if it were wheat. Babies died of hunger or the diseases of hunger. And then the Black Pest came.

It was swift and pitiless. Boccaccio tells how the terror began with buboes, tumors in the groin or in the armpits, some as large as a Mary apple, some the size of a quail's egg. And from here, the groin and armpit, this deadly infection spread to the whole. Mysterious dark spots—black or purple—appeared on the thigh or the forearm, small at first then growing larger in size, and these spots proclaimed the swift approach of death. Death was sometimes instant, a plentiful gush of blood from the nose or mouth, and then no more. Before the dark spots appeared, even before the buboes, a man walking in the street might put his hand to his forehead, draw a deep breath, and fall dead before he could cry out: a long sigh and then extinction. Sometimes death was more leisurely, with fever raging for a week, the limbs wasting and the body sunk in diarrhea and vomit, and then silence. Always it was a most unkind death. The sick became foul, all the matter from their bodies drenched in an overpowering stink, their breath, their sweat, their spittle and shit so putrid no one could bear to stay with them. Besides, to be in the presence of the dying was—with few exceptions—to guarantee your own death.

Master and servant alike gave over all decency. Brother abandoned brother, husband abandoned wife, mothers—it is hard to believe— abandoned their own children. Corpses multiplied, too many for decent Christian burial. The dead who once would have been borne to church with tapers and the singing of dirges were now attended by one or two of the surviving family and by a priest who performed his office swiftly and with small solemnity. Many died in the public streets and sometimes whole families who died at home went unnoticed until the stench from their putrefying bodies alerted their neighbors who would drag the corpses into the street to be carried off to any empty grave. The graves filled up until, desperate, the living stacked the dead like lumber in a common pit, covered them with dirt, sprinkled them with holy water. It was the best they could do.

At this time a new profession sprang up, the *becchini*, corpse carriers from the rank of peasants who would shoulder the bier and carry it to the nearest churchyard where, blessed or not blessed, bodies were consigned to the waiting pit. Maddened by their unholy task, the *becchini* themselves sometimes turned murderous, raping and robbing the families of the dead. What, after all, did they have to lose?

And so the living fled the city. As the Pest raged on, some abandoned all good sense and, brutalized, mere animals, gave themselves over to license and folly and lusts of the flesh. Others sought refuge in the high country, isolated from human contact in the clean air, where crops withered in the fields and cattle wandered untended. Still others prayed and fasted and reformed their lives.

Whatever they did, death waited patiently. Boccaccio says that in Florence the pestilence carried off one hundred thousand souls between May and November alone. At Avignon, his Holiness Pope Clement VI waited out the Pest sheltered between two fires that were kept blazing on either side of him whether he sat to his dinner or knelt to his prayers. It was thought that fire would purify the tainted air, but in the end the heat grew too much for him and he decided that the will of God would be better served by taking refuge in his castle on the Rhone. By November the Pest died down and he returned to Avignon, and so the Church of Rome—in a manner of speaking—was preserved.

Such was the *pestis atra* of 1348 in Italy. It had come upon us for no reason—or for our sins; who can say?—and it left for no reason, and afterward everything remained almost as it was before. We had abandoned industry and rule and prudence, we had committed license and theft and rape, we had abandoned hope and shame. And this held true for all of us: the clergy, the nobles, the peasants, none were without blame. But human nature itself had not changed. The Pest withdrew, slowly, gradually, and once more peasants went to the fields, lawyers began again to twist the law, men and women married and made children and sometimes fell in love. Knights went on crusade. The Pope retained his throne, demanding prayer and penitence and a tithe on all income. Dukes and princes ruled their duchies and their kingdoms. There were fewer workers. There was more land. And in the end the Black Pest passed.

But the Black Pest had not passed for good. It returned and was to return often, with its old savagery and indifference to rank. Every twenty years it returned, the foul dyer liked to say, but he spoke in ignorance, because I knew that in my own life it had returned with ferocity in 1400 and had claimed my mother, and now here it was again in 1417, lying down with me in my narrow cot, staking its claim, hot, determined. There is no set date for dying.

Yes, we have come back to me.

I lay with my hand in my groin, touching that terrible swelling, certain I would die at once. I said a Hail Mary, slowly, but the end did not come, and so I took up my Rosary and began to tell my beads. Before I had completed the first joyful mystery, the Annunciation to Mary, I had fallen asleep. Or if not asleep, into a feverish state where everything was at once very clear and very confused.

I was in the city square and they had nailed the cat to a post and I was to batter it with my shaven skull. But it was not the black cat I had seen that morning. It was the white cat from the courtyard where I had met Maria Sabina. She was calling to me from the edge of the crowd. "You must not strike the cat," she said. "The cat is sacred to me." I looked over at her and was astonished to see she was bare to the waist. I pointed at her breasts. "It's nothing," she said. "It's perfectly natural. How could it be a sin?" The crowd was shouting for me to attack the cat. A trumpet blared. "It's time. It's time." A small boy ran at me from the crowd and began striking my legs with a stick. "You're not a real monk," he said, "or you would kill the cat." He poked the stick under my robe and lifted it above my knee. "Strike him, strike the monk," someone shouted. "Show us his balls!" "If he has any!" This was Spinetta, the dyer's wife, as I knew it would be. The cat screeched and a new shout went up. There was the shrill of the pipe and the beat of the tambour and suddenly I was naked before the crowd. Their laughter rose and grew louder and louder. Maria Sabina shouted out, "It's all perfectly natural. How could it be a sin?" She placed her hands beneath her breasts, displaying them to the crowd, and she was laughing. Everyone laughed with her. The little boy danced around me, possessed, slapping at my privates. I began to be aroused. Suddenly there was a silence and a shudder as the little boy pointed, saying "Look! A bubo!" The crowd fell away from me then, and Maria Sabina pulled her robe across her breasts, decently, turning away, and the little boy became a golden-haired child with a wooden begging bowl. Silence everywhere until the cat let out a long shriek of pain and terror and I turned to her, both of us naked, and rammed my head into her belly while she clawed and tore at my scalp and the sweat poured down my back and the blood poured down my face and the pounding in my brain went on and on until I woke and felt a cold cloth on my forehead and a young monk whispered, "Jesus mercy," and I fell asleep.

In the long silence I lay suspended between sleep and waking. My cell collapsed to the size of my cot. The ceiling descended on me. I could not draw a breath. This is the fever, I told myself, this is the *pestis atra*. Soon it will be over and I can die. I will be bundled in a sack and thrown in a grave with lime on me to hasten corruption and I will rest. But the ceiling pressed on me and the breath was crushed out of me and I tried to cry out but there was no sound. And then I was back at the fair and once more they had nailed the cat to a post and I was to batter it with my shaven skull. "I cannot," I said. "I will not do it." But as I looked about, the cat had become a woman. It was Maria Sabina, naked, waiting on what I would decide to do. "How could it be a sin?" she said, and smiled, beckoning. "I cannot," I said, and as I said it, I shed my cowl and my robe. All my clothes fell away and I kissed her breasts and lay her down in the center of the crowd and embraced her. The crowd shouted their delight. A little boy sprinkled us with rose petals from a wooden bowl and danced around us while I labored at my pleasure, and labored on until my loins seemed about to burst and finally there was release. I was alone then on my cot. The walls had withdrawn and the ceiling had ascended. Someone held a cup of water to my mouth and I swallowed greedily until the water ran down my face onto my chest. It was cool and fresh and I was still alive. Father Alfonso sat on the stool by my cot and ran his hand across my brow. "A nightmare only," he said. "*Misere Domine.*"

Time had ceased to have any meaning. Day and night were the same, with darkness at noon and blinding light in the deep hours.

The nightmares returned, never quite the same, but always painful, hysterical crying, people calling out for water, a terrible stench, suppurating black filth, and the sound of feet running. Water drunk down greedily, pouring out of the side of the mouth, cracked lips, sunken eyes, black and purple smudges on the chest and arms. The clank of the cart sent out to collect the dead. Prayers sung for the funeral procession, the flickering candles, strangers cleaning up the poisoned blood, the vomit, the yellow shit.

It was this way for seven days and on the eighth the fever broke as the bubo ruptured. Black pus mixed with blood sprang from the wound in my groin and ran down my legs. The cot was soaked with it. The stench was unbearable. A young monk, a novice from the main Friary of Saint Francis, made the sign of the cross and with a clean rag mopped at my groin and leg. He turned aside to vomit—he could not help himself—and then came back to his filthy task. He prayed while he worked, drawing off the black matter and pressing gently on the thigh to force out more of the infected blood, and when it seemed there could be no more, he stopped and looked at me.

"You have survived the pestilence," he said. "You are very blessed by God."

He had a bucket of water beside the cot, and he bathed the wound and put on it a poultice of rosemary, cumin, long grass, and pig dung to kill the infection and induce healing. "You have survived," he said again, and sat on the stool beside my cot and told his beads. When he was done, he bathed my forehead with cool water, slowly, lingering, and before he left, he kissed me on the lips. He was being Saint Francis, of course, kissing the leper. He was a dedicated novice.

I fell asleep and dreamed an angel had come to my cot and breathed life back into me when I was dead. I awoke with Father Alfonso by my side.

"They are all dead," he said. "Our Brothers in Christ."

I could not understand.

"You and I have survived, useless and sinful as we are. All the others are gone. God's ways are indeed mysterious."

He was silent for a long while.

"You have brought the pestilence among us, Brother Luca," he said. "It was God's will that our Brothers should suffer and die this terrible death. It was God's will that you and I, sinners, should survive. But it is God's will too that you should leave the Order of Friars Minor."

I made no response to this. How could I, dazed still from seven days of fever and guilty for the foul death I had brought among the Brothers who were my care and duty?

"When the pestilence is at an end and it is once more safe to go into the city, you must leave here. God has his plans for you. Whatever they may be, they do not lie among us."

"Yes," I said.

He fell silent, then he said, "Maria Sabina. She too is dead." He looked at me for a long time. "May God have mercy on your soul," he said.

CHAPTER 7

I was seventeen, old for an apprentice, but my natural father took pity on me and paid the initial fee that contracted me as student to the painter Cennino Cennini. His was a small *bottega*, but it was in Florence, that center of all the arts, where painters and sculptors seemed to spring up from the ground, and I was free at last to study with a master and to try my hand and my mind at making paintings.

At his command I visited the merchant, my father, in his wool office. I knelt before him, head bent, and tried to summon words of thanks for treating me like a son, but he cut me off when I had scarcely begun. "You have your mother's face," he said, and he ran his fingers through my thick hair. "And her hair." He seemed lost in thought for a moment, then he said: "You could have been my son except that you were born in sin. That is my fault. You too are my fault." He sighed. "But it is never too late for penance and so I have paid your fee as an apprentice and I have signed your contract. You have failed me as a Franciscan, Luca. Do not fail me as an artisan." It was the first time I had heard him use my name. "You must make your life a sacrifice to God."

* * *

THE CONTRACT HE had signed put me under vow to submit to the direction of Cennino Cennini, my master in all things. I was to practice the virtues of obedience, constancy, and silence. And above all I was not to marry or attempt marriage without my master's permission. Finally, I was committed to remain with him until such time as I would become skilled enough to be recognized by the Confraternity of Saint Luke as a master painter, perhaps five years, perhaps more. He, in turn, was committed to teach me, to provide me food and lodging, and to care for the good of my soul.

I was excited to be alive and to be in Cennino's *bottega* and to be in Florence, that great city of artisans. And I was grateful. It was the year 1417 and as I stood on the hill above the city, I looked down on the Cathedral of Santa Maria del Fiore where Brunelleschi had begun work on the soaring red brick cupola that would become the wonder of this age. Beside it Giotto's slender, perfect campanile lifted toward the sky, and just beyond it the towers of the Bargello and the Badia appeared to bow toward one another. In the distance stood the four bridges that spanned the yellow Arno. It was a city fortified by seven miles of stone walls, with eighty watchtowers, and within those walls there were a hundred churches and fifty piazzas and more than twenty huge *palazzi* where lived the magnificent lords of the city, the Pazzi, the Strozzi, the Brancacci, and the two families struggling for dominance: the Albizzi and the Medici. But it was the artisans and their work that made the city so exciting: Brunelleschi and Donatello, della Quercia and della Robbia and Uccello, Ghiberti creating the bronze doors of San Giovanni, and Masaccio painting the Trinity at Santa Maria Novella. And Cennino d'Andrea Cennini, my master—of lesser fame, but fame nonetheless—who had set himself the task of putting down in writing the principles by which a craftsman may come into possession of all he needs to know in order to make pictures. A craftsman's handbook. It was the morning of a bright new day in this world and it was exciting to be alive.

My master Cennino was a man in middle age who earned an adequate living as a painter but who never enjoyed those commissions from the Operai del Duomo that would give him the chance to prove himself a great artisan. His painting was for private patrons: a John the Baptist for a family chapel, a Virgin and Child for an entrance hall, a wedding chest, a birth tray, a commemorative plate, any of which could be rejected if it was not pleasing to the patron. He was not embittered by this. He lived in hope and the conviction that good work was its own reward. He was a fine draftsman and a skilled colorist but his great strength was as a teacher. He worked, he said, to preserve the tradition of Giotto and Taddeo Gaddi and Agnolo Gaddi, his own master. Cennino could teach anyone anything that required craft alone. He was not God, however, so he could not teach genius.

There were three apprentices in all, and after a day's work, and sometimes in the middle of the day, the master would put aside his painting and take us through the city from church to church, and he would point out paintings that he said we must study, making copies, teaching ourselves the difference between ambition and accomplishment. "See, only see," he would say. "We paint with the mind as much as with the hand. There is no substitute for genius."

Cennino wrote notes as he taught us—the two other apprentices were younger and more accomplished than I—and his Craftsman's

Handbook mirrors the careful and difficult training he offered us. He undertook to teach us the principle of the plane and how to place figures in a foreground and how to represent a woman's head, or a man's, and the systems of the body. These were advanced lessons, abstract and very hard to master. To prepare for these we first learned to grind paints, to draw on a little panel with a leaden stylus and with a pen. We learned to cut the quill, to tint the paper for drawing, to trace and to copy from nature. To apply size to board or cloth, to gesso and gild and burnish, to temper and lay in, to pounce, stamp, and punch, to mark out, paint, embellish and surface a panel. These were never-ending tasks. The work of an artisan is in large part preparation. He taught us to work on a wall, to plaster, to paint in fresco. Varnishing, illuminating, the preparation of mosaic gold. To work on cloth, to make crests and helmets, caskets and chests, to model in glass for windows, bowls, reliquaries. To make life masks and to make death masks.

As for me, I had ability enough to satisfy but not enough to matter. "You work hard," Cennino said, sadly. "You are very devoted."

This was daily life for me in the *bottega* of Cennino Cennini, not made easier by the fact that he had me transcribe his notes each night.

I remember thinking I too can do this, I want to do this, and after all it was understood that no special gifts were required for the apprentice. Hard work and constancy would accomplish whatever could be accomplished and the rest would depend on the will of God. The will of God became clear for me as more and more often Cennino had me spend my day copying out his notes, keeping his accounts, writing up contracts in the common language of Florence first and then, for legal purposes, in my halting Latin. Like the others, I posed for him: as John the Baptist, as Jesus feeding the multitudes, as anonymous men in the crowd. I was still asked to assist in painting backgrounds and draperies, the less demanding parts that did not really interest him, but in truth I had become his amanuensis.

Still, I was paid my six florins for the first year, eight for the second, and ten for the third. I was saving them to marry Alessandra.

W HEN MARIA SABINA died of the Pest, Alessandra had done the only thing she could do. She came to Florence to find work as a prostitute. It was only a few years since the magistracy had legitimized prostitution and indeed had sponsored a house for this purpose near the Mercato Vecchio. This was not in the interest of fostering fornication or adultery; on the contrary it was—officials said—to counter the fervent and growing vice of sodomy. Men who could not marry were pleasuring each other. Better by far to indulge them in a vice that was at least natural. Alessandra was young and beautiful and she was willing to please. She had a room near the Mercato and, though she never lacked for clients, she kept Sundays for me. It was the custom that on Sunday apprentices were free to use the day as we wished. I spent the morning sketching but in the afternoon I walked out with Alessandra and we had congress and talked the foolish talk of lovers.

"Do you love me? In truth?"

"I love only you. I loved Maria Sabina, but that was a worldly love. Not like this." Without thinking I placed my hand lightly on her breast.

"But this is worldly love. I am a whore."

"You are not a whore at heart. You are a dear and gentle girl. You are a saint."

She was pleased at this and we made love once again.

On another Sunday, in another month, we talked of marriage. The poor could marry where they loved and so, in this sense at least, we were more free than the great folk.

"I would be better for you if I could. I would be beautiful, with yellow hair and a fine figure. And a virgin as well."

"Does it make you sad? To whore?"

"It makes me sad only when I think of you. You were a holy Friar."

"A Friar, for a while, but never holy."

"Would you choose to be one still, if it were not for . . ."

"I would have found you, wherever you might be."

She was silent then, thinking, and when at last she spoke, her voice was different. More soft. More low. "I would have been a nun, if..."

I was ashamed then, and for no reason I could think of. We did not make love that day.

Nonetheless we planned our future. We would marry once I finished my apprenticeship and had freedom and money to do it. In our talks we came back always to the subject of love and our lives, as if we were great folk and mattered.

"Have you ever been truly, truly in love?" she asked me, caressing my shoulder as we lay side by side.

"Isn't this being in love?"

"This is what I do. I give pleasure."

"Yes."

"Is this what you long for? Is this what you want?"

My years in the Friars Minor had done little to prepare me for talk of love. I was twenty years old and I hungered after something but I did not know what. Not love, I think. Not even a sense of belonging. My hunger was not for anything in the future or even in the present. It was for something past, and I did not know what it was.

"I want to have been born someone else."

"Cennino," she said.

But it was not that at all.

"Masaccio," she said. "Or Giotto."

I put my tongue against her upper lip, lightly, and moved my body against hers and our conversation was lost in the familiar motions of sex.

"We will marry," I said afterwards. "For love. And soon."

* * *

I WAS NOT prepared, then, for Cennino's visit to my bed that night. He sat on the edge of my cot and said, "It's all arranged. I am passing you on to Lorenzo Ghiberti, a second cousin and a friend, who will take

you among his *garzoni*. Perhaps you will have more success with him."
He paused and put his hand on my shoulder, reassuring me. "It will
be a great honor for you to work for the man who is creating the great
bronze doors of San Giovanni. Even sweeping his floor." He paused
again as tears came to his eyes and he said, "You will never be a master
painter, my son, and I cannot afford to keep you on." He embraced me
for a moment longer than necessary—the other apprentices lay quiet,
listening—and then he said, "You will be happy with Lorenzo."

I had one of my spells that night: the roaring in my head, the great
pain, the dimness of my eyes, the flailing arms. The others pretended
not to hear. No one held me. No one told me it would be all right.

And so it came about that at age twenty I was being given over
once again. We have no lasting city here, Augustine said, and I was
proof of that. I had failed to please the wool dyer and I had failed to
please the Brothers of the Order of Friars Minor and now I had failed
to please Cennino d'Andrea Cennini. And, it goes without saying, I
had failed to please God. This alone should have filled me with fear,
but I had little fear of God or love for him or concern for his holy will.
I was hungry for something I did not know or understand.

Ghiberti, when I was presented, turned from his work and cast a
long hard look at me and said, "Yes, he is fair indeed." And to me, he
said, "Why do you stand there with your hands folded in front of you.
You look like a Friar."

"I was a Friar, my lord. They made me leave." He smiled suddenly,
and nodded in agreement with himself. Three months later, when I
had proved useless to him in casting, sanding, finishing, and polishing, he smiled again—not kindly—and said, "He is handsome but useless. Send him to Donato. Donato will find use for him."

In this way—not at once, but in the fullness of time—I came to
understand that love is not always what it seems and that some hun-
gers can never be satisfied. I was hired on as an assistant to Donatello,
the chief artisan of Florence.

1420–1423

CHAPTER 8

I HAD FAILED with Father Saint Francis and in different ways with Cennino and Ghiberti and I was sick with desire for Alessandra, who alone did not hold me a failure. But I would not see her until Sunday and today was Wednesday and, rejected and shamed, I was now about to meet the great Donato di Betto Bardi, called Donatello, *orafo e scharpellatore*, goldsmith and stone carver.

He stood before a clay armature, looking from the comely wax head he was modeling to the model himself who sat in front of him on a little platform, anxious and uncomfortable. This was to be the head of Louis of Tolosa, the boy saint who gave up his kingdom to become a Franciscan mendicant.

"We won't disturb him while he's working," Michelozzo said.

Michelozzo was of course Michele di Bartolomeo, Donato's chief assistant, who stood with me while I waited to be presented to my new master. I felt like a dwarf beside him. He was broad and tall, with huge rough hands, and so heavily muscled that his evident strength was the first thing you noticed about him. It was for reason of his size they called him Michelozzo: Big Michele, a gentle giant. The second thing you noticed was the warmth of his eyes. They were gray, going on blue, and they looked kindly on whatever they saw.

Like all apprentices in Florence, I had heard of Michelozzo but I had never thought to meet him. He was but a few years older than me and already an accomplished goldsmith and indeed something more: he was one of those rare, invaluable men who could paint fresco and carve marble and who knew everything about the difficult task of casting in bronze. It is impossible to believe, but from the age of fourteen he had been a die-engraver for the Florentine mint. Now at twenty-four he was employed by Ghiberti to assist in casting his bronze Saint Matthew for the Or San Michele and his famous bronze doors for the Baptistry. At the same time, out of love for Donato who had no gift for management and no sense of money, Michelozzo had put himself in charge of Donato's *bottega* and spent time here whenever he was not needed by Ghiberti. Michelozzo organized the paperwork for Donato's commissions—insofar as it was possible to organize that chaos—and he took charge of the apprentices, paying them and feeding them and allotting them tasks he was sure they could complete. Now he was taking charge of me.

"That is Lo Scheggia, the Splinter." Michelozzo indicated the thin young man with flax colored hair who looked so uncomfortable as he sat posing for Donato. "He is Masaccio's brother."

Masaccio. The most exciting painter alive. It was a great new world I was entering and I could not find breath to answer him.

At Donato's side there was a wooden table and on it was the *bozzetto*, a miniature clay model of the bronze statue of Saint Louis that he would eventually produce. It was the figure of a young man wearing the cope and mitre of a Bishop. The *bozzetto* was less than two feet high and only roughly finished, but it carried a sense of authority and mystery. At this moment Donato, fierce and attentive at his work stand, was modeling the head, life-sized, from wax.

Michelozzo pointed and said quietly, "First the armature, then a wax model, then the clay encasement, then we pour the bronze. You'll get to know the process. It may be you know it already?"

"Yes," I said. "Well, no."

He nodded agreement and, seeing that Donato would be much occupied for some time, Michelozzo offered to show me about the shop, but in truth we were both so fascinated that we remained there watching the master at work.

I had attempted sculpting from clay and wax in my studies with Cennino and I had seen Ghiberti at work during my few months apprenticeship with him, but now in Donato I was seeing a new kind of artisan. Michelozzo had said we should not interrupt him at work, but it seemed to me that nothing short of the Final Trumpet could have interrupted him. He bent over the *bozzetto* with an intensity impossible to describe. His hands were quiet, they seemed to rest on the air. He had long thin fingers that hovered above the wax as if he were conferring a blessing. As I watched him, he seemed to slip out of time. I had seen this look once before on Father Alfonso at the moment of consecration and I had seen it in paintings of Father Saint Francis rapt in ecstasy. Donato looked as if he might levitate or, if the trance should end, as if he might fall down dead in the place where he stood. I thought the wax would melt beneath his gaze.

I thought I myself might have one of my spells.

I turned to Michelozzo, hoping he would say, "Enough," but he too was caught up in the sight of Donato at work and was unwilling to turn away.

"Should we go?" I asked finally, though it was not my place to speak.

Michelozzo said nothing, not even when a boy arrived from Ghiberti with the message that Michelozzo was needed. He must come at once. Michelozzo nodded agreement but, raising his hand in dismissal, he continued at my side watching the master at work.

Donato had been famous for as long as I could remember: his marble statue of St. Mark and his bold St. George had dominated the eastern face of Or San Michele for years now. In my mind, he was not of this world and so to see him at work in his *bottega* came as a shock. He was dressed like anybody, in shirt and drawers, with a length of towel around his head to hold back his hair. His face was smoothly shaven, and I would discover later that beneath that head towel he had a mass of red-brown hair the color of my own. He was short and square and I wanted to think him handsome, though he was already a man of thirty-four. He had a nose like a blade and even in profile he gave off a sense of great power. His looks were completely unremarkable. It was only the intensity of his gaze that set him in a world apart.

He was staring, now at the boy's head and now at the wax model. The boy—Masaccio's brother!—must have felt that intensity because his leg began to tremble and his hands clenched in his lap. I wondered if he too was subject to spells.

Donato picked up an ivory finishing tool, and after a moment put it down again. He raised his right hand over the sculpture, hovering there. He touched the right cheekbone with his index finger and then with his thumb. He stared for a long time at the wax head as if he might somehow perfect it just by looking, and then he raised his eyes to the boy and stared at him, an inquiry of some kind.

The sculpted head looked absolutely flawless to me.

Whole minutes seemed to pass. "What are you thinking?" he asked, but it was not a question and Lo Scheggia did not answer. The boy's leg continued to tremble and my own legs trembled in sympathy with him. How was it possible to be stared at like this and not crumple to the floor?

Finally Donato shook his head, no. Quietly, still deep in thought, he approached the posing platform and placed his hand gently on the boy's head. He touched his right cheekbone and then his left. Once again he shook his head. "You can take a rest now, Scheggia *mio*," he said, and his voice was very soft.

He came over to us and put his hand on Michelozzo's shoulder. "It is impossible, Lozzo," he said. "It is not possible."

Michelozzo said nothing but it was clear that Donato expected a response.

I was watching them closely.

"Tomorrow," Michelozzo said, "all things will be possible."

They exchanged a look. Michelozzo's look was merely sympathetic, understanding, but Donato's was a look of love and need. For an instant I felt a twinge of jealousy, but I did not know of what or of whom.

Michelozzo raised his hand, farewell, and left us for Ghiberti.

Donato stared after him and then, with a pained look, sat down at a work table littered with drawings for the statue. There were piles of them, sketches of Lo Scheggia in a Bishop's mitre and cope, some with him holding the crosier and some of the crosier alone, but most of them were sketches of the boy's head, a handsome young man who looked determined in some images and desperate in others. Donato shuffled the drawings for a moment and then pushed them into a pile to the side. He had decided to get on with this matter of duty.

"Now," Donato said, and looked across at me. His intense stare that could melt wax had disappeared completely. "*Dimmi*. Tell me everything."

I fell absolutely mute.

He asked where I was from, who my father was, why I had agreed to be a Brother of Saint Francis and why I had left the Order and I answered him in single syllables, as if I were not only frightened but slow of mind as well. He was interested that I had been a Franciscan Brother.

"Louis of Tolosa was a Franciscan," he said. "And a saint, of course. And a fool."

I was not sure what to make of this.

"He gave up a kingdom to become a beggar," he said, as if in explanation. He shrugged and for a long while he sat there silent. "Do you read Greek?" he asked. "I read only Latin and very little of that. Enough to know the old stories. Abraham and Isaac, David, Susannah and the Elders."

An orange cat that I had not seen before suddenly leaped onto his lap and then onto the table where it curled up on his drawings. "Do you like cats?" he asked. "Lots and lots of cats?" He tickled the orange cat beneath the chin. "They keep down the vermin."

He lapsed into silence again and then, a second time, he asked my name.

"Luca," I said. "I'm sorry."

"Luca is a good name for a painter. Saint Luke, as you know, painted the Virgin Mother. We revere him for that, though he was probably just a sincere painter and not a very good one. We do little painting in our *bottega*—wedding *cassoni*, mostly—but there are always things that need doing, Lozzo will tell you, and there is always someone to show you where you've gone wrong."

He smiled and again he seemed to drift off in thought.

"Nencio"—he meant Ghiberti—"says you are gifted, though he does not say at what." He shot me a sharp look and then turned away. "A gift, plus hard work, and you'll fit in well here."

He shifted the drawings on his desk, gazing for a long moment at one of the full-length sketches and then at one of the head alone. He picked up a stylus, twisted it between his fingers, and handed it to me. "You must have this," he said, and I could see that with its ivory handle and fine point it was of some considerable value. "You must draw constantly," he said. "Do you draw all the time?"

"No, my lord," I said, so nervous that I told the truth.

"Good," he said, "*designe sempre*. Drawing helps to train the eye as well as the hand. Drawing . . ."

As he spoke, it was clear that he was reciting merely and that his mind was elsewhere.

"You will learn from the others, and from me too, I hope. By watching. And doing. You'll like them. That meager boy with the red hair is Pagno di Lapo. We call him Rosso. He is in first youth, only twelve or thirteen, but he shows promise of being very good with stone. And, in time, with fine marble." He paused, thinking, and then he said, "I like him." He shook his head, as if dismissing some thought. "The boy over there is Francesco Bottari. Even at his young age he shows clear to be a carver in relief." He smiled to himself. "He is very fair. And the others, Rinaldo Franco and Caterina Bardi. Caterina is family." He gestured to a far corner where a young woman was applying gesso to a panel. She was dressed like a boy—her skirts were hitched up about her legs—but she was very clearly a girl and, seeing her, I longed for Alessandra. "My cousin's daughter. She paints." He did not mention Masaccio's brother, Lo Scheggia, who I noticed had returned to the posing stool.

Donato stood up suddenly. "Go and give a greeting to Rosso and the others. I have to get on with this." As he left the worktable and moved toward his sculpting stand, he turned back to me and said, "If you have need of money, there's some in the basket." He pointed up to the ceiling where a small wicker basket hung from a rope.

At that moment he seemed to disappear. Certainly he stood there, square and solid in front of the wax head, but the Donato who had welcomed me and made pointless, polite conversation was gone. I felt a deep hollow in my chest. I was too nervous to think what this meant. While he talked to me he had seemed an ordinary man, but as he moved away he became once again the terrifying artist I had first seen at work. I clutched to my chest the ivory-handled stylus he had given me.

I met the others, nervous likeable young men who frightened me by their quick wit and their rare accomplishments and by how comfortable they all seemed at work in Donato's *bottega*. I was not comfortable with them. I was new and a possible threat, I suppose, but I sensed they made a show of politeness because I was older and came recommended by Ghiberti. Caterina alone seemed pleased to see me.

In truth I gave them only half my attention. My mind was fixed on Donato who stood motionless before his work stand as if incapable of movement. He did not stir. The air itself seemed to have congealed around him. He was looking only, from the wax head beneath his hands to the model posing for him, and again back and forth, and again. He said nothing and there was no expression I might read on his face. He seemed resolved to stand there forever.

"You can go now," I heard him say at last.

Lo Scheggia slipped from the posing stool, grateful, and went outside to the privy closet.

Donato stood looking at the empty stool. Then he looked long and hard at his unfinished sculpture. At last, expressionless still, he leaned forward and drew the sculpture to him. He crouched above it, lowering his chin to the crown of the wax head and hugging it close, embracing it hard. He pressed the sculpted face against his chest, harder and harder, until there was a small cracking sound and the head shattered. A long minute passed. He pulled away from the ruined sculpture finally—bits of wax and clay clung to his shirt—and, still with no expression on his face, he placed a rag over the shattered head and held it there for a moment.

The apprentices continued talking, knowing it was better to pretend not to notice, and I joined in their talk, thrilled and frightened at what I had seen and what it all meant to my new life.

CHAPTER 9

MORE THAN A year would pass before Donato took any real notice of me and during that year my life in the *bottega* gradually changed so that I was no longer an outsider. I became an anonymous part of the comings and goings of the *bottega* and little by little I was accepted by the other apprentices—young, all of them, except for Lo Scheggia—but during most of that year I was largely ignored by Donato himself, even as he ignored the abandoned Saint Louis. The statue had been commissioned more than two years earlier for a special niche in the Or San Michele and Michelozzo remained mindful that at some future time Donato would have to complete it. And he remained mindful of me as well, though I could not have guessed what he intended either for the statue of Saint Louis or for my place in the *bottega*.

On that calamitous afternoon—my first among them—Donato had turned from the shattered statue and packed everything away in the storage shed: the innumerable sketches, the battered armature, the crushed wax head. He looked to have lost all interest in completing Saint Louis, now and forever. He went on to other things—minor ones—a sandstone *tondo* of the Virgin and Child, a bust in terracotta, a coat of arms—gilded—of copper, some decorative work for a frieze. And then he returned to another abandoned project—a major one—the prophet Isaiah. It had been commissioned by the Operai of the Cathedral four years earlier and had long since been completed but not yet surrendered for judgment. It stood on wooden blocks outside in the courtyard, a statue over six feet tall carved of white Carrara marble and cloaked beneath a shroud of heavy sail cloth. The shroud was removed and here stood Isaiah: wisdom in old age rendered live in marble, the seal of the divine encounter written plain upon his face. To any observer it was Isaiah, there could be no doubt, but in truth the statue began as a portrait of Donato's uncle Niccolò, a finisher of leather goods who could no longer work because of his age and his mangled hand. Donato had found the hard lines of his face and the balding head and the crippled hand sympathetic and convincing as marks of the prophet. Now he wanted time to think about the statue despite repeated demands of the Operai for its delivery. Uncle Niccolò as the prophet Isaiah? He returned to work on it and Saint Louis be damned.

Meanwhile Michelozzo helped me settle into the life of the *bottega*. It was a working *bottega*, like Ghiberti's, and the sounds of hammering and sawing and the sharp chink of iron against marble rang in the air. There was the smell of wood chips and the sweet tarry smell of paint and the smell of sweat. There was dust everywhere. At times it was like working in the *campo*, with too many people coming and going. Donato had many assistants in addition to his chief assistant, Michelozzo, who oversaw this constant motion. Nanni di Bartolo, who had helped in roughing out Isaiah's robes, was there all the time and stonecarvers came in now and again to cut huge blocks to the rough shapes of statues. And there were artisans hired for a particular piece of work—experts in copper or silver—and sometimes too there were hangers-on who were simply eager to be linked in any way with my lord Donato. And of course there were apprentices who occupied workbenches and trestle tables and there were men delivering work materials—wood and wax and marble, sacks of lime, barrels of plaster—and there were others, visitors and friends, who seemed to have no purpose but to look on. To be sure, it was not always so. There were times, especially late in the day, when it seemed no one worked there except the apprentices and the master. Cosimo de' Medici himself had been known to visit at such an hour, Michelozzo said. The great Cosimo ever avoided crowds but he rejoiced in visiting Donato.

The *bottega* was huge, a vast rectangle divided into sections by work benches and partitions. At one side of the room was a long table covered with quills and styli and piles of paper: commissions of every kind, as well as sketches of work in progress. This table was supposed to be Donato's command post, though in fact it was more often Michelozzo who occupied it. The idea was that from here Donato could see everything going on in the room and have instant knowledge of what was being done and what was being neglected and who needed assistance and who might give it, and thus the *bottega* would become a model of economy and efficiency. But Donato was renowned for abandoning a work in progress while he gave himself over to a fresh commission or a brave new idea that came to him in the night or as he crossed the Ponte Vecchio or sat dozing over a midnight cup of wine. His work was always late, therefore, and contracts had always to be rewritten. No one in the *bottega* seemed to notice and no one, saving Michelozzo, seemed to care.

Working here was a continual excitement to me, and it seemed right and just that Donato's *bottega* opened onto the Corso degli Adimari cat-a-corner to Giotto's Campanile. There was a small door to the street for coming and going and beside it there stood great double doors wide enough to admit a cart loaded with granite or marble and these doors were generally kept barred except for deliveries. At the far end of the *bottega* there was another small door and, beside it, a set of matching double doors that gave onto an outside garden area and a courtyard used for carving heavy sculpture. A garden shed with a long overhang protected work in progress from the rain and snow, and a separate shed provided a stall for the donkey, Fiammetta, a patient, smelly beast used for carting materials. A flock of brown and speckled chickens scratched about in the courtyard for grain; they were a nuisance, Michelozzo said, being always under foot, but their eggs were essential for fixative in painting. Two black cats and the fat orange one that was Donato's favorite kept watch over the chickens or curled up in a patch of sunlight or fought among themselves for amusement. A well with a hand pump stood in the center of the yard and, just beyond it, a small furnace for smelting ore. Close in against the outside wall was a privy closet for our physical needs.

Inside the *bottega* Donato maintained a separate chamber walled off from the huge public work area. It had a lock on the door and a cot where he might spend the night if he worked too late to cross the Ponte Vecchio to his rooms. Here too he kept his most private papers. No one—except Michelozzo—was granted entrance to this room.

✷ ✷ ✷

From the start Michelozzo was my friend and my unexpected patron. It was not only my awkwardness that commended me to his attention, but my knowledge of Latin and my ability to attend to the fine details of the *bottega*'s commissions. Also, I was strong and he could see I would be able to assist him in casting bronze, which was his specialty. As the year went by he let me help in organizing the works in progress. Since I was much older than most of the other apprentices and since I was so much less talented than they, no one seemed to mind that I passed on to them orders that came from Michelozzo and thus from Donato himself. Michelozzo settled me among the apprentices and, with great patience and to the limits of my ability, he taught me to sculpt in marble.

At first they all seemed nervous likeable young men who terrified me by their quick wit and their rare accomplishments and by how comfortable they all seemed at work in Donato's *bottega*. Caterina was older, more gifted, and as a relative of Donato, she stood a bit apart.

As they got to know me, they explained about the basket of money; it was really for Michelozzo to dispense when you had need, but if he wasn't there and you had an emergency, you could lower the basket and help yourself to whatever money you needed. It was the ongoing joke that Donatello—so they all called him—was too unworldly to care about money. He would give you anything, but cross him in some other way—on design or workmanship or the pains necessary to get something right—and he would kill you. He had thunderous rages, they said. He would shout long and threaten much. He had been known to take a hammer to a marble bust, shattering it in a hundred pieces, rather than sell it short to a patron who accused him of charging overmuch. They were bursting with such stories and they were proud to work in the *bottega* of such an important and dangerous man. They made small mention of his kindness and generosity, of his booming laugh, of the late nights he spent with them drinking deep and telling fond stories of Cosimo de' Medici and wry stories of working for Ghiberti. I would come to understand that the obvious point of each tale was that the great Donatello was unlike any sculptor before him; the less obvious point—but the real one—was that they were unlike any apprentices before them, chosen as they were by him.

I came to know them well, all except Pagno di Lapo. He was a boy of twelve or thirteen, silent and surly with the others but full of light and charm with Donato, who thought him greatly gifted and called him *Piccolo Mio*. I did not trust him, though he gave no reason why I should not, unless it was his sliding smile. During this time I shared a small room with two other apprentices, Francesco Bottari and Rinaldo Franco, across the Ponte Trinità next door to the Palazzo Frescobaldi. Lo Scheggia lived at home with his brother, Masaccio, and of course Caterina Bardi lived with her own family. Francesco and Rinaldo were youths of fourteen and fifteen and I was expected to look after them, whatever that might mean, and I did so by making sure they were in bed each night before I locked the door. I did not want to inquire what they did with their free time. They were serious young workers, gifted beyond my own capacities, and though I suspected they sometimes visited whores near the Mercato Vecchio and undoubtedly pleasured themselves privately in ways I knew only too well, I made a point of not inquiring. Next door to us, in a little house rented from the Frescobaldi, Donato himself lived with Michelozzo. They had two rooms and a small kitchen garden as befitted men of substance and accomplishment. It was whispered by apprentices of Ghiberti—and, I must acknowledge, by others as well—that Donato and Michelozzo were lovers, sodomites, but I who saw them together each day knew that this could not be true. There was never that curious physical tension between them that is the mark of desire. They were simply men who loved one another. And in truth the laws were clear: the ultimate penalty for sodomy was death by fire.

Gifted, but not gifted enough, I held a special place in the *bottega*, but it was not one of expertise as a craftsman and so it did not rankle. I got on with the others, I helped keep peace at work, I was useful and needed no special care.

In this way, Michelozzo brought me, little by little, to the attention of the master himself.

✳ ✳ ✳

Raw and clumsy as I was, Michelozzo took pity on me and instructed me in the basic needs of Donato's *bottega*. For weeks he let me grind paints and embellish panels and assist at plaster casting, but then it came time for work in sculpture.

"You paint well, and we always need painters, but if you are to be of use to the master, you must learn to carve. Painting and sculpting are very different things." He looked at me hopefully and nodded agreement with himself. He was teaching an idiot, he knew, but he was very patient. "Painting fills a particular space. You see?" He indicated the flat oaken wedding panel that Caterina was painting: Solomon meets Bathsheba. "But painting remains flat. Sculpture has depth. Not only the illusion of depth, but true physical depth. You can walk around a sculpture. You can touch it. It has life and motion from behind as well as from the front. If it is well done, you can feel it breathe."

He walked around Caterina's painting and I followed him, noticing—not for the first time—that Caterina was full of figure and fair to look upon.

"Also, a sculpture—and this no painting can do—a sculpture moves into the space of the observer. You are the observer being observed. You see?"

"I see. I see."

Caterina allowed me the thin edge of a smile.

"Sculpting is not painting."

"No."

"Donatello takes rough stone and creates this new life, this . . . Only look at what he is doing."

Donato was out in the courtyard making changes to Isaiah's robes. As he worked, quickly, deftly, the shapeless gown that Nanni di Bartolo had rendered now began to reveal the body beneath it, the thrust of the leg, the arms that gave shape to the flowing sleeve. The Operai had at last been shown the statue and with gratitude they had paid more than the contracted fee and still Donato worked to perfect his Isaiah.

"Do you see?"

"I see."

Michelozzo smiled at me and put his hand on my shoulder as we stood watching my master at work. We both knew I would never sculpt like Donato. He was thinking this, I knew, though my own thoughts strayed to Caterina.

Michelozzo went to work with a will, teaching me first the proper use of chisels for carving wood and stone. He was thorough and demanding and he did not wait long before starting me on my first carving, a marble bust of Rinaldo, one of the two young apprentices in my care.

On an afternoon in May with the sun warm on my neck and the sweat pricking on my brow, I first came to Donato's notice. I was lost deep in work and concentrated all in knots as I rolled the wax into strips and lay them on the frame of my *bozzetto*. Michelozzo stood by my side, encouraging me, silent. And so I did not hear Donato come into the little shed where we worked and I was surprised when he said, "How does it go?"

Michelozzo explained on my behalf—since as always I was speechless—that it would be a small bust. My first. We would use scrap marble.

Donato glanced at the sketches that lay on the worktable. "Rinaldo," he said. "A handsome boy." He smiled at Michelozzo and Michelozzo returned the smile. Donato examined the rough wax mess I had produced. "Rinaldo has a fine hand with marble. When you've completed his bust, you should ask him to sculpt you in return."

I nodded agreement. He looked at me then, curiously, as if he were noticing me for the first time though I had worked in his shop every day and, as an errand boy for Michelozzo, I had brought him papers to sign and reminded him of appointments and commissions and schedules. I thought he might turn away but he continued to look at me, for a long time, in a new way.

"You should start to mold that wax before it hardens," he said. He turned then and went back inside the *bottega*.

Michelozzo said, "He has seen you now and he will remember."

To BE REMEMBERED or not to be remembered was no matter to me. It was enough to be one of the six apprentices in the *bottega* of Donato di Niccolò di Betto Bardi. Donato was the most accomplished and the most innovative sculptor in Florence, and if in Florence, then in the whole world. And he was not alone. Lorenzo Ghiberti, absorbed in the sculpting and casting of his first bronze doors, nonetheless kept his eye on the work of my master and, as you can see in his second set of bronze doors, he learned from it. Masaccio—Big Thomas—was in and out of the *bottega* as a friend and student of the master. He was twenty years old and would be dead at twenty-six, but now he was still alive and at work on the San Giovenale Triptych and much preoccupied with color and with Uccello's laws of perspective. Uccello himself spent a long afternoon showing Donato—and the few others who tried to understand—how to look at a sphere with seventy-two facets in the shape of diamonds and how to draw it and what the results might be. He was twittering and slightly mad and Donato was kind but firm with him, taking in what was useful and dismissing the rest with thanks, while Uccello returned to his solitary house in the hills and his paintings of every kind of animal, to his sad wife and his cages of wild birds. Donato's oldest friend and companion, Brunelleschi, was in and out, working in secret on his miraculous dome, and my friend Michelozzo was there, whom I called Michele, learning from the master and keeping accounts for him and leading him out of the financial disaster he seemed to want to embrace. The great patrons would sometimes appear: the Medici—old Giovanni di Bicci and Cosimo himself—and Niccolò da Uzzano, the Rucellai, the Riccardi, and even the Albizzi who would later try to destroy Cosimo, our patron. The entire world came around to see what Donato was creating and to applaud the work and to ask a favor. And among all these, invisibly, I too was there, a man in years but still a boy in the craft of sculpting, unskilled, unsubtle, but full of hope and not yet possessed by the demon of . . . of what exactly I could not yet say.

IT WAS A sweltering day in June—hot in the way that only Florence can be hot—and the huge double doors to the courtyard had been thrown open in hopes of a breeze. There was none. The sun seemed to have settled over the city with the intention of putting it to fire. We had all laid aside our stockings and doublets and, dressed only in our long shirts, we gave ourselves over to lethargy. The stone floor was cool on our bare feet.

I was at the big table doing the accountant's work Michelozzo had assigned me and I had finished sorting through the sheaf of commissions still unfulfilled. I had separated out the commissions that were fulfilled but not yet paid for—a *tondo*, a marble bust, two *cassoni*—and I had begun to add up the sums owed and the sums paid. But it was June, and hot, and I was distracted from thoughts of money by thoughts of Alessandra. I was set upon continually by desire for her. By—I must tell truth—by a lust that never seemed possible to slake though she was always willing to try. I shifted Donato's commissions in my hands, but my mind was on her body, the soft skin of her inner thighs and the sweet mound there. I began to sweat and I began to go hard. It was lust, I knew, and I pressed my legs together to make myself harder. Yes, it is lust. And lust is evil but, since we are not angels, it is necessary. But was it only lust? I shut my eyes to see her the better and thought, Surely this is love.

Suddenly, the master was standing before me, and I realized he had been standing there for some time, staring. He had, as Michelozzo promised, remembered me. I leaped to my feet.

"How old are you, Luca?" he asked. "About twenty-three?"

"Twenty-one or maybe twenty-three."

"Sit down. Sit down. And you were a Franciscan brother for a time."

I nodded and sat down.

"Louis of Tolosa was twenty-three when he died. He was a Franciscan mendicant."

He was thinking aloud, not truly looking at me now, and then suddenly he was, and it was as if he was seeing me for the first time. It was that same look he gave to whatever he was sculpting.

The look of a great artist is not a devouring look or even a penetrating look. It is illumination, as if a great light is turned upon you and all the dark places of your mind and heart are suddenly revealed. It is how God will look at you at his Final Judgment. It is naked, it is not decent.

I felt myself go hot under his stare, and then cold, and I began to sweat. My leg began to tremble and my sight went dim and I had fear of the worst but—a great mercy—the spell did not descend on me. I felt tears come to my eyes. I had never been looked at in this way. Would I be found out? Would I be acceptable?

Donato had already turned away.

"Rinaldo," he called out, "set up a new armature. I am going to sculpt my Louis."

CHAPTER 10

"WHAT DO YOU want?" Donato said, but it was not a question, it was merely something he was saying to himself as he sketched. I was seated on a low stool while he sat behind his huge worktable. "Lean forward a little. Bring your shoulders down. Good. Now a quarter turn to the left."

He had been sketching me—or rather my head and shoulders—for more than an hour. He wanted not only my features but a sense of depth and volume.

"What do you want?" he said again.

At last I found my voice and said, "I want to marry."

"Good," he said. "That's very good." And after a moment he stopped drawing and asked, "What did you say?"

"I want to marry."

He smiled then. "A handsome boy. But you're so young."

"I'm twenty-one. Or perhaps older."

"Does she have a family, a dowry?"

"She is a street woman. I knew her sister in Prato."

"You want to marry a prostitute? You *frati minori* are full of surprises."

"I was not a very good Brother."

"Is she comely?"

"She is very beautiful. Her name is Alessandra."

"And you love her."

I did not hesitate. "Yes."

"Even though she has been with others?"

"Yes."

"With many others?"

I said nothing.

"And without a dowry."

"Yes."

"You'll need more money."

"I need your permission."

He made a gesture that seemed to say his permission was not important, though in truth I could not marry without it. He went back to his drawing.

"And I will need money for a room. I cannot well ask that she move in with me and Francesco and Rinaldo."

"They might like that." He smiled. He was amusing himself. "How much do we pay you now?"

"Twelve florins a year and a new pair of stockings." I wanted to be clear: "A new pair of stockings each year."

"You'll need at least thirty florins. I'll tell Michelozzo. Or you can tell him if I should forget."

I had not intended to ask his permission to marry until he was done with the Louis statue and then, if I had less fear of him by then, I thought I might dare ask. I was overwhelmed. I could think of nothing to say.

"Thirty florins. And a new pair of stockings," he said. "Each year."

A MONTH BEFORE Alessandra and I were to marry, there came a letter from Prato. I had received a letter only once before—an appeal for money from Spinetta, the dyer's wife, some years past when she learned I was apprenticed to Cennino, so I was convinced that the boy who brought it was in error. But he was a messenger by profession and assured me that if I was the Luca di Matteo apprenticed to Donatello, *orafo a Firenze*, then the letter was for me. I signed the note of receipt.

The letter was from Spinetta, written in a fine hand that could not have been her own. It was again a request for money. Her life was difficult beyond imagining, she wrote, her poverty crippling. Her oldest son had been scalded in a dyeing vat and could never work again. The next two boys were young, and sickly in any case, and together they earned less than enough to keep them in food and clothing. Agnolo, coming on to nine years old, was always in trouble. He had tried to run away. He was wild and uncontrollable, a young animal. Could I send money? Any little thing would help to keep them alive, but surely I could spare more than a little. I should ask the rich and famous Donatello, she said, since he was known to have pity on the poor. She assured me I had always been her favorite and that she counted on me now and she remembered me in her prayers day and night, storming heaven on my behalf.

I folded the letter and, to keep from thinking on it, put it away in my sandalwood box with my few special things. It was an odd collection: the New Testament in Latin that the Fratelli had let me keep when they turned me away and some charcoaled sheets I held in high value. There was a sketch I had made of Alessandra naked and one of the courtyard in Prato with the well and the white cat, and another of Lo Scheggia that Donato had drawn and then thrown out when he abandoned the earlier Saint Louis. And the ivory-handled stylus that was my first gift from Donato. There was also a single gold earring I had found days earlier in the Mercato Vecchio. It was valuable, surely, and engraved with tiny laurel leaves. I was keeping it to give Alessandra on her feast day. I put Spinetta's letter at the bottom of the box and tried to forget about it. I was resolved that I would not reply.

I WAS POSING now, no longer for the bust alone but for the full length statue of Saint Louis. It was early evening, a scorching July day, and all the others had left the *bottega*. Donato was caught up in his work, taking advantage of the late light, when all at once it came to him to sketch me in episcopal robes. He hauled out three light canvas throws from where they hung on a storage rack and with much care, as if he were clothing me in heavy damask, he draped one around my front to make a gown and the other two around my shoulders, so that in a very short time I looked like a poor man's bishop. I bore all the elaborate paraphernalia but what should have been brocade was in fact canvas and what should have been a bishop was an inept apprentice awash in sweat. Donato was caught up in the travesty. He arranged the gown in front, tying it with a cincture so that the light canvas draped like rich material, and he doubled back the shoulder pieces to make a kind of collar on the mantel and then he stood back and admired his work. He fussed with the folds, pulling and pushing the stiff fabric to make it hang like rich damask.

"We need episcopal gloves," he said. "And a crosier. And we'll make you a mitre."

I was too uncomfortable to move, too drowned in canvas to speak.

"How do you feel? Do you feel like a bishop?"

"I don't know how a bishop feels," I said.

"Do you feel like a saint?"

"I feel like I'm being smothered."

"You look like you're being smothered." This was not Donato speaking. It was a man of the nobility, magnificent in his bearing, dressed all in red and with a servant in black and gold by his side. I knew at once it was Cosimo de' Medici. He was famous for being rich and powerful but he was famous for being ugly as well. He was tall and lean and his skin was yellowish. His eyebrows met in the middle of his forehead and the eyes themselves were small and narrow. His chin protruded in an uncomely manner. I could see why people said he was ugly, but he smiled as he greeted Donato with a greeting that was open and hearty and at that moment he appeared a man of supreme elegance and beauty. It was well known that women found him attractive.

"My friend," he said, and embraced Donato with feeling, kissing him on one cheek and the other and then kissing him once again.

"My lord," Donato said, returning the embrace.

"I am just returned from Rome. Your work goes well? And yourself?" His voice was deep and rich, a pleasure to hear. He was completely at his ease with Donato, but even more remarkable was that Donato seemed completely at ease with him. They were like old friends, not like patron and artisan. I could not help staring and he must have sensed my look because he glanced over at me and smiled. It was said that he was never too grand or too busy for even the little people and this seemed to be true. His servant waited patiently by the door, his hands folded before him, a small dagger at his right side and a velvet purse worked with gold thread hanging at his left. It appeared they had come on foot.

Donato led my lord Cosimo out to the work yard and showed him the huge Abraham and Isaac he and Nanni di Bartolo, working together, had nearly completed for the Or San Michele. It was a marvel, though Nanni's work on the boy Isaac seemed to me less wonderful than Donato's Abraham. Also there were two marble heads in bas relief—a sibyl and a prophet—for the Porta della Mandorla, completed and ready for delivery, and as always there were statues in progress: blocks of marble that in time would become the Jeremiah and the Zuccone and stand in niches on the west walls of Giotto's campanile. At the moment, however, they were merely two massive blocks of marble, cut to size and crudely marked for first carving by the apprentices. Even now Donato could see that these rude stones would become great wonders and Cosimo, a connoisseur of all the arts, looked on and must have known this as well. He smiled and put his hands together, palm to palm. He was ugly, perhaps, but he was bold and heartening to look upon.

Meanwhile I stood, swathed in canvas, without moving as I watched the two great men move among the marbles outside, talking about sculpture which always fascinated Donato and about rare books and the new learning which did not. It was hard to believe that the rich and famous Cosimo who inspired fear by his power and his silence was the same person as this cheerful man talking now with my master about an ancient statue of Marsyas he had bought in Rome and would like repaired—or perhaps even copied—for the courtyard of his palazzo.

They came back into the posing room and seemed surprised to find me still standing swathed in my mock episcopal robes, my hands folded at my chest and sweat pouring down my face. "This is thirsty work," Cosimo said, smiling at me. Donato apologized and began to remove my canvas robes piece by piece while Cosimo said merely, "The fault is mine," and went to have a word with his servant. Before they left, the servant discreetly handed me a tiny red velvet sack in which I found a newly minted florin. The sack itself was a work of art.

When they had gone, Donato said to me, "Write this down. For my lord Cosimo de' Medici: a small gold coffer tooled with the family crest and a jeweled clasp, this to serve as a kind of tabernacle for a Greek prayer book newly brought from Byzantium. Three designs. No fixed fee. No fixed date for delivery." He paused and thought for a moment. "It is a handsome commission. I leave the design of it to you."

I wrote out the receipt and placed it on his worktable on top of the other commissions. My task! My design!

Because I overflowed with happiness, I sent Cosimo's florin on to Spinetta, a salve to my conscience, an answer to her prayers.

✷ ✷ ✷

On the evening of August 20, Alessandra and I were married at the church door of little Santa Maria in Campo and then proceeded inside where mass was celebrated and our marriage vows solemnized.

Donato was there and Michelozzo and Masaccio and all the apprentices. Afterward Donato made a plentiful feast with fish and fowl and venison and—because it was a wedding celebration—the testicles of a boar. To end the feast there were honeycakes, soft and hard, and comfits of every kind. We drank wine late into the night.

The apprentices had made for Alessandra the present of a handsome *cassone* that Caterina had painted with a scene of Mars wooing Venus, in which mine was the face of Mars and Alessandra's the face of Venus. Our marriage bed had been bought with an advance against my thirty florins. That night Alessandra and I lay together as man and wife and she conceived. Our son, Donato Michele, would be one year old before my lord Donato would finish the Saint Louis of Tolosa.

* * *

In time my three designs for Cosimo's gold coffer became thirty in number, but they were of no interest to Donato who now neglected everything—the towering Zuccone, the prophet, the sybil, commissions large or small—while he concentrated on the Saint Louis of Tolosa. He had finished the *bozzetto*, and had begun the full-sized statue.

He was working now on the body. This was to be his first full-sized bronze statue and he deliberately set himself new challenges: he wanted his Louis to look as lifelike as his Isaiah and he wanted the bronze to have the soft folds of cloth. He posed himself the further problem of how to make the finished statue look like me, the model for it, at the same time as it captured the sanctity and mystery and determined character of the boy Saint Louis himself. It was to be a real person who was me and Louis at the same time. In bronze. And finished in gold.

He had built an armature of wood approximately the size of the finished statue, a manikin fantastically fleshed out with a composition of clay, cloth, hair, and horse dung to create a headless bishop ready for the application of beeswax from which the actual cast would be made. But there remained problems of size and problems of material.

The Saint Louis was to be immense, nearly eight feet tall, and Donato was charged with the problem of how to cast it in a single pouring and the further problem of how to create the illusion of masses of brocade modeled first in wax and then in bronze. What he wanted, of course, was the thing itself, a young man, his heart beating hard, suffering. And to suggest a living body beneath those episcopal robes.

He agonized for weeks. He went back to his initial sketches, he restructured the *bozzetto*, he had me pose for him again and again until I began to think I had become the unwilling saint himself. He despaired of getting it right. He had, of course, considered sculpting it in pieces, but it was the cloth—or rather the appearance of cloth—that would not come right. The wax he was modeling continued to look like wax.

"It's wrong," he said aloud. "It's all wrong."

He said more, mostly to himself and all of it despairing.

This trial and failure went on for a long time.

"The wax won't speak," he said.

He said, "The wax is dead."

And he said, "I can't make it live."

"Why not just soak *me* in wax, robes and all?" I waited, but he made no response. "And then cast the statue."

He paused, his hand caressing the air, and then he stood back from his work and stared at me for a long moment. He gazed at the manikin he had constructed, nodded in agreement, and smiled.

"Yes," he said. "I have it now."

I was confused, but happy that he was happy.

"I have it!" he said. He was exultant.

He left his work stand then and came to me where I stood, motionless, on the posing platform. I did not move. I did not know what his intention might be. I thought he would adjust my pose.

He pushed the hair back from my forehead and smoothed his palms over my brow. With my head between his hands, he looked at me long and searching, his eyes upon my eyes as if he saw me in a new way, and then he kissed me full on the lips. It was a soft and searching kiss. His mouth lingered there on my mouth, his hands on either side of my head as he held me firmly in his grasp, and his lips were warm and hard. It was a lover's kiss.

"I have it now," he said, and went back to his work stand, smiling, happy.

The kiss was done, forgotten. He might have been kissing a statue, for the little it meant to him.

He had discovered how to breathe life into his Saint Louis and he was full of joy . . . and as indifferent to me as to the manikin of wood and hair and dung he was about to abandon.

CHAPTER 11

HERE MY LIFE changed forever. We say that all the time, we point to a foul or fair moment in our lives and say, yes, here is where everything of a sudden went wrong, or right, and that is why today I am damned or saved. But in this case, it is true. My lord Donatello—who looked at me and into me and who knew me as none other has—kissed me on the mouth and changed my life forever. That night, Alessandra being large with child, I lay with Caterina who it seemed had long been willing. And when I left her I took money from Donatello's hanging basket and went to the Mercato Vecchio where, in a meager passage used for that purpose, I stood against the wall with an easy whore, and after that with another.

Alessandra and I would have three more children—healthy, all of them, until the Pest of 1437 claimed the youngest two—and I would remain faithful to her, after a way, and keep her close until the end. But on this last day of May, 1423, Donatello had kissed me like a lover, and though I was never again to feel his mouth upon my own, however much I was to think on it, this careless act of his made me his abject creature and so I would remain forever. Even in heaven or in hell.

CHAPTER 12

THIS KISS WAS nothing to Donatello, caught up as he was in his discovery of how to complete the Saint Louis. He abandoned the manikin in its robes of clay and created another that he threw together quickly and with ease. It was rudely done but in form very much like me, with my sloping shoulders and my narrow hips and even my way of standing with a slight twist to my back and my weight heavy on my right foot. Once again he postponed work on the head until later.

On this new manikin he hung not clay robes but robes of fine brocade—gown, cope, gloves, mitre—and he arranged the folds and rearranged them until they said what he wanted them to say. And then he did a bold thing that had never yet been done. He painted the brocade with watered clay. It was a fine mixture that looked more like dirty water than like clay. He used a brush and quick, deft strokes that let the water sink deep into the cloth and after several applications and before the cloth grew too stiff to alter form, he went to work arranging the folds.

The living cloth began to dry and harden as he shifted the curve of the drape so that when the clay water dried, the fabric took on the look of bronze that would reflect the light and create deep shadows. The cloth, weighed down and growing stiff, seemed nonetheless to billow outward. You could see at once that beneath those dramatic folds the saint's body was not so much clothed in the episcopal robes as weighed down by them, the burden almost unbearable.

The process took more than a week but at the end Donato had his workable core. Now he brushed the hard brocade with a thin coat of the finest beeswax. The liquid wax molded itself to the stiffened cloth, catching and keeping the texture of brocade while quickening the light and dark folds of the fabric. Then he laid on the wax in long sheets and, while they were still soft and pliable, molded them over the clay robes. As the wax hardened, he fell to carving in earnest. He began with the heavy twist of fabric that served as a clasp for the cope and from there he moved to the collar—twisting, cutting, smoothing out his errors—and then to the luxurious knot of silk thread at the meeting of glove and crosier. I watched him carve, no longer as an apprentice but as a conspirator.

I do not think he held memory of the kiss.

It was thunder weather. All day the sky had been heavy and overcast as if it might send down a deluge at any minute. It was hard to breathe and the noises of the *bottega* seemed louder in the gathering silence. Everyone's temper was on edge. Donatello was at work completing the wax Saint Louis and all the apprentices were occupied at their several tasks when the great Cosimo made one of his surprise visits. Of a sudden he appeared at the door, splendid in his red cloak and *cappuccio*, accompanied as was his custom by a single servant. There were a few seconds of quiet while, one by one, we became aware of his presence and stared too long for courtesy, and then the ordinary noise of the *bottega* resumed.

Donatello at once covered the statue with a work cloth and turned to greet the great man. They embraced.

"My good friend," Cosimo said.

"My good lord."

They smiled. Cosimo remembered always that men wish to be treated with equality. Donatello remembered they were not equals.

"I'm returning to Rome," Cosimo said, and my mind went immediately to his Byzantine prayer book and the golden coffer I had sketched so many times. "But first I have a new undertaking for you. And for Michelozzo too, of course. His Holiness Pope John the Twenty-Third"—he meant the anti-Pope, one of the three who reigned in 1415—"desired at his death that a great tomb be raised to his memory, of marble and bronze, to be lodged within the Baptistry. Michelozzo would design it. You would execute it." He paused. "There would be a handsome fee, of course." The fee seemed to be especially pleasing to him.

"Of course."

"His Holiness has left, as well, his greatest personal relic: the finger of Saint John the Baptist. A golden reliquary would be required."

"Of course."

"Of your exquisite craftsmanship."

Donatello nodded in agreement. No matter how much work there was in the *bottega*, no matter how far behind he was in that work, Donatello would refuse Cosimo nothing.

They walked together to the work yard and I hastened to the pile of boxes where Michelozzo stored the records of Donatello's commissions. I found the sheaf of sketches I had made for Cosimo's golden coffer and placed them in the center of the huge worktable. Months earlier Donatello had glanced at the sketches, and nodded twice at the particular design I now carefully placed on top of the pile. It had merit, I thought. It had become my favorite.

While they were outside rain began to rattle on the roof, and as the full force of the shower burst on them Cosimo and Donatello came in from the wet. There was a crack of thunder and a short shiver of lightning.

"Ah," Cosimo said, shaking off the rain and approaching Donatello's worktable, "the tabernacle for my book? You are at work on it. Well done. Well done." He examined the sketch with evident pleasure.

"My lord," Donatello said. "As you see."

"Very handsome. The family seal. The laurel wreath. A jeweled clasp."

"As you see."

"Spare nothing. And perhaps when I next return I will be able to look upon the thing itself?"

Donatello smiled. Cosimo was a member of nearly all the committees that had commissioned Donatello's work and he, better than anybody, knew that Donatello's work was always astonishing and always late. Waiting was the cost of dealing with genius and Cosimo was an expert at waiting.

"And our Michelozzo? He goes well?" His voice, hearty and pleasant to attend, softened noticeably as he asked for Michelozzo. Cosimo loved Donatello for his great artistry but his love for Michelozzo was more personal; they were friends of the soul; they studied the principles of architecture together.

"He works with Ghiberti today. They are casting 'Pentecost' for the north doors."

"A marvel."

There was a loud crack of thunder followed by a long silence and a new onrush of rain.

"God agrees," Donatello said. He believed still that his friend Brunelleschi should have had the commission for the Baptistry doors.

"And the Saint Louis?"

"Nearly done."

"And may I . . . ?"

Donatello nodded, not willingly, but led him to the posing area where he removed the work cloth. Cosimo studied the wax sculpture for a long time and asked, "But how will you be able to cast it? It's so large."

"Lozzo is an expert," Donatello said. "He'll do the casting."

Cosimo nodded and continued to look at the statue. "*Miracolo*," he said.

They embraced and he made to leave, but before plunging out into the drenching rain, Cosimo turned and said—as if Donatello might not know this—"He'll need a head."

* * *

THE HEAD AGAIN. He made a false start and then another until, frustrated, he let go the head and worked on the marble Zuccone and the two busts—a prophet and a sybil—long since commissioned for the Porta della Mandorla. Then one day, for no reason other than he saw me of a sudden with a different eye, he returned to the head of Saint Louis with a bold energy. The wax *bozzetto* he produced, carved in less than a week, seemed to me perfection itself. He worked with speed and fury, pausing only to confirm with his fingers the shape of my brow and my cheekbones and the line of my teeth. It was a marvel of invention. In another week the head and the whole was set for casting.

To the core of the statue he had applied liquid wax and to the wax, once hardened, he had applied layers of clay in increasing thickness. The whole would be bolted together, core and clay with the wax in between, and when it was heated the wax would melt and the bronze would be poured into the hollow left by the wax. It was an ancient technique.

He and Michelozzo broke the statue down into eight pieces and each was cast as a separate sheet, the head remaining till the last. The clay mold was bolted to the core and heated slowly, slowly—heated too fast, the wax would boil—until the wax began to melt and run out of the vents at the bottom. And then the molten bronze was poured into the mold through the funnel at the top, replacing in exact detail the wax that had run out the bottom. When the metal cooled, the bolts were removed and the clay armor stripped away and, behold, not the flawless wax that had been encased within but in its place a bronze mess, an eighth part of Saint Louis, that would now be carved and chased and polished. It seemed to me a disaster. All the fine detail was gone, the bronze had clotted, the brocade looked to be canvas. I gasped at the ruin of Donatello's work.

He himself was pleased, however, and chisels in hand, he set about carving away the unseemly clots, chasing the hard bronze, polishing the smooth surface until it was ready for gilding. Each finished piece was heated—evenly and for a long time—above a charcoal fire. This would strengthen the statue to resist foul weather but, more important, the transformative mixing of the chemicals would cause the gold to adhere to the bronze in a way no ordinary gilding process could produce.

At the end the pieces were bolted together invisibly from behind. Constructed thus, the back remained unfinished and so would fit into the Or San Michele niche. The work was all but complete when—we had become this close—he let me put my mark upon it. The *putti* at the base of the niche are his in design but they are executed by me. To celebrate the birth of my son, Donatello assigned the making of these to me as a gift. That they stand there still—my poor work beside that of the great master—is a mark of his generosity and love.

A solemn music here. A change in tone. You've noticed? All is not what it seems. It never is.

During those weeks Donatello spent gilding the Saint Louis, I worked at carving the *putti*, making them frolicsome and antic, like Donatello's own. In the end I was satisfied that the work was my best. But when Donatello looked upon it, he regarded the *putti* in a long silence, a fatal silence, but then because I stood beside him, hoping, he placed his hand on my shoulder and said, "Well done, Luca. You have done well."

I could hear the disappointment in his voice and I knew that only his kindness kept him from pointing out the hundred places where my chisels had gone wrong. My *putti* were common, awkward, ugly; they were as unworthy of his great Saint Louis as I was of him. I felt a tingling in my leg and my foot began to tap, tap, tap and, though I tried to brush it away, that dull gray cloud descended upon my eyes.

I made to cry out but no sound came. I lost all breath. The sculpting of the Louis was done, and my own sculpting of the *putti* had failed, and I would lose my master now, forever. Blood rushed to my head, pulsing. There was a roaring sound, and in my nose there was the stink of the dyer's vats, and I made to cry out though no sound came. Donatello's hand tightened on my shoulder and I began to shake and I could not stop. "*Mio figlio,*" he said. "*Mio tesoro.*" I heard the care in his voice and for a moment my vision cleared. But then I saw my work with Donatello's eyes: these *putti* were not angelic babies, they were tiny men, deformed and loathsome. They had betrayed me. They had lost me his love and I was falling, falling.

I snatched up a chisel and made to lunge at the *putti*. I would efface them from this world.

He threw his arms around me and shook me hard. He pried the chisel from my hand and helped me to his private room. I lay down on his cot and he sat beside me, shushing me, be quiet, be quiet, *figlio mio*. He sat there, trembling himself, and placed his hand softly on my arm. And at his touch my terror fell away.

I lost all sense. I was in a green meadow, the sun upon my brow and cool water flowing nearby. I was safe from all harm. I was not alone. No ill could befall me ever again, no mad pulse of blood within the brain, no dissolution of the heart.

I fell asleep, his hand upon my arm a promise of salvation.

1427

CHAPTER 13

I~T IS TIME~ to talk of Michelozzo and Donatello—and of me—and what we did in the *bottega* before Agnolo entered our lives, but that is all too much for now—I am unwell today, I am discontent—so instead I will talk of Donatello only, and of the things I learned from filling out the forms for his taxes.

Taxes ever were and are and always shall be. But in 1427, the year of the *catasto*, a new kind of wealth tax was introduced by Rinaldo degli Albizzi in hope of injuring his great enemy Cosimo de' Medici and at last bringing him to his knees. Here was a tax that skipped over the poor and taxed the landowners and the merchants and the people who had all the money. The *catasto* obliged every Florentine citizen to declare in writing an account of his property, debtors, and creditors. As business people Donatello and Michelozzo fell under this obligation and I liked it much that it fell to me to tally what they owned and what was owed to them, for they were partners now. I grew close to both of them—they were my fathers, they were my brothers—and of Donato I learned much that I had longed to know.

I have his tax declaration to hand since I have always been a grand conservator of notes. What I learned about his finances did not surprise me but what I learned about his family pleased me much.

Niccolò, Donatello's father lived long enough to see the marble David, though he was addled in his brain and had no proper sense of what his son had accomplished. He died in 1415.

Orsa, his mother, was eighty years old and still sound of mind and body. She was a small woman with eyes like a ferret and, though frail of hearing, nothing escaped her view. She longed for only one thing: to die. But she could not die. If mothers live past child bearing, it would seem they live forever.

His sister, Tita, five years his senior, was a dowerless widow with a sickly son, Giuliano, aged eighteen. He was crippled in his legs and he was given to fits and he could not speak. Small wonder then that Tita was a sour woman, jealous and self-pitying, who resented Donatello's kindness to her son. She had a thorny, unforgiving wit. Donatello told me once that Tita's heart had grown so bitter that it had shrunk to the size of a walnut. I was uncertain if he meant this in truth or if he was being figurative in speech or if this were some cruel jest. He was sometimes *intricato* in thought and in word.

Orsa and Tita and Giuliano lived in a warren of rooms next to his new *bottega* in the Via degli Adimari. Donatello was their sole support.

As for the tax itself Donatello claimed to owe one florin, three lira, and ten *piccioli* and to be without any property except thirty florins' worth of tools and equipment for his art as a carver in partnership with Michele di Bartolomeo Michelozzi.

"I am owed," he says, "one hundred eighty florins for a narrative scene in bronze which I did some time ago for the Cathedral of Siena. Also from the convent and monks of Ognissanti I am owed thirty florins for a bronze half figure of San Rossore. I rent a house from Guglielmo Adimari in the parish of San Cristoforo. I pay fifteen florins a year." He then lists creditors—goldsmiths and bronze casters and assistants—to whom he owes a total of one hundred fifty-six florins, not counting the thirty florins he owes for two years back rent. Donatello hated paying taxes.

Michelozzo signed and filed Donatello's tax report though it was I who did all the preparatory work. You can see how quietly useful I had become.

My life was full and good this year of our Lord 1427.

Alessandra gave me a third son, Renato Paolo.

I was now indispensable to the workings of our *bottega*.

And I had become the trusted friend of the greatest sculptor of our time. It is no small thing to have had the love of so great a man. How, then, did I become possessed . . . so that in the end it seemed the necessary thing was murder?

In truth it was the fire I feared.

Now, dying, I put aside my discontent to ask how different things would be if Donatello had not changed my life with that kiss and if that sharpened chisel had not come so readily to hand. I think, I pray. I remind myself that God permits these things. But in my dark heart I know the cause was fear . . . of Donatello used against Cosimo, Donatello denounced as a sodomite, Donatello stripped and at the stake, and I at fault for all that goodness consumed by flames.

1429

CHAPTER 14

IN THE YEAR of our Lord 1429, in one day, a great shame descended on the Florentine Republic. It was a bright November morning with an early frost underfoot and a hard cold sky above, a promising day for sunshine and merriment and sharp business for the vendors of onion tarts and sugared apples and those small meat pies that are eaten in hand. The wine taverns had been at serious business since dawn. The Piazza San Marco was crowded with city people and with country folk who had come in from the hillsides around Florence to witness the first public execution for sodomy within memory. Not for sodomy only, of course, but for the rape and mutilation of a ten-year-old boy.

Piero di Jacopo was to be burned at the stake and his ashes thrown into the Arno. It was Piero's ill fortune to have raped the one child whose violation could concentrate the attention and the powers of the two great warring families of Florence, the Medici and the Albizzi.

Piero di Jacopo was a coppersmith from Bologna in the employ of Franco Severini, a servant to the estate manager of the Medici. As fate would have it, the boy he raped was the son of Marcello di Angelo, a servant to the estate manager of the Albizzi. Determining di Jacopo's punishment, therefore, became a bitter contest between the Medici and the Albizzi. But in the end, since the accused was a notorious sodomite and since the violated child remained even now in medical care, judgment went to the Albizzi and di Jacopo was sentenced to death.

By sunrise it seemed that all the city had poured into the Piazza San Marco and waited, eager for the ceremony to begin. Somehow everyone knew the ritual: the prisoner would be led out, the indictment read, and then—tied to an ass—he would be paraded through the principal streets of the city to the Place of Justice to be burned at the stake. The excitement increased as the wait grew longer. A dense crowd, thick with the smell of wine and garlic, clustered around the church steps in anticipation. Children had ceased to run about and even the dogs had given over their quarrels and seemed to be waiting. The guards stood to attention, holding the crowd a little distance from the church steps.

At last the San Lorenzo bell began to toll its death knell and the church door was thrown open. A priest appeared—a Prior of the Benedictines—vested in a ceremonial cope of black velvet rich with gold embroidery and carrying a tall processional cross. He was followed by a young boy in a red gown and he in turn by a procession of six priests robed in black and holding before them huge black candles. They in turn were followed by two guards who led di Jacopo out onto the church steps. A great cry went up—"Sodomite! Burn him!"—and the crowd surged forward to get a better look at him. He wore only a long white shirt and his feet were bare and he shivered in the morning cold. He limped when he walked because of course he had been tortured into confession. But he had the comfort of knowing that because he had confessed his sins, mercy had been granted him: he would be hanged until dead before the fire was lit. But that would be later. Now he was the central event in this celebration of justice.

The cries to burn him continued on and an old woman threw a stone but she was restrained at once by the guards. This was to be an orderly ceremony, to warn and to instruct.

The Benedictine Prior handed off his gilded processional cross to the young boy in the red gown—this was the boy's task, to hold the crucifix and by his own tender years to remind the crowd of the violated victim—and then, representing the Church militant, the Prior stepped forward and in a stout voice made his proclamation.

"In the name of Christ our Savior, praise and glory to God our Father. Amen. The trumpet of the Lord and the voice of the Highest shall call out on the day of judgment: 'You who are worthy, come,

O blessed of my father; and you who are unworthy, O accursed ones, go into the eternal fire.' "

He continued these holy denunciations for some minutes and finished with a malediction for di Jacopo and an exhortation to the rest of us.

"Do justice on the body of this sinner, as righteous sons of God and servants of our holy Church." He sketched a great sign of the cross over the crowd. "May the mercy of God our Father and the merits of his son, our savior Jesus Christ, descend upon you and remain forever. Amen."

He stepped to the side then so that the citizen representative appointed by the Curators of the Night Curfew—the Otto di Guardia— could pronounce the indictment on behalf of the Republic. This was Ser Bonaventura degli Buondelmonti, a man well advanced in years, chosen for this task by reason of his large family and his well-known detestation of the sin of sodomy.

A brief drum roll summoned attention and Buondelmonti began to read out the charges. "Theft, extortion, corruption, soul murder." He read slowly. He had difficulty making out the script on the parchment and he was further afflicted by a catch in his voice and almost at once the crowd, attentive until now, began to grow restive. Buondelmonti labored on: "Sodomy, active and passive, continued and repeated over many years." He paused and looked up. "The rape of a child under the age of ten, the severe laceration of his anus, injury to his head and arms." He looked up once more and with difficulty cleared his throat. "Kidnapping and violation, debauchery, perversion, and other enormities hateful to God and man. These crimes cry to heaven for vengeance."

"Burn him!" someone shouted.

"Enough of this! Let us see him burned!"

When at last Buondelmonti ground to a stop—"Vengeance now and punishment for eternity!" he cried—the crowd greeted his words with shouts and cat calls.

There came a pause, with much shifting about of Church and Republic officials at the top of the stairs. Nobody knew what came next.

"Strip him," someone called from the crowd.

At this, the guards led di Jacopo forward and steadied him between them. Then, grasping his shirt at the neck—one on either side—they gave a single hard pull and tore the shirt from neck to hem. Instantly he was exposed to the crowd, naked, shivering. There was laughter and whistling and applause. He tried to cover himself but the guards tied his hands behind his back and a long cheer went up from the crowd. His privy parts were raw and swollen and this was what they had longed to see: he had been punished in the place of his crime. They shouted obscenities, they cursed his soul, and di Jacopo lowered his head in shame. He was exhausted already and it was early in the day.

The young boy in red had gone into the church and now he reappeared carrying a huge crown. It was a bishop's mitre, a mockery painted white and gold, and on either side was scrawled the single word *sodomia*. One of the guards set it on di Jacopo's head and turned him in a circle. The crowd whooped their satisfaction as he turned and they could see from the burn marks that he had been tortured in his anus as well as in his privy parts.

The mitre began to slip and they forced it down harder upon his brow.

Now the boy returned with a placard on a short cord. The boy showed no sign of being ill at ease. In truth he seemed pleased, as if he had rehearsed this role for many weeks and knew he was performing well. The guards tied the placard about di Jacopo's neck so that it hung down before and behind. *Sodomia*, it said, and below that was a list of his crimes. The crowd applauded.

"Cut off his nose!"

"And his ears!"

"Cut off his *cazzo*!"

There were cheers—they wanted blood—but di Jacopo's punishments had already been pronounced in law and he was obliged to give up his life but not his nose or his privy parts. Still, some in the crowd cried out for more.

From the side of the church an ass was led out and brought to the foot of the stairs. The guards huddled di Jacopo roughly down the church stairs and untied his hands so that he could grasp the hair at the ass's neck. They half-helped and half-pushed him onto the back of the frightened beast and, as they pulled at di Jacopo's legs so he could straddle its back, he let out a terrible groan and fell forward on the ass's neck. They propped him up and, once he was steadied, they whipped the ass forward.

Buondelmonti led the procession. He was followed by the Prior with the tall processional cross and then the young boy in the red gown and then the six priests with the black candles and finally the battered Piero di Jacopo who was slumped over the ass. The soldier with his drum brought up the rear. It was a lusty and colorful procession with the great men in their crimson robes, women of every estate in fine silk or crude wool stuff, children scampering through the legs of horses, the colorful costumes of the soldiery, and at the center the condemned man naked on an ass, a mitre and placard proclaiming his crimes. They would process from the Piazza San Marco to the Piazza della Signoria where di Jacopo would be whipped around the square. From there they would move to the Mercato Vecchio and through the Street of the Furriers and on past the Stinche—that notorious prison—and wind through the principal streets of Florence past the Basilica of Santa Croce to emerge beyond the city walls at the area prepared with a platform and banks of straw and firewood that would become for him the Place of Justice.

The procession began and at once calls for his blood rang out.

"Kill him now!"

"Kill him here!"

"Cut off his balls!"

"His balls! His balls!"

"Cut off his *cazzo*!"

There were screams of pleasure.

I turned away. I could watch no more of this. The rage and the lust. The spectacle had at once become a terrible sight, obscene, and I was reminded—who can say why?—of being a child of six and watching the dyer Matteo and his wife Spinetta as they labored, naked, furious, at their pleasure. I was sick at heart and I sought the safety and comfort of the *bottega*. Still, I looked back and recognized among the heaving, pushing crowd many of the men who came and went in our *bottega*—servants, merchants, buyers and sellers. Our apprentices were there too, eager and uncertain, and as I paused at the corner of Via del Cocomero I saw Donatello himself, hanging back from the crowd, watchful and, I thought, troubled as well.

As I skulked through the silent back streets to the *bottega* I thought of my own three sons and how, like that bloodied crowd, I too would cry out for the death of any man who violated them. I hurried on my way.

I found no one at the *bottega*. Michelozzo, I knew, was in Pisa but I had thought to find Caterina at work or Pagno di Lapo, but no one responded to my knocking. I stood leaning against the door, wondering. Why should I care about this wanton sodomite? Why should I not witness this act of justice?

I returned to the Piazza della Signoria where the crowd had gathered in a huge circle to see him flogged. He had been lightly whipped around the circuit of the Piazza and was tied to a horse-post for the serious whipping. A ring of guards kept the crowd at a little distance so that everyone might see. Di Jacopo's guards had removed the *sodomia* mitre and the placard, and now a uniformed officer, a specialist with the whip, was laying on twelve stripes to the counting of the crowd and the beating of the drum. This officer was an expert who knew just how to swing the whip so as not to lay open the flesh too soon—the prisoner had to survive to the place of execution—and loud cries of approval rang out as the whip moved down from di Jacopo's back to his buttocks and curled around the tensed body to tease lightly at his privy parts. Di Jacopo writhed at each new stripe. The Prior stood to the side, at once a witness and a judge, and beside him, shivering, was the young boy in red who seemed no longer to enjoy his part in this morality play. The boy shifted from foot to foot, and at each crack of the whip he flinched and turned away. He could not be above ten years old, a child still, like my own Donato Michele.

Finally the guards untied the prisoner and put him again upon the ass, and with much shouting and cheering the procession continued on to the Mercato Vecchio. Here they came to a halt as the crowd milled about, eager for more. Again di Jacopo was pulled from the donkey, again he was tied to a post—there was the roll of the drum—and again he was given twelve stripes. Someone threw a rotted lettuce and someone else a pear and within minutes they were pelting him with whatever rotten fruits and vegetables came to hand. The mood was merry suddenly and some in the crowd began to sing bawdy songs that celebrated the joys of sodomy. They were comic songs that everybody knew and took in good part.

At the Street of the Furriers they made a long stop. This was the place where the crime against the boy had been committed and here the aged Buondelmonti read out the charges once again, slowly, with solemnity. As each was read the drum rolled and the whipping officer laid another stripe across di Jacopo's back. Blood spurted from the shredded flesh. Again the crowd counted out the blows and again there were shouts of pleasure and vengeance. The officer laid on the whip more lightly now since he feared di Jacopo might not last. He must not die before the execution.

The sun was moving higher in the sky and, though it was November, it promised to be a fair day. The mood had changed again—the list of crimes had done that—and the crowd began to grow restless as the morning grew hot and the procession moved too slowly for their aroused expectations. Once more there were shouts of "Burn him!" and "Let us see him burn!" but the vested priest and the boy in the red gown and the six priests in black and the half-conscious di Jacopo clutching at the ass's neck proceeded on—a lesson in endurance—with one last stop before the Stinche, the prison where criminals of every kind were immured in stone cells awaiting their fate. Sodomites, it was said, met special treatment here.

This was a place of reverent fear—at night you could sometimes hear the screams of the tortured—and so Di Jacopo was made to kneel on the cobblestones and bow his head to the ground three times over, a humble gesture to his fellow criminals. Shouts of "More!" and "Whip him!" came from the crowd, but di Jacopo was too weak for more, and the guards hauled him back onto the ass where he collapsed. They propped him up until he came to himself and then, with the Prior's approval, the procession moved on.

But the crowd was not pleased. Those stripes on his back and buttocks were not bloody enough. Bowing to the cobblestones was no kind of vengeance at all. Only those far gone in drink were laughing now and the larger number seemed angry at the slow progress of the ceremony. They wanted more—and still more—and they wanted it now. They wanted pain. They wanted blood in plenty. They wanted that processional cross to be rammed up his asshole, far up and twisted, they wanted his balls to be cut off and stuffed into his mouth, they wanted his *cazzo* sliced in little pieces and thrown to the dogs.

They wanted his dying to go on and on without end.

The little boy in the red gown covered his eyes and began to whimper and one of the guards laid his hand on the boy's shoulder, comforting him. I wondered was he a father himself that he knew how to console the boy. And at this moment I saw Donatello, his face drawn and pale, his mouth tight in fear or anger. He is seeing himself, I thought. He is himself a sodomite. I turned away from a thought I had never allowed myself to think before, but at this moment I saw it was so and I hated myself for seeing it. I turned back to di Jacopo. Better he than Donato at the stake.

We came at last to Santa Croce but the whipping officer decided di Jacopo would not survive further stripes and, at his command, we passed on through the city walls to the Place of Justice by the river.

The Arno was at full water, a clear yellow, and scrawny trees along the banks were still in leaf and the day seemed festive suddenly. Huts of the very poor had been cleared away and the ground smoothed to make a kind of arena for the spectacle. In the center of this arena they had erected a high platform with banks of straw and firewood heaped around it, and in the middle a mighty gibbet from which di Jacopo would be hanged. Everything had been carefully planned and now a certain formality descended on the crowd. The procession, led by the Prior and his retinue of priests, wound in a huge circle around the arena in a ritual act, as on Easter Sunday in the Piazza della Signoria when we reverence the Eucharist. The clergy moved to the left and the civil authorities of the Republic moved to the right and the guards formed up in an inner circle to ensure that the ceremony would be carried out according to plan.

Di Jacopo was dragged from the ass but he immediately collapsed. The two guards got him to his feet and shook him till he came around and then held him up by main force. They seemed uncertain what to do next, so one of them went to consult Buondelmonti.

Buondelmonti left his body of officials and went to consult with the Prior and after a long moment the matter was decided. It was time for the central event. One guard trussed di Jacopo's arms behind his back and the other guard placed a halter around his neck. They dragged him up the stairs to the platform and stood on either side of him and waited while once again, though in shorter form, Buondelmonti read out the charges. No one listened. All attention was fixed upon di Jacopo, who stood on the black box beneath the gibbet, his head bowed, his lips moving.

The drum rolled. A guard adjusted the noose, tightened it, and then stood down. And—a great wonder—the sun dipped behind a cloud and then slowly reemerged.

The crowd pressed forward. Di Jacopo lifted his head and tried to say something but his voice was lost in the general noise. He struggled against the ropes around his hands. The drum roll ceased and there was a keen silence.

Some one of the watchers shouted "Jesus! Jesus!" and the cry was taken up by others and the Savior's name rang along the city walls and echoed off across the Arno. It was as if they were calling out for Jesus because di Jacopo could not. No one knew why this was happening.

The shouting stopped and, in the silence that followed, the signal was given, the drum rolled again, and all at once the black box was jerked from beneath his feet. There was a short barking sound and di

Jacopo's body plunged forward and down. His head snapped back and his legs flailed out wildly. How could there be any life left in him? Finally his legs stopped flailing and his body twitched and his head hung to the side at an impossible angle. Still, he appeared to be breathing. A man nearby, deep in his wine, shouted out, "Die! Die!" but the cry was not taken up. Everyone was concentrated, waiting for the precise moment of death, as if the devil himself might appear to lead off a new soul to hell. The moment was long in coming.

At last it seemed he was dead. A guard stepped forward and hooked an iron collar about di Jacopo's neck and attached it to the gibbet. This was a precaution to ensure that when the fire took the body it would not fall among the ashes before it was thoroughly burned. The iron collar would hold him upright, more or less, until what remained of him fell to pieces. As the collar was attached the hanging body twitched and the crowd gasped. Di Jacopo was not yet dead. Still, he was dead enough to proceed.

There was the roll of drums and the guards lit their torches. Everyone tensed with anticipation. At four different corners the torches were touched to the straw and wood and at once the flames shot high about the platform. At last, after all this calling on Jesus and the high solemnity of the hanging, here was what they had come to see: the sodomite burning at the stake, justice done, and virtue restored to the Christian community of souls.

A cheer went up from the crowd. "Death to all sodomites," someone shouted and the cry was repeated amid much laughter and cheering.

Off to the side I could see the little boy in red with his face buried in the guard's tunic. He was weeping uncontrollably and the guard, pretending not to notice, nonetheless patted the boy's back in a show of comfort.

After its first flaring the fire burned slowly, but a sudden wind came up and turned the fire away from the body. The crowd groaned, but then the wind shifted and the straw at di Jacopo's feet caught fire, and then his hair, and he stood chained to the pillar like a human torch.

I turned away, sick at my stomach, and fought a passage through the crowd. I thought then, yes, the thing most feared in secret always comes to pass, though I did not know what that might mean for me.

The body was a living flame. They laughed. They shouted. They heaped fresh wood upon the fire and stoked it well so he would burn and burn. I stood and watched. When the flesh of his face began to peel away, they threw stones to see if they could dislodge the head. But the head would not give way and so they let fly chunks of wood to make the arms fall off. Bit by bit the right arm gave way and fell into the fire. A cheer went up and they doubled their efforts until the left arm too gave way. It was a merry game.

They shouted and they danced and they cheered until the body was ashes and they carted it off to the Arno.

The joy of it all. The stink of it. It was a vision of hell.

* * *

Do you wonder that I feared for Donatello?

Attenzione! It is ill done to think that in the middle of my life—a married man with children—I suddenly became a sodomite. I did at certain times think it myself, because I loved him at those times more than I loved my wife and my sons and it hurts even now to say it. But here is the hard truth: I loved him with a cold, keen love. It was of the heart and head only. In time you yourself may judge with what honesty I speak.

1430

CHAPTER 15

It was one of those sweltering days in June when the young Agnolo—then in his sixteenth year—first entered the life of my master Donatello.

The sky was a hard blue, the sunlight so relentless that it struck the marble and dazzled the eye and left you for the moment blind. The birds were silent, the cats had disappeared, the whole city seemed to be at sleep. It was hot, it was sweltering, and we had been at work since dawn. Both of the great doors stood full open—the delivery door from the Via Santa Reparata and the door to the workyard—but dust hung heavy in the air and not the slighest breeze stirred. No one spoke. We worked in our undershirts, barefoot, with no stockings, tired in the heat and ill disposed one to another. We were all nervous at our work because Donatello was expecting a visit from my lord Cosimo.

Cosimo de' Medici was a man of great and unfathomable mystery. He spoke little and listened much, he was a man of enormous wealth who lived—in public, at least—with notable modesty. He was open handed and even profligate with his gold but he could be frugal as well, and even mean. I had observed him closely over the years. He studied politeness and generosity and, apart from his magnificent clothes, he was without ostentation. He preferred a donkey to a horse for daily use and he went about with but a single servant. He loved the busy traffic of florins and was known to have said, "Even if I could wave a magic wand and create money, I would continue to be a banker." So it was not just the money he loved. He was a man of middle age—younger than Donatello, who was forty-four—but he looked older, perhaps because his mind was much on death. Donatello told me once that Cosimo had had a twin brother Damiano who died at birth and thus they were truly Cosmas and Damian, united in life and death, as in the Litany of the Saints. For this reason—the lost brother—he was ever mindful of dying and of the life to come. He belonged to a pious confraternity that met together for prayer and penance, and later in his life, for the sake of his soul, he would spend a vast fortune on the monastery of San Marco. And yet in every other way he was the most worldly of men. He had a particular love for Donatello who loved him much in return.

My master Donato was at this time at work on the Santa Croce tabernacle that shows the angel Gabriel announcing to the Virgin that she is to be the Mother of God. It is a relief in sandstone, generously gilded, and has the look of two fully rounded statues. In truth it seems not so much two statues as the living presence of the angel Gabriel and the Virgin Mary. She is a creature of supreme beauty and intelligence and, despite her initial fright, she accepts what must be. Caterina Bardi, Donatello's niece, posed for the Virgin Mary, and—let me say it once again—at the top of the tabernacle and teetering above it on the right and left are my two boys, Donato Michele and Franco Alessandro, holding one another in fear of the height.

Agnolo had once again come to the *bottega* to ask for money, not because his soldier had thrown him over but because he got bored during the day and found pleasure in causing me discomfort. In truth he had called here several times before and on this day chance alone brought him to Donatello's notice.

Agnolo appeared at the open door of the *bottega*, leaned in— shy—and called to Pagno di Lapo who was sharpening chisels near the door, asking that he call me away from work for only a moment.

"Tell him his brother has a message for him," he said.

Pagno came and stood by me where I attended Donatello as he cut in details of the angel's wings for his Annunciation. When at last Donatello stood back and studied the effect of his chisel work, Pagno took that as permission to speak to me.

"Your brother is here," he said softly. "He has a message."

I looked across the room at Agnolo, who stood at the doorpost, smiling, his straw hat clutched in his hands. He looked up at me and scuffed one foot against the other. He was wearing only a shirt and those strapped boots the soldier had given him. I made a sign that he should wait there.

"I thought you said you didn't have a brother," Donatello said and continued to study his work.

"He's not my brother."

Donatello looked from his angel to me, and seeing I was uneasy, he cast a glance at the door where Agnolo continued to wait. His glance lasted for some time.

"He doesn't look like you."

"He's not my brother."

He looked at me again, comparing us. "He has yellow hair and a broad forehead and eyes that . . . he is very comely."

I said nothing. My master Donatello was forty-four years old and was still taken with comely youths. There was nothing I could say.

He put down his chisel and gave me all his attention.

"What is he called?"

"Agnolo. Agnolo Mattei."

"So he is your half-brother?"

"He is no brother of mine at all. Neither his father nor his mother was my father or mother." I spoke with some heat. "My father was a merchant. My mother was the merchant's slave. She died at my birth and I was forced to live my early years with Matteo and his wife. This Agnolo is their son. He is not my brother."

Donatello had rarely heard me speak with passion and never with such anger.

"He only wants money," I said.

"Then we must give him some."

He put down his chisel and went to the rope that hung from the ceiling and lowered the basket with the money in it. There was a scattering of *piccioli*, some silver florins, and a single gold florin. He took out several *piccioli*, hesitated a moment, and then put them back and took out a silver florin, a large sum, enough for a man to live on for weeks.

"No," I said. I spoke in anger still.

Donatello paused, thinking, and then he raised the basket and tied off the rope. "I think so," he said.

As Donatello approached him Agnolo bowed his head, a quick jerky movement, and then bowed once more, solemnly. Donatello smiled at him and Agnolo returned the smile, his white teeth flashing, his eyes darting from Donatello's face to my own and then back to Donatello.

"You are called Agnolo Mattei?"

"I am Luca's brother."

"Then you're mine as well."

"He's not my brother," I said.

"Peace, peace," Donatello said. And to Agnolo he said, "Have you been in the city long?"

"A year, almost."

"Then you have a place to live."

Agnolo simpered and said nothing.

"And friends."

Agnolo looked down at his boots.

"Those are very handsome boots."

"They were a gift."

"A handsome gift."

There was a silence then and I did nothing to make it easier.

"I came to see Luca," Agnolo said.

"I could not run my shop without Luca. He is greatly valued here." There was another silence.

"I've seen you before," Agnolo said. "In the Mercato."

"Yes."

"And on the Ponte Vecchio. On the far side."

"I live there. With Michele di Bartolomeo."

"Yes."

"Have you seen him as well?"

What were they playing at, I wondered? This seemed less a first meeting than a deliberate flirtation. It was clear that Agnolo was prepared to spend the afternoon in this way and I worried that Donatello was also.

"He only wants money," I said.

"Then you must give him some," Donatello said and handed me the silver florin. He nodded to Agnolo and went back to his work.

I gave Agnolo the coin and a hard look along with it. I waited until I thought Donatello could not hear me.

"You have no shame," I said.

"He likes me. I can tell."

"He only gave you the money because of me."

"But he gave it."

"You must never come here again. This is where I work. Don't come here!" My voice had risen in anger and the others had begun to cast glances at me.

Pagno laughed silently and shook his head.

I turned back to Agnolo but he had disappeared. I stepped out into the street and there he was on his way to the Mercato, tossing his coin in the air and catching it, careless, defiant.

At the horseblock outside the door the great Cosimo de' Medici stood looking after Agnolo, a broad smile on his face. I bowed to him and retreated into the *bottega*.

At once Pagno approached me with a knowing grin. "A little problem with the boy?" he asked. Pagno was one of those men who sees sin everywhere, in everyone, as if the greatest pleasure lay in sniffing out the failings of others. He was twenty-two years of age and had never known love. No, nor sex either, I thought.

"He's my brother," I said and turned away from him.

"Oh? Your brother? Indeed!" Pagno said.

In another week Agnolo returned. For the past two days it had been raining and the *bottega* was heavy with the stink of wet wool and sweat and the earthy smell of cut marble. Lamps were lit throughout the vast room and flares were set beside the Annunciation where Donatello was at work. I had finished feeding the chickens and was in the workyard pulling down hay for Fiametta when Agnolo arrived, drenched through, stamping his feet against the wet.

I came back into the workplace and noticed him at once. He was standing at the door, his hat in his hands, aware every moment that he was being looked at. His hair was drenched, his clothes clung to his body. He looked a misery. The orange cat ran to him and rubbed herself against his leg and he shoved her away with his foot. Good, I thought, let them all see his heartlessness: he has rejected the cat. But of course no one cared. It was just a cat.

At this moment Pagno went to him and said something and they both laughed quietly, like conspirators. I went up to them and Pagno gave me a look and said, "Your brother."

I waited till Pagno left us, then I said, "I told you not to."

"I came in out of the rain."

"What do you want? You couldn't have gone through all that money in these few days. And you're not supposed to come here."

Agnolo hung his head, a penitent.

"Well?"

"I know. I'm sorry."

"Well, what do you want?"

"I want nothing. I wanted only to see you." He looked beyond me to where Donatello was at work on the Annunciation.

"Nobody wears boots like those except soldiers and whores," I said.

"I know. I know."

"And everyone knows how you paid for them."

"They were not payment, they were a gift," he said. He ignored me then, done with pretending to penitence, and instead tugged at the hem of his shirt to shake off the wet. He looked around the room boldly. His eyes darted from Donatello to Pagno where they stood together talking and then to the other assistants and apprentices.

"So many people work here."

"And we're always busy. That's why you must not come here. We have work to do."

"There's a girl over there."

"Yes."

"Do girls make good stone pickers?"

"She paints. And she makes designs."

"She is very fair. Is she your mistress? Or Donatello's?"

"It's not like that here."

"It's like that everywhere." He gave a small poisoned smile.

"You should go," I said. I could not think how to make him leave.

Meanwhile Pagno had lowered the money basket and raised it again and now he approached us, his mouth stretched in a grin.

"This is from your brother," he said, and dropped a few *piccioli* into Agnolo's outstretched hand. "Donatello is busy now."

"You are most kind," Agnolo said, and slid the coins into the small embroidered pouch he wore at his waist. "I am your servant."

Pagno nodded his head, glanced at me, and left us.

"I know his kind," Agnolo said, once Pagno was out of hearing. "He'll do you a shrewd turn and rejoice in it."

"And you?" I said.

"I? I'm just a poor boy of sixteen looking to please God." He laughed then and ducked out into the rain.

✳ ✳ ✳

The next time I saw him he was inside the *bottega* itself, sitting on a stool next to Caterina as she painted the inside lid of Cosimo's wedding chest. The painting showed Queen Esther, bare of breast, pleading before the King that he should spare her people. Agnolo sat watching, his feet planted firmly on the stone floor, his legs apart, playing the man. Caterina was absorbed in her painting, but she could not keep herself from turning now and again to respond to him as he talked. He had a way of fixing her with a glance that lasted a moment longer than necessary and seemed to send a message . . . of interest perhaps or of desire, if she preferred to regard it that way. He was a very practiced young man.

"I've met your brother," Caterina said.

"He's not my brother."

"Luca is ashamed of me," Agnolo said. "Can you believe such a thing?"

"No. Not Luca," Caterina said and looked at me, an admonition.

It was clear she was taken with him. How could this be? His head was too big for his body and his body was soft and girlish. His skin was sickly white.

"I must get on with this *cassone*," she said and turned back to her work.

Agnolo shifted his attention to me. "I talked to your friend, Michelozzo," he said. "He told me Ser Donatello is away in Pisa."

"Buying stone," I said. "You should let Caterina get on with her work." I took his arm and, reluctantly, he got to his feet.

"Michelozzo is very big. And handsome."

He meant to annoy me so I did not respond.

"How old is Michelozzo?"

"Come. I'll walk you out to the street."

"Does he play the boy to Donatello?"

I struck him then, an open hand to his cheek that left a stinging red mark. He raised his fist as if to strike back, then thought better of it and left. Everyone pretended not to notice, except Pagno, who cast me that glancing smile of his.

* * *

IT WAS SOME time before Agnolo returned. Once again I was not there when he arrived—I was occupied in the storage area overseeing delivery of a large packet of wax blocks—and when I came out to the main room of the *bottega*, there was Agnolo deep in conversation with

Donatello. They were standing together before the tabernacle of the Annunciation as Donatello explained to him what was happening in the scene before them.

"You see, the Angel Gabriel kneels before the Virgin and he has come in much haste," Donatello said. He pointed to the feathered wings, still unfurled, rising behind the angel's head. "Mary is startled, she is afraid, as who would not be? She has been at prayer and she is still clutching her book in her arm, see here, as she rises from her chair and makes as if to flee." With his long fingers he traced the book and the arm and the figure rising from the chair. "Notice that the lower part of her body has turned away from the angel, her right foot is poised for flight. Do you see? And now the angel greets her, 'Hail, full of grace!' And at the angel's words she turns back to him—notice the upper part of her body—and attends his message, so we see her face in profile, her hand above her heart. Her eyes are fixed on his eyes and she says, 'Behold the handmaid of the Lord.' And in that moment it is done. She is to be the Mother of the Christ." Donatello stepped back and looked at his work, not altogether satisfied.

He had never explained to me what he was working on or what he hoped to achieve. He had never explained to anyone, until now.

"And this is all marble?" Agnolo asked.

"Limestone. The very best there is for carving."

"You are very skilled."

Donatello laughed softly at this. They stood there in silence for a moment and then Donatello placed his hand on Agnolo's shoulder and squeezed it gently. Agnolo gave no sign that he felt the hand. Then, in the way he had done with all of us at one time or another, Donatello reached up and ruffled the boy's hair. Agnolo shrugged his shoulders and pulled away. Donatello stepped back from him.

If there had been an offer, Agnolo had turned it away and Donatello recognized that. I watched to see what would happen next, but nothing happened. They continued to look at the Annunciation and then Agnolo said he had to go.

"To meet a friend?" Donatello asked.

Agnolo flushed and looked at the floor. After a moment he lifted his eyes to Donatello and gave him that look I had seen him give Caterina, lingering a moment too long, and with a kind of promise in his eyes.

"Could you spare a few *piccioli*? A loan only. I will repay you."

Donatello went to the basket and took out some money and gave it to him.

Agnolo looked at the coins in his hand. "So few?"

"Easier for you to repay," Donatello said.

* * *

IT WAS IN this way that Agnolo became a frequent visitor to the *bottega* of my lords Donatello and Michelozzo. The assistants and the apprentices seemed to accept him as just another presence, here for a few minutes or a few hours and then gone again on his way. Caterina in particular seemed pleased by his visits. Michelozzo did not.

Agnolo made a show of repaying Donatello's few *piccioli* and a week later borrowed some more. Donatello gave without hesitation, as he gave to anyone in need, but finally one day he said, "How do you plan on repaying me?"

Agnolo had watched Caterina posing for Donatello and now, without hesitation, he said, "I can pose for you." He lowered his glance. "If you find me comely enough."

"You are comely enough."

Agnolo cast him a long look.

"As Ganymede, perhaps." Donatello paused. "The beloved of Zeus."

"Ganymede."

"Or as the boy David." They continued to stare at one another, Agnolo eager, Donatello curious.

I could not understand his fascination for the boy. He seemed to think he was in truth a new Ganymede, the perfect boy, with his thick yellow hair and his long, thin body, like a girl's. Everything about

Agnolo was girlish, especially his hair. He fussed with it constantly, pushing it back and tossing it to the side, calling attention to it. One day he arrived with the sides cut shorter than the back, so that in the front it fell in thick curls about his ears but in the back it hung down until it touched his shoulders. He wore a farmer's hat—a *galero*—a ridiculous affectation, with a laurel wreath around the crown—and of course he was never without those expensive leather boots, the gift from his soldier. To me he appeared laughable, the toy of sodomites. I could not abide him.

"We'll talk of this later," Donatello said and returned to his work.

"And where is your soldier these days?" I asked. "You seem to spend a good part of your day with us."

Agnolo took no offense at this, and merely said, "He's in Lucca, fighting. He could not take me with him."

"And you would go if you could?"

"It would be my duty."

"Duty? Are you his bride?"

"He gives me gifts and I am faithful to him. I am not like some of the boys. I am not for sale at the Buco."

"But you were for sale at the Buco. That is where he bought you."

"You want only to hurt."

And he was right. I did want to hurt him. And to spare my master Donatello, since it was clear how tightly he was wound in Agnolo's web.

"And Donatello?" I asked. "You are faithful to him as well?"

"My lord Donatello is a great worker in stone, but he is an old man of more than forty years. I have no designs on him."

"But does he have designs on you?"

He smiled, then, on one side of his mouth. "Most men do," he said. And then he added, as an afterthought, "I would rather Caterina."

And so the situation was impossible. He would pose for Donatello and Donatello would wind himself tighter into that web and in the end it would all come to no good. I knew this and I think Donatello knew it as well.

Agnolo, stripped to his underdrawers, stood on the posing platform while Donatello sketched him from every angle. I stood behind, watching him sketch. It was August, one of those sweltering days in Florence when the heat is unendurable, and Agnolo was hot and restless.

Donatello was trying to encourage him to hold his pose.

"You have just killed Goliath with a stone from your slingshot. You have cut off his head with his own sword and now you stand with one foot on his severed head. It is not your triumph, it is God's."

"It's too hot."

"Stop moving about."

For a few moments he stood still and the only sound was Donatello's stylus scratching against the paper.

"I get itchy standing here." Agnolo flicked his thumb against his waist and then slipped one long finger into his crotch. He let it rest there.

Donatello gave a quick intake of breath. I could hear the lust in his throat.

"Keep still."

"As you wish." But in a moment he touched his crotch once again, as if by chance. I thought I saw Donatello's hand falter.

I turned away from them and found myself facing my lord Cosimo who had come in unannounced and stood there watching. He never interrupted Donatello at his work. I made him a small bow and he nodded in return. His servant Giacomo stood, silent, beside him.

Donatello had stopped sketching. Agnolo stood there motionless. There was a great silence and a pulsing in my ears as if I knew what was about to happen.

"Take off your clothes."

"I've taken them off."

"Take off all of them."

"Even my boots?"

"Leave the boots on."

Agnolo tugged the cord that held up his drawers and they fell to his feet. He kicked them aside and stood there, utterly comfortable in his nakedness. After a moment he raised one foot and rested it on the posing stool. He raised his hands to his hips. "Now what?" He looked down at himself to see how he must look to Donatello and he was satisfied by what he saw.

It was at this moment that my lord Cosimo finally spoke. "Goliath, conquered by the boy David."

CHAPTER 16

I<small>T WAS NOT</small> clear to me what Cosimo de' Medici intended when he said, "Goliath, conquered by the boy David." Was he referring to the scene before him, with Agnolo as David, his boot resting on the head of Donatello? Cosimo was a quick, hard man and, though he loved Donatello, he knew his nature well. Or was he suggesting that here was the subject of a new sculpture? Donatello had carved two Davids already, one for the Duomo and another for the Martelli family, both of them in the old fashion, both of them in marble, both of them clothed. Agnolo would make a new kind of David altogether. There had not been a naked statue in perhaps a thousand years.

"Clap him in bronze and you have your David," Cosimo said.

"If he would stay still long enough," Donatello said, smoothly, as if a naked boy in his studio was no rare thing. My lord Donatello was changing each day, becoming more subtle and more devious as he suited himself to Agnolo.

"We must persuade him," Cosimo said, and they drifted off to Donatello's worktable where they discussed the more immediate business at hand. As keeper of notes, I joined them.

First to hand was the war against Lucca. Brunelleschi had been hired as a consultant on battle plans and it was his grand idea to mount a new kind of attack: instead of relying on a mercenary army and its feeble forays into the outlying areas of the city, he would quite literally swamp his adversaries: he would divert the river Serchio in such a way that it would flood the city out. The *Consigli* were enthusiastic and Cosimo had gone along with them. Michelozzo had been at Lucca for the past two months and had sent back word that he despaired of "the crazy scheme." The scheme had been impractical from the start and was now proceeding so slowly that Cosimo, speaking for the *Consigli*, was inviting Donatello to lend his expertise as war engineer. Donatello never refused a commission and he readily accepted this one. I made a written note of the commission and a mental note that this could not turn out well, not for my lord Cosimo and not for Donatello either.

Cosimo then moved on to the next order of business, the delays with the Prato Pulpit. Two years earlier Michelozzo had signed a contract with Prato in the name of the partnership—*La Bottega di Donatello e Michelozzo*—to produce an outdoor pulpit for the Cathedral of San Giovanni for the celebration of the feasts of the Virgin and for the display of the holy sash that was the cathedral's most prized relic. The contract was precise: the pulpit was to be supported on a fluted pier constructed at the corner of the new façade and to be of the finest white Carrara marble. All the details were very specific, all of it agreed to by Michelozzo and Donatello. I myself had inspected the contract and had made revisions in our native language that were later put into lawyer's Latin, and so I was well aware that it specified completion of the pulpit in no more than one year, and now here we were in August of 1430 and the work was scarcely begun. It was Cosimo's business this day to remind Donatello that the contract had been negotiated through the Medici banks and Cosimo himself was being made to look negligent. I made a note of this while Donatello assured him he would attend to the matter at once.

Finally, Cosimo wanted to talk of the soul and its perdurance after death. I excused myself because this was an intimate matter between two men of genius who shared a love and trust of each other and, for Cosimo at least, a great fear that beyond the edge of life there loomed the possibility of an eternity of fire that would burn but not consume. I wondered at the time if I had ever entertained such a fear myself and I wondered if Donatello—prey as he was to unnatural lust—shared Cosimo's fear of eternal fire. I had little time to worry about the next life, however, since this one—with a wife and three sons to feed— kept me sufficiently occupied. Besides, I was not important enough to catch the eye of God and hold it. It was one of the advantages of being a little person.

When it seemed right to do so, I returned to my lords Cosimo and Donatello and found their talk had moved from eternity to the more pressing problems of mortality. The Pest had returned to Florence this summer and Cosimo was about to leave for Verona where the infection had not yet caught on. The disease seemed to have lost some of its original force since the decimations of 1400 and 1417. It continued to reappear, in summers usually, and it remained as cruel and as fatal, but the victims now were fewer in number and often weakened by other ills to begin with. Children were most vulnerable, but thanks be to God my boys were sturdy and, until now, lucky as well. Cosimo had only two sons, Piero who was fourteen and Giovanni who was nine, but like any father he was most eager to protect his family. Later, I would discover that he was eager to leave Florence to protect his family, not from the Black Pestilence but from that other pestilence, the family Albizzi. They were conspiring against him and in little more than three years they would succeed in placing blame on Cosimo for the failure of the war against Lucca and for "crimes against the state of Florence."

"The David," he said, turning to me. "In bronze. Life-size. For display in my garden."

He cast a glance across the room to where Agnolo was standing, clothed now, fiddling with his hair. Cosimo looked frankly at Donatello and smiled, a strange kind of amusement.

"When you can find the time," he said.

CHAPTER 17

FOR THE NEXT months—in truth, until the very end of the year—creating Cosimo's David seemed the sole concern of the *bottega*.

Michelozzo had returned from the increasingly hopeless war on Lucca and assumed oversight of the Prato Pulpit and, having long since completed the overall architectural design, he now took on responsibility for the sculptural work that Donatello had put aside. This included a new balcony composed of seven marble sections bristling with child angels who hold between them the arms of the Commune of Prato. But even before Michelozzo could settle in and lay chisel to stone he was summoned by Ghiberti—with the intervention of the Operai—to assist in casting sections of the Baptistry doors. These were the second set of bronze doors for San Giovanni and they took precedence over all other public art works, so Donatello had no choice but to let him go. He put Pagno in charge of the frieze for the pulpit—scrollwork and laurel leaves—and promised that very soon, just as the Prato contract specified, he would sculpt the *putti* with his own hand. But not now. Not the pulpit and not anything else.

And so Donatello was at liberty and set to work sketching Agnolo from every angle as he worked out on paper the possibilities he would explore in clay. He seated Agnolo so that his head and the sketch and his own eye were all at the same level. He sketched the head and neck for the latter half of a day. The next morning he had him stand and turn beneath the angle of the light so that the unexplored planes of that soft, smooth body came newly into focus. He had him face front and back and side. He had him lean forward from the waist, then back. He had him stand with his left knee bent, his full weight upon his right leg, and then reverse the pose. He was searching for the angles with the greatest show of power and resilience. He was searching out the bronze David.

"You're about to hurl a heavy stone. Bend back a little. Feel the weight of it." He was taking great patience with the untutored Agnolo.

"I don't know how."

"This is not difficult. Relax. Now make as if you have a stone in your hand and you're about to throw it."

Agnolo made a feeble effort at throwing an imaginary stone. He stood up straight and still. He looked ridiculous.

"Like this," Donatello said. "Your right leg forward, your upper body bent back so that your right arm can gather to a force, and your left arm across your chest supporting the other end of the slingshot. In a slight crouch."

Agnolo folded his arms across his chest and stood there.

Donatello held his patience as if this stupidity were a normal thing in a model.

"Right leg forward," he said. Agnolo stretched out his leg as if he were about to dance. "Put your weight on that leg. Lean into it. It's bent at the knee. Good. Now lean backward from your waist. More to the side. The right side. Good. Now crouch a little. No, just a little, and now pull your right arm back and down. Your right hand is holding the sling with the stone in it. Hold it back, and down. Now with your left hand reach across your body to grasp the other end of the sling. Good. Now look up at your enemy." Agnolo looked at Donatello. "No, look up. Look up over your left shoulder. Pull the shoulder down a little. See? You feel the tension through your entire body. Your right foot curls down with the effort. Good. You are about to launch a stone that will fell Goliath in a single blow. Good. Very good. Now hold that pose while I sketch you."

Agnolo held the pose for a moment, pleased with himself. He discovered at once that posing was not easy—all his limbs ached—and from this time on Donatello was hard put to encourage him.

"You are a poor shepherd in the hands of God. He is using you to perform His holy will."

"You are one of the great heroes of the Bible."

"The King has clothed you in his own armor but you have put it off because you find your strength in God alone."

Agnolo was a boy without education of any kind, but he was quick to respond to approval.

"The king has summoned you to fight for Israel. You alone."

These brief hymns of praise were pleasing to Agnolo but almost at once he began to make difficulties. First it was a question of posing nude while someone drew pictures of him. This was degrading. This was beneath him.

Donatello, who had not considered this nicety, shot him a hard look and left me to deal with the matter. I was, in truth, made speechless by Agnolo's complaint.

"What?" I asked. "Why?"

"I am not a whore. Only whores pose nude."

"On both points you are in error," I said.

"What do you mean?" He was not indignant. He did not understand.

"David fought Goliath with no weapon but a stone. He has to be nude."

"But no one else is nude."

"No one else is David."

This seemed to please him, but a moment later he said he would not pose nude unless someone else was nude. "Ask Caterina," he said, smirking, and Donatello, who was listening, made as if to strike him.

Well, he would not pose nude, he said, unless some third person was present.

Donatello's face darkened and he frowned. It was a mark of anger we had all learned to fear.

"To protect you?" he asked.

Agnolo stared at him, a provocation.

"From me?"

Agnolo said nothing.

"Are you afraid for your reputation?"

"I am unused to posing. Nude."

"I can find any number of boys who will be glad to pose. Nude."

"Some boys will do anything," Agnolo said.

Donatello fell silent, but I sensed that this was an insult he would not soon forget.

Thus, it was agreed that I should move my worktable nearer to the posing alcove so that, by merely looking up from my notes, I could see Agnolo and, if there were need, intervene to protect his virtue. I thought that Donatello would not concede this, but the boy had a power over him I could not understand. Agnolo glowed with satisfaction.

A DRAFT UPON Cosimo's bank arrived that morning and I immediately inscribed in my *quaderno* the date, the amount, and the quantity of bronze it was expected to buy. The draft was an advance of fifty florins against materials—tin and copper and fine white wax—and another thirty to urge the project on. Donatello cared little if it were thirty or forty or one hundred. So long as his bills were eventually paid and the materials for his next project were readily available, he was indifferent to money. It was only with Agnolo that he seemed to count his coins and, even with Agnolo, he made up for a moment of stinginess with countless acts of generosity. "He's just a boy," he would say to me and reach for the rope to the money basket.

Agnolo preened and fawned and pouted.

DONATELLO GAVE HIM a new, easier pose, and—to ease the dreariness of posing—had him alternate it with the first. "Stand straight," he said, "your weight is on your right leg, your left leg is extended. No, less extended. You are about to throw the stone. It is curled in your left fist and you hold it at your left shoulder. Do you see how easy? You are looking off to your left. Calmly. You see Goliath and you are not afraid. You are in the hands of God."

"What about my right hand? What is it doing?

Pagno, who had stopped his own work to observe the new pose, leaned into me and made an obscene comment.

"Nothing," Donatello said. "It's hanging by your side. Is that easy for you? Is that comfortable? We can alternate the poses when you tire."

But Agnolo made new difficulties. Now it was a question of money. He chewed on his lip and rubbed one booted foot against the other and finally came out with it: he could not possibly live on the few *piccioli* Donatello paid him.

"You must tell him I need more," he said.

"Tell him yourself."

"He won't speak to me."

"Don't play the fool."

He hesitated and then he said, "He is offended that I know he wants me."

"He does not want you. You make too much of yourself."

"I need money."

"You need, you need," I said. "Ask your soldier for money."

"He's in Lucca, fighting. He doesn't know my needs."

Once again my contempt rendered me speechless.

"I'm standing here naked," he said.

"Then cover yourself. Put on a cloak."

"But I should take it off for him? I'm your brother."

"You're not my brother. You're the son of the wool dyer and his wife."

And so it was agreed that Donatello would pay him a weekly sum, due always in advance. This did not include the odd trips to the hanging basket, sometimes by Donatello, sometimes by Agnolo himself, and once—and this astonished me—by Pagno di Lapo who slipped the boy a handful of change. What, I wondered, could explain this?

* * *

THE MONEY ISSUE settled, Agnolo found himself hard-pressed for another source of complaint. It was not long, however, before he lit upon the Black Pestilence. He was not feeling well. He was hot. He had a fever. He wanted to lie down in Donatello's privy chamber. He needed a cold drink. He was bored. He might die of boredom. Or of the Pest. In response, Donatello gave him the key to his privy chamber. He sent an apprentice for a cold drink, or a hot one, whichever the moment required. He assured him that boredom did not cause death. He promised him the Black Pestilence would pass when the weather grew colder. It always had. It would again. "And then I shall freeze," Agnolo said.

Besides, he said to me, Donatello did not respect him. Tell him so.

I told him so.

Donatello assured Agnolo he had the deepest respect for him. He could not possibly respect him more, not if he were a saint, not if he were an angel. His respect fell just this side of worship.

For this Agnolo rewarded him with a smile and one of those looks that lasted a moment too long and this encouraged Donatello to ask for one final pose.

"David has just killed Goliath and now he stands looking down at the severed head. He holds Goliath's sword in his right hand and a stone in his left. Goliath's head lies at his feet. No. Beneath his feet. Try this: David stands with his left foot on Goliath's head as he looks down at him in triumph."

I was sent to the workyard for a block of scrap marble that would serve as Goliath's head.

Agnolo assumed the pose with surprising ease and speed. In truth he was learning the difficult skill of posing for a sculptor. But he quickly grew tired and assumed his usual girlish pout before Donatello could complete even his first sketches. Donatello resorted to his little hymns of praise—"You are God's vengeance against his enemies." "You will be the great King of Israel."—but these did little to change Agnolo's ill humor. He sulked. He pouted. And, in his boredom, he resorted to seduction. He fluttered his eyes and touched his hair and tipped his pelvis forward, an offering.

Donatello, insulted and enraged, sketched him exactly as he was, a bold youth who could be bought for a pair of soldier's boots. This would become the pose of the bronze David.

* * *

It was November now and, for Agnolo's comfort, Donatello installed a small wood stove in the posing area. It was no good, Agnolo said, it did not cast enough heat.

"Stop moving."

"I'm trying to stay warm."

Donatello ignored him.

"Look, I'm cold," Agnolo said. He tugged lightly at his privy member which, as he intended, began to stiffen. "Look."

Agnolo had taken his provocation too far and Donatello would not have it. He put down his stylus. Slowly, deliberately, he crossed to his worktable and shifted through a small pile of sketches and then went out into the courtyard where Pagno, by another small wood fire, was chiseling floral scrollwork on the support brackets for the Prato Pulpit. Donatello engaged him in conversation. He pointed out places where the cuts were not deep enough, where proportions were amiss. He visited the privy. When he returned to the posing area, he appeared calm, disinterested.

"Enough for today," Donatello said, and he did not so much as cast a glance at Agnolo. He turned instead to me.

"Does your work go well?" he asked, and I said yes, it went well, but I was concerned about commissions that were overdue. Not only the pulpit but the Annunciation and the marble reliefs for Cosimo and the score of other neglected commissions. Could he review them with me? Could he find the time? Perhaps now? And thus, together, we closed out Agnolo and he was left to dress and put away his privy parts and his hurt feelings and go home.

The next day Agnolo did not appear until noon. It was not his fault, he said. He was unwell, he had a fever, he would probably die of the Black Pest. What difference did it make anyway? Donatello knew well enough by now what he looked like. And why was he still sketching? Why didn't he move on to the next thing, the *bozzetto*? From this I knew Agnolo had been talking with Pagno.

"You cannot well begin without a *bozzetto*," Agnolo said, proud of his intimate knowledge of the technique of sculpting.

Thus Donatello moved on to the *bozzetto* and for the next long days I watched with some wonder as he took a bunch of sticks and wires and hammered the wires into wood and twisted those wires to the rough shape of human limbs, metal bones he would convert to living flesh. As he applied the clay, the form of the boy began to come into being, the legs looked less like sticks and the arms took on shape and solidity. He moved slowly, steadily, following the sketch of the pose.

During this period of making the *bozzetto*, there was no need for Agnolo to pose. But perverse as he was, he came to the *bottega* nonetheless, hanging about in everyone's way. He watched Caterina as she worked at the second of Cosimo's *cassoni*, the one where King Solomon meets the Queen of Saba. He sat on a stool by Caterina's side and asked if he could help her. Could he grind the paints? He leaned against her as she worked. He let his knee touch hers and he put his hand on her back. He played the modest lover. "Enough," she said, pretending to annoyance, but it was clear she enjoyed Agnolo's attention.

He drifted off to Pagno who was still chiseling foliage on support brackets for the Prato Pulpit and asked if he could help. "What could you possibly do?" Pagno asked and looked about, pleased to be seen dismissing him.

Agnolo returned to Donatello who, anxious and annoyed, shrugged off his neediness and told him to go away and let be. The *bozzetto*, it seemed, was a failure.

"It is impossible," he told me. "I cannot do this David in bronze."

"Tomorrow," I said, trying out the words of Michelozzo.

The next day Donatello did not come to the *bottega* at all, nor on the day following. I sought him at his home where Michelozzo met me at the door and said Donatello was not himself, I should be patient, all would be well soon. Another day went by and we waited.

✶ ✶ ✶

Meanwhile Agnolo, with nothing to occupy him, turned to me for the attention he could not live without.

"Why are you always writing?" he asked. "What do you keep in that notebook?"

"It's my *quaderno a casa*," I said. "It's a book of commissions, work that has been ordered but not yet completed."

"Am I in it?"

"You're in the *campione*, the general account book. You're a liability."

"Because I model for the David?"

"Because you cost money and provide nothing."

"As always, you speak only to hurt."

I asked pardon for offending his lordship and returned to my *quaderno*. He stood beside me, saying nothing, until I began to feel sorry for being hurtful. In truth I had changed since Agnolo had come among us: I took pleasure in finding fault with him. Alessandra had noticed it and made comment and, of course, so had Pagno di Lapo.

Alessandra was pregnant again—our fourth son—and she was given to saying hard things with a sharp tongue. "You resent his closeness to Donato," she said, and there was nothing but truth in her voice. "It is small of you, Luca, since he loves you so."

"He loves nobody, not even his soldier."

"I meant Donato."

"Donatello is obsessed with him."

"It is a passing thing. Agnolo is only a boy."

"A boy possessed by the devil."

"Luca," she said, and that ended her rebuke.

Pagno was more to the point. As always he seemed to imply more than he said. Words for him were another tool for carving.

"You've changed since your brother has come among us."

"He's not my brother."

"You've become querulous and testy. You're always short of patience. Why do you suppose that is?"

"He wastes our time. He costs us money."

"But he is pleasing to Donatello."

"He is useful to Donatello."

"You too were once pleasing to Donatello," he said.

In my anger I made no reply. Pagno himself pleased Donatello . . . beyond all reason. He had been Donatello's prize apprentice and now he was the prize assistant, allowed to sculpt beyond his abilities and trusted beyond all measure. Given the chance—and in the end he would be given it—he would execute the two angels on the support braces of the Prato Pulpit and ruin them. Pagno had been the most comely of Donatello's youths and was grown now into a handsome man of twenty-two years, tall and lean, with a high, broad forehead and eyes that were sometimes green and sometimes blue. Later he would be the model for Donatello's bronze Daniel in the group of seven saints on the great altar at Padua, where it pleased me to see that his low chin betrayed his true weakness. I was ever keen to number Pagno's failings.

"He is useful to Donatello," I said again. "Only that."

"So are we all," Pagno said. He paused. "And he seems to have taken the eye of my lord Cosimo de' Medici."

Donatello returned to the *bottega* on the third day. He was pale and he looked unwell and I wondered if he had passed these lost days in drink. He spent the morning in his privy chamber and in the afternoon he returned to his worktable where he went back over his earliest sketches, scores of them, dissatisfied, angry. Almost at once he began a new *bozzetto*: David triumphant, his foot resting lightly on Goliath's severed head. A gift for a soldier.

Agnolo assumed that pose once more, pleased to be the center of interest, excited to be nude and looked at and—as he thought—desired. The *bottega* was alive with tension once again. There was a heavy silence in the air as when a storm is threatening. Donatello worked in a fury. "You have killed him and you have cut off his head. It was nothing to you. You have the stone in one hand and his sword in the other. Your foot rests on his head. You are young and you have great power. And you are beautiful to look at." Agnolo smiled and leaned forward. "No. Lean back. Look down. Your foot is on his head. How do you feel? What do you want?" He went on and on this way, returning always to David's beauty and his power. "You are burning in your beauty," I heard him say, and I set it down in my notebook because it was ridiculous and embarrassing, and I watched as Agnolo assumed that pose, burning from within.

The *bozzetto* began to take form. Donatello completed the limbs bit by bit, fleshing out one arm and then another, one leg and then another, so that as it moved toward a fullness, the whole body seemed to be growing from the inside outward.

Agnolo was much more cooperative now. He held a pose without fidgeting and he kept his complaints to himself, though it was now late December and the wood stove gave off little heat. He shivered and he chafed his arms and legs but he did not complain.

"A little longer," Donatello said. "And then you can have a rest." Agnolo sighed to let us know how heavy a burden this posing had become.

The arms and legs and the long torso were completed before Donatello had well completed the neck and head. He had left the private parts unformed, a blob of clay without shape, as if somehow this shameful part was not important. I noted this and so did Agnolo, but it was Agnolo who asked him about it.

"In good time," Donatello said.

"You didn't leave enough clay for my *cazzo*."

"We're still in the early stages.

Agnolo pouted.

Donatello ruffled his hair but Agnolo pulled away from him.

"You are tiresome," Donatello said. "And more."

"I'm a good model, all the same."

"You are the best model."

"Then why don't you show me as I am, here?" and he pointed at the unfinished blob of clay.

Donatello did not reply, and I expected him to offer a rebuke but he only smiled to himself and placed a clean wet cloth over the *bozzetto* to protect it from drying out.

WINTER IN FLORENCE that year was wet and unforgiving. A cold fog descended on the city, and though the weather had brought an end to the Black Pestilence, everyone was unwell with afflictions of the head and chest. The light in the *bottega* was gray and for much of the time Donatello worked by rushlight as he finished the neck and head. The wet clay was clammy to the touch. Agnolo spent a week in bed and when he recovered he posed for shorter and shorter periods, huddling between times in woolen blankets. Despite all the delays, the day came when the *bozzetto* was finished.

Donatello was pleased with his work, though he examined it as if it were an enemy who had come to threaten his life. He studied it from every side. He turned the revolving stand again and again. He felt the arms, the legs, he smoothed the blade of the heavy sword. He touched the soft and sagging buttocks and he ran his finger the full length of the feather on Goliath's helmet from where it touched

David's ankle to where it disappeared high up between his legs. He stood back farther and farther and he was pleased. The effect, even in this preliminary sculpture, was of a boy satisfied with what he had done, indifferent to death, and at ease in his nakedness. He asked to be gazed upon.

All this time Agnolo was caught up in admiration of himself. He saw the *bozzetto* as an extension of his own person and he wanted to know more and more. He could not get enough.

"Tomorrow," Donatello told him, and put the *bozzetto* under cover of a wet cloth. He was filled with excitement, I could tell, but he was determined to see the completed miniature in the hard light of morning before he pronounced it done. Agnolo would have to wait.

It was late in the day. Most of the others had left. Michelozzo had come in to see how Pagno was getting on with scrollwork for the Prato Pulpit but left almost at once to get back to Ghiberti who was well along in the process of casting the bronze doors. Pagno himself lingered until Donatello finally told him he could go. My own presence he took as a given; I was there because I was always there; I didn't matter.

Now there remained only the three of us.

Agnolo was dressed for January in heavy stockings and a woolen shirt beneath a thick quilted over-vest. He had already put on his outer cloak and, disappointed, was preparing to leave when Donatello said to him, "Wait." And then, as if this had not been his plan all along, he said, "Come here," and his voice was honeyed. Agnolo took off his cloak and tossed it on my worktable.

Donatello removed the wet cloth from the *bozzetto* and his hands were trembling. "Look!" he said. "The *galero*, first of all, the peasant's hat you wore all last summer is David's now. He is a peasant, a shepherd. The king has dressed him in his own armor, a helmet of brass and a coat of mail. But David put off the armor and went out to meet Goliath armed only with a slingshot and stones. See here," and he pointed to the stone in David's fist. "We know this from the Bible."

But Agnolo was not interested in the Bible. He wanted to hear only about the statue.

"Look." Donatello turned the *bozzetto* face forward. "You can see here how the right leg bears the weight of the body while the left knee bends as he places his foot upon Goliath's head. The right arm and the sword make a long, uneven triangle that runs the whole length of his body while the left arm makes a small perfect triangle on the other side. They please the eye. The long sword pulls your attention down to the head beneath David's foot."

Donatello traced the lines of the statue as he talked.

Agnolo fidgeted at his side. He was not interested in triangles or swords.

"Tell about the feather," Agnolo said.

But Donatello was moving at his own pace. "Notice the curved line of the body on the left and the swelling movement of the flesh here, on the right hip." Donatello touched the right hip of the statue and then, with the tip of his fingers, touched the right hip of the boy standing next to him. "Just here," he said. "You can feel the slight bulge."

Agnolo put his hand to his hip and nodded.

"Now notice this side." He turned the stand on its pivot so that they faced the statue in its left profile. "Notice how the stone in your fist is in perfect line with your shoulder and your foot." He touched Agnolo's shoulder. "And with the angle of your elbow." His finger drifted slowly in a straight line from Agnolo's shoulder to his elbow and then, turning away, he pivoted the statue another quarter turn. "From the back your hair falls down to the top of your shoulder blades, and note here the slight twist to your spine and the swell of your buttocks." Donatello touched the statue here and let his fingers trace the curve of the buttocks. He lingered there but he did not touch Agnolo. They stood silent for a moment and then Donatello said, "Beautiful."

He turned the statue to its right profile and pointed out that the sword and the right leg carry the eye firmly down and up despite the diagonal lines of the forearm and the thigh.

He turned the statue once more full front.

"Goliath's head," he said, "and the helmet . . ."

"More about David," Agnolo said.

It was as if Donatello had been waiting for this.

"Note the setting of the eyes," he began and Agnolo leaned in closer, his pleasure undisguised. Donatello, with the tip of his finger, traced the outer lid of the statue's eyes and then repeated the gesture on Agnolo himself. "You can feel the weight of my finger tip and you can feel the flesh beneath it as it responds. Is this not so?" Agnolo nodded and Donatello went on, slowly, languorously, describing what he had done with the *bozzetto* and tracing on Agnolo himself the set of the eyebrows, the breadth of the forehead—he used both hands, gently, scarcely touching him—the high wide cheekbones, and the perfect lips.

I stared at my account book, unable to look up though I could see what Donatello was doing—his finger tracing the shape of the mouth—and I could see Agnolo's response. He was enraptured, his face kindled with passion.

They stood facing one another and Donatello ran his fingertip across the boy's upper lip, saying nothing, only looking into his eyes. "Perfect," he said, "perfect," and I could see Agnolo tilt his lower body in toward Donatello and I could see Donatello lean in toward him until they touched. There was no shame on either part, only desire and need.

Without casting me a glance, Donatello said, "Cover the *bozzetto* with a wet cloth and lock the door when you leave." He took Agnolo by the hand and they moved slowly down the long room and disappeared into Donatello's privy chamber.

* * *

A<small>ND SO IT</small> was a surprise on the next morning—a cold January dawn, heavy with mist—that Agnolo did not appear at the *bottega*. Nor on the next day. Nor the next.

Good, I thought, he is well gone. And I was hard put to conceal my joy.

1431 – 1432

CHAPTER 18

So Agnolo was gone and there would be no sculpting of the David until he came back. I had hoped life in the *bottega* would return to normal, but after his first fit of annoyance with the boy, Donatello grew half mad with anger and frustration. He was enraged at first that he could not continue with his sculpting but then his rage gave way to worry about the boy himself. He was perhaps ill. Perhaps the Black Pest, even during these winter months, had stolen upon him and borne him off just as he had feared. Or perhaps, taken by force in a sodomite tavern, the boy had been raped and murdered and his body was even now lying in some filthy alley behind the Mercato . . . or was being carried toward Pisa on the swollen waters of the Arno. We must find him. We must search him out.

In truth none of us save Donatello seemed sorry that Agnolo was gone. The *garzoni*—assistants hired for their specialized skills—were caught up each in his own task and the apprentices, who worked hard and resented all the attention lavished on the boy, were plainly relieved to see him gone. Pagno di Lapo seemed to me indifferent. "He's run off with that sodomite soldier," he said, "and he'll come back when the soldier casts him off."

I did not say, "All this fuss over a pair of boots." I bit my tongue instead. But I wondered if this might be a new coyness, yet another assault on Donatello's patience. How many rival soldiers could Donatello endure? I had no concern for the wretched boy himself; he was vain and stupid and a whore; it was Donato in this new frightening blindness I was concerned for.

Pagno had less concern for Agnolo's welfare than for the *bottega's* commissions, he said. The Prato Pulpit, for instance, was being completely neglected. It was long since time for Donatello—or Michelozzo—to carve the child angels for the cornices. Still, it was Donatello he worried for, and what the boy's disappearance meant to him. "You must find him," Pagno said, "he's with his soldier." And in Donatello's hearing, he said, "After all he is your brother."

As if echoing Pagno, Donatello said, "You will make inquiries? You will find him for me?"

"Of course," I said. "You need only ask." But I added, "He is not my brother."

I KNEW THAT Agnolo lived with other boys of his kind in the warren of inns and rooming houses on the far side of the Ponte Vecchio, but I set out with little hope of finding him or—more unlikely still—anyone who might know of him. "A comely boy of sixteen? With fair hair? And willing?" They are thirteen to the dozen here, runaways and wild young boys and even the sons of good and noble families, ripe for danger and deviltry.

I went at nightfall, half frozen by the January cold and muffled in a double vest, a long cloak wrapped around me twice and a heavy wool scarf to shield my face against the fog. It was a damp night with rain just starting to fall and a dim moon that provided no light at all. Here and there flickering night torches lit a main street and gave safe passage to people hurrying home from work, but I turned from the main streets to the back alleys and the haunts of prostitutes and cutpurses and criminals of every sort. In such doubtful company and in such darkness and danger, how was I to discover the whereabouts of Agnolo Mattei? And yet, though it seemed impossible, it was not long before I chanced upon a gang of three young toughs who loitered at the head of an alley and who, by their youth and eager appearance, looked as if to welcome me and whatever I might have to offer. I asked about Agnolo—I mentioned his soldier friend—and they claimed to know him. "He wears boots like those of his soldier and he calls himself a sculptor," one of them said, laughing. "A sculptor!" He was as tall as Michelozzo and as broad. I gave him a few *piccioli* and asked at what house I might find the boy. "Ask for him at the Buco," he said. "It is a special house." They laughed at this fine joke. "Or at the Sant' Andrea or the Chiasso or the Fico!" I pretended patience. "And what of yourself?" another said. "Do you want for company?" I said I wanted only to find the boy. "He is lost," I said. "He is my brother." "Oh, he is surely lost, your brother," he said and added quickly, "everyone should love his brother." They were sturdy boys—*bravi*, you would think to see them. The tall one gave a quick embrace to the boy nearest him and let his hand linger on his buttocks shamelessly. He looked carefully to see my response. The third simpered and said nothing.

I thanked them and came away and sought out Donatello. I was struck of a sudden by how tired he looked, and how much older than his years, and I blamed Agnolo for this. Nonetheless I reported what I had learned, that we should look for him at a tavern called the Buco.

"I know the Buco," Donatello said. "It's an evil place."

The next night we went there together. It was the worst of the January weather and snow was falling lightly as we crossed the Ponte Vecchio. Most of the shops were shuttered for the night and, despite the number of people crossing back and forth, the air was quiet and we could hear the Arno rushing beneath us. I thought of what Donatello had said about Agnolo's dead body being borne off to Pisa on the swollen river and I shuddered to think I had wished him just such a fate. "*Miserere mei Domine,*" I said. Donatello, who could not know what I was thinking, cast me an odd glance and said, "Ever the Franciscan." I took that unkindly and wished Agnolo ill all over again.

The falling snow had begun to gather in the streets, transforming the filth and the slops and the debris of the day into mounds of white and silver, a disguise that for a moment turned the ugly into something beautiful. There was the scent of woodsmoke from the evening fires and I wished we could forget Agnolo and walk on like this together until the night was over. But almost at once we came to the end of the bridge and the start of the Via Lambertesca where the snow turned dirty and the street itself became a stream of mud, dangerous underfoot and ugly to look upon. We reached the alley called Buco from which the tavern takes its name—the tavern is still there today, I am told, and still a haunt of sodomites—and we paused before the door, ill at ease. There were no windows onto the street. Only a hand-lettered sign above a narrow door indicated this as a place of business. "Taverna Buco," the sign said, and beneath the lettering someone had scrawled what looked to be an erect penis.

"We'll find him, surely," I said for want of anything else to say.

The door opened upon a tiny entrance the size of a coffin where still another door opened into the main room of the tavern itself. I pushed the door inward and at once we were assaulted by the din of drunken laughter and the clash of tankards against wood and the roar of voices raised in mindless anger and pleasure and surprise. A great fireplace against one wall heated that end of the tavern, but the chimney drew poorly and smoke poured back into the room and stung the eyes. The noise was constant and the air was thick with the smell of spilled wine and sweat and wet woolen clothes. Serving maids came and went in haste. Tavern boys delivered flagons of wine and ale. A barman, thin to the point of emaciation, was heartily at his work with wine casks and tankards and a handcloth to slop away spills. The Buco had the look of a typical Florence tavern, except that a narrow stairway led to the floors above where there were tiny rooms that could be rented by travelers . . . or by sodomites to entertain their guests, boys and women alike, with rent to be paid by the hour or the night or, in special cases, for longer periods if money was no problem and the need was unremitting. All this was known to be true, though little of it had ever been proved in court. To me it looked like any other tavern in Florence.

Before I had adjusted to the shouts and laughter and before I could well see through the smoke-filled air, we were approached by the tavern keeper who surprised me by bowing slightly to Donatello and greeting him, "Ser Donato. Welcome to my tavern." I could not tell if the tavern keeper knew him from the past or merely recognized him as the great sculptor he was. From his greeting it was impossible to know with surety.

"*Benedicite*," Donatello said, and I wondered if he was mocking me.

"Our tables are full, as you see, but I'll make up a new one especially for you." He signaled to a boy and said "Another trestle." The boy flashed us a broad and willing smile. He was no more than fifteen with a great mass of black curls, a gap in his front teeth, and the awkward, unformed body of a growing youth. He wore the new tight stockings—one leg red, the other yellow—that were meant to show his thighs and buttocks to advantage. Like Agnolo, he was shamelessly for sale.

"I'm looking for a boy," Donatello said, and when the tavern keeper raised his brows in inquiry, he added, "my apprentice, Agnolo Mattei by name, in training to be a sculptor."

"There are many boys," the tavern keeper said, "with many names."

"Wine, then," Donatello said and the tavern keeper left us. A serving woman appeared, fat and happy, with her breasts much on display, and in her hands she bore two small tankards of wine. It was of poor quality and faintly sour. The Buco was not patronized for the quality of its drink.

"Agnolo, the sculptor," she said. "He fancies a farmer's hat in summer and a soldier's boots all the year through." She was pleased to show she knew him. She was that kind of loose woman who is motherly by nature and a prostitute by necessity. They are not uncommon even today. My Alessandra had been one of those . . . Alessandra who today is a nun of the Order of Preachers of San Dominic, Sister Maria Adriana, O.P., may she have long life.

We finished our wine and took leave of the tavern keeper and in the falling snow we made our way back across the Ponte Vecchio. We did not talk about what we had seen at the Buco—a life as far from the *bottega* as life in a Muslim seraglio—nor about what we would have done had we found him there. We walked in silence, listening to the crunch of snow beneath our heavy shoes. Reluctantly I suggested the other taverns known for prostitution—the Sant' Andrea or the Chiasso or the Fico—and I was relieved that Donatello did not have the heart for it. Nor did he want to be alone.

Back once more at the *bottega* he lit a fire and we huddled by it while he ran his worries through his mind and I sat thinking murderous thoughts about Agnolo who was responsible for so much misery. I longed to be home now with Alessandra and my boys. For this misery too, I blamed Agnolo.

"Where do you think he could have gone?"

"To his soldier, I imagine." I waited for a response and then, because I could not help myself, I said, "Or to a new soldier."

Donatello shot me a hard look.

"He is not famed for fidelity," I said.

"He claims you speak only to give him hurt. I wonder if he is right."

"I speak the truth."

"Always? I think you are very hard on him."

"Yes."

I could not bear to have Donatello think ill of me but no more could I bear to think of them alone together in Donatello's privy chamber. I tried to force from my mind the thought of what things they did there and I wondered if, in the madness of love, I might be willing to do such things. I looked at Donatello, my father, my friend, and in truth I knew not what I could do. There was a long silence while we carefully studied the fire. It was burning low.

"He could have been arrested. It was late night when he left . . . here"—had he been about to say, "when he left my bed"?—"and it could happen that he ran into a gang of toughs, or soldiers on the lookout, or the Onestà . . . ." His voice drifted off into silence.

"He is too quick. He is too clever."

But his mind had fixed on this. He has been arrested, Donatello said, he is in the dungeons of the Bargello, they are torturing him, that small body.

"Tomorrow," he said. "Tomorrow you will go inquire. You must."

I lowered my head and said nothing.

"He's only a boy."

"I'll go," I said, "and I'll find him. Or news of him."

✳ ✳ ✳

The next morning, ripe with fear and wearing my new cloak and my red *capuccio*, I set out to find the offices of the Ufficiali di Onestà.

At the Palazzo della Signoria the guard at the main entrance said he had no knowledge of the Onestà. He yawned. What exactly was I looking for? A young man, I said, perhaps a prisoner. Well, there are no prisoners here in the Signoria, he said, with a wink and a half-smile. If I was in search of a prisoner I should go to the Bargello. But, he added, there are prisoners everywhere in Florence, not all of them in the city jail. I thanked him for his help. He nodded wisely and wished me well.

At the gates to the Bargello I asked for the offices of the Onestà. I was referred to the Office of Information, inside, to the left. There I found, between two armed police, a tiny man with a luxurious black mustache who sat behind a table thick with papers scribbled over in red and black and green: an official's desk. Two men were ahead of me in line and I waited while their business was dispatched—with a certain amount of fuss and a good deal of contempt for the nuisance they caused—and then it was my turn.

"The Onestà?" He licked one side of his mustache and then the other. He had the white watery eyes of the near blind and, despite the sinister mustache, he had a kindly look. "What is your business with the Onestà?"

"Only an inquiry."

"About what matter?"

"About a prisoner."

"In the Bargello?"

"That is what I need to find out. If he is in the Bargello."

"You won't get that kind of information. They won't tell you." He licked his mustache again and shuffled the papers before him.

"Thank you for your help."

"They can't tell you." He chuckled, pleased. "They don't even know."

"Thank you."

"No one knows. Once in there, you're gone forever. Sometimes."

"Thank you."

"You'll see."

He waved his hand in dismissal and, as he instructed, I went outside and down the stairs and turned right. It was icy cold below stairs. I wandered in a dark corridor until I came upon a door with a small plaque that said Ufficiali dell' Onestà and, beneath it, a smaller handwritten card that said Ser Paolo Ruggiero del Pagone, Conservatore di Legge. There was no guard at the door and no sign of anyone else in the corridor, so I knocked softly and, when there was no answer, I knocked a bit harder. I waited and knocked once more, harder still. I turned away and started back down the corridor when I heard the sound of a door opening. I looked back and there in the doorway marked Ufficiali dell' Onestà stood a huge man with a bald head and the black gown of a cleric. He was peering anxiously into the dark corridor. He was enormously fat, with tiny slits for eyes and no chin at all and he was murmuring apologies.

"Ser Paolo at your service," he said and squinted at me. "I was unaware . . . I do apologize . . . I was pissing . . . the smell . . . it is a problem of control . . ."

The air was close and fetid. In truth the room was stale with the smell of old clothes and wet paper and over all the strong sharp smell of urine. Ser Paolo's skin was very white, like the belly of a fish, as if he had never been exposed to light. I wondered if he slept here.

He waved me inside the office, a narrow room with a table and two chairs and many wooden cases stuffed with notebooks and account books and the bits of paper that accumulate in any place of business. Some of the oldest of these documents were of rolled parchment, yellow as butter, with wax seals still attached. Some had ribbons dangling from the wax. Some were recent, with no seals at all. A small window at the top of the rear wall admitted what little light there was in the room.

Surely this could not be the headquarters of the Ufficiali di Onestà, a powerful branch of the government of the Republic. The Onestà had as its commission to protect the purity of convents and monasteries and—a more recent commission—to prosecute sodomy. And this airless room was their headquarters? This could not be.

I made as if to leave.

"Sit, sit!" he said, and put on a pair of spectacles the better to peer at me. He saw at once that he had mistaken me for someone of importance—my red *cappuccio*, a gift from Donatello, had misled him—and thus he had wasted his apology on a nobody. He looked startled at this and his tone cooled noticeably.

"Your business here?"

A young man had gone missing and I was looking for him, I said. His name was Mattei, he was a bit wild, and I wondered if at some time in the past week he might have been arrested on suspicion of loitering.

"Loitering," he said, and readied his notebook and his stylus. He paused to caress the cover of the book and to lay the place-ribbon straight along the binding. "By loitering"—he squinted up at me—"by loitering you mean . . . sodomy?"

"I only ask," I said.

"Your name?"

"Luca di Matteo," I watched, anxious, as he wrote it down. He wrote slowly and with care, his tongue between his teeth.

"Di Matteo. Mattei. He is your son?"

"No relation," I said, "it is a common name."

"It is a common name. Alas, it is true." He asked what trade I plied. I paused. "Engraver," I said. "Assistant to a goldsmith."

He wrote 'engraver,' slowly, as if it were a great labor. "Employer?"

"Whoever will hire me." He squinted, displeased, and overcome by folly I said, "The great Lorenzo Ghiberti."

He raised his eyebrows in surprise and wrote down "Lorenzo di Cione Ghiberti" and underlined the name.

"Well!" he said, and puffed out his cheeks. He looked exactly like a frog.

I was eager now to leave but that was not possible. The interrogation, once begun, must go on until he was satisfied. He continued to ask questions and I responded with lies and he wrote down everything I said. Your residence? I am a visitor from Prato. Then you should ply your trade in Prato. Your residence here in Florence? I made up the name of a rooming house in Santa Croce. Near the Basilica, I said, in the area of the stables and the bake houses. Your interest in this boy? He is the son of an acquaintance; I am inquiring on his behalf. By name? He is a merchant in Prato. Of what name exactly? I drew a deep breath: Ser Lapo Mazzei. And then, improvising, I said the boy goes by Mattei to spare his father shame. Ser Lapo Mazzei was an important merchant, known even in Florence, and he recognized the name at once and entered it in his book. He asked more questions and I answered them, some truly, some not. He squinted at me and wrote down what I said, his tongue fixed between his teeth.

When he had exhausted his store of questions, he asked once more what it was I wanted. He seemed truly to have forgotten. I repeated that I was looking for a boy called Agnolo Mattei who may have been arrested. He shook his head and, to my great surprise, he smiled. "No," he said.

"No? It is certain?"

"No one has been arrested since before the Christmas feast. Our laws, like all the laws of our great Republic, are better kept than punished. Public decency is our first priority."

I did not know what he meant so I said nothing.

"We want no more burnings at the stake. If your friend Agnolo is a practicing sodomite and if he confesses voluntarily, he will be pardoned. If he is denounced by someone else, however, we may decide to take action against him." He spoke gravely, reciting a lesson. "That is how we proceed: we value honor first and then denunciation. Onestà is not a name only. It is a promise."

"No. Yes. I see."

"And do you wish to confess anything yourself?" He squinted and leaned forward, his stylus poised above the page.

"No. Nothing."

"Do you wish to denounce?"

I told him I did not wish to confess or denounce. I was done. I was grateful.

All at once he bent forward and clutched at his stomach. His pale skin grew whiter still. "Go then quickly," he said, "because I must piss again. It is a sore affliction." As I moved to the door, he said with urgency, "Go. Only go!"

I could hear the gurgle of urine in the night jug as I closed the door behind me and, with a huge sense of relief, I left to his ledgers and his piss pot the Conservatore di Legge Ser Paolo Ruggiero del Pagone. I made my way quickly along the dark corridor and up the stairs and out again into the world of air and light. Ser Paolo Ruggiero, farewell, farewell!

✶ ✶ ✶

I T WAS FREEZING outside but the clean air was welcome and, though I was greatly agitated to have told so many lies—and all of them written down by a government agent—I was much relieved to be able to report to Donatello that Agnolo had not been arrested. I had this on the authority of the Conservatore di Legge himself.

"He has simply gone away then."

"It would seem so," I said.

"With his soldier."

I said nothing.

"I had thought that was behind him." He laughed, ironically.

"It may be he will come back."

"Then damn him!" he said. "Let him rot in hell and his soldier with him."

I was not prepared for his response.

"If he comes back, turn him away. I will not see him. I will have nothing to do with him."

"As you wish, my lord."

With that he went to his work table and for an hour or more he sifted through the pile of commissions. Some were for work under way and some for work that had long since been abandoned. He set about rearranging them in their order of importance. "Prato," he said. "We have been neglecting Prato. Tell Pagno to come and talk with me at once."

"My lord," I said.

He removed the wet cloth from the *bozzetto* of the David and stood for a moment gazing at it. He touched the shoulder and let his finger drift down the arm to the hand that held the stone. He moved that same finger to the helmet of Goliath and pressed hard against the severed head. I turned away, embarrassed, but I looked back in time to see him lift a hammer and take aim. With a single great blow, he shattered the perfect *bozzetto* in a hundred pieces. He stepped hard upon the shards of clay and ground them to dust beneath his foot. He was mad with rage, surely, but I studied him keenly and to my eye he appeared calm.

That was the moment when I realized, with a terrible tug at my heart, that it was not just a sexual attraction Donatello felt for the boy. He was—fatally—in love with him.

"Clean away this mess," he said and then he went outside to tell Pagno di Lapo to begin carving the child angels for the cornices of the Prato Pulpit.

CHAPTER 19

AT LAST DONATELLO could rest. And so could I. Agnolo, that poisonous child, had disappeared, Pagno di Lapo was joyfully occupied carving his two *putti* for the Prato Pulpit, and Alessandra had just given birth to our fourth boy, Giovanni Marco by name. He had his mother's deep green eyes and broad forehead and her full mouth. He was perfect. It is true that too often during these years I looked lightly upon my good fortune in having Alessandra for wife and four fine boys to better me in carving . . . for surely they would be more gifted than I. I loved them with a full heart, Alessandra most of all, but I never told them so and I have lived to know the full taste of that regret . . . Still, here was a time to rest, as Donatello rested, free at last from that terrible sting of the flesh.

All of us had long speculated on that sting and wondered just what form it took and who was its chief object. During my earliest years in the *bottega* I had worried that Michelozzo might be the lover of Donatello. Michelozzo had become—after Alessandra—the center of my life. He was a great artisan, a man of strength and integrity and it pained me to think he might, even for a moment, even once only, act the sodomite. It was unthinkable. He and Donatello shared work and they shared a house and I could not help fearing they shared a bed. Sometimes it is hard to tell the difference between fear and knowledge.

Later, after the burning of Piero di Jacopo, my fear became more immediate. Sodomy among distinguished men was not unheard of and, in truth, among the great artisans, it was not uncommon. Moreover it was noised about that Michelozzo was not the first of

Donatello's lovers, that Brunelleschi had been there before him. Nearly thirty years earlier, at a time when I was still the squalling brat of the wool dyer and his wife, the young Brunelleschi had, in a fit of anger, gone off to Rome to explore the ruins of ancient temples and to unearth the secrets of architectural perspective . . . and, some said, to live in sin with Donatello. The stay in Rome came about in this way.

In 1401 the Officials of the Florence Cathedral—the Operai—declared a public competition to select the artisan who would make a set of bronze doors to celebrate the passing of the Black Pestilence of 1400. The doors, which were intended for the north side of the Baptistry, were meant to rival the great south doors of Andrea Pisano. Artisans from Florence and Siena and Assisi competed, five finalists were chosen, and each was given a year to submit a bronze panel depicting Abraham's sacrifice of Isaac. Though there were thirty-four judges, they quickly agreed on the final two competitors: Ghiberti and Brunelleschi. In the end, the votes of the Operai were evenly divided between the two and so the judges offered the commission equally to Ghiberti and Brunelleschi, splitting the work and the money between them. Brunelleschi, insulted and on fire with rage, refused the commission altogether and went off to Rome to dig through the ruins. While he studied the inner life of statues and sought out the secrets by which the ancients turned public buildings into works of art, he practiced as a goldsmith to support himself. Donatello was nine years his junior—a passionate sixteen—when he went with him to Rome.

I say "passionate" of the young Donatello because a year earlier he had been arrested in Pistoia for fighting with a German named Anichinus Pieri, wounding him with a large stick that caused much bleeding. It is not true that this was a lover's quarrel. It was a case of two boys proving they were men. A court document of 24 January 1401—Donatello kept it; I have it by me today—warned "the Florentine" that he would be fined one hundred gold florins should he again violate the peace of Pistoia. Donatello found this an excellent time to go with Brunelleschi to Rome. He went there as an apprentice gold-smith and returned two years later as a master craftsman.

So there were Brunelleschi and Michelozzo to consider, but most mysterious of all was Donatello's love of Pagno di Lapo. Pagno was a middling sculptor—he had no sense of how a body occupied space and whenever he attempted a *putto*, for instance, the result was always a miniature man, malformed and ugly. And yet Donatello insisted he was a sculptor of talent. Was he deceived by passion? Was it the fascination of his red hair and those eyes that were now blue and now green depending on his malice at the moment? "*Piccolo mio,*" Donatello called him at thirteen and, despite his low chin, Pagno had grown into a handsome young man, tall and of some physical strength, with a quick wit and a sharp tongue, and he moved as si-lently as a cat. He was forever enticing Donatello but, at a mere touch on his shoulder or a tousling of his hair, he would resist and pull away. I saw it happen but I did not understand.

I did not understand any of these attachments at that time, though in my old age I have come to have some sympathy for them. Love robs us of our strength—of mind as well as of character—and we cease to know who we are. In truth we become strangers to ourselves. I did not know it then, though Pagno knew it and so did Alessandra, but I was just such a stranger to myself.

Over the years I had become a spy and I had perfected my spying skills by watching Donatello at work. That intense stare, that ability to exclude from sight everything that was not the focus of his vision, had—in a worldly way—become my own. Nothing escaped my notice, not Michelozzo's glance at Donatello, not Donatello's suppressed smile, not the heartstrings' jump of pleasure or delight that showed subtly on the face. I was a spy, and I was good at seeing the intent of things. I could hear the words they only meant to say, the touch that they intended, the dangerous thought left unformed in the mind. I do not exaggerate.

When Agnolo entered our lives, spying became for me an obsession. He had ruined Donatello and ruined the David and he had ruined me.

But now, *gratia Dei*, he was gone. And we could rest.

"You have changed," Alessandra said, "You're a different man." She was nursing Giovanni Marco and her face was peaceful though her voice was firm. I had come to recognize that tone. She was about to deliver hard truths that she felt were needful for her to say and good for me to know. "You begrudge Pagno his high favor with Donato." She let that hang in the air for a while and continued to suckle the baby. She began to sing him a lullaby.

She was the picture of motherhood. She had grown more beautiful and more plump with each new birth, her green eyes soft, her hands delicate. She could have posed for the Virgin with Child.

"Pagno is only what your jealousy makes him," she said. "He is of no importance."

Giovanni Paolo sat on the floor at her feet twisting a bit of red yarn in knots while the two older boys were building a fortress with small wooden blocks I had made for them and painted to look like stone. Donato Michele at eight years was too old for this, but he played at knights and soldiers to entertain his brother. Donato, the oldest, was ever the giving child. Franco Alessandro, two years younger, was not. Still, here was a lovely family picture . . . until Alessandra spoke once more.

"Jealousy is beneath you." She paused. "You are better than that." She paused again. "You are better than him."

I was ashamed and angry and so I began to play with the loose ends of wool on her loom. Alessandra did weaving by the piece—fine wool, chiefly, though sometimes rough silk—and she was paid well for her work. This was illegal, of course, but everyone did it and we were always in need of extra money. Even then, more than thirty years past, it cost a fortune to raise four boys.

"Don't play with that," she said. "You'll throw me off."

Finally I said, "I am not jealous of Pagno."

"Of Pagno and of poor Agnolo too. It's as well that he's gone off . . . to wherever he's gone."

"He's corrupt."

"You're obsessed by him. He is in your mind like a poison."

"He is not."

Alessandra looked at me in that way. I lowered my eyes. She took the baby from her nipple and laid him across her breast. She tapped him—pat, pat, pat—and he coughed up a small mess on her shoulder, gave a heavy sigh of satisfaction and fell asleep. Of a sudden I was overwhelmed with love for her.

✴ ✴ ✴

LONG AGO, IN our first year of marriage I asked her how it could be that we had made love so many times without conception and yet, once we married, she conceived immediately. I was wondering aloud and, if she was offended, she did not say so. She explained about the weed called *daucus carota* . . . and I now include this information as part of my confession to lighten the burden of listening to my sin. This is not advice, it is an explanation only, and my reader is free to pass it on to women who may find it useful or you may keep it for your own delight, an odd thing, good to know in itself.

The *daucus carota* is an acrid weed, a kind of wild carrot that grows by every roadside, and in late summer it produces a white lacy flower. In fall, you take the dried seeds of the flower and you grind them to a pulp, a greenish mess that is foul-tasting but very effective. You cannot swallow the seeds whole; they will do no good. You take one teaspoonful of this paste and you swallow it after sex and you will not conceive. No one knows why, but chemists say it causes slipperiness in the woman so that the man's seed cannot take hold. And later, when you want to conceive, you simply stop taking the *daucus* remedy, and if you are in all other ways healthy and of good disposition, you will conceive. It is as simple as that. Is this not a good thing to know?

Alessandra and I had married for love—or what we took to be love—and, as sometimes happens in marriage, we continued to feel love for one another even after the pleasures of the flesh had become a common, if necessary, thing. Many marriages exist on nothing more than physical pleasure snatched here and there in moments of desire or demand, and so we considered ourselves fortunate to have found in each other someone who shared our loneliness and need and that feeling of not knowing who we are or why we are here.

We lived well. I was a clerk for Donatello, an accountant of sorts, a reminder of tasks, and a sometime sculptor. Donatello never thought of money and so it was only with the birth of each new child that he remembered my growing needs. He paid me well: eighty gold florins at the time of Giovanni Marco's birth. Thus we could afford to send Donato Michele to study with the Franciscans and in the new year Franco Alessandro would join him. The two youngest boys were taught by Alessandra, who tended the little garden, washed and cooked and cleaned the house, took charge of bills and payments and, to our mutual satisfaction, took charge of me as well. And our four boys.

All I know about love I learned from Alessandra. Maria Sabina—may God have mercy—taught me everything about the body's pleasures, but the love of God I learned from Alessandra. It is a hard love, like Donatello's bronze: heated to the melting point and hammered afterward to a fine finish. This much I have learned. There is no love without pain. Forgiveness costs everything. Memory is itself the source of suffering. This is not the *Novum Testamentum* but it is true nonetheless.

These things too I include as part of my confession. To lighten the burden of sin and the boredom of telling. But perhaps I grow antic.

It is my sons, my sons, my lost sons that I repent. Because who is guilty if not me?

✷ ✷ ✷

With Agnolo gone, we could rest at last. Alessandra was my rest. She knew my little infidelities—what did they matter; they were meaningless—and she forgave them. She knew I was a failure as a sculptor and she forgave that as well. And she knew, better than I, my love for Donatello.

Which Donatello you ask? For indeed there were as many Donatellos as there were people who loved him. He was a different man with Michelozzo than with Pagno. And he was different still with me. It was not simply that he was changeable, a chameleon who responded to each of us as we were. He was a great deal more complicated than this.

He was a man of infinite capacity and each of us took from him as much as we could hold. This, I suppose, was the nature of his fascination for us as well as the source of our frustration. He turned his gaze upon us and for that little time we existed in a way we had not existed the moment before. For that time he was totally present, no other person existed for him, and he was transparent to us. We knew the man himself and he knew us. Everyone wanted to plumb the depths of who he was—as in truth they do even today as they examine his sculptures—but there was no easy explanation of his character then and no secret that could resolve the mystery of his genius now. There was always more to him than we could know.

Alessandra recognized my love for him and accepted it.

I did not tell her of that secret kiss—so many years gone by now—and that cry of discovery and delight that had meant nothing to Donatello but that to me had been an invasion and an assault. In that assault I knew I had been discovered. I did not tell Alessandra that.

CHAPTER 20

Dᴜʀɪɴɢ ᴛʜᴇ ɴᴇxᴛ eight months Donatello became again his old self, working continually, moving from statue to *cassone* to tabernacle as the mood or inspiration struck him, regardless of contracts and commissions and money owed or promises made. We were at ease now, all of us, and we gave ourselves over to the work of the *bottega* without the continual distractions caused by Agnolo and his need for attention. A single glance at my account books revealed how much we were behind in all our work.

The Prato Pulpit, for instance, was far from finished though Donatello and Michelozzo had in 1428 contracted to produce a pulpit for the Prato Cathedral, installed and ready for the feast of Our Lady on September 8, 1429. Money had been advanced and the project begun. It was begun again, and again, and it was abandoned just as many times because some new proposal was more pressing, more interesting, more challenging. Besides, Michelozzo had to finish his design for the lower half of the pulpit—the support pillars and the cornices—before Donatello could begin the figures for the balustrade. And, alas, Michelozzo was in Pisa, Michelozzo was in Lucca, Michelozzo was casting bronze for Lorenzo Ghiberti. Eventually Michelozzo completed his design and work proceeded on the cornices and balustrade. But then there were problems with the marble; the quality was poor, it was not uniformly white, it was streaky, pocked. New marble was ordered. But by then Donatello was occupied with the *bozzetto* for the bronze David and could think of nothing else. Pagno complained, Pagno begged, and finally he was given the opportunity to demonstrate his skill with fine marble. He carved the two *putti* for the brackets that would support the cornice. They were disastrous—ugly and deformed—and they were added to the heap of rubble used by apprentices for practice work. By now it was 1431 and the work was still in progress. The Prato Pulpit, as it turned out, would not be completed for a decade.

Meanwhile, in Agnolo's blessed absence, Donatello finished carving the magnificent Annunciation to the Virgin for the Cavalcanti chapel. I recalled with envy how he had explained the work to Agnolo in the early days of that seduction. "You see, the Angel Gabriel kneels before the Virgin," Donatello had said. "Mary is startled, as who would not be?" I could see him as he raised his long fingers and traced the book that Mary held, and the arm, and the figure rising from the chair. For that second I had hated him.

But now, with Agnolo gone from our lives, we stood together before the completed Annunciation and I softened toward him. The sculpture, in its simplicity and its beauty, was itself a source of grace.

"It needs a frame," Donatello said. "A canopy or a frieze." To me it seemed perfection as it was. "Putti," he said, talking to himself. "Looking down. In awe. In fear." He put his long hand on my shoulder. "Your boys. Your oldest two. Let me use them for the *putti*."

That is how it came about that my sons Donato Michele and Franco Alessandro will stand forever in the Basilica of Santa Croce, clutching one another in fear of the height as they look down on the Virgin at that stupendous moment when she assents to be Mother of the Christ. My boys appear again, of course, in the Cantoria that Donatello executed for the Duomo, but here they are most themselves, alive and full of mischief, as I would choose to remember them.

The Annunciation was finished, save for a few bits of ornamentation left for Pagno to complete, to ease his disappointment at seeing his Prato carvings cast aside. Donatello turned at once to his several postponed commissions for Cosimo de' Medici. First came two matching marble panels, one of the Crucifixion and one of the Ascension. Then a gilded coffer that would hold a manuscript copy of *Aesop's Fables* in the original Greek. And then the long delayed bronze bust of Cosimo's wife, Contessina de' Bardi.

For the Crucifixion and the Ascension Donatello devised a new kind of sculpture, *rilievo schiacciato* he called it: on a flat marble panel he carved a relief of such thinness that it appeared to be a drawing, as if by using a stylus instead of a chisel he had forced the marble to release the forms trapped beneath its surface. The setting is Golgotha and those dim forms, as you gaze at them, become the figure of Christ in his last agony and, kneeling at the foot of the cross, the Virgin Mother and Mary Magdalene and the apostle John. As you continue to gaze at the figures, the background too moves to the surface and you become aware of angry clouds troubling the sky and a darkness settling over the scene. The face of Christ is taut with agony and the face of his Mother taut with grief. The matching panel, the Ascension, shows Christ surrounded by his apostles, the Virgin Mother kneeling at his feet, as he rises into heaven. He ascends into a summer sky and Donatello has so ordered the lines of sight that as you observe the figures you are forced—like the apostles themselves—to look up in expectation and in hope. These are masterful works, unlike anything I have seen before or since, and they adorned the facing walls of Cosimo's private chapel in the palazzo on the Via de' Bardi. The tiny chapel was without windows and lit only by wall sconces so I am sure they could not be well seen but it was enough for my lord Cosimo to know they were there. Later, when he built the great new Palazzo Medici on the Via Larga, he moved these marble panels to the family chapel which was well lit and where they could be seen to advantage. They are there even today.

The gilded coffer was to be companion of the one I had designed for Cosimo's Greek prayer book nearly ten years earlier. As you would expect, I had kept the original drawings—I was ever a devoted collector of papers—and so with speed and some skill I brought the coffer to completion. This time I was allowed to do the work myself. I adorned the coffer with the Medici family seal, I cast the laurel wreaths and gilded them, I attached the jeweled clasp. My finished work was a perfect match for Donatello's original. It was my masterpiece. The twin coffers stand at either end of the altar in Cosimo's chapel, a Byzantine prayer book on one side and *Aesop's Fables* on the other, with Jesus on the cross between them.

We went together to present the coffer to my lord Cosimo at his palazzo on the Via de' Bardi. The name itself will tell you that the palazzo belonged to Cosimo's wife although, since their marriage, Cosimo had gone far toward making it his own. The immense double doors that fronted the Via de' Bardi now bore the Medici family crest—four balls within an ornate shield—and they were flanked on either side by decorative iron rings in the form of laurel wreaths that held torches against the night. Like all noble palaces of Florence, the Bardi had originally been a fortress and it seemed so still. The thick stone walls on the ground floor provided storage rooms where food and weapons had once been stacked against attack; these rooms were now workshops for the palace, stores for grain and wine, and shelters for the family horses and carriages. And, of course, the palace kitchens.

We were greeted by two servants in full livery—I recognized Giacomo as one of them—and we followed them through the entryway to a huge courtyard paved in stone. In the center stood an ornate well crowned by a small statue of the bearded Marsyas playing a flute, the same Roman statue Donatello had repaired for Cosimo years earlier. Giacomo showed us to a vaulted staircase that led to the first floor balcony where Cosimo himself met us. He greeted Donatello with an embrace and a kiss on either cheek and he shook my hand with some warmth. My hands were sweating and I feared to drop the coffer, bundled in a crimson velvet cloth and clutched beneath my arm. Cosimo led us through two vast reception rooms to his private quarters. I scarcely had time to look around me. The public rooms were a blur of great wealth. Ornate marble floors, gilt ceilings, and walls painted with scenes of triumph from the Bible and mythology: the walls of Jericho tumbled down, Hercules wrestled with the Hydra. Cosimo's private apartment was a series of rooms that unfolded, one from another. There was a sitting room with carved chairs and a long table, a study where he kept his huge collection of books in Latin and Greek and our native Italian, a bedroom, and his tiny chapel—scarcely more than a closet—where he daily made his prayers. I believe there was a bathroom, all unto itself.

At a gesture from Cosimo I settled the coffer on the long table in his sitting room and he removed the velvet cloth. The coffer glowed in the dim light, and I watched with pleasure as Cosimo traced the laurel leaves with a stubby finger, caressed the gilded edges, and tried the jeweled clasp.

"It is a perfect match," he said to Donatello. "A beautiful, rare thing for my Aesop."

Donatello bowed and said that the design was mine.

Cosimo seemed surprised, but he smiled and came to me and took my hand. I did not say what I was thinking: that the execution had been mine as well. All work that came from Donatello's *bottega*—no matter who had produced it—came from the hand of Donatello and with his approval. High lords did not pay Donatello for work by his assistants. He had been generous to acknowledge that the design was mine.

Wine was brought and Cosimo toasted Donatello's good health and great talent and then they talked at length of other commissions Cosimo had in mind. The bronze bust of his wife, Contessina de' Bardi, already agreed upon. A bust of Niccolò da Uzzano, quickly, before he dies. And after that he desired another bronze, a decorative piece, whimsical, something like the *putti* on the Annunciation Donatello had only now completed. A cupid perhaps, or a baby Pan, holding a butterfly or a little bird. He left it all to Donatello.

This Pan, this dancing baby, would of course become the Atys Amorino, a pagan *putto* with tiny wings on his back and on his heels. In his outstretched hand he holds a butterfly and he is laughing with delight. He wears only leather pants, open in the front, to reveal his waggling privy parts. He is filled with pleasure in the butterfly and in the world and in himself. He is the perfect pagan. "He is the spirit that was Greece," Cosimo would say when it was completed, but to me he was the spirit that was Donatello . . . if only Agnolo had not come among us.

Cosimo himself escorted us to the door of the palazzo and stood bidding us farewell as if we were old friends who had stopped by to exchange a greeting.

He turned suddenly to Donatello and asked, "How does it go with my bronze David?" He knew that Donatello had taken a hammer to the *bozzetto*—such news is never secret—but he asked nonetheless.

"Slowly," Donatello said.

"Ah, yes," Cosimo said, and nodded agreement. "Yes. Of course." Then he turned to me and said, "You must encourage your brother to be of help." He looked me full in the face and said, "I shall remember you." He clasped my hands in his.

I could not have been more surprised by the words or by the gesture. Cosimo was a man of extraordinary warmth beneath all that silence and it was a warmth I would have need of later as I lay in prison in cursed Padua. We said farewell.

I write this down for what reason? Because it happened and because I would have you know that no less a critic than Cosimo himself approved my work and because he loved my lord Donatello enough to include me in that love.

All this came about because Agnolo had left us and Donatello was himself once again and so was I, free for a time of what Alessandra called my poisoned feelings.

Agnolo came back into our lives once more in August, 1431.

CHAPTER 21

AGNOLO WAS STANDING at the door in easy conversation with Pagno di Lapo. They were laughing together, like old friends. It was a warm day in August and Agnolo had left off his stockings and was wearing only a dirty white shirt and that ridiculous farmer's hat. His hair was long and scraggly and his feet were bare. I approached them and said, "It's well for you that Donatello is not here," and I found that in my anger I could scarce get the words from between my teeth.

Pagno looked at me in surprise, but Agnolo gave me a wide smile and said, "He's not here. He's at the Palazzo Bardi, sketching Big Contessina." I should have struck him for his impertinence, but I was so astonished that he knew of Donatello's whereabouts that in truth I did not know what to do.

"Agnolo is newly back from Lucca," Pagno said.

"You're not allowed to be here. Donatello has forbidden it."

"I'm only standing outside. I came to offer a greeting."

"Go away!"

"He is always hurtful," Agnolo said. "Why is he like this?"

Pagno turned to me and then to Agnolo and then back again to me. There was no more to say. I waited for Agnolo to go but he did not move.

"I looked for you everywhere," I said. "My lord Donatello looked."

"I told Pagno where I was going," Agnolo said. He turned to Pagno and said, "I told you."

"And I told you," Pagno said to me. "I said he's gone off with his soldier. You asked me and I told you."

"But you didn't say you *knew*. You let us chase around the city looking for him! You let us go to the Buco!"

"You went to the Buco?" Agnolo laughed, incredulous, pleased. "Did you enjoy it?"

"I told you he was in Lucca," Pagno said.

"They're very friendly at the Buco." Agnolo was amused.

I found myself speechless with anger and frustration. Here I was a man of thirty-one years, an accomplished artisan with a wife and four sons, being made fool of by a rent boy, a *bardassa*, who had exploited my lord Donatello and was even now mocking me with what he had done. I turned away in fury.

Agnolo and Pagno continued to talk, defying me, until Pagno slipped him some coins and Agnolo took his leave.

"Donatello must not know of this," I said, and my voice shook with anger.

"Donatello will want to know he's back," Pagno said.

* * *

DONATELLO WAS, AS Agnolo had rightly said, at the Palazzo Bardi making sketches for the bust of Cosimo's wife. He was there almost every morning for a week and when he returned he began at once on the *bozzetto* from which he would model the bust itself. He worked quickly and well, as was his way.

I did not mention to my lord Donatello that Agnolo had returned to Florence nor that Pagno had known him to be in Lucca all those months, but I continued angry at Pagno that he had spoken truth about Agnolo's disappearance but in such a way that we were meant to think it was not so. All my anger at Agnolo was now concentrated on Pagno and I wished him ill.

"What's wrong with you?" Donatello asked me. "You do not concentrate."

"Nothing."

"Well, try to concentrate."

"As you say, my lord."

"Never mind 'my lord'. Only pay attention to what you're doing."

What I was doing was helping prepare the framework for the bust of Contessina and in truth I had just badly formed the wires that would support her left shoulder.

"It's Pagno," I said.

Donatello sighed and shook his head. He was well aware there was discomfort between Pagno and me.

"He knew all along where Agnolo was."

Donatello said nothing but he paused with his trowel poised above the bucket of clay.

"And now he's back. He was in Lucca the whole time we searched for him at the Buco."

Donatello said nothing.

"And I had to go to the Ufficiali di Onestà," I said

"They inscribed everything in a record book," I said.

"I told them lies. They have my name," I said.

"And now he's back?"

"I saw him. He came to the *bottega*."

"Turn him away if he comes here. I don't want to hear his name again."

"I did. I told him to go."

"Enough."

"Pagno gave him money."

He was silent then for a long time and I knew not to say anything more.

Now at least Donatello would not be surprised if he came upon Agnolo in the street, and I further hoped that I had done Pagno some little harm. I was thinking this when Donatello of a sudden said, "Pagno is kind and generous. We should all be more like Pagno."

AGNOLO WAS STANDING at the door, careful not to come in but just as careful to be sure we could see him from our work stations. I was bent over my account books, pleased that so many of our commissions were completed or were near completion, when I looked up and there he was, staring straight at me, not bold and confrontational this time but meek and penitent. I looked from him to Donatello who labored at his bust of Contessina, and I rose immediately and went to the door.

"Go!" I said.

He lowered his glance and gazed at his bare feet for a long minute and when he looked up there were tears in his eyes and he said, "I'm sorry."

I was astonished. I could never have imagined him crying and here he stood with a tear starting down his cheek and more to come. I softened at once, but reminding myself that Donatello had said his name was never to be spoken here again, I told him, "Go. It is too late."

He turned and left and I went back to my work. I was of course angry at Agnolo but surprised at my feeling of pity for him and so after a few profitless minutes staring at my account book, I got up and went outside to the privy. One of the new apprentices was using it and so I waited, looking back into the *bottega* at the figure of Donatello, consumed with his work.

How can it be, I thought, that such a man as he could fall in love with such a boy as Agnolo. It could not be a question of physical attraction because Agnolo was mere skin and bones. In truth he had a fine, handsome head and wondrous yellow hair but he was soft and girlish and his behind was flabby and without form. Yet he was desired by many, so it must be that I simply did not understand the nature of his beauty. Caterina herself was taken with him. And, I suspected, so was Pagno. All the same, the source of Agnolo's fascination remained a mystery to me. He was quick of wit in a vulgar way. He was keen to please when he was in the mood to do so. He was ready with a smile. But he was a soulless, selfish child. Still, he had once amused Donatello and made him laugh, so perhaps he had rare qualities that I failed to see. Or perhaps the Donatello who fell in love with Agnolo had qualities that I failed to see. I preferred the Donatello at work now on the bust of Contessina. He was a man of forty-five years—already in his late middle age—too old for the foolishness of first love and too wise to give over his good sense to a boy who sold himself at the Buco. Donatello was sane once more and I was resolved to keep Agnolo at a distance from him.

I finished in the privy and when I came out, calmer now, who should be waiting at the door but Pagno di Lapo.

"What?" I asked.

"He's back again. I thought you should know."

"I sent him away. He left."

"But he'll never really leave," Pagno said. "Not altogether."

"And you? What do you propose to do about that? You were once cold to him, but your temperature seems to have changed greatly."

"I feel bad for him."

I gave him a look that meant I knew the truth about him. It was a quizzical look, and I would say that I had learned it from Donatello except that Donatello *did* know the truth.

Pagno was defeated for the time and went away.

* * *

THAT NIGHT WHEN I returned home Alessandra greeted me with the news that Agnolo had been to our door. His soldier had left him. He was desperate for a few coins.

"And you gave them to him."

"So would you have."

"His heart is broken, I suppose. He's abandoned and alone."

"He was near tears," she said.

"Awash in tears, I have no doubt."

"He said he was sorry. And I think he is."

"Sorrow, like the request for money, comes readily to his lips."

"Even whores can be sorry," she said. "It is not an easy life."

Supper that night was uncomfortable and I blamed Agnolo. The dread Agnolo, ever the sower of misery even in his absence.

* * *

DONATELLO, PAUSING IN his work, looked up and saw Agnolo standing at the entrance to the *bottega*. He crossed to the door and pushed it shut.

He went back to his sculpting stand and with great calm resumed work on the bust of Contessina de' Bardi. It was coming along beautifully.

Agnolo stood across the street from the entrance to the *bottega*, a penitent, barefoot, wearing only his shirt and that straw hat he fancied. Donatello had shut up the *bottega* and turned the lock on the passway door, when I spotted Agnolo waiting to be noticed. I tried to block Donatello's view but of course he saw him at once.

"He looks ill."

I made as if to move on but Donatello hesitated. He reached for the purse at his waist, touched it, and then thought better. We walked in silence to the Piazza della Signoria where we parted and each went our way.

The next night, after we closed the *bottega*, Agnolo was once again stationed across the street. This time Donatello did not hesitate. He crossed the street and with only a glance at the boy he handed him a silver florin.

"For the love of God," Agnolo said.

"No. Because you need it," Donatello said. And we walked on.

This was the beginning, however, as I knew it must be.

The next night when Donatello told me he would shut up the *bottega* by himself, I knew that the moment of his surrender had come and Agnolo would again have his way. And so it was. I waited in the Piazza and watched from a little distance while Donatello bought him a meat pie. They stood together in awkward conversation for a short while and then, without a touch or a gesture, they said farewell. Donatello went off toward the house he shared with Michelozzo, and Agnolo went on to some tavern, I suppose. He looked the penitent no longer. He had a jaunty walk and his hat was tilted in a carefree way.

Toward noon of the next day he appeared at the doorway where he was greeted by Pagno di Lapo with a smile, which made me think that Pagno must know that Agnolo was no longer an exile. They went out together through the rear doors of the bottega to the courtyard where Pagno was carving a set of *tondos*—the Annunciation in one and the Virgin Mary with the Child Jesus in the other—that had been on order from the Linen Guild for more than a year now. I waited for a while and then made the privy my excuse for going outside where, to my astonishment, I found Agnolo, with chisel and hammer, hacking at a discarded chunk of marble. I approached them and asked Agnolo what he thought he was doing.

"Getting the feel of hammer and chisel," he said. "Pagno is showing me."

Donatello appeared suddenly, his eyes piercing, his look hard. "You are not to disturb Pagno at his work," he said. "You'd better go."

Humbly, like a beaten dog, Agnolo left the *bottega*. We did not see him for several days.

* * *

IT WAS A cool day in late September when he next appeared. He was wearing new stockings and shoes with thick leather soles and he had left off his silly hat. He looked clean and his hair shone in the light. He had found a new patron, I supposed, but his attitude was as humble as when we last saw him. He went directly to where Donatello was working and stood at a little distance, silent, until Donatello took notice of him. He looked the boy up and down and then smiled a bitter smile I had seen only once before when a client had tried to cheat him of a fair price for a sculpture he had executed. It had surprised me then and it surprised me now.

"New shoes," he said. "New stockings."

"They were a present," Agnolo said, as if he were acknowledging his unworthiness of such gifts.

"From a new soldier?"

"From my old soldier. A present for memory's sake." Donatello continued to look at him—with contempt, I thought—but then Agnolo said, "It is true, I have played the whore, but I have put all that aside."

"Aside?"

"I want to work for you. I want to change my life." He hesitated and then he went too far. "I know I am unworthy."

Donatello gave another bitter smile and said, "Yes," but whether he meant work or worthiness I did not know. And then he said, "Speak to Pagno and he will give you some money."

"If you treat people like whores, they will act like whores," Agnolo said with a sudden flash of his old self and then he retreated behind his pretence of humility.

I could see Donatello falling again into Agnolo's trap and I could not endure it. "If you act like a whore," I said, "people will treat you like one."

They both turned to look at me. In their absorption with each other, they had forgotten I was there.

"Your brother is annoyed," Donatello said.

"He's not my brother," Agnolo said.

"He's not my brother," I said.

Donatello laughed as if he were in truth a happy man.

Agnolo became a regular presence in the *bottega* as I knew he would. In October the weather grew suddenly cold and that provided him an excuse to hang about with his continual offers to help grind paints and carry wood or marble or, as he said more than once, to model for anyone who wanted to draw him. Or sculpt him. Clothed or nude. None of us knew where or how he lived.

Caterina did a sketch of him as the boy David and another as the young Joseph and then a whole gallery of sketches from the Bible and from Greek mythology. She had the excuse of needing these figures for her *cassoni* and Agnolo was eager to please. They spent much time together. The two new *garzoni*, Matteo di Bartolomeo and Betto d'Antonio, were entertained by what they called this new romance of the plain girl and the pretty boy, though in truth nobody thought Caterina plain. Pagno kept his distance, both from Agnolo and from me. Since he had Donatello's favor, no one else mattered to him.

By the end of November Donatello had completed the clay bust of Contessina de' Bardi. To the dark red clay he applied wax in increasingly thick layers and, once it had hardened, he modeled the bust in fine detail: the nose straight, the chin firm, every line and wrinkle designed to produce the impression of nobility. Her thick neck was heavy with jewels, her fine eyes were deeply set, and the trace of a smile brightened her face and welcomed our glance. There she was, the wife of Cosimo de' Medici, in a wax model that could be shattered in an instant. It was frightening to look upon a perfect work of art sculpted in a medium—mere wax—that would be melted away and replaced by bronze. I have never lost my dread of this moment preceding the great transformation. Is it death and resurrection we fear? Or death and no resurrection?

Liquid clay was painted on the bust and built up gradually and allowed to dry. The core and the dried clay were yoked together. Vents were introduced. The core was heated slowly, gradually. And finally the molten bronze was ready for pouring. Everyone gathered around, at a little distance so as not to be in the way but close enough to observe master artisans at work. Agnolo for once left off trying to impress and watched with curiosity and respect. This was always the moment of greatest danger and excitement, since a successful cast depended not only on the physical strength of the men pouring the molten liquid but also and especially on the skill of the artisan who had calculated the thickness of the wax that would be replaced by the molten bronze.

Michelozzo and Donatello worked together as one. In truth their partnership was based on just this mutual need. The final result could never be guaranteed but this casting proceeded without fault, and the newly cast bronze—rough and edgy though it was—required only a minimum of chiseling and chasing. The bust was to be an Epiphany gift from Cosimo to his wife and so, as soon as the bolts were removed and the casing chipped away, Donatello fell to the work of finishing the bronze with eagerness and determination. He completed the bust and presented it to Cosimo well ahead of time and Cosimo, true to his nature, was most generous in his thanks and in his payment. All was well with Donatello.

But Agnolo had seen for the first time how a bronze sculpture comes into being and, thinking on the David, he was set afire with vanity.

He waited until the bust of Contessina had been delivered to Cosimo, and payment was received, and Donatello once more approachable. "I could pose for you," he said. "You could continue with the David."

Donatello looked at him. He had been expecting this.

"If it would please you," Agnolo said.

Donatello continued to look at him, kindly, but not eager to succumb.

"I know how to pose now and I would be no trouble," he said.

"I would not go away with anyone. I have no soldier," he said.

"I have no friend at all," he said. "Only you."

So, at the end of this year Agnolo once again began to pose for the David. The Florentine army could have learned something from Agnolo at the siege of Lucca. Agnolo's siege had taken only a few months and Donatello had surrendered completely.

To lessen the sting of his capitulation Donatello made it a hard rule that Agnolo must be present in the *bottega* after first light and stay as long as he was needed, that there could be no absences, no spells of anger or boredom or petulance that spoiled the work time, and that if he ran off again with a soldier, with anyone, they were done with each other. This was his last chance. This was final and forever.

"Just as you wish, my lord. Just as you say."

Donatello then arranged for Agnolo to share a room with three of the apprentices and agreed to pay him an apprentice wage. He bought him a new winter cloak of thick brown wool, and when Agnolo protested that he preferred green, Donatello gave the brown cloak to Pagno and bought a green one for Agnolo, less expensive and less warm but without any doubt green.

There was a spirit of Christmas in the air and Donatello and Agnolo were both well pleased with the bargains they had struck.

CHAPTER 22

THE NEW YEAR came on cold, there was ice in the street, and for a few days snow pushed hard against every door. The *bottega* was freezing. The smell of wet wool and wet stone mingled with the smell of burning wood so that the air tasted of vinegar and the smoke stung our eyes. It was a relief to duck out into the snow and draw a breath of fresh air.

Donatello and Agnolo huddled by a brazier in the posing section. Agnolo posed for him without clothes and without complaint and Donatello worked rapidly and surely, sketching him in the pose of the destroyed *bozzetto*, his left hand on his hip, his right hand clutching the sword and his left foot resting on Goliath's severed head, and all of it saying, Look at me.

"You can rest in a minute," Donatello said. "Don't move until I tell you."

But Agnolo needed no indulgence. He was present in mind as well as body and he assumed the pose Donatello asked and held it as long as there was need. He had become a good model.

Donatello moved on to the *bozzetto* and in less time than seemed possible he constructed a wooden core and, with wires and rods and clay, he roughed out a scale model of David triumphing over the fallen Goliath. He worked with economy and speed and great satisfaction.

He was pleased with Agnolo and he had good reason. At first light each morning Agnolo was at the *bottega* and ready for work. He never complained. He expressed gratitude for the small gifts Donatello gave him—a cap of rabbit fur, a set of woolen gloves—and he never asked for extra money. He got on well with the apprentices whose room he shared and at the end of each day he offered to tidy Donatello's work space, though he knew that was my job and I would relinquish it to no one. It appeared that Agnolo had given over the whim of becoming a sculptor and had resigned himself to the glory of living forever in Donatello's bronze.

"I could be of help," he said.

"You help by posing well," Donatello said.

"But there are many other things I could do." He was clever enough to pretend he meant no more than the words he said.

"You do enough," Donatello said. "We have an agreement. We must not go outside its limits."

"But I . . ."

"Enough," Donatello said, and I could see that Agnolo would have to work very hard to break down this new unyielding attitude.

At the end of January the weather broke momentarily and our spirits rose. Work was proceeding well for all of us and there was the false feeling that the hardships of winter were past. At just this time I discovered that Agnolo's thoughts had been inclined toward Caterina, and his thoughts—as always—had led to action and thus, to my horror, he had lain with her. I learned this from Michelozzo who had learned it from Pagno di Lapo.

"I have spoken to her, firmly," Michelozzo said, "and you must speak to Agnolo."

I thought of Caterina and that boy at play with her. I hoped she knew of the *daucus carota* and its preventive powers, since a child by Agnolo was not to be thought upon.

"Do you hear?"

"Agnolo is a fool," I said. "And so is Pagno."

"But Donatello must not know of this. For his own sake. And for Agnolo's as well." Michelozzo thought for a minute. "You have never seen him in anger."

I could not believe he was serious. I had seen Donatello crush the wax head of Saint Louis against his chest and I had watched as he took the hammer to the David *bozzetto*. "I have seen him in anger."

"He will not suffer betrayal," Michelozzo said. "Not again."

I said I would speak to Agnolo as he would have me do. "In a brotherly way."

Michelozzo smiled his sad, knowing smile.

He was leaving, he said, for Trebbio. Cosimo had appointed him as his official architect and the first order of business was a design for a new villa, indeed for a castello. He was eager to begin work. He would keep me in his heart, he said, along with my master Donatello.

* * *

"It was but a single time with Caterina," Agnolo said, looking penitent but then, incapable of restraint, he offered me a huge smile, "and excellent too!"

This is how it was to deal with Agnolo. He lived for the moment. He had no care for the consequences of his actions. He was incapable of understanding danger. It was as if he lacked all sense of right and wrong, of sin and forgiveness, of love and betrayal . . . although, to be sure, he was able to imitate any emotion that was asked or desired. He had the charm of innocent wickedness.

Donatello, I told him, would be enraged. Donatello would throw you out, forever. He listened and nodded. Donatello would be hurt beyond remedy by your betrayal. Here he lowered his eyes and put on the mask of sorrow and penance, as if he understood what it meant to be hurt. He should be a traveling player, I thought, taking on a new character with a new cloak, feigning emotions he did not feel, moving his audience to false tears and vows of repentance. I could find no way through to him.

"Donatello loves you," I said in anger and frustration. Agnolo smiled. "He should not, but he does. And I will not see him injured in this way." He listened, wanting more. "Caterina is his niece—not that that matters—what matters is that you have betrayed him."

He was astonished. "How have I betrayed him?"

I saw for that instant he was sincere. In truth, he did not understand.

"I've promised to be here each daybreak and to pose without complaint. I did not take a vow of chastity."

"You refuse to understand. You're like a child."

He gave me a wide smile. "I am a child. Until eighteen."

He was referring to the laws of the Ufficiali di Onestà who arrested but only rarely prosecuted sodomites beneath the age of eighteen years.

"One day your age will not protect you," I said, and gave over. It was not possible to make him hear what he did not want to hear.

FEBRUARY HAD BEGUN with a week of fair weather—the snow disappeared, a warm wind blew from the west—and it seemed almost as if spring was about to bloom. We cast off our heavy cloaks and drank deep of the fresh air. Even Donatello seemed to relax. He was well advanced on the core of the life-sized statue. On the next morning he would begin the actual sculpting of the head, but this night when we finished work, and after I had tidied away his tools, Donatello said he would stand us to a tankard of wine. Everyone had left for the day excepting me and Agnolo—and of course Pagno di Lapo who lived in fear he would miss something Donatello might say or do—and we went to the San Giovanni tavern in the Piazza della Signoria. We drank a flagon of wine, watery but sweet, and in good cheer we departed each for home. Agnolo went back to the room he shared with the apprentices but later that night, goaded by the sting of the flesh or perhaps only by the need for excitement, he wandered off to the Via tra Pellicciai—the ill-famed Street of the Furriers—to see what might happen.

The next morning Donatello was early at his sculpting stand. He was in good spirits, ready to work.

"Have you seen the boy?"

I feared to answer and my heart tightened at the thought that of all mornings Agnolo had chosen this one to stay late abed.

Donatello patted the clay with his wet fingers and looked about the *bottega* impatiently.

I looked about as well and saw that the three apprentices who shared the room with Agnolo were all at their tasks. I approached the youngest, Antonio Carpacci, and asked if he knew where Agnolo might be, but Antonio had not seen him that morning. Or the previous night. I dared not tell Donatello this. Caterina, too, knew nothing of him.

The rest of the morning was long and slow and at mid-day Donatello told me to come along, and we walked together in silence down the Via Larga to the Ponte Vecchio and across the bridge to the apartment houses where Donatello's assistants had their rooms in the Via del Gufo. No one was there, of course, and it was too early in the day to try the Buco and there seemed nothing further we could do.

"Where could he have gone?"

"It may be Pagno would know."

Donatello shot me a quick look. "Always Pagno," he said.

"They share confidences," I said, to defend myself.

"Agnolo does not share," he said.

We returned to the *bottega* and Donatello approached Pagno at once. I could not hear what they said, but it was clear that Pagno had no idea where Agnolo might be.

The rest of the day was marked by my careful silence and Donatello's self-control. He left the *bottega* early with orders for me to lock up.

Everyone had finished for the day and I was putting the lock to the door when Agnolo, looking white and exhausted, appeared behind me.

"Let me go in," he said. "I need to use the privy."

I unlocked the doors and waited for him outside the privy and after a few moments there he was standing beside me, full of sudden energy and bravado.

"I was arrested," he said, as if this were some new and wonderful adventure. "I was brought before the clerk of the Onestà."

I stared at him in disbelief.

"I was in prison for the whole night."

"In truth, you stink of it," I said. "You should be proud."

"They let me go with only a caution."

"First," I said, "Donatello must never know of this. "Next, sit down and tell me what happened. In the end, I will tell you what you must do. Now sit."

Insensible creature that he was, he sat down and poured out his story. He had left the San Giovanni Tavern and returned to his room in the Via del Gufo but none of the apprentices was there and he was bored and feeling lusty and in need of some liveliness, so he went back across the bridge to the Sant' Andrea Tavern near the Via tra Pellicciai. There an older man of good quality—he had a fur-lined cloak—snatched off his cap and said he would not return it unless Agnolo agreed to service him. My cap and a silver florin, Agnolo had said, and the man responded, the cap now and the florin afterward. They went together down a narrow alley and the man at first fondled Agnolo's privy parts, and then worked at his own, and when at last he was ready he lowered the flap on the front of his stockings and was scrabbling at Agnolo's rear, roughly too . . . "Enough," I said, "so they arrested you." But he went on and, in short, what happened was this: two police appeared suddenly out of the dark and arrested them—*in actu*, or nearly so. At once the man in the fur-lined cloak claimed it was all a misunderstanding, that he had gone into the alley to relieve himself and this boy, whom he had never seen before, was there relieving himself as well, and the boy had propositioned him while he was making water and he had said no, but the boy had said he would service him for a silver florin, so it was the boy who was at fault. The police led them off to the Bargello and turned them over to the guard at the Onestà who put them in the holding cell until the morning when they went before the clerk to be charged, separately, as sodomites.

I listened fascinated, I confess, but in horror of what would follow.

The clerk of the Onestà, he said, wrote down his name, his age, his home address, his place of work, the name of his parents—"I gave your name, as you are my brother"—and then he asked Agnolo if he wished to confess.

"Was he a fat, fat man?" I asked, "with no chin and white skin all sickly?"

Agnolo thought a moment and said, "He smelled of ginger and ink . . . and piss especially."

So it was the same clerk, and now he had my name and my true place of employment and my connection to a confessed sodomite. My mind clouded and for a second I thought I would go unconscious. How long was it since I had had a falling fit?

"So I told him this was my first time. And he let me go. With only a warning."

"Because you are under eighteen."

"I told him I was fifteen."

"And you gave them my name. And Donatello's?"

"They asked where I was employed. I had no choice."

So it was disaster, worse than I could have guessed. I sat across from Agnolo, my head in my hands, thinking they have my name, they have my name, and this is only the start, this will follow me the rest of my life.

"But I did not name names."

I looked up at him.

"I did not name Donatello. As a partner."

"What are you saying?"

"Or you."

I truly did not understand.

"They want names. They want you to name all your partners in sodomy. You don't have to tell the truth. You only have to give a name."

"But you did not mention the name of Donatello."

"I would never mention Donatello. And besides, he has lost interest in me . . . in that way."

"You must tell no one you were arrested. Not Donatello, not Pagno, no one."

"Not even Caterina?"

He was impossible. "No one," I said.

✳ ✳ ✳

Two days later the warm weather ended abruptly. Heavy rains blew down from the mountains and cold settled hard upon the city, freezing the mud in the streets and making it a penance to walk from our rooms to the *bottega*. Everyone was impatient. Carving marble outside became impossible, even with the small comfort of a brazier and the limited shelter of the canopy. Everything was damp. Everything smelled of wet stone. Inside, the *bottega* was airless and dark. We worked by rushlights that flickered and went out and so needed constant attention. The *garzoni* complained—softly—that they could not see and they could not breathe and the apprentices went about looking aggrieved and put upon. Caterina and Pagno labored together on the unfinished *tondi* of the Virgin and Child. Only Donatello and Agnolo were in high good spirits.

After his day's absence in the holding cells of the Bargello, Agnolo returned to the *bottega* and to the posing stand without a word of explanation. He was standing in position when Donatello arrived the next morning. Donatello was startled and pleased, and he offered no rebuke nor any comment whatsoever on Agnolo's absence. He fell to sculpting the clay head at once.

✳ ✳ ✳

I left my account books and, seeing Caterina alone at work, I went to her and said, "He's back. And all is forgiven, it would seem."

"He was in jail. He was arrested," she said.

"It appears he is irresistible, our Agnolo," and when she offered me a hard look, I said, "Even to you."

"A single time," she said. "An experiment."

"I would think you'd blush for shame. A woman of thirty years, a boy of sixteen."

"Do you think women have no curiosity? Do you think we do not desire loveliness in our beds?"

I was shamed by this talk and could think of no response, because in truth I knew that women feel the same needs as men, at least such needs of the body, but I did not want to imagine Caterina with that boy.

"And he is very lovely."

"He is a . . ." I was about to say, "He is a whore," but I recoiled from the word just in time, as Caterina drew herself up and looked at me with disdain.

"I had thought better of you," she said.

At that moment Pagno joined us. "Donatello does not know," Pagno said. "You must not mention about Agnolo's arrest."

"Is there anyone who does not know!" I said.

"Only Donatello," he said. "And if you care for him, you will protect him."

Enraged, I went back to my work table.

* * *

During his break from posing, Agnolo approached Donatello and whispered, "I have failed you, my lord." He was the very image of penitence and I wondered would he confess to Donatello now that he had played the whore, that he had been arrested, that he had involved me—and the *bottega*—in his disgrace.

"You are posing well today," Donatello said. "It is no easy thing."

"I drank too much and . . ."

"You are here now." He placed his hand gently on Agnolo's shoulder. "Only be here."

MICHELOZZO MOVED OUT of the house he shared with Donatello and three days later Agnolo moved in.

"It is easier this way," Michelozzo said to me.

"And you?" I asked.

Michelozzo shrugged and gave me that sad, understanding smile. He thought well of me and I felt guilty for his trust and his approval.

I went back to my work but I could not concentrate. That it should come to this! That Michelozzo should move out and Agnolo move in. To his very house. To his bed? Agnolo must have seduced him beyond his reason. I thought, I will go mad. I will not endure it. I felt myself falling, my arm went numb, there was that roaring in my brain.

I told Donatello I was ill and must go home. At once.

"Lie down in my little room," he said. "You work too hard. You must have a rest."

But I would not lie down in his little room. I would not stay and listen to the loving words passed back and forth between this old man—however much a genius—and this wanton boy, no better than a whore. I had suffered enough outrage for this day. I was going home. Let them lock up the *bottega* and do filthy things in that little room and, only see, they would find themselves in prison and rot there for the rest of their lives. I did not care. I went home.

CHAPTER 23

DIZZY AND CONFUSED, I took to bed and fell asleep at once. I woke some time later with a pain in the right side of my head and, when Alessandra asked how I felt, I found that I could not speak. My mouth seemed full of wool, my tongue stumbled, and my words came out a muddled, shushing sound. I felt as if someone was driving a small nail into my skull. I tried to get up—I had to get back to the *bottega*—but I found I could not move my left side. I had no feeling there, not in my arm, not in my leg, and I lacked all strength. I tried to explain this to Alessandra, but I could not make myself understood, so I picked up my left wrist with my right hand and let the arm fall. "It's dead," I said, though the sounds I made were unintelligible. For some reason, I found this funny and began to laugh. Alessandra, who remained always sensible in any crisis, got a bowl of cool water and placed a wet cloth on my forehead.

"Stay," she said, "only rest," and to assure me a little quiet, she sent the boys out to play.

I fell asleep and when I woke it was night and the pain was gone. Alessandra was leaning over me, asking if I felt any better and I said in my normal voice, "Yes," and she smiled and kissed me softly on the mouth. She slipped out of bed then and went to heat the broth of a chicken, but when she returned I was again asleep and could not be wakened. In the morning I could move my left arm and I could speak a little but I could not manage to stay awake. I drifted off, only half-conscious and, it seemed to me, only half alive.

Alessandra sent to Donatello to say that I was ill. Though the weather remained foul, he came through a blizzard of sleet and rain and sat by my side. I slept through his visit like one who was dead. "A good sign," he said. "The sleep will heal him." He said a prayer to the Virgin and left me to continue sleeping.

A day later he sent a doctor referred to him by Cosimo de' Medici. The doctor prescribed bleeding and cupping, but after they drew my blood I was weaker and more light-headed than before. The doctor promised that in time I would recover, but he did not say when that time would be.

Cosimo, hearing of this, asked his favorite priest to visit. This was Antonio Pierozzi, Prior of the Dominican monastery, a most learned and spiritual man who would years later become Archbishop of Florence. He came to our small cottage and sat by my bed and, when I could not speak to make my confession, asked instead a few simple spiritual questions: Who made you? Why did God make you? Do you believe in the saving blood of Christ? I heard him ask these questions, and I was eager to respond, but my tongue could make no sense of my words, and I nodded merely. Donatello stood beside him and waited for his advice.

"*Acedia*," the Prior said. "If this Luca were a monk and this cottage a monastery, I would say he suffers from *acedia: tristitia de bono spirituali*. He is alive in body but not in spirit. He is fatigued in the face of God's omnipotence. He can do nothing to save himself. We must pray for him." He loved to teach and he warmed now to his topic. "*Acedia* is a refusal of Christian joy. It is a condition, not a sin, though it can become a sin when it embraces the luxury of despair. I have observed this sometimes in the Brothers of Saint Dominic, I have recognized it in myself, but I have never seen it in a layman." He paused for a long moment. "Does he pray much, this Luca? Is he greatly given to the spiritual life?"

Donatello responded that I had once been a Franciscan Brother, that I had left the Order following a bout of the Black Pest, that I was a good husband and father but beyond that he could not answer for any man's spiritual life.

"The Pest," the Prior said. "Could it be the effects of the Pest, I wonder."

"He has been known to have spells," Donatello said, and when the Prior merely looked at him, he went on. "A trembling of the limbs and

I believe severe pains in the head and a kind of violence of feeling. I do not say madness, not that, but a leaving of himself and the sudden need to destroy."

I listened in disbelief. Madness? The need to destroy. Could Donatello be right?

The Prior nodded. "A contagion of evil," he said, "from the Black Pest. Those who survive are never the same again."

He continued to sit beside my bed while Donatello stood beside him and I lay there saying nothing, no longer sure if I was unable or merely unwilling to speak. I had not thought of any need to destroy. I had not thought to blame the Black Pest. I had never heard of the contagion of evil.

"I will pray for him," the Prior said, and he blessed me with the holy oils on my hands and feet and on my brow and on my lips.

I fell comfortably asleep and dreamed that I was an apprentice again in Donatello's *bottega* and I had only now completed the sculpting of the *putti* for the base of the Saint Louis statue. I was pleased and proud of my work—it was honest and honorable like my lord Donatello himself—and then for one terrible moment I saw my work through Donatello's eyes and the roaring in my brain began and the pain and the blindness and I snatched up a chisel and struck out with it and suddenly I was falling, falling. "*Mio figlio,*" I heard him say, and "*mio tesoro.*" His hand was on my shoulder, comforting, consoling, and at his touch I was calm again, at peace in a green meadow, and all my terror fell away. The dream faded and returned once more. And faded. And returned.

I went on like this, half living, half dead. In the end it was Donatello who cured me, though that was not his intention. He cured me by accident. Out of his own terrible silence and out of his need to share his worry and his grief, he made me his confidante.

It came about in this way. The boys were playing outside in the neighbor courtyard, Alessandra was spinning fine wool at the front door, and Donatello, who had tried without success to engage me in conversation, sat quietly by the side of my bed. "You need a cat," he muttered, "A cat can be a great consolation." After a long while he cast me a sidelong glance and said softly, "I am not a bad man, you know. It is not such a case with me." He fell silent and then began once more, scarcely audible, as if he were talking to himself. "I am foolish, I am an old man who should know better, but I am good to him. And I make no demands." He wrung his long hands together. "No demands of the kind you think."

He shifted uncomfortably on the stool by the bed. In a voice so soft I could barely make out the words, he said, "I need him." He muttered something else. "He breaks my heart."

I would not hear such things with my eyes open. I closed them.

"I know about him, you can be sure. I know he was arrested on the Pellicciai and I know why. But what does it matter? I have always known him for what he is. He is not going to change."

I tried to speak, to warn him against Agnolo, but I could not get my tongue around the words.

He leaned against the bed and whispered in my ear. "I love him. What can I do?"

"Let him go," I said, and these were the first understandable words I uttered since that day two weeks earlier when I had left them together, cooing, at the *bottega*.

He showed no surprise at hearing me speak and answered simply, "I cannot. I will not."

He rose and left, saying goodbye to Alessandra. She brought me wine mixed with water and I slept, at peace now, and when I woke she found me able once again to speak, and hungry, and alive. And, most strange to say, happy.

I lay in bed for a week and then another, strengthened by the good care of Alessandra and the shy visits of Donatello, and then the weather turned mild—it was the beginning of March—and I returned to the *bottega*.

I was eager to work and eager to play out my new role as confidante to the master Donatello.

CHAPTER 24

Aᴛ ᴛʜᴇ *ʙᴏᴛᴛᴇɢᴀ* they took it as natural that I had been ill and was ill no longer. Caterina smiled at me and Pagno said, "Well done"—whatever he meant by that—but Donatello and Agnolo acted as if I had never been gone. I wanted to tell them what a narrow reckoning I had had but they were greatly pleased with each other and had no need to know. Michelozzo alone seemed moved to see me. He gave me a great embrace and said how happy he was at my return.

I was happy too. Donatello had confided in me unseemly things he had not told others. He was in love with Agnolo. "He breaks my heart." The thought itself was unworthy, degrading. Here he was, a man of eminence, the most accomplished craftsman in Florence—I place him ahead of Brunelleschi and Ghiberti and, in truth, all others—and this artisan without peer was brought low by desire for this nobody, this Agnolo, brought so low that he was moved to confess to me that he asked no sexual favors from the boy. Still, and this was the great thing, he had chosen me to share his secrets. Me only. I was shamed that he should tell me these things, as if he were some ordinary man who had never sculpted the Saint George or the Louis of Tolosa or the bronze David that was even now coming alive beneath his hands. "He breaks my heart." In this weakness and pitiless need Donatello was no different than me and he had confessed as much. I was his confidante.

I could tell at once that something had changed since that evening when I had watched Donatello take Agnolo by the hand and lead him to his privy chamber. Things were different between them now. Work on the statue was well advanced and there was no longer any need for Agnolo to pose. In truth, there was no need for Agnolo at all and yet he continued to hang about. He could not understand that Donatello had moved into his own mind and heart, that he was bent now on one thing only: the making of this statue. The unformed David had become more real to him than Agnolo in the flesh.

"Go ask Caterina for a task," he said, and Agnolo went away to bother Caterina.

It was a joy to see the master wield his shaping tools. The clay had been brought to the necessary finish and the wax had been laid on thinly, then thicker, until it was exactly the right depth for carving. Donatello had roughed in the features of the face and now, with a sharp knife, was bringing them to a keen perfection. I watched him as he disappeared into his work.

Agnolo returned. "She has nothing for me to do."

"Grind colors for her."

"She says I do not grind fine enough."

"Go ask Pagno for something to do."

"Pagno says I should pose for you."

Donatello sighed. "In a while," he said. "Sit there and wait and after a time I will need you to pose again."

Agnolo stood by, watching him as he worked.

But, watched in this way, Donatello was no longer with the statue. He found himself half at work and half in love. He made a gash in the wax lip and threw down the knife. "Go!" he shouted. "Go home and let me work!"

We all pretended to be busy while Agnolo put on his cloak and hat and, without a word, left the *bottega*.

This is how things stood between them: Agnolo had become the supplicant, Donatello the desired one.

Nonetheless, Donatello left the *bottega* at once in pursuit of the boy.

Donatello pretended now and again that he needed Agnolo to pose for him: to refresh the mind, he said, to reaffirm the design. Agnolo fell in gladly with his requests.

In mid March the winter suddenly ended and mild weather settled on the city. Michelozzo had just returned from Trebbio with the plans for Cosimo's castello and I rose to greet him at the door. In a moment Donatello left off his work and approached us joyfully, welcoming Michelozzo with a shy embrace.

"It went well?" he asked.

Michelozzo began to talk of Siena and the bronze panel for the Baptistry and I seized upon this opportunity to give them privacy while I engaged once again with Agnolo. Since my return to the *bottega* I had made daily efforts to become his confidante as well as Donatello's.

"Your work goes well," I said.

Agnolo relaxed his pose and sat down on the little resting stool Donatello had provided him. Agnolo was still not sure he should trust me.

"Your posing pleases him."

"He likes to have me near at hand."

"He is a happy man these days."

Agnolo nodded.

"He is happy because of you."

He covered his privy parts with his hand, casually.

"You are good for him, I think. He trusts you."

"He asks nothing of me. I only pose for him. It is not what you think."

I assured him once again that he posed well and that he made the master happy. I returned to my accounts, annoyed. Any stranger in the street could have him, but he would be won over by me only with the greatest patience.

Donatello returned from his talk with Michelozzo. The Feast of Herod for the Siena Font had been accepted by the Cathedral with great thanks. Final payment was to follow immediately. Donatello was in good spirits. "Make a note," he said to me, "and let me know when the payment is made." He rubbed his hands together and anyone seeing him at that moment would think he cared about the money when in truth it meant nothing to him.

"Our David," he said and at once Agnolo stood and assumed the pose of David in triumph, proudly naked, his foot resting on the head of Goliath.

* * *

THE MESSENGER WORE a uniform of black and silver. He was a young man with the newly fashionable long hair and short doublet. He stood at the passway door to the *bottega* and waited for someone to come to him. Pagno approached him and asked his business. He must present a summons, he said, to one Luca di Matteo of the *bottega* of Donato di Betto Bardi, Orafo e Scharpellatore of Florence. It was a summons to appear before the Ufficiali di Onestà.

I heard my name and approached them. I confirmed I was that same Luca di Matteo, at which the messenger handed me a thrice-folded card that said inside in a florid script, *Citazione*, with a time and place designated, and next to Purpose was the single word *Interrogatorio*. Pagno leaned in to read the card but I folded it quickly and asked the messenger, "When?"

"Yesterday," he said, "but I found you neither at home nor at work, so I have been sent again today. A third time and the guards will be sent to summon you." He seemed pleased at this bit of news.

I told Donatello I must leave, but he was by now deeply involved in shaping wax for the left arm of the David and only nodded his assent. Agnolo, naked and content, smiled at me. I could see how greatly I would be missed if I disappeared into the dark cellars of the Bargello.

The walk to the offices of the Onestà took only a few minutes and the young messenger chattered the whole way. He was new in the job, his father had arranged it through a friend, a relative of the estate manager of Rinaldo degli Albizzi. He prattled on but all I heard was the name Albizzi, the bitter enemy of the Medici.

He led me through the same doors and down the same corridors I had traveled in my search for the disappeared Agnolo. All at once we stopped before the door with a plaque that said Ufficiali di Onestà and beneath it, in smaller script, Ser Paolo Ruggiero, Conservatore di Legge. The messenger pinched his nose between thumb and forefinger, winked at me, and thumped the door soundly. Ser Paolo himself poked out his huge bald head and said, "Yes? Yes?" and beckoned me in. He waved away the messenger with the back of his hand—the young man laughed, mocking—and urged me to sit down.

I was assaulted by the stench of urine. He must be ill, I thought, with some dread disease. And so fat! In a city of fat men, he was gigantic.

He took my summons, glanced at it shortly, and went back behind his desk where he began to shuffle papers and notebooks until he found the one he wanted. Then he examined my summons carefully, compared it with the pages he had opened in his notebook, and sat back satisfied.

"You are Luca di Matteo. Also called Luca Mattei."

I nodded.

"A common name."

"Yes."

"A name also held by Agnolo Mattei. No relation, you say."

"No."

"He claims to be your brother."

"He is no relation. His father took money from my father to raise me."

"A complication, but not a relation. You are a bastard then?"

"Yes."

"You know your father?"

I gave his name and Ser Paolo nodded and wrote it down. He went on like this for some time, asking questions he had asked in his previous interview, and then he said, "There are discrepancies. You said you were visiting from Prato. You said you were an engraver. You said you were in the employ of the great Ghiberti—I underlined his name—you said you lived in a rooming house in Santa Croce. Near the Basilica." He paused and looked hard at me. "Why so many lies? Truthful men do not lie."

"No," I said.

"Agnolo Mattei, that youth who you say is not your brother, has confessed to a single crime of sodomy, but he is beneath the age for punishment and besides he is self-confessed, and he has given your name as well."

"But I am not a sodomite."

"No. He did not say that. He said you were his brother and you worked as an assistant to Donato di Betto Bardi"—he paused significantly—"famous for his works of sculpture."

"Yes."

"Donato di Betto Bardi has not been denounced as a sodomite."

"No."

He stared at me with his squinty eyes to see my reaction.

"Is he a sodomite?"

"No. He is not a sodomite. He is a very great artisan."

"He is, without doubt, a great artisan. That does not mean he is not a sodomite."

"I know him well. I have worked for him for many years. I know him to be a man of honor and decency."

"And yet he is not married, though he is a good age."

"He is married to his work."

"So are many great artisans, I notice."

He paused then and looked at me hard and long. I waited.

"You are known to the great Cosimo de' Medici."

For a moment my heart stopped and I could not breathe. It was not good for small people to be named with the great in this way.

"The lord de' Medici is a close friend of your master Donatello." I continued to look at him, horrified and silent, and he went on. "You know this?" He turned toward me a little book bound in red leather. I shook my head, no. "It is a collection of foul epigrams that celebrate the sinful pleasures of sodomy. *Hermaphroditus* . . . by one Antonio Beccadelli. This Beccadelli is a sodomite. He has dedicated his book to Cosimo de' Medici, praising him for his openness of mind and his easy acceptance of the luxuries of sin." He leaned toward me. "And Cosimo de' Medici has accepted the dedication." He waited. "With pleasure, it would seem." He waited again. "The lord Cosimo is a friend of your master Donatello, you have said it yourself."

"I have not said it."

"But it is true." He sat back, satisfied. "It is true nonetheless."

I sat there, confused, frightened.

"Do you have anything you want to say? Anything?"

I assured him I had said everything I could and should.

"But if you had information, you would offer it?" He was silent for a long moment. "I am not suggesting you become a spy. But should you see where danger lies, you would act to prevent it."

I only looked at him.

"It would be sad to see harm come to the great Donato di Betto Bardi through his association with others who themselves are not . . . careful."

Still I said nothing.

He dismissed me then and from the corridor outside the door I could hear the torrent of piss and the sharp cry of pain as he relieved himself.

I resolved to tell no one of this, not even Alessandra.

"HE ASKS NOTHING of me," Agnolo said. "I wish he would ask."

"Do you offer?"

He paused, silent, unsure if he should trust me. Then he decided we had become friends.

"I do offer. I offer and he says no. He says it is not like that between us."

I listened and a great peace spread through me.

"Good," I said, but then I thought of my *interrogatorio* with Ser Paolo and his determination to discover if Donatello was a sodomite and I went cold.

"Only take care," I said.

* * *

DONATELLO ASKED ME to stay after the others had left. He locked the door and led me to his privy chamber where he lit a rushlight and poured a cup of wine for me and another for himself.

I had been in the chamber once before, insensible, and I had glanced inside many times when the door was open, and I knew it to contain his most valued things. There were several books in Latin and even some in the native language, there were paintings by Uccello and Massolino and designs for projects too important to be left outside among the pile on his great work table—I noticed drawings for the new Medici castello—and there were projects abandoned for a time but too weighty to be abandoned for good, there were letters and contracts and a Brunelleschi crucifix. A small table stood next to a cot, and there was a stool and several jugs of wine.

Donatello sat on the cot and propped himself against the wall. I took the stool and did my best to conceal my excitement at this new intimacy. He drank his cup of wine and poured another. Finally he looked at me and said, "It is your brother, Agnolo." He gave me a half smile. "He is driving me mad."

"He wants to be needed," I said.

Donatello put down the cup and covered his face with his hands. He sat that way for a long moment and then he uncovered his face and he had become an old man driven to despair.

"What can I do?" he said. And to my joy and shame he told me everything. "He does not understand. He can't. He won't. He is a satyr. He throws himself at me like a wanton and it is my fault, it is all my fault because of that night you know about, you remember, when I had him here on this same bed, three times over, in my lust and my rage for him. He remembers that lust and he thinks that is what I want. And I confess to you it is, I want him, but there is a love that I want still more, and he does not understand. Sometimes I ache for him, I want him so. He comes at night into my bed and he is young, and his smooth body is so yielding, and I want to take him in my arms and hold him hard, hard, until our bodies melt into one another and we are but one thing and I devour him." He put his hand to his forehead and rubbed away the thought. "No, not devour him. Did I say devour him?" He rubbed his brow again. "That may be what I mean. I want to possess him whole. *Is* it so wrong? You have been a Franciscan brother, Luca, tell me, is it so wrong?"

"We are weak men. We know what is right but we do what is wrong."

"Do you understand what I mean when I say I want his love and not just his body?"

I understood but, jealous, I said nothing.

"You are a good man, Luca," he said, and I kept this in mind as he poured another cup of wine and talked on and on for hours about his love and his lust and devouring the smooth body of that damned Agnolo.

Toward midnight he fell asleep and I returned home to Alessandra who was too tired to make love with me and so I satisfied myself at the side of the bed and slept a disturbed and bitter sleep for the few hours remaining to the night.

I had in truth become Donatello's confidante but at a great price.

* * *

"THERE IS NOTHING for me to do. I stand about all day and do nothing. Caterina says I am no use to her because I do not grind the pigments well even when I've ground them to a powder and Pagno says I dull his chisels when I use them but when I try to sharpen them he says I chip the edges. The apprentices think I am a fool. The *garzoni* call me a *bardassa*. And Donatello fails even to see me." He paused and looked at me, hopeful. "You are my only friend."

In this way I became Agnolo's confidante.

✳ ✳ ✳

T HE STATUE WAS progressing beautifully. The head and neck and shoulders were the young David come alive in wax. The face expressed nothing. There was no triumph in his look, no sense of awe and horror at having killed Goliath and beheaded him. No exhaustion. No godly fear. Only that indifference Agnolo had showed in the days when he was the desired one.

"Look at me," he said now. He had undressed and was standing at the posing platform, the living David, naked, impatient for attention.

Donatello was smoothing the wax beneath the arch of David's chest and either did not hear or did not want to hear. I looked up from my work table and shook my head no, a message to Agnolo.

"Look at me," he said again, and pressed hard with his foot against the marble block that served as Goliath's head. The muscles in his leg rippled and he smiled at the effect.

"I'm working!" Donatello was in no mood for real flesh. He put down his ivory smoothing chisel and picked up a hooked awl with which to shape the nipples. He leaned in closer to his work.

Agnolo pouted for a minute and then, never having known restraint, he said. "Look what I can do." And again, "Look at me."

"Go!" Donatello shouted. "I cannot work with you here. You're driving me mad. Just go away!"

Agnolo went all red with anger and embarrassment. He pulled on his stockings, catching his toenail on the parti-colored cloth and tearing it, and he threw on the rest of his clothes and flung himself through the door. Meanwhile Donatello bent over his work in a terrible silence. When he was sure Agnolo had left, Donatello went out to the privy and did not return for some minutes. He came back and his face was gray with anger. He stood before the statue, staring. After a long while he turned to me and said, "I can't work with him here. He must be made to stay at home. You must see to it. You can talk to him."

"I will talk to him," I said.

"After all, you are his brother." And, with a half smile, "I beg you."

✶ ✶ ✶

"He says you are not to come to the *bottega* while he's working. He cannot work with you there."

"Are you so sure?"

It was the day after Donatello's explosion and, as soon as I saw that he had resumed work on the David, I left the bottega and sought out Agnolo at the house he shared with Donatello. Agnolo had just risen from bed.

"He said to tell you not to come," I said.

"He repented of his anger and I forgave him." He gave me that coy look of his. "I raised the young man in him and he had me twice during the night. He desires me still."

I shook my head. "But he does not want you at the *bottega*."

"Then I'll find other places to go."

"You anger him at your own peril. You have been arrested once already."

"He knows and he forgives that."

"But the Onestà . . ."

"Donatello will protect me. He is mad for me."

"And who will protect Donatello?"

"Cosimo," he said, giggling, "and his fat wife."

I left him to get through the day in whatever way he would.

Caterina was the first to mention what I had noticed immediately. Donatello was in good spirits once again but he was not working on the David.

"It is hard to say which David he prefers," she said, "the one in wax or the one in the flesh."

"For shame," I said.

"The shame is not mine."

"We are behind in commissions. The pulpit, for instance."

"Love," she said airily. "Love is the great destroyer." She returned to the *cassone* she was painting, Amor in pursuit of Dido.

Donatello had left off work on the David. Suddenly he was caught up in Michelozzo's plans for Cosimo's Castello di Trebbio and then he returned to work on the Prato pulpit. He was anxious, he said, about payments for commissions that had been fulfilled and not yet paid for. What about the three hundred florins for the Baptistry panel in Siena? The money had come, I said, it was in the hanging basket. But what about the Tabernacle of the Sacrament for San Pietro in Rome? Had we ordered the marble from Pisa? Why was the shipment late? Why was nothing completed?

The David stood there, unfinished, a reminder and a rebuke.

Donatello was dismayed. He was back at work on the David but it was going badly. He could not concentrate and his hands and eyes were no longer sure. "What can I do?" he asked me.

Agnolo had taken to going out nights and not returning until long past curfew. He was bored staying home all day and wandered instead through the markets and back alleys in search of amusement. He met boys his own age, professional *bardasse* who talked of their lovers and the gifts they gave them and the adventures they had by night. Agnolo joined them, just for fun, just for excitement, he assured Donatello, but all the same he did not return until dawn sometimes and always disheveled and exhausted. He lay abed in the mornings and was out again each evening. This could not go on.

"It cannot," I said. "Think of the dangers."

Donatello looked at me as if he were uncertain what I meant.

"The Onestà," I said. "He could involve you."

He was silent and I felt I must say it. "He already has."

Donatello showed no surprise.

"When I was summoned for my *Interrogatorio*, they asked me about . . . well, about you . . . and I assured them there was not a trace of truth in it."

"In what?"

"That you were . . . you know." I waited for a response. "Nor Cosimo either, despite the dedication of that book."

Donatello offered no show of surprise or interest in what I had said. He turned from me quietly and went back to work on the David. Work went well for the rest of the day and that evening before leaving the *bottega* he said to me, "You do well to say little of this. You are a good man, Luca."

I went home to my wife and boys, grateful for God's mercy and love.

✳ ✳ ✳

"He is an old man," Agnolo said. "He gives me presents and he loves me but he is old and clumsy in bed. I stay with him only to be kind."

✳ ✳ ✳

April came, and the soft rain fell, and everyone was glad of the weather, except Donatello, except Agnolo.

CHAPTER **25**

O<small>N</small> 17 A<small>PRIL</small> in the year 1432 the Commune of Florence established a special magistracy called the Ufficiali di Notte, the Officers of the Night, whose task was to seek out and punish those who practiced "the abominable vice of sodomy." Earlier offices had prosecuted sodomy as part of their commissions, but the Ufficiali di Notte was the first magistracy with sodomy as its sole target.

Attenzione: I now write a section full of dates and facts . . . because they interest me in themselves and because I have the documents before me and because I must somehow wear out my length of days before I am allowed the great sleep that never ends. Indulge an old man, and I will tell you of the Ufficiali di Notte and its nice complexities.

Sodomy was nothing new or unusual in Florence: among the Germans a sodomite is even today commonly called a *florenzer*. In truth so common was florenzing that nearly a century ago Pope Gregory XI wrote "there are no two sins more abominable than those that prevail among the Florentines: the first is usury and the second is so unspeakable that I dare not mention it." The unspeakable sin was sodomy.

Fra Bernadino of Siena did not fear to give voice to the unspeakable when he came to Florence in 1424, and again in 1425, to give the Lenten sermons. He awoke one night, he said, to find every street and courtyard ringing with the voices of unborn children crying out against the cursed sodomites: "to the fire!"

"When you see a grown man who is without wife, there you will discover the evil vice. They are so blind in this their wickedness that no matter how beautiful a woman may be, to him she stinks and is displeasing, nor will he ever want to yield to her beauty. Burn them at the street corners," he cried out. "All of them, burn them with their fathers and mothers and all who support this unnatural vice. Away with them! To the fire! To the fire! To the fire!"

Bernadino did not immediately have his way. It was not until 1429 that Piero di Jacopo was burned at the stake.

This new magistracy—the Ufficiali di Notte—was the Commune's most recent, and most desperate, attempt to control "the Florentine vice." You must not think that in Florence there were sodomites on street corners from sunup to curfew, stockings down, buggering one another for the amusement of passersby. It was a vice practiced by few, but it was a vice that commanded the attention of the church and the nobles and therefore the officers of the Commune.

In truth it was a vice more jested about than practiced. Beccadelli's little book of Latin verses made that clear: sodomy, with all that fuss about behinds and holes and horns, was the stuff of jokes; the act itself was intrinsically funny, the position for both partners was shitty. Here was a sport to ridicule, and yet more than a few young men of eighteen, hot with first lust, found it a sport worth playing. They were from good families mostly, men of substance and promise, who considered it no more than rough fun to take a teenaged boy from behind. They were not sodomites for life, they said, but for the moment. They were real men, they took the active role, the giver. The receiver was a boy, young enough so that no permanent shame attached to him but old enough to know what he was doing. He was like Agnolo, an adolescent— rebellious, at liberty in the streets—willing and sometimes eager. The sport might last an hour or a day, but when the boy turned eighteen, the game was over. He married if he could, and if he could not, he played the man, the giver, and—reversing roles—he found for himself a boy not yet eighteen, passive and willing, et cetera, et cetera. It was a game, a romp. But at thirty, everyone agreed, a man must marry. No matter if he had come to enjoy the sport, he must leave off sodomy forever and make an end to it with marriage and a family.

To be practical, to be frank, let me say this straight out. Sin is, by its nature, complicated. It does not always corrupt. It is, after all, Adam's first gift to man. And so it was that my beloved Michelozzo had been Donatello's boy. It is true. I hate it, and it remains mysterious to me, but it is true. And then at forty-five years Michelozzo married and had eight children and so what harm to anyone that he had been Donatello's lover? And Donatello in his youth had played the boy to Brunelleschi—I can say it now; they are both gone—and both of them remained good men. And my son, my son, my Franco Alessandro! It is, in all, a great mystery.

Preaching and mockery and denunciation had been tried but had accomplished nothing. Fra Bernardino of Siena had come to Florence and shouted himself hoarse, and for a time good Christians spat on the ground when they passed the Buco and the Sant' Andrea, but Bernardino's preaching had little lasting effect. Parents were urged to forbid and condemn, and they did . . . and their counsels were greeted with the customary indifference of the young.

But we must have laws, the clergy said. The laws must be enforced, the nobles said. And so laws were made and were, in general, ignored.

Let there be some solace, the Commune said. If they must fuck, let them at least fuck women as God intended. Choosing fornication over sodomy, the Commune legalized certain brothels "for the easement of young men who could not yet afford marriage." In truth this was a scandal, but it was the lesser of two scandals. The brothels flourished . . . and so did sodomy.

Over the years there were repeated attempts to legislate morality and stamp out sodomy.

In 1403 the Commune established the Otto di Guardia. This was to be the central criminal agency that would seek out and destroy political conspiracies and, as an afterthought, punish crimes against morality. The Otto di Guardia fought conspiracy with great success, and there was always a new conspiracy to fight, but morality was less important than conspiracy and the *Guardia* showed little interest in such crimes.

Then in 1421 the Ufficiali di Onestà was appointed to regulate prostitution and to supervise the city's official brothels and to crush out sodomy. But how was this to be done without a police force and without scandal to the citizenry? The Onestà soon found itself no more than a legal office mired in its own paperwork. Only in sensational crimes did the Onestà push for trial, as they had with Piero di Jacopo in 1429, but his death at the stake, popular though it was, had proved a municipal horror no city administrator wanted to see repeated.

And so it came about that in 1432, in a mood of desperation, the Ufficiali di Notte was established to crush out sodomy now and forever. Or, failing that, to make the practice of it so dangerous that the streets would be safe from sodomites, more or less, and citizens could sleep soundly knowing that their sons and daughters were as pure and virginal as they themselves had been in their youth. One last attempt to legislate virtue.

There were six Ufficiali and three assistants for all of Florence, and from the start they knew they must depend on anonymous denunciations. How else could you apprehend criminals guilty of sodomy? Anyone could accuse anyone else simply by placing his name in one of the denunciation boxes that hung in the Duomo and in Orsanmichele and in San Piero Scheraggio. Once each month the Ufficiali would open these *tamburi* and examine the denunciations and decide which to investigate and which to ignore. Personal politics, they promised, would not be a consideration.

New laws laid out specific punishments. For the first conviction, males over eighteen years were fined fifty gold florins. For a second conviction, one hundred. And so on with increasing fines until the fifth conviction, when the penalty became death by burning at the stake. For males not yet eighteen, the fines were smaller, from ten florins for the first conviction and twenty-five for the second on up to five hundred for the sixth, and death by burning if by that time the youth, a hopeless sodomite, had reached his eighteenth year.

Since the Ufficiali di Notte could not function without help from citizens, they offered the usual rewards: informers were guaranteed anonymity and—more important—one fourth of the sodomite's fine. It was an easy way to make money and an excellent way to punish an enemy. But how could the Ufficiali know if the denunciation was true or merely malicious? And how could they guarantee anonymity? And, if the informer's name leaked out, how could they prevent the taking of revenge? Inspired by these doubts, then as now the Ufficiali employed "secret explorers," spies whose job it was to investigate accusations before the officials proceeded with formal charges. It was a complicated web they wove, made more complicated still by the practice of revoking punishment for any sodomite who denounced himself, confessing his crimes and naming his partners.

Informers, secret explorers, anonymous accusations, self-denunciations and the naming of partners: you can see the danger of having even one enemy in the city of Florence. Or worse, a friend caught in a judicial trap.

* * *

In the spring of 1432 Agnolo was arrested once again for sodomy. He admitted only to anonymous partners, two in number, and confessed he had received gifts from them, a leather belt, a silver buckle. When pressed for names, he denounced a known sodomite who was already under arrest. He accused himself and, under the new law, was allowed to go free.

The next day ten florins disappeared from Donatello's hanging basket and on the day after that Agnolo fled—so he told Pagno—to Rome.

There was a great silence in the *bottega*.

Donatello locked the unfinished David in his privy chamber where it would remain, cracked and crumbling, for more than a year.

"He is dead to me now," Donatello confided. "Now and for good."

TIME LOST

CHAPTER 26

GOOD, I THOUGHT, he is damned forever . . . and I meant Agnolo. My master Donatello once more folded in upon himself, saying little and showing nothing of his feelings, but I felt certain that this time was the last time. He would not forgive Agnolo again.

I was wrong, of course. Agnolo fled to Rome in spring of 1432 and he would not return until late summer of 1433 when once again, incredibly, all would be forgiven. And the time between—wasted, wanton—would be forgiven as well. Except by me. During his absence carvings for the Prato Pulpit lay in the work yard still only half complete, the life-cast of Niccolò da Uzzano was forgotten, and the clay David stood in Donatello's privy closet, drying out, cracking, turning into a mockery of itself.

A week after the wretched boy's disappearance Donatello himself packed off for Rome . . . though not in pursuit of Agnolo, he insisted. It was a matter of work to be done and money to be made. Michelozzo shook his head and said nothing. Two weeks later, having conferred with Cosimo and having bought time with the importunate members of the Prato Commune, Michelozzo joined Donatello in Rome. They had a Papal commission to fill, he said, and there were rich promises of memorial statues, marble tombs, tabernacles. Suddenly we were asked to believe that Donatello and Michelozzo had become interested in profit, they who never knew what was owed them or gave thought to what they owed.

I was left behind in Florence with Pagno, who was put in charge of the *bottega* . . . a temporary arrangement, Michelozzo said, but he could not look at me as he said it. Pagno again, as ever. It would be a matter of a month, perhaps two, until Donatello should return with the commissions for me to write up first in our common language and then in Latin for the sake of the tax laws. At that time, as befitted my age and accomplishments, I would replace Pagno. But one month became three months and then four, while Pagno preened and crowed as manager of the *bottega*. Though he pretended to consult me on all matters of commissions and payments—he was ever sly and subtle—it was I who made all the important decisions and guaranteed that work was accomplished in due order and on time. My exile—so I still think of it—was further occupied with transcriptions of Latin and Greek manuscripts for Cosimo de' Medici. It was I who made the first copies of Cicero's *De Oratore*, a text I came to hate as I copied it out with care and deliberation for the fiftieth time. Cosimo delighted not only in acquiring these manuscripts but in making gifts of them as well.

Meanwhile time stretched on intolerably as Donatello and Michelozzo labored in Rome on the great marble slab that would become the Giovanni Crivelli tomb in Santa Maria Aracoeli and the even more splendid Tabernacle of the Blessed Sacrament for San Pietro itself. And they did much fine work in gold, work of great beauty executed at great profit.

Yet it was time lost, all of it, lost. Anyone could have done these things.

In Rome Donatello carved a small wooden John the Baptist as a boy very like the lost Agnolo, so I am told, but Michelozzo says that is not so, that Donatello was happy at this time and that he had put Agnolo from his mind. But in this I do not believe him. I think he lies only to spare me.

I am saddened even now to say that I regard these Roman sculptures with a certain bitterness since I had no part in them: the writing up of the commission was completed by some sticky-fingered lawyer in Rome and even today, among my many papers from the partnership of Donatello and Michelozzo, there is no trace of contracts or commissions for their work in Rome; only the odd note from Michelozzo promising to return to Florence—soon—and wishing me well.

It was not until 1433 that they returned to Florence—Michelozzo in April, Donatello in May—and then in truth only because the Prato Commune had run short of patience and had begged Cosimo to intercede. "Donatello is *intricato*," they said. "He is unreliable. He has again and again violated the terms of his contract." They were threatening to sue for completion of their Pulpit, but Cosimo intervened and sent Pagno to Rome to tell Donatello and Michelozzo that they must return to Florence and finish the Prato Pulpit. It was not a request; it was a command.

They returned and a second contract was drawn up, this one calling for new balcony ornamentation for the Pulpit with a firm date fixed and new money advanced.

To soften the harsh urgency of his summons, Cosimo rented them the Inn of Santa Caterina and two adjoining little houses for five florins a year—nearly a gift outright—for use as a much enlarged *bottega* with a foundry and a work yard and with lodgings for his apprentices. This new *bottega* stood where the Via Longa meets the Via de' Gori and where, in 1443, Cosimo would erect the great new Palazzo Medici designed and built by his favorite architect, Michelozzo. But for now it was Donatello's *bottega* and the time forever lost was about to be redeemed.

It is here that Donatello would carve the immortal *Cantoria* for the Duomo and the two sets of bronze doors for the sacristy of San Lorenzo and it is here that he would finally bring to completion the fatal Medici Boy.

We were hardly settled in the new *bottega* when, without warning and without reason, Agnolo came back. Incredible as it must seem, he was accepted into Donatello's life without rebuke. In truth he was accepted without warmth and without forgiveness either—it was a chill homecoming—but he was accepted nonetheless. He hung about uselessly—"a decoration," the apprentices said—while everyone else worked hard at their given tasks, but for once he did not complain and did not put himself forward. He made no offers to grind paints for

Caterina or to carve marble for Pagno or to pose for Donatello. He was simply there, modest and humble, as passive as the donkey Fiametta.

I knew him, of course, and I knew his calculations. He was waiting to be noticed and therefore loved. I, in turn, was waiting to see what would happen.

1433–1434

CHAPTER 27

W<small>HAT HAPPENED NEXT</small> took all the world by surprise. Cosimo de' Medici, in his forty-fourth year, the richest and most admired man in Florence, was arrested and charged with treason. This was the work of Rinaldo degli Albizzi, a man whose hatred and jealousy of the Medici had led him to plot against Cosimo for years, to fabricate plot after plot, and finally to bribe the Signoria successfully and convince them to put Cosimo under arrest. He wanted nothing less than Cosimo's death and it was his great mistake that he settled for less.

The plot unfolded over a period of years but, as I think of it now some thirty-six years later, it seems to have begun at the foolish siege of Lucca, when Cosimo resigned from the war committee and took his family away with him to Verona. The blame for the disastrous war with Lucca naturally fell on the Albizzi, and the crushing financial burden as well, and this is when Rinaldo's conspiracy against Cosimo took fire.

To crush the Medici Rinaldo would first have to take control of the Signoria. This took time and much money, but by spring of 1433 Rinaldo had bought the votes of six of the nine members of the Signoria. He then paid off the debts of Bernardo Guardagni so that he could be elected Gonfaloniere—head of the Signoria—and with Guardagni in office Rinaldo was ready to spring his trap.

Rumors were circulated about Cosimo and his ambition. He acted modestly and went about with only a single servant, they said, in order to distract honest citizens from his prodigious wealth. He was a friend and intimate of sodomites and perverts. He was a usurer, not a banker, and his donations to the poor and his civic building projects were hypocritical gestures to buy men's good will in this life and God's mercy in the next. His famous sympathy with the little man was a ruse to disguise his drive toward absolute power. What he intended in fact was to hire *condottieri* and, with their aid, to overthrow the Republic.

These rumors drifted back to Cosimo but he shrugged them away as the cost of doing business in Florence. The rumors spread, growing more vile and vengeful. Finally words led to actions and one night the Medici insignia that framed the great palace doors were publicly desecrated with black paint and a week later with human shit. This happened not once but several times until finally, when those same doors on the Via de' Bardi were smeared with blood, Cosimo chose the way of caution and withdrew from the city to his newly fortified palace at Trebbio in the Muggelo.

$$* \; * \; *$$

First, however, he took care to protect his money. Only Cosimo would have thought how to do it and only he would have been able to execute his plan.

On a single day in May he emptied his palace vaults and transferred three thousand gold ducats to the Benedictines at San Miniato al Monte, nearly five thousand gold florins to the Dominicans of San Marco, and to the Venetian branch of the family bank over fifteen thousand gold florins. To end the day right, he transferred all his family stocks in the Florence Commune to the Medici bank in Rome. Do whatever they might to him, the Signoria would have no access to Cosimo's wealth because, though they might dare to tear down his palace, they would never dare to move against the monasteries.

I was witness to this transfer of gold, and I am proud to say I was a participant in it as well. Cosimo had long depended on me to copy out in my best hand the rare manuscripts that he collected, and over the years he had come to value my loyalty. Thus it came about that on the third day of May I was summoned to his palace and told to

bring Fiametta, saddled with the stout leather *borsette* used for haul-
ing limestone and marble, and to come quietly with no show of haste.

It was a fair day to be out in the streets and I was flushed with
pleasure at being singled out by Cosimo for some important task.
Secrecy always makes the heart beat faster.

I was admitted to the palace through the small side doors and,
since Fiametta could not well fit through the opening, the great fortified doors were swung open long enough to admit her, and then they
were closed again. In the courtyard a dozen men set about their business. They worked in silence, bringing out sacks from a storeroom
within the walls and piling them in a neat circle around the central
well. Cosimo was there, standing beneath the arch of the stairs, and
his lady was there as well, and Giacomo stood silent behind them. I
bowed from the waist but they gave no mark of seeing me and I realized that, officially, this was not happening.

Cosimo's men selected four heavy sacks and packed them firmly
in the *borsette*. They placed cypress chips on top and tightened the
straps on the pouches. They stepped back, silent still, and waited. And
then Giacomo appeared from beneath the arch of the stairs and approached me where I stood beside Fiametta. I noted that even here
in the courtyard Giacomo wore the sword and dagger that seemed to
mark him out as Cosimo's special servant. He said simply, "Monas-
terio del San Miniato al Monte. You will be expected." I was not told
what was in the sacks and I knew not to inquire. I guessed that it was
a cache of rare books. I did not suspect that I was bearing through the
streets of Florence three thousand gold ducats.

I walked beside Fiametta half consumed with pride in my secret
commission from Cosimo de' Medici and half consumed with fear
that I would be discovered. I knew only that great things were afoot
and I was playing a part in them, though I grew more anxious as I
approached the city gates.

I passed through the Porta Romana with no trouble from the
guards and it was with a sense of relief that I ascended the great hill
to San Miniato where the Prior was expecting me. He seemed both

anxious and annoyed at my arrival, as if he had feared I might not come and was troubled afresh now that I had. He unbuckled the straps on one of the pouches and put his hand deep in the pouch and rummaged about. We could hear the dull clink of metal on metal. He nodded then and made a sign to two of the Brothers who were standing by. Without a word they shouldered the bags of gold and disappeared into the sub-basement of the larder. When they reappeared, the bags safely stowed away, the Prior dug down into the side folds of his habit and brought out a velvet purse embroidered with the insignia of the Medici. He slipped it into the breast of the leather apron I wore and beat lightly on my shoulder. "You have," he said ceremoniously, "done well." When I was safely back at the *bottega*, I took out the purse and discovered ten gold florins.

It was yet a good thing to be a trusted friend of the Medici.

✷ ✷ ✷

With his money safe and only his palace exposed to confiscation, Cosimo spent an easy summer in the safety of the Mugello surrounded by family and servants and visiting friends. In Florence the insidious rumors died down and Cosimo concluded that perhaps his worries had been unfounded. All the news from the Signoria was reassuring and Bernardo Guardagni, the new Gonfaloniere, in particular seemed to have turned friendly. He sent messages regularly to Cosimo informing him of news of the Signoria and seeking his advice on matters of tax reform and sumptuary laws.

Cosimo was still in the Mugello in early September when an urgent message came from Guardagni summoning him back to Florence. The Signoria was about to make important decisions, he said—though he gave no indication of the nature of those decisions— and Cosimo's counsel would be essential. Cosimo was wary, as always, but he returned to Florence, without a retinue and without any sense of what was about to happen.

On September 4, as requested, Cosimo presented himself at the Palazzo della Signoria where he received a warm welcome from Guardagni who was vague about the matters to be discussed and who asked Cosimo to wait for three days—"a little patience, my dear friend, it is essential"—until the Signoria would hold their official meeting. Cosimo returned to his palace and waited. During this time he visited his bank and moved further monies from Florence to Venice.

On the morning of September 7 Cosimo arrived early at the Palazzo della Signoria and found the council already in session. There was no sign of Guardagni or any welcoming committee. Instead the captain of the guard, without any explanation, led the way past the council chamber and continued on up the stairs. Cosimo paused at the chamber doors, wondering what this could mean, and then he looked behind him and discovered two more guards, pikes in hand and swords at the ready. Stricken, he realized that the trap had closed on him and it was too late to resist. They continued on up the endless flight of stairs—two guards behind and one in front—until at the very top of the tower they reached the prison cell called the *alberghettino*, the little inn. The captain opened the door to the cell and stepped aside to let Cosimo enter. The two guards took their positions on either side of the door. Then the captain, reciting a formula, assured Cosimo he had been arrested on solid legal grounds as his subsequent trial would make clear and for now he was a prisoner of the state. He moved forward and opened the three windows that looked down on the great piazza far below. Cosimo moved slowly toward the back wall. For an instant he felt sure they intended to fling him from those windows, but the captain only turned to him and said that until further decisions were made the *alberghettino* would be his home. The captain bowed and left, locking the door behind him.

Cosimo looked around him at the long rectangular room with its narrow windows opening onto the great piazza below and realized that this prison might become his tomb as well.

Wʜᴀᴛ ꜰᴏʟʟᴏᴡᴇᴅ ᴡᴇ know from Cosimo's own confidential note-books, his *libri segreti*. After a week of fasting, since he refused even to taste the prison food and since everyone agreed that poisoning was both a danger and a possibility, Cosimo was permitted to have meals brought to him from the Palazzo Bardi, though guards were assigned to supervise the cooking and the delivery of his food. He was allowed no visitors at all. When he insisted on seeing his confessor, a priest was brought to hear his confession and give spiritual counsel, though even at these private times some government official was always present. What was specifically forbidden was any communication between Cosimo and his friends, his family, or his bank.

The personal guard assigned by day was sympathetic to Cosimo, however, and like most guards he was susceptible to bribes. Thus, in a matter of days messages were passed into and out of the *alberghettino* and in time Guardagni, the Gonfaloniere himself, accepted a bribe of a thousand florins. In return Guardagni found himself too ill to attend the council that would decide Cosimo's fate and so delegated his vote to another Priore who had already been bribed by Cosimo's people. In his *libro segreto* Cosimo noted that the price was low; he would gladly have paid ten times more to guarantee Guardagni's timely illness.

Meanwhile ambassadors from Venice and Rome had arrived to protest this persecution of the Medici whose banks were so impor-tant to them. In Cafaggiolo Cosimo's brother Lorenzo was raising an army among Medici followers and readying them to march against Florence. And in the city itself there was a mood of unrest, a rising distrust of the Albizzi and a concern for Cosimo who had for so long been a defender of the poor.

His trial came down to this: Cosimo was accused of raising him-self above the rank of ordinary citizens—a high crime against the state—and of conspiring to take over the city and become its despot. The penalty was death.

It was a terrible situation for everyone. The council, threat-ened on all sides, had no choice but to go forward with the trial.

Desperate to have all this behind them, they met in haste and on 28 September, after a long dispute about death versus exile, they chose exile over death. Rinaldo degli Albizzi exhausted himself arguing for the death penalty—it was well deserved; it was essential for the safety of the Republic—and he was on fire with rage but he could not bend the council to his will. Their decision was binding. By decree of the council Cosimo was banished to Padua for ten years and his brother Lorenzo to Venice for a period of five. Both Cosimo and Lorenzo, and the entire Medici family, were forbidden to hold office in Florence for however long they should live.

Cosimo was summoned from his freezing accommodations in the *alberghettino*. He stood before the full council—this great man now a lowly prisoner—and the decree of banishment was read aloud to him. He made no effort to refute the charges. He merely insisted that he had always declined to be nominated as a government official, that as a citizen he had paid taxes in excess of what was required, that he had supported the war against Lucca with money and men, and that he remained a simple law-abiding citizen of the great Republic of Florence. He concluded by accepting the judgment of the Signoria which he would obey without question. "I will go into Padua most willingly; in truth I would go wherever you might command, whether to live among the Arabs or any other people however strange and distant they might be. I am, Signori, the loyal servant of our state."

But knowing the Albizzi and their gangs and foreseeing treachery in the streets below, he added a demand that he expressed in the form of a request.

"One thing I beg of you, Signori, that since you intend to preserve my life, you will make certain that it should not be taken by wicked citizens, and in this way you be put to shame. Take care that those who stand outside in the Piazza desiring my blood should not have their way with me. In such a case my pain would be small, but you would earn perpetual infamy."

The Signoria took his meaning and, aware of what would befall them individually if harm should come to Cosimo, they took care to spirit him out of the city by night through the Porta San Gallo, and under armed guard they turned him over to men of his house who would escort him through Ferrara to his exile in Padua. This took place on 28 September 1433.

* * *

WHEN NEWS OF Cosimo's exile spread in the city—and it spread almost at once—a kind of panic started among the friends and debtors of the Medici. The levy of new taxes was inevitable, of course, but it was anyone's guess what other burdens the Albizzi might lay upon them. Meanwhile friends of the Albizzi celebrated openly, though there were some who suspected they had merely postponed a terrible retribution by sending Cosimo to exile rather than to death. The Palazzo Bardi was confiscated in the name of the state and the Medici banking tables disappeared from the Mercato Vecchio, but for a while the life of the city continued on as it had. There were no prosecutions of Medici servants and—so it seemed—there were no secret lists of Medici followers who were marked out for "accidents." Still, no one felt secure.

"Now it will begin," Agnolo said.

"What will begin?"

"The persecution of men like me."

This was not like him. Had he become a man who had some sense of himself, who understood how he failed to fit into the world?

I thought for a while and then said, "You make too much of yourself," but as I turned over in my mind what he had said, I realized he could be speaking truly. Under the Albizzi there would surely be persecution of men like Agnolo. And if Agnolo was in danger, so too was my lord Donatello.

CHAPTER 28

A SHUDDER RAN through all of Florence at the exile of Cosimo. It was an unimaginable thing and it affected everyone. In the taverns men drank less and talked more cautiously. At the banking tables in the Mercato Vecchio business slowed and even the chink of coins seemed more discreet. In our *bottega* there was the constant strain of things unsaid and the suspicion of friends who might at any moment be revealed as enemies: Donatello knew that as an intimate of Cosimo he was being watched by the Albizzi. He took care that in speech and action he was ever restrained.

But as the constant spy, I noticed there had been a thaw in the relations between my lord Donatello and the newly humble youth Agnolo. For months now Agnolo had made himself useful in the *bottega*, running errands, feeding the chickens and looking after Fiametta, doing whatever he was asked to do but without his old insistence on being noticed at all times. And now my master Donatello seemed to have softened toward him.

"How do you live," I asked Agnolo, "you two alone in that small house?"

"Peacefully. He asks nothing of me."

"He is fifty years of age. There is little he could ask."

Agnolo gave me a wry look and then a half smile. "It's little you know about these things," he said.

"Then you must tell me," I said, but he withdrew into the humble, quiet, self-possessed Agnolo he had lately become.

I could tell nonetheless that there was increasing warmth between them.

∗ ∗ ∗

Early in July, when Cosimo's arrest and exile were still unimagined, Donatello had taken on the commission to create a great marble pulpit for the new sacristy of the Duomo. It was to be of the finest marble. It would be placed above the door of the sacristy on the south side of the Cathedral as a complement to the pulpit of Luca della Robbia on the north. I have the documents before me and what I find of greatest interest is the strict determinations of the contract. It is as if from the very start the Operai of the Cathedral had learned from Prato to deal firmly with Donatello, however *intricato* he might be. They demanded a guarantee that "Donatello must finish each piece within three months after receiving the block, which will be furnished by the Operai but for which he must give security through a reliable bondsman."

Donatello read the conditions of the contract and smiled that cryptic smile. All through July and August he worked at the design of the pulpit. By September, when Cosimo was arrested and sent into exile, Donatello had already produced in miniature the magnificent pulpit that would become known as the Cantoria—the singing choir—for its frieze of babies who riot in joy at hearing the proclamation of the Good News. He made preparations, slowly, to carve.

He was distraught for a while at Cosimo's exile, but he allowed nothing to come between him and his work . . . and he found other consolations as well.

∗ ∗ ∗

Rinaldo degli Albizzi had driven his great enemy from Florence and, though he now found himself unofficial ruler of the city, his own position was not what he had hoped. For one thing, the enormous

Medici wealth he had planned to secure for himself had disappeared into Rome and Venice and, locally, into monasteries that he dared not plunder. For another, Cosimo remained popular in Florence while in Padua he was welcomed as a visiting dignitary, rich and distinguished and much to be admired. And who could tell what Cosimo's followers might be up to?

Rinaldo found it increasingly difficult to rule. The ancient noble families that had supported his attack on Cosimo remained supportive in words but when it came to gold florins their support wavered. The banking families, too, were reluctant to provide financial backing since they regarded the regime as unstable and perhaps even illegal. Increasingly, through manipulation of the Signoria, Rinaldo assumed the role of despot, banishing Medici supporters who called for Cosimo's return and thus depriving the city of further tax revenue. Frustrated and furious, Rinaldo grew daily more erratic.

His remark to a friend ran round the city. "You should not lift your hand against the mighty or, if you do, you should make certain to finish them off."

Cosimo meanwhile managed to have his exile commuted from Padua to Venice where he joined his brother Lorenzo and where, through his spies, he kept a close eye on events in Florence and on the several conspiracies mounted to bring about his recall. Ever the good citizen, he distanced himself from all these plots, waiting, watching.

* * *

DONATELLO SEEMED HAPPY. In truth he was never a man you would describe as happy, but there was a new ease about him now, a kind of comfortableness, as if his work on the *Cantoria* was enough for him and he longed for nothing else. I had no difficulty guessing the cause for this new satisfaction.

"You're sleeping with him," I said one day to Agnolo. I caught him up as he came from Fiametta's stall, a sack of feed in his arms. "Aren't you." I said it confidentially as if I knew this to be a fact and as if I did not disapprove.

He looked at me, distrustful, and then he said, "We get on well."

"Even though he is a man of fifty years."

He said nothing.

"And you are—what?—eighteen?"

"Sixteen."

"I grow older but you do not. How is that possible?"

"You grow older, Luca, and you grow more sly."

I laughed in appreciation of his wit and ruffled his hair in the way of Donatello with his apprentices. Agnolo looked at me, wondering if he should trust me. I smiled at him. He was easily won over.

"We do sleep together, but that's all it is."

"It seems to make him happy."

"I could make him happier still. I would gladly give more."

"Tell me."

"He likes to hold me only." He thought about it. "He likes to run his hands over me. He likes to touch me. Sometimes he holds my *cazzo*. He doesn't do anything with it, he just holds it." He went on and I found myself growing hot with anger as my mind wandered to the picture of the two of them in bed. "But he won't fuck me," Agnolo said. He looked to me for sympathy and understanding. "He presses against me and he grows hard so I know he could do it if he wanted to, but he doesn't."

At once I felt attacked and I had to struggle not to strike out at him.

"He says he loves me. But he won't fuck me."

"And yet he will," I said, forcing a smile. "You can be sure he will."

* * *

In Venice the Doge himself welcomed Cosimo into exile as his special guest. Cosimo and his family were made comfortable in the monastery of San Giorgio Maggiore, a sprawling, beautiful building on an island at the entrance to the Canal' Grande. This was the kind of country retreat that Cosimo particularly enjoyed, he said, a place where he could live quietly with family and friends and pursue his study of Greek philosophy.

If you did not know Cosimo the man of business and politic, you would think this the whole truth. It was in part truth since it was the contemplative Cosimo who so loved rare books and the things of beauty created by my master Donatello and those others—Ghiberti and Fra Angelico and Uccello and della Robbia and the wanton, half-crazed Filippo Lippi. And of course the fine mind and architectural genius of Michelozzo had always been Cosimo's great delight, and his conversation as well, so to thank the monks of San Giorgio for their hospitality he resolved to build them a library and he invited Michelozzo to design it.

The request came by messenger in plain clothes to the new *bottega* Michelozzo occupied now that his partnership with Donatello was so thinly observed. They still had mutual contracts—the Prato Pulpit, chief among them—and of course Michelozzo would still oversee the casting of bronze for Donatello, but their lives had moved in different directions and thus, for the present time, they maintained separate *botteghe*. It was a peaceful, friendly separation, but I saw behind it the thin, manipulative hand of Agnolo Mattei, model and whore.

Cosimo's invitation to join him in his Venetian exile was a great excitement to Michelozzo. He had long been Cosimo's favorite architect and an intimate friend as well, so it seemed only natural for him to join his patron in Venice. He told the messenger that he would come at once. He put aside all his commissions at hand—among them were plans for the new Palazzo Medici—and, sending ahead a great trunk full of sketches and designs, Michelozzo set out to join Cosimo in exile. It was a cold clear day in November of 1433.

* * *

By January Donatello had made small progress with the Cantoria. The marble provided by the Duomo was not the pure white that had been agreed upon, and so Donatello sent it back and gave himself over to the marble Feast of Herod that was to have been an Epiphany present from Cosimo to his brother Lorenzo. The idea was to achieve in marble the same miracle of perspective you find in the bronze Feast of Herod he had cast for the Baptismal Font in Siena. He put the Cantoria from his thoughts and was at once thoroughly caught up in his work for Cosimo.

The January cold was bitter. There had been a dusting of snow during the night and it was good to be inside the *bottega* with the smell of wet wool and stone and the sharp, stinging scent of quick-lime. A gray-striped kitten had replaced the departed orange cat that had been Donatello's favorite and it was rioting now among the chickens and the two aged cocks were hard put to defend them. There was dust everywhere. Amid the noise of hammering and the hard, chunking sound of metal upon stone and the horseplay of the two new apprentices, we all found ourselves—for some unknown reason—in good humor.

"My lord Cosimo is enjoying his exile, I think."

Donatello looked at me askance. "Exile is exile," he said. "To be away from Florence is to be absent from the world."

"And yet you were willingly absent from the world . . . in Rome . . . for more than a year." I could play with him this way now.

"I was with Michelozzo." He paused, remembering. "We were much in the world."

"And I was with Pagno. With Pagno we were not much in the world, even though we were in Florence."

He cast me a look of annoyance and would have said some sharp thing about jealousy or envy except he was too well disposed toward the whole world to bother catching me up short. He worked without stop as long as the light held out.

At the end of the day he was in the mood for celebration. The Feast of Herod was not nearly finished but he could see already that the carving in marble—thin as paper—would be as fine in its own way as the bronze of the Siena font. It would perhaps be finer.

He had dismissed the others and we had worked together for a short while by rushlight but then he feared to spoil the carving and put down his chisels.

"A drink," he said. "To keep out the cold. A deep drink of good wine for the old *scharpellatore* and his young *tesoro*, so badly neglected for a year and more. For shame. For shame. And such a handsome Louis of Tolosa you were." He ruffled my hair as if I were still one of his apprentices.

"Tell me about Rome," I said. "Tell me about Michelozzo."

We were sitting now at his long worktable and by the light of a single candle we drank wine as he told me about Rome and the disgraceful luxuries of the Vatican and about Michelozzo, the most talented gold worker of our day.

"And designer of buildings," I said. He did not reply and I said, "My lord Cosimo is of that opinion."

"Michelozzo, yes. And Brunelleschi."

They too had been lovers—Brunelleschi and Donatello—what a small and incestuous world Florence had become, a stew of emotions. I longed to say, Tell me about Agnolo, but I dared not move ahead so rapidly. I decided on silence. And so I was astonished to hear myself say, "Tell me about Agnolo."

It was as if he had not heard me.

He filled his cup and drank deeply and said, "A bishop it was, or it may have been a cardinal, who confided in Cosimo that in his reform of the clergy he hoped to persuade the priests to stop gambling. Cosimo listened in his sympathetic way and then replied that first he should persuade them to stop using loaded dice."

He laughed that deep infectious laugh and I could not resist laughing with him. I could see he was beginning to feel his wine.

"Cosimo enjoys a good jest even when it turns on himself. He is quick witted and of a humorous turn of mind. For all his wealth, he has the same love of dirty jokes as the poorest of us.

Cosimo . . . Beccadelli knew he was on safe ground when he dedicated *Hermaphroditus* to Cosimo."

"But holy mother church has condemned that book."

"It is a harmless book."

"It celebrates the joys of sex," I said. "And the joys of sodomy."

"Harmless as well."

"But the church says . . ."

"The church." He shook his head sorrowfully and emptied his cup of wine. For a moment he said nothing and I wondered if I had gone too far. And then, as if he suddenly remembered what I asked, he said, "We get on well, Agnolo and I."

"And yet you do not fuck him. So he says."

"That would be to lose him." He went on then at length about not using Agnolo for his own satisfaction. The whole matter came down to love, he said, what love could bear and what it could not. I had no idea what he was talking about. For me, from my first encounter with Maria Sabina, fucking was a natural and normal expression of love. I did not understand this anxious planning of what you might do in bed. And so I listened with care, hoping to understand the mysterious love of Donatello for Agnolo. It was lust that bound them, surely, a perverted lust. I was thinking exactly this when Donatello paused and said, "And so I love him."

I knew this, I had heard it before, but now, alone with him in this freezing *bottega*, it was as if Donatello had plunged a knife in my stomach and turned it.

"I know," I said. "You love him." We were silent for a long time and then I said, shyly, exploring, "Was there not a time when you felt the same for me?"

He looked at me, uncomprehending. Then he took a sip of wine and sat back and looked at me sadly. "Luca," he said. "Not in that way. Never in that way."

"And yet you kissed me." I spoke coldly and I was bitter in my mouth and in my heart.

"Ah, Luca. Sometimes I do not know myself."

"You seemed to know well what you were doing then."

"I think you do not know yourself either, Luca." He gazed at me with that terrible focus he brought to sculpting. "*Tesoro mio*," he said softly. "I will be more kind."

And then, as if he had disposed of the matter, he put aside his wine, sighed deeply, and began to number the virtues of his friend and patron, Cosimo.

"Cosimo de' Medici is not the man he appears. He is kind and generous and he loves artisans. He has a fine mind. He knows beautiful things. He studies Latin and Greek and pursues the study of philosophy." On and on he went. And in this way, with handsome talk of Cosimo de' Medici, the matter between us was settled . . . for a time.

✳ ✳ ✳

THE GREAT MISTAKE of Rinaldo degli Albizzi was in allowing Cosimo to leave Florence alive. The lesser mistakes followed fast upon the new year. In February Rinaldo exiled the rich and powerful Medici supporter Agnolo Acciaiuoli who had publicly called him a dictator and a few weeks later he exiled Mario Bartolommeo de' Medici, a distant cousin of Cosimo, on grounds of sedition and conspiracy against the Signoria. These were difficult and unpopular decisions and they served to further alienate the already distressed *grandi* of Florence. Cosimo himself remained silent and aloof in Venice, content to let others do his conspiring for him.

By March Rinaldo was facing nearly constant opposition and there was the feeling in the city that the spring thaw might see rising discontent among the *popolo minuto* and a corresponding unease among the *grandi*. Meanwhile there was no Medici money available to run the city and no bankers willing to lend—as Cosimo himself put it—"so much as a pistachio nut."

In May the Albizzi welcomed to Florence the Pope—Eugenius IV—who had been forced to flee Rome in disguise pursued by vicious mobs that burned and looted the holy city and rioted in the Vatican itself. Rinaldo himself welcomed the Pope and installed him and his court in the monastery of Santa Maria Novella. It was another mistake. The Medici had been and would be once again the Pope's personal bankers.

The Albizzi could look forward to a difficult summer.

* * *

THE DAY AFTER the Pope's arrival in Florence a messenger came from Cosimo in Venice. For me. It was addressed to Donatello, of course, but the burden of the message was for me personally. I have it by heart.

My lord Cosimo sent greetings to Ser Donatello, *orafo e scharpellatore*, and begged to be remembered to his fellows Pagno di Lapo Portigiani and Luca di Matteo. He wished the blessings of God and our Republic on all singly and together and hoped we were enjoying good health and good work. He regretted that so many of his own commissions were suspended for this time but he rejoiced that Michelozzo di Bartolomeo was working well and that the library of the monastery of San Giorgio was proceeding according to plan.

In a leather wallet the messenger carried, Luca di Matteo would find a manuscript of Cicero's letters to be copied in triplicate in his best hand and put aside safely against the end of our exile, nine years hence.

So there it was! Cosimo de' Medici writing to me! But what followed meant the end of my rejoicing.

He wished once more the blessings of God upon Ser Donatello and all his works and, in a *post scriptum*, he said he looked forward on his return to viewing Donato's bronze David, triumphant and joyful, with his foot on the head of Goliath.

This *post scriptum*, however casually intended, proved sufficient to enflame Donatello with his old madness. The Prato Pulpit lay unattended in the workyard. The marble relief of the Feast of Herod was far from completion. And the Duomo Cantoria, for lack of the right marble, had barely proceeded beyond the stage of design. And now, of a sudden, there was talk of the bronze David. Not talk, to be sure, since Donatello did not mention the David to anyone, but I knew from his look when he read the letter—and he read it over again many times— that the fire had been started and that in very little time we would be back again to posing and sculpting and perhaps this time to forging in bronze the statue he seemed doomed to complete.

✴ ✴ ✴

SUMMER WAS AN unbroken succession of sweltering days. Everyone was listless, the customary noise of the *bottega* sank to a low murmur, even the chickens seemed too tired to lay eggs. The entire city lay smothered beneath a blanket of heat. Rumors continued to circulate that Cosimo's exile would not be permanent, but no one seemed to care. It was enough to get through the day.

Perhaps because of the heat, perhaps because he was not born to lead, Rinaldo degli Albizzi relaxed his hold on the city government to the point that he neglected to fix bribes for the summer elections of the new Priori. He awoke one day to discover that five of the nine Priori were Medici loyalists and the power of the Signoria was no longer entirely in his hands. Rinaldo considered refusing to seat the new Signoria, but even he could see that this would be to overreach himself by much and to guarantee revolt. The new Signoria was seated and, indignant at their treatment and determined to show their independence, they took advantage of Rinaldo's absence at his summer villa to move definitively against him.

When he reentered the city in September, refreshed and eager for work, Rinaldo was greeted by a summons to report immediately to the Palazzo della Signoria. He knew at once that rebellion was at hand and, sensing the possibility of imprisonment in the *alberghettino*— and would he, like Cosimo, emerge alive?—he rode straight to his own palace and called to arms his private bodyguard that numbered more than five hundred men. He gave orders for them to occupy the church of San Pietro Scheraggio near the Palazzo della Signoria and to await orders to attack the palazzo, to burn all the Medici properties, and to take the city by force. The Signoria countered by sending its own troops into the piazza and barricading themselves inside the palazzo with food and supplies enough to withstand a lengthy siege. Civil war seemed inevitable. Days went by and nothing happened. Troops on both sides became restless, standing at attention and ready to fight but with no orders given. Finally the Priori smuggled out messengers to the Pope in his sanctuary at Santa Maria Novella and Eugenius was persuaded to summon Rinaldo to a conference. Rinaldo knew this could not be good. He arrived with fewer than his original five hundred troops; they had begun to dessert as time passed and rumors swirled about a huge mercenary army levied by the Signoria and only waiting for the signal to attack.

Rinaldo joined the Pope in his court at the monastery and through the long afternoon the troops waited in the piazza outside the church. The Pope was grieved by this unrest, he said, he wished only for peace. And, of course, for a strong and stable government in Florence that might guarantee his eventual return to Rome. Meanwhile what could he do? He spoke sympathetically of the Medici in exile and to Rinaldo he promised he would do what little he could to protect the life and property of the Albizzi family during whatever period of conflict might come upon them. He droned on and on.

Rinaldo remained closeted with the Pope, determined whatever the cost to win his support. As darkness fell the troops began to disperse and by the time Rinaldo emerged late in the night he was greeted by the few stragglers who had remained hopeful till the end.

And the end it certainly was. Two days later, on September 28, 1434, Rinaldo degli Albizzi was banished from Florence and Cosimo de' Medici who at his death would be named *Pater Patriae* was recalled from his exile in Venice. Almost a year to the day after his banishment my lord Cosimo returned to the city in triumph.

Cosimo, the humble David, had brought down Goliath with not so much as a stone.

WHEN MY LORD Cosimo visited our *bottega* a month after his return, Donatello was able to show him the life-sized model in wax that would become—once it was cast—the first free-standing bronze nude in more than a thousand years.

Agnolo stood beside the model as if he alone were responsible for it.

1435

CHAPTER 29

THE WAX DAVID was a work of such perfection that Donatello himself seemed reluctant to risk it to the clay and fire that must come next. It was life-size and gleaming as it stood on the low workstand where Donatello had put his last strokes to it and pronounced it done. This was a special moment because Cosimo de' Medici had been invited to view his statue and we watched as, stunned in admiration, he gave way to its magic. He looked and looked and after a long while he leaned forward and pointed to the laurel wreath on David's hat. "Ah!" he said, because of course the laurel was sacred to the Medici family. And then he noticed the laurel wreath beneath Goliath's head, making of it an offering to a jealous God. He studied the helmet closely and gave a small gasp of pleasure as he realized that the medallion on Goliath's helmet was a copy of a medallion from his own collection, ancient, Roman or perhaps Greek. On the medallion a chariot is pulled by three winged children while a fourth child pushes it from behind. They are true Donatello children, plump and full of charm. High on the chariot sits an imposing male figure shaded by an umbrella and before him a fifth child kneels in worship. Here, in a medallion emblazoned on the helmet of the stricken Goliath, is the triumph of pride brought low.

Cosimo could not have been more pleased. He leaned forward and let his hand trace David's buttock and thigh and then he turned to Donatello and gave him a warm embrace. He kissed him on both cheeks once, and then again, and whispered some word of thanks or astonishment—we could not hear it—before turning back to the statue and gazing at it with wonder.

The whole world has come to know and marvel at the bronze statue as it stands glowing in the courtyard garden of the new Medici palace. But to see it for the first time—so fragile in its thin coat of wax—was to confront a vision of what was possible for humankind: this frail boy, armed only with a stone and the mighty strength of God, had brought down the enemy of the people of God. Cosimo, who had just brought down the Albizzi, must have seen himself in David, just as surely as Donatello saw himself in Goliath. Look at Goliath's head and tell me these are not the sunken eyes, the scruffy beard and the blade-like nose of Donatello.

"There will be much gold for this," Pagno whispered. "I have never seen my lord Cosimo more pleased."

"Donatello does not care about gold," I said.

"No, but it makes his work possible."

I could not argue with that and so I turned to my accounts where, in truth, I found that we were much in need of gold. As always we were behind in our work, and several of our major commissions, though completed or nearly completed, had not been paid for. Only Cosimo was beforehand with his money and so we were not surprised when a week later a huge shipment of copper and tin arrived—some three hundred pounds altogether—so that the casting of the David could go forward at once.

Our *bottega* had formerly been the Inn of Santa Caterina and so we had to create our own foundry before we could cast the David. Donatello installed a new furnace for smelting the bronze and a new crucible for melting it, though he kept his old oven for heating the clay mold because he trusted it. He knew its oddities and its range of temperatures and he could depend on it to bake the clay mold slowly so that, when the wax had melted out and before the bronze was poured to replace it, he could further strengthen the clay by heating it to a higher temperature. The stronger the mold the less danger of imperfections in the pouring.

He installed a new drum bellows also, an old invention newly perfected by Michelozzo. Two men mount the twin bellows where they stand with a stout cord in hand. They shift their weight from foot to foot and, as they depress one bellows with their heels, they pull on the cord to raise the skin of the other bellows, allowing air to flow inside and fan the fire. Everything depends on the heat of the fire.

Beneath the pouring platform a pit was scooped out and filled with sand that was damp and porous. This would become the casting pit where the sand would support the individual pieces to be cast and would serve to cool the bronze once it was poured.

I took great pleasure in seeing the foundry come together. I had been charged with the installation of each of the related pieces and in the end even Pagno di Lapo acknowledged that it was a model foundry, as fine as Ghiberti's. The casting itself—if all went as planned—would be a matter of a week.

All other work in the *bottega* came to a halt as we held our breath to see if the miracle in wax could be reproduced in bronze.

∗ ∗ ∗

THE CASTING OF David was planned for the first week of January. The days were cold but not freezing and the sky remained clear, a good casting weather. We rolled back the huge doors that gave onto the courtyard of the *bottega* so as to accommodate the terrible heat of the furnace and to allow fresh air to circulate through the foundry.

Michelozzo was concerned about the timing of the pour. Two strong men working together could manage a crucible of about 150 pounds or two gallons of molten bronze. To pour more than that would tax their ability to control the flow of the metal. The poured bronze would take at least two days to cool, followed by a day or more to break open the clay molds and remove the finished bronze. If everything went smoothly the casting would require a week to complete.

Donatello had painted the wax David with many coats of clay and he had separated the several parts in which it would be cast. The hat with its laurel trim was to be cast separately from the head. Then the body in a single section to below the knees, and a separate section from the top of the boots to the bottom of the sandals. The sword itself would require a separate casting, though the hilt of the sword along with the right hand that gripped it was to be cast as a single piece. In the same way Goliath's head and the laurel wreath it rests on were meant to be cast as one, but out of concern for the intricate details of the helmet and its medallion Donatello decided to cast them separately. Each of these pieces presented a problem all its own in the pouring, the casting, and in removal from the clay mold.

As always on a casting day much of our time would be taken up with preparation, each of us with an assigned task. Donatello himself had prepared the clay molds with their flues and wax vents and he had placed the individual sections in the order they were to be fired: first the hat and, if the pour went well and the bronze did not clog, then David's head and trunk, and his sword. That would be the total casting for the second of January.

Four special assistants were hired for this day, men with knowledge and experience who had worked on Ghiberti's bronze doors. Two were in charge of the clay molds as they entered and left the oven while two others positioned the molds in the sand of the casting pit once the wax had been melted away.

Two of the apprentices were in charge of the bellows. They were young and inexperienced but they had been practicing for days. They knew that, once the furnace was fired, there was no room for error: temperature must be kept at a constant heat and that would depend on the deft use of the bellows.

Pagno and I, as two of the strongest, were assigned the task of pouring the bronze from the crucible into the individual molds.

Michelozzo supervised the mixing of tin and copper and lead: 90 percent copper, 10 percent tin, and a tiny addition of lead to lower the melting point of the bronze mixture and to allow the molten bronze to pour more easily.

Donatello himself supervised every step of the pour.

∗ ∗ ∗

THE *BOTTEGA* BRISTLED with the excitement of the first casting. We were all aware that this was a special moment and that our task—and our privilege—was unique among Florence's craftsmen. This was to be the bronze David, life-size, a free-standing nude, such as had not existed since ancient times, and sculpted by the greatest artisan of our day. Agnolo was beside himself with expectation.

The morning was cold but the heat from the furnace was overwhelming and the acid smell of the melting bronze burned in our noses. Even worse, bits of ash from the fire flew at our eyes. We all wore heavy leather aprons to protect us from the fire and around our necks we had twisted thick towels for further protection. Pagno and I stood on either side of the furnace, raised above it on a low platform, and that extra height gave us purchase on the two heavy rods that supported the crucible and would enable us to control the flow of molten bronze as we poured it into the molds.

We began with David's hat. It was fired in the oven, the wax was drained out, and then—to further harden the clay shell—it was fired at a still higher temperature to make it strong enough to resist the melting force of the molten bronze. Everything was moving along smoothly. The empty mold was allowed to cool a little and then the two special assistants from Ghiberti's *bottega* transferred it to the sand pit immediately below the crucible. The mold was heavy and they carried it in a kind of cradle they balanced between them. It had a great weight and they groaned in an unseemly way as they carried it. Our apprentices—who would never allow themselves such a groan—had prepared a hole to the right size and as Ghiberti's assistants lowered the mold into the pit, they scooped the moist sand around it to secure it in place. This was the easiest part of the process. What mattered here was to keep the mold—the hardened shell—intact, with no chips or splinters within that might cause the finished bronze to blister or clot.

Meanwhile, under Michelozzo's careful eye, the molten bronze had been stirred and heated to exactly the right temperature and consistency. It was a beautiful and terrifying broth and I stared into the crucible, marveling that this liquid was the most important step on the way to the completed statue. Pagno and I waited for Michelozzo's signal to pour. The mold was firmly in position in the casting pit, the temperature and viscosity of the bronze exactly right, and at last Michelozzo gave the signal, pointing first at the crucible and then at us.

We took a deep breath and began our work. Carefully, steadily, we tipped the crucible until the molten bronze bubbled at the lip and then flowed—slowly, slowly—into the funnel at the base of the hat. We poured steadily with no jiggling or jerking of the rods that might cause an uneven flow.

It was good to feel the strength in my arms become the controlling force that made the bronze flow perfectly. Pagno and I worked well together since this was no time to compete and because, for all I did not trust him, I acknowledged that he was strong and had some gifts as a pourer of bronze. The effort was tremendous and the sweat coursing down our arms made it difficult to sustain the evenness of the pour, but it was yet early in the day and we were glad to perform so well. We finished pouring the hat, slowing the flow of bronze as it gathered in the funnel, the sign that the empty mold was now full. We tipped the crucible back into position above the furnace and rested. Pagno smiled at me, satisfied, and unable to help myself, I smiled back at him.

Michelozzo checked the fire to make certain the right temperature was being maintained. He said nothing but he looked satisfied at our work. Donatello, more anxious than I had ever seen him, hovered above the mold while it was lifted from its place beneath the crucible and placed further down the casting pit where it would settle and cool for the next two days.

The hat appeared to be a success, though of course we would not know for certain until the mold was broken open and the backing scraped away from the new bronze. But for now, in anticipation of success, there was a moment of pleasure and satisfaction for all of us as Donatello examined what we had done and, from the look of it, found our work satisfactory.

He gave orders then to proceed with David's head. The mold was placed upside down in the pit and, at the signal from Michelozzo, Pagno and I repeated what we had done with the hat, pouring slowly so as to control the flow of the bronze while being careful not to jerk the crucible from its fixed position on the furnace. It was exhausting work and required more strength and attention than you might think. Once again we worked together as one to create an even and smooth pour. And once again the funnel indicated the empty mold was now filled and we tipped the crucible back into position on the furnace and stepped back from our completed work. Donatello seemed pleased. Pagno and I exchanged a glance—he smiled yet again—and for the first time since I had met him I felt some affection for him.

We could now move on to casting the upper body and the sword. I call it the upper body but in truth it was the largest piece to be cast and it extended from the base of the neck down to the joining of the leg and the boot, including the belly and buttocks and the private parts that had so deeply disappointed Agnolo. "My *cazzo* is twice the size of that," he said, "even at its smallest it is bigger than that." Donatello was hard pressed to convince him that decency must be observed, that it was merely a symbolic *cazzo*, that nobody would think less of him because the penis on the statue was not of the immensity of his penis in real life. "We must not offend," Donatello concluded, "with too much reality," and that at least for a time had seemed to satisfy Agnolo's vanity. The casting of so large a section worried me. To sustain a constant pour at a very low volume would tax all my strength but I was determined not to fail my lord Donatello nor let Pagno see me as the lesser man. We leaned back from the poisonous smell of the bronze and waited for Michelozzo's signal. He gave it and we bent to the controlling rods and tipped the crucible at exactly the right angle and held it there truly. The pour took a long time. The sweat poured into our eyes and down our arms, but we held the rods firmly and the pour was a success. Gratefully—the strain was over at last—we tipped the crucible back into place.

And then we poured the sword.

The first day of casting, then, was a great success and we were all pleased at Donatello's approval. He thanked me especially for my nice care in pouring. Michelozzo had said almost nothing. He had more experience in casting bronze than any of us and in truth he was more skilled than Donatello, but it was his nature to defer to others and to Donatello in particular. So it was enough for me that he looked on and nodded his approval.

Agnolo was full of joy. He had been allowed to watch and he was careful not to get in the way of our pouring though he was everywhere at once, excited and impatient to see himself reborn in bronze. Now that the first pour was done, he could not wait for the moment when the molds would be cracked open and his new self would emerge.

✳ ✳ ✳

The poured bronze rested in the sand pit for the next two days while we made preparations to fire and pour the molds for the rest of the statue. And then at first light on the third day the rested molds were cracked open and the bronze was removed, first the hat and then, with some anxiety, the head. They were rough and for the moment ugly, with the air vents and gates in need of removal, but we had all seen what Donatello could do with chasing and finishing and we had no doubt that here was the head of the David he had carved in wax. We gathered about while the trunk of the statue was cracked open, the body from shoulders to boots. There was difficulty breaking through the shell and we drew back nervously while Donatello worked to free the bronze. It opened at last with a sighing sound and the harsh clank of a chisel on fired clay. Something had gone wrong. The shoulders and the chest were perfect, but Donatello stared in disbelief as he examined the left leg where the bronze had failed to take, leaving a hole the size of a penny in the front of the thigh. Perhaps there had been a bubble in the mix, perhaps the layer of wax at this point had been too thin. Whatever the reason, the result was disaster, I thought. There was a long silence and then Donatello let out a soft moan and sat back on his heels

He lowered his head and for a moment I thought he was crying. I could readily understand why. The lost wax method of casting was ever a gamble, since once the wax had been melted away the original statue was gone forever and only the bronze remained . . . and if the bronze was imperfect there was nothing to be done except start again to build up the statue from the beginning. I tried to think of something to say, but of course no words were possible at such a moment. Agnolo had at first rushed forward to see the ruined thigh, but even he had the good sense to pull back and say nothing. It was Michelozzo who took on himself the burden of consoling Donatello.

"It can be patched," he said softly. "In the end it will be well."

Donatello remained bent over the wounded thigh and nodded in agreement. It could be patched but it would not now be the flawless statue Donatello had conceived. Michelozzo helped him to his feet. We all made ourselves busy with something else, anything else.

David's thigh was not ruined, but it was badly damaged. But ruin was in all our minds as we continued our work. We finished finally, gratefully, and then we scraped out the inner shell—the clay, cloth, hair and horse dung—that had supported the original wax David. The bronze was ready now for assembly and for chasing. For all the rest of this day we worked in silence.

* * *

It was the second day of pouring and we were well advanced in our task. Pagno and I had poured molten bronze from the crucible into the several separate pieces of the statue—steadily, without feint—and we had stood up well to the test of strength that required. We were exhausted and the sweat poured liberally down our chests and arms, but we had only two more pieces to pour—Goliath's head and the laurel wreath on which it rests—and we were confident we would finish before nightfall.

The day grew frigid as the hours went by but the increasing cold offered us little relief. The crucible seemed to grow heavier with each minute and Pagno and I, on either side of the furnace, could feel ourselves weakening as we prepared for the last of the pourings.

"Are you ready?"' I had to shout to make Pagno hear above the roaring of the furnace and the shouting among the apprentices.

"Always," he said and managed to smile even as he rubbed ash from his eyes.

Goliath's head was to have been cast next. Agnolo was eager to be of help and, with one of the apprentices, he mistook the order of pouring and instead positioned the laurel wreath next in line beneath the crucible.

"The head," I shouted down to him. "The head is next."

Donatello was occupied in conversation with Michelozzo and did not hear me. In truth I did not know if it mattered. I looked into the crucible and I could feel the heat singeing my eyebrows. There seemed to be plenty of bronze left and what did it matter if we did the head last? I shrugged and said nothing more.

Michelozzo gave us the signal to pour. We tensed and I could feel the terrible strain on my arms as we tipped the cauldron and the molten bronze poured slowly into the mold. The pour was agonizingly slow but—God's mercy—it went smoothly. We began to tip the crucible back into rest position and as we did so I was seized by a cramp in my right arm. I lost purchase on the control rod I held clenched in my fist. The crucible began to shake and the molten bronze sloshed about freely. And then I lost control of the crucible altogether. But, a stroke of good luck! The crucible fell back into position above the furnace rather than forward into the casting pit. No one except Pagno had seen this happen. And Agnolo, of course, who was everywhere and into everything.

"Are you all right?" Pagno asked.

I pretended not to hear.

"Can you go on?" he said, shouting now. "Michelozzo could take your place."

"I can help," Agnolo shouted. He was standing next to the pouring platform and trying to get a foot up on it.

I pushed him away.

"I'm fine," I said to Pagno. "My hand slipped from all the sweat." I wiped my hands on the towel around my neck. "I'm fine."

By now the assistants had moved the mold for the laurel wreath from the casting pit to the sand pit and replaced it with the mold for Goliath's head. They steadied the head beneath the crucible and checked to see that it was braced firmly in place. Pagno and I waited for the signal to pour. I flexed the muscles in my right arm to shake out the cramp and I worked my fist open and closed. I could see Pagno watching me.

"I'm all right," I said. "I'm ready."

Michelozzo heard me and looked to see what I meant. He saw me flexing my fist and judged that I was ready and that Pagno was ready and he gave the signal to pour.

We tipped the crucible slowly, steadily, and the molten bronze began to flow into the funnel opening. This would go well, I could see. I glanced over at Pagno who was all concentration. Goliath's head was the last piece to be poured and then we would be done and never mind the heat. An ash stung my eye but I blinked it away. The bronze was flowing into the mold, evenly, beautifully, when suddenly—again—my right arm tensed and my hand shuddered on the control rod. My arms shook. Sweat poured down my face and I tried to shake it away when suddenly Agnolo leaped onto the platform.

"Let me help," he shouted. "I can help."

He grabbed my wrist, and pressed hard on the rod I held. The crucible tipped violently and at once the molten bronze shot from the crucible and overflowed the funnel and poured down into the pit. Michelozzo shouted a warning and at the same moment there was a scream of pain from one of the apprentices as the molten liquid splashed on his naked arm. Donatello leaped to my aid and pulled Agnolo from the platform and then turned to the stricken apprentice who continued to scream in pain and terror. Michelozzo hugged the apprentice to him, murmuring, "Yes, yes, it hurts, I know, I know," and he rocked the boy back and forth in his arms.

Donatello turned back to Agnolo and, in the silence that followed the uproar, he fixed him with that terrible look and shouted, "You whore! You stupid, stupid whore."

Agnolo recoiled and seemed to shrink into himself.

Donatello moved toward him, his hand raised in anger.

"No!" someone shouted. It was Pagno.

Donatello stopped and said softly, "Get out. Just get out."

Agnolo fled.

Donatello turned once more to the apprentice who lay crying softly now in Michelozzo's arms. "*Piccolo mio*," he said. "We'll take care of you." He stroked the boy's hair and laid his hand on his cheek.

Pagno was dispatched to find a doctor.

So ended the second casting of the David. The apprentice would recover, with only a nasty scar on his arm to recall the day. Donatello would recover as well, at least for a while.

But for Agnolo this day had seen the great betrayal from which he would not recover. Donatello had called him a whore, before everyone. So much for his professions of love.

✶ ✶ ✶

By a stroke of luck Goliath's head was cast to near perfection. The molten bronze had overflowed the mold, but somehow that had not proved the disaster it might have been. The plumes in Goliath's helmet would serve to mask the imperfections caused by the sudden gush of bronze and Donatello's expertise in chasing and finishing would take care of the rest.

The casting in truth had not been a total success. There was a small hole beneath David's chin and, though most of us failed at first to notice, there was a piece of finger missing below the second knuckle of the hand that held the sword. But the main problem was the hole in the left thigh. It would require a patch and no matter how perfectly the patch was applied there would always be evidence of an imperfection. "Good," Michelozzo said. "Otherwise they would think you were God."

✷ ✷ ✷

DONATELLO AND MICHELOZZO worked together cleaning the bronze pieces, getting rid of all traces of holes and stems left by the gas vents, and then welding the clean bronze pieces into the finished statue. They patched the hole in the left thigh and the smaller hole beneath the chin. They disguised the imperfections in Goliath's head. They tested the statue for weight and balance. This took over a month. The raw bronze was then hand polished and ready for the patina.

Applying the patina took a matter of weeks. It was a shade so dark that in the shadows it seemed nearly black and it lent to the bronze a luster and a warmth that seemed like flesh itself and made the viewer want to lean forward and touch it.

During all this time Agnolo never appeared in the *bottega*. Donatello worked with his usual concentration, lavishing all his care on the bronze boy he was daily bringing closer to perfection. And then one day it was done.

Donatello stepped back and for a long time gazed at what he had accomplished.

Cosimo too gazed—in wonder and gratitude—at what he had accomplished.

Agnolo came to the *bottega* and looked upon the statue and smiled. "A whore," he said, "and no doubt stupid, but he defeated Goliath, didn't he."

Agnolo would not forget and he would not forgive.

Before the week was up he left Donatello's house and bed, vowing never to return. And, to my astonishment, Donatello did not seem to care. It was as if having captured the boy in bronze, he had no further need for him in the flesh. Such are the limits of love and art, I told myself.

1437–1443

CHAPTER 30

On the second day of July in the year 1437, my two youngest sons were carried off by the Black Pest. Renato Paolo was ten years of age and Giovanni Carlo a tender eight. Oh my sons, my sons! What did they ever do to merit such a cheerless end? Or what did I do to cause it? Even now in my oldest old age I weep for them. One day they were fine young boys—stout and sturdy and of a sweet nature—and the next day they were racked with fever, their armpits and groins purple with buboes, and the deathly smell! In the night they died, even before the Pest had begun to sweep through the city.

I held Agnolo to blame, for he had visited them earlier that week and brought the Pest with him. Two years had passed since he left Florence for Prato, vowing never to return again. He pretended then that he had been betrayed by Donatello who had called him whore before his entire *bottega* but in truth he had been betrayed by one of his patrons, a known sodomite, who saved his own neck by naming Agnolo to the Ufficiali di Notte. Brought before the *magister* Agnolo claimed to be seventeen years of age and so not responsible, but this was his third appearance in court and so they fined him fifty florins—Donatello paid—and urged him strongly to leave Florence for a more benign climate. Two years had passed and he was back in Florence . . . in need of family, he told Alessandra, but as always he was in need of money. He was more than twenty-one years by my reckoning and still able to trade on his youthful looks but he was beginning to see his empty future and—I know him—he hoped to insert himself in my family. He had the good sense, and the wiliness, to approach me through Alessandra.

"I've come to see you," he said. "And to flee the Pest in Prato."

"Who is the pest this time?" I asked. "Another soldier?"

"The Black Pest," he said, though he paused to smile at my little jest. "There have been many deaths."

I had come in from work on commissions for the sacristy of San Lorenzo and found him sitting on a stool next to my wife with my two youngest, Renato Paolo and Giovanni Carlo, seated one astride each knee. I did not like the look of this and said, "Get down!" and to make my chiding seem less angry I tousled their curly hair. They climbed down, obedient as always, and went to stand beside their mother. Franco Alessandro, who at twelve was attentive beyond his years, sat cross-legged on the floor looking up at Agnolo. Franco had grown into a vain young man, concerned always with his shirts and his stockings and the length of his yellow hair, so it displeased me that he was much taken with Agnolo. My oldest, Donato Michele, already half-Franciscan, sat at the table, watching.

"I trust you've not brought the Pest with you," I said.

"Agnolo has been ill," Alessandra said, and it was true he looked even thinner than I remembered and he had an annoying cough. I had only lately seen the bronze David in Cosimo's garden and marveled that such a skinny wretch could have inspired so perfect a statue. I breathed a silent curse, for which may God forgive me, though I meant it and mean it still.

"What illness?"

"In my breathing. I cannot well breathe."

"You had best learn how or your life will be short indeed."

"I am well once again, thank you."

There was an awkward silence.

"Does my lord Donatello know you are in Florence?"

He said no.

"And do the Ufficiali di Notte know?"

There was another awkward silence, which I made worse by asking how much money he needed this time. He lowered his head and looked into his empty hands. He coughed and muttered something I could not hear and I asked him to repeat it.

"Our mother has died and I owe burial fees," he said.

"She was never my mother."

"She is dead all the same. And buried."

"Luca," Alessandra said, pleading for him.

"And I am apprenticed to a wool carder. In Prato."

"Apprenticed? At your age?" Nonetheless I was impressed.

I went to the other room where we kept the money box and took out ten florins. Donatello paid me nearly ninety gold florins a year, but our two older boys were at school with the Franciscans and the cost of food was ever higher and it is an accepted truth that you spend however much you earn, so I felt I could not well afford this. Nonetheless I gave him the money and, cheered by such easy wealth, he accepted Alessandra's invitation to share our supper.

Less than a week later my two youngest sons were carried off by the Pest. They were so young and so tender, loving in their innocence, and they would have been a comfort for our old age, for Alessandra and me. Instead they were taken away, cruelly, on a dark day. I cursed Agnolo and I must allow that for a time I cursed God as well.

I have said before that I cannot imagine God sending me to hell—I am not important enough for him to notice—but cursing God is another matter. He does not wait for death to catch you up. I know, since this day marked the end of all comfort in my life and I began to glimpse now and then—in tiny flashes, caught by candlelight—the narrow cubbyhole prepared for me in hell. This cannot be, I thought, and turned my mind away. I had a wife still, and two fine boys, and I knew—for my two youngest—that it is natural to die.

Yet even now I blame Agnolo for their deaths, just as I blame him for betraying Donatello and corrupting Franco and driving my wife from our marriage bed into the convent. And for my own discomfortable imprisonment, *miserere mei Domine*.

CHAPTER 31

Sᴇᴘᴛᴇᴍʙᴇʀ ᴛʜᴀᴛ ʏᴇᴀʀ was a long patience. The days were hot and the nights airless. We lay abed, unable to sleep and unable to stop thinking of our two youngest boys carried away by the Black Pest. We still had our oldest, Donato Michele and Franco Alessandro, and they were a great consolation to us, but the loss of our two youngest was still very much with us and, instead of bringing us together in grief, seemed to thrust us apart. I blamed Agnolo for this, as I blamed him for everything, and Alessandra seemed to blame me.

"You are unjust to him," Alessandra said. "It is wrong to wish him ill."

"I don't only wish him ill. I wish him dead."

At that moment it came to me: some day I will kill him. At once I put the thought from my mind, but of course it would not go easily. A mortal sin, an eternity in hell. But he has done me great harm and Donatello much harm and it was right that he should die. And then, No, I thought, I could never do such a thing.

"He would be better dead."

I felt Alessandra go rigid at my side. For a moment I wondered if she too thought that some day I would kill him.

"It is the death of your own soul to wish him dead."

"Our sons are gone. I lay the blame on him."

"Did I blame you for my sister's death? And yet you made love with her that same afternoon she lay dying."

I was silent then thinking of Maria Sabina.

"But I did not bring the Pest to her."

"Nor did Agnolo bring the Pest to us. The Pest is in the hand of God and he strikes where he will. We must accept."

"So Agnolo is the agent of God? I would think he was rather the agent of the devil."

"Is it not bad enough our sons are gone? Why make it worse by such sinful thoughts? They are with God."

I wanted to say, 'There is no God. Death is the only God we all obey," but the thought frightened me and I said nothing. For a second I saw again that cubbyhole in hell reserved for me. I began to tremble with fright and I reached out for safety.

"Alessandra," I said, and put my hand to her breast the way I did when we were to make love, but she pushed my hand away and turned from me.

"It is too soon," she said.

I turned my back to her. Two can play at this game and I would show her that I would not be first to ask for love. In this I was mistaken. I asked again, repeatedly, and was refused. She had taken against me, like God. Never again in our married life did we make love.

CHAPTER 32

TIME PASSED AS it does whether you are happy or not and by my fortieth year I grew more bitterly silent as Alessandra grew fatter and more distant from me. She worked at her weaving and gave herself over to frequent prayer, perhaps because Donato Michele at seventeen years had chosen to enter the Order of Saint Francis and she wanted to be a worthy mother. Donato was a bright boy and virtuous and his Father Superior told Alessandra that perhaps one day he would make a priest.

Perhaps one day, I thought, Alessandra will again be a wife to me.

She had little time for me and no patience with my ongoing anger at Agnolo or my disappointment that Pagno was permitted to carve marble and I was not. With Donato Michele now a Franciscan novice, Alessandra grew more impatient with me and more indulgent with Franco Alessandro who at fifteen years was impossibly vain and lazy. He was apprenticed to a carpenter and was away from home much of the week but his requests for new things remained ever the same: a belt, a money pouch, new parti-colored stockings with one leg red, the other green. Worse than this, though he was a sturdy boy with a strong manly face, he fussed with his long yellow hair more than any young girl. He has never recovered from Agnolo's visit, I thought, but I refused to let myself think what this might mean.

What it meant was clear to everyone when in October of that year he was arrested and accused of sodomy. His was a first offense and so he was fined ten florins and released. He did not name his partner; he claimed not to know him.

Alessandra was in tears beyond comfort and I was in a rage that I thought might bring on my first fit in years. There was that familiar roaring in my brain and then I seemed to lose control of my arms and legs and my eyesight went dim. I will kill him, I thought, and for a moment I did not know whether I intended my son Franco Alessandro or that devilish spawn Agnolo whom I held responsible for all things ill. I will kill him, I said to myself, and for a second, as the pain thrilled through my brain, I wondered if I might some day—in just such a fit—kill him indeed. The roaring passed and the pain diminished and I realized that Franco is my son and I his father and it was Franco's foolish vanity that had brought him to this, not Agnolo, and so I determined on a calm but firm talk with him. I would be fatherly and forgiving. I would not rage at him.

"Franco," I said. "This is not good."

"It was not my fault," he said.

"Then let us reason together. How did it come about that you were arrested?"

"It was all a mistake. It was all meant to be a jest."

I composed myself to listen to a string of lies.

"We were acting the fool, Giovanni and Marcantonio and I, pushing and shoving one another, when two older men stopped us in the street. They were not soldiers but they were dressed like soldiers and they told us to stop and spend a minute with them. All on a sudden one of them snatched Giovanni's hat and said he would not give it back unless he, you know, surrendered to him. I said, "Let's go. Let's get away from here." We were on the Via tra' Pellicciai and we knew it was a bad place to be after sunset. But the soldier would not give back Giovanni's hat unless Giovanni went with him. Marcantonio tried to snatch back Giovannni's hat but the other soldier—he only looked like a soldier—caught him by the arm and led him off to the old convent where there was a shed that opened onto the street and they went inside the shed. Then the first soldier took Giovanni to the shed. I was alone in the street and I was afraid, so when another man came along—this one was a soldier truly—I told him what had happened to my friends, and he listened carefully, but then he snatched away my hat and said I had to go with him. I said I wouldn't go and he began to shout for anyone to hear that I had just serviced an old furrier but that I would not service him though I had taken his money. So I went with him down the alley where we ran into two officers from the Ufficiali di Notte and, while the soldier made his escape, they arrested me for sodomy. And that is the full story."

I looked at him, my son of fifteen years who was now almost a man, and I tried to believe him. These things often began with a snatched hat, I knew. No one knew why the hat should take on such significance but certainly it was true of female prostitutes that they made off with a man's hat in order to force him to pay for sex. It had happened to me more than once and in truth I had entered happily into the game. And so I believed that a soldier or someone who looked like a soldier had snatched away Franco's hat. What I could not believe was that my own son was so easy, that he had put himself in a place and a situation where sex of that nature was likely to occur, and that he had been willing to bend over and let himself be penetrated. That he could be like Agnolo was more than I could bear.

"The full story," I said. "But it raises so many questions. Why were you there on the Via tra' Pellicciai? Why do you hang about with boys who—do not deny it—make themselves available to soldiers? Or, I think, to anyone who has a few coins and is thick with lust? What would your mother think to know her son is a *bardassa*? She who prays night and day!" I was beginning to shout. "*Are* you a *bardassa*? Has it come to this? What shame to your brother!"

"I am not a *bardassa*. I never take money."

I stopped then and listened to him. He never took money. So, this was not his first escapade. There must have been previous times when he was not caught. My anger faded and my heart ached for him, a poor vain boy. Playing at this kind of seduction was not rare among the rich and the noble—nor in truth among the very poor—but it was a thing that could not be borne by men of middle rank. Such men were sober and responsible, we worked hard, we married young. We were not seduced by the backsides of wanton boys.

And yet today, some twenty-six years later, the Florence vice is more common still and prevails among all levels of men, as if it is a necessary ritual for boys in their early teens, something they grow into and out of and it does not matter. But it does matter and it did. For this was not something Franco Alessandro would grow out of.

"Never again," he promised on that day in 1440 and he wept most bitterly in my arms. I wept as well. But I sensed even then that he was lost to me forever.

CHAPTER 33

Donatello claimed not to miss Agnolo, not to care about him any longer, but I did not believe him and what I saw convinced me that Agnolo remained very much in his mind and heart. He had been pleased to hear that Agnolo was apprenticed to a wool carder—his own father had been a wool-carder—and from time to time he asked if I had news of the boy. The boy was now a man, of course, but in Donatello's mind he was still that sixteen year old who, posing for the David, seduced him and stole his heart and remained still in possession of it.

Donatello had grown old—he was more than fifty years of age by now—and it seemed that with the exile of Agnolo he had lost interest in both his work and his life. Those good days when he would gather us all together at the end of a work day and we would joke and drink and he would say witty things about Ghiberti or intimate things about my lord Cosimo de' Medici, those days were gone. He no longer laughed and he seemed always a little lost. He had never been of easy approach on any personal matter and now he seemed more remote than before. Still, I took courage and asked him outright about Agnolo.

"Do you miss him?"

Donatello gave me a sharp look.

"He is in Prato," I said, "carding wool. It is not far off."

"He was dear to me," he said, "once."

"He is a man now and has perhaps given up his evil ways."

"His evil ways were my evil ways."

"He is ever in need of money," I said.

"And your evil ways? Of mind and tongue?"

"I could not help myself and so I said it. Sometimes . . ."

"Do you think the tongue corrupts the heart, Luca? Or does it work the other way?"

"I think you are hard on me. I want only to help."

"It is good that you have Alessandra."

I did not mention that Alessandra had grown cold to me and that I was forced to find my ease with whores. Of course it may be he knew this and was being sharp with me. With good reason he was called *intricato*.

He was silent for a while and then he said, "Yes, I miss him."

"He could still be purchased, I think. At a bargain price."

"Don't," he said. He looked at me, suddenly a very old man, and drew me to him. He was crying and I could feel his head shaking against my breast. For a fleeting moment I felt good to have brought him down. He pulled away then, his beard wet with tears, and said, "Come. We have work to do."

* * *

He was lethargic, dull. He came late to the *bottega,* worked indifferently, and left even before dark. His mind was elsewhere and besides, though there were few new commissions, there were a great many works not yet complete. Of these the Cantoria mattered most. The marble was costly and the Duomo was committed to holding Donatello to contract. He worked dutifully but he had scarcely begun carving the right side of the frieze when his attention wandered to other commissions.

He passed off work on the dancing children of the Cantoria to his new assistant, Agostino di Duccio, and of course to the ever-present Pagno di Lapo. He had laid out the design for all the dancing children and he had done the preliminary cutting and now he allowed them to do carving that once he would have insisted on doing himself. Occasionally he would correct Pagno's errors and sometimes he would be moved to take chisel in hand and show Duccio how to carve out a plump leg as it showed from behind a pilaster, but mostly he left them alone to complete the relief as best they could.

If the Cantoria failed to engage him in the old way, the lesser commissions were a positive annoyance. The Prato Pulpit he dismissed in disgust, finishing the carving as if he were attacking an enemy. But at last it was done.

✳ ✳ ✳

FRANCO ALESSANDRO WAS arrested for sodomy. It was his second arrest. We paid the fine of twenty-five florins and he was released. There was a long silence in our house, and in my heart I had begun to despair of him.

For no reason I could allege, I blamed Agnolo for this.

✳ ✳ ✳

COSIMO HAD MUCH to occupy him. After his return from exile he had taken great care to remain in the background of political events and though he could have made himself the supreme power in Florence he chose merely to exile the Albizzi and their followers and to maintain the laws and offices unchanged. He announced his return to political life by accepting the office of Gonfaloniere for January and February of 1435 and then, having served the Republic as its visible head, he withdrew into the private life of a banker, retaining first approval of any candidate nominated for office, however high, however low. Without bloodshed and without rancor, Cosimo had quickly and effectively taken control of the government of Florence.

All this time, despite his involvement in politics, he remained mindful of his artisan friends. They needed money and so they needed work. His particular concern for Donatello had begun after the completion of the David. Donatello seemed downcast, defeated, as if by surrendering the finished sculpture he was losing something of himself. Cosimo responded as he invariably did, with praise, with devotion, with money.

By way of thanks—and in addition to the five hundred gold florins he paid on completion of the statue—Cosimo presented Donatello with a gown and cloak and *capuccio* in the finest red wool of the nobility, a thing worthy of the maker of David. And then, when the statue was mounted on a marble column in the center of Cosimo's garden, he gave a banquet in celebration and, in addition to his extended family circle, he invited Ghiberti and Brunelleschi, Michelozzo and Uccello, della Robbia, Fra Angelico, della Quercia and the unspeakable Filippo Lippi. It was a gathering of my lord Cosimo's dear friends, artisans of extraordinary skills, each of them in debt to him for work commissioned and work yet unimagined. Donatello was the guest of honor. He wore the red robes that Cosimo had given him and he drank much and marveled at the attention and praise they lavished on him, but in the end he found the attention tiresome and the praise meaningless. These were his gifted friends and sometimes his competitors whose loving admiration for him was limited by their own ambitions. There was jealousy here as well as love. He knew this and he was happy when the banquet was over.

Though he wore the red robes on the Feast of the Most Holy Name of Mary and again on the Feast of San Lorenzo, he was glad to give them back with thanks and apologies as being too grand for a simple artisan whose father had been a wool-comber. Cosimo understood and, taking back the robes with some reluctance, promised that nonetheless they would remain friends and collaborators . . . as even now there stood in his garden the beautiful bronze David that was proof of the importance of their collaboration.

* * *

Franco Alessandro was arrested once again, his third arrest.

"Are you *trying* to disgrace us?"

"I'm sorry. I beg pardon of you and mother."

"Are you trying to be another Agnolo Mattei?" I spat out the name.

"I am an evil son."

He would sin again and would be punished again and so would we all. We paid his fine of fifty florins and begged him to sin no more.

* * *

MICHELOZZO HAD BY now completed plans for the new Medici palace—a more controlled design than the grandiose palace Brunelleschi had earlier proposed—and my lord Cosimo was pleased with its strength and modesty and its quiet grandeur. There was a garden and a formal courtyard for display of statuary and there were separate apartments for members of his family and of course a private chapel for Cosimo himself.

The new palace was not Cosimo's only concern. More and more he worried about the fate of his immortal soul, and the more he worried the more he invested his great wealth in works for the church. He poured a small fortune into the sacristy and chapel of San Lorenzo and a large fortune into the restoration of the Dominican monastery of San Marco.

He chose Michelozzo as architect and gave him a free hand. Michelozzo designed a new cloister with twenty-eight columned arches, an *ospizio* for the ill and the aged, a refectory, a chapter house, a second cloister, and a long corridor of cells for the monks, one of those cells reserved from the beginning for Cosimo's personal use. It was to be a place where he could spend days and nights at prayer and meditation and where Mass could be said for the good of his soul. Fra Angelico painted frescoes in each of the cells and along the corridor, making of the passageway a veritable entrance to paradise. In Cosimo's private cell, Angelico painted a fresco of the Adoration of the Magi, in which Cosimo himself may or may not have been represented as one of the wise men. Angelico was not readily given to flattery.

At this time Michelozzo chose at last to marry. At nearly forty-five years, he was nearing old age when he took as his bride the young and beautiful Francesca di Ambrogio, a tanner's daughter of nineteen years. She reminded me much of Alessandra when I first knew her, a lively girl with green eyes and a full figure, a good bearer of children and with the attitude of a devoted wife.

For the wedding of Michelozzo and Francesca, Cosimo gave an enormous banquet in the courtyard of his old palace on the Via de' Bardi. It was a rare mild day in January and the courtyard was alive with flowering shrubs brought in for the occasion and in the center stood the bronze David, mounted on a marble pillar and surrounded by wreaths of laurel. As a friend of Michelozzo—and, I like to think, as transcriber of manuscripts for Cosimo himself—I was invited to attend the banquet. There was much eating and drinking of rare wines and there was music and dancing and it was good to see Donatello give away his great friend to this tanner's beautiful daughter.

As it happens Francesca was true to her appearance; she was indeed a devoted wife and a good bearer of children. In my own lifetime she bore Michelozzo four sons and four daughters and they all survived. None of them has his genius but they are all beauties and all devoted to him. And Michelozzo, as he deserves, is supremely happy.

* * *

Franco Alessandro was arrested for sodomy—his fourth arrest—and now lay ill in the cellars of the Bargello until the fine of one hundred florins would be paid and names named and the sentence of one hour in the pillory carried out. We were ruined now. We had fifty florins in our savings box and my lord Donatello loaned us another fifty and we paid the hundred florin fine.

Franco Alessandro was released from prison and by the mercy of some jurisdictional accident he was spared an hour in the pillory. No one knew why. A check mark next to his name, a question raised by some City Eminence, some sleight of hand? He was spared the pillory and its torments thanks to Cosimo de' Medici, but we were not to know this until two years later when Franco was arrested once more and Cosimo yet again came to his aid.

We welcomed Franco home this one last time. Another arrest would mean a two-hundred-florin fine and exile for life. Alessandra was convinced it would come to that. I too feared the worst. I had watched Agnolo's madness play itself out over all these years and I knew that Franco would not easily give up his reckless way of life. In truth I was torn between rage and anguish. We had lost our two youngest sons to the Black Pest, and our oldest Donato Michele had given himself to God in the Order of Saint Francis, so it was sad to think our one remaining son should be such bitter gall to us. Alessandra felt only love for him but I felt love and hate together, the frustration of all my desires and my hopes. He made me want to cry on his shoulder and cry out against him all at the same time. He was our hope and our salvation, dashed.

We had tried everything, of course. At first we thought his wanton behavior was a lark, a sign of what might happen if your only interests were clothes and how you looked in them. Franco had been a handsome child, sturdy, with strong shoulders and good arms and hands. He might have grown into a carver of marble or a caster of bronze but from his earliest days his great interest was his hair and his clothes and the impression he made. Vanity, we thought, a woman's vanity, or a preening noble's, we hoped it would pass.

I was horrified at what he had come to but Alessandra was determined to offer him only love and understanding. She continued on this way after his second and third arrests, telling Franco she understood and she loved him still.

"What is it you understand?" I asked, furious, and when I asked him, "Do you think it makes you loved?" he would give no answer, choosing the silence of the victim instead of confessing his sins and changing his life thereafter, amen.

We did what parents could. We scolded, we cursed, we threatened to throw him out of our house and dismiss him from our family . . . forever. We pointed out the neighbors' ridicule, we urged a show of manliness in this effeminate world, we called upon the honor of the di Matteo name. He remained dumb. We pleaded and we threatened and we tried to argue reasonably. In the end he agreed, he offered apologies and submission, but then a little time passed and he was once again curling his hair and slipping out at night with his band of young friends, all of them in parti-colored stockings, tight about the backside and the fork in front, an offer clearly on display.

Now he was back after being arrested for the fourth time. He was silent still. He would let neither Alessandra nor myself near him. He refused to see his brother the Franciscan. He would not go to confession. When he had been home from prison for over a week I determined on a firm talk with him. I waited till long after dark and then I entered the bedroom and sat on the edge of his cot. I could tell he was not sleeping but he gave no sign that he knew I was there.

"Franco mio," I said softly.

He stirred beneath the covers but said nothing.

"Franco. Why?" Of course he did not respond. If he could easily have answered "Why?" he would long since have done so. But I went on talking softly, reasonably, and he listened. When I had run out of new ways to ask the question "Why" and new entreaties that he not do this to us—the shame, the cost, the waste of his young life—he suddenly responded.

In a strong clear voice, with no regard for the time or the darkness, he said, "Do you think I choose to be like this? This is who I am. This is what I am." And he turned from me to face the wall. I sat there, wondering, and then because I could think of no other response, I repeated Alessandra's words to him, "I know. I understand." And for a short while I felt I had spoken truth.

Franco had left us. He did not say where he was going. He simply disappeared the morning after our talk and I was torn between relief and fear of what might happen next. Alessandra was already preparing for what she was convinced would happen next.

"I need money," she said. "I need one hundred sixty florins."

I laughed at the idea of such a sum. Donatello paid me ninety florins a year, and it is true he gave me generous gifts—the fifty florins I had borrowed were a gift, he said—but that an artisan's accountant should lay hands on that much money was surely a jest.

"I know it will take some time. We will have to live frugally."

I was stunned. I fell speechless once again.

"It is not impossible," she said. "I have saved forty florins myself."

"That cannot be."

She lifted a loose flagstone in the bedroom and took out a small leather sack. It contained forty-one florins."

"How is this possible?"

"I spin fine wool and save every *picciolo*. And I save the living money you earn from Donato."

"Forty florins is a fortune. For such a sum we could buy a slave girl or a mule."

"With one hundred sixty more we can free our son."

"When he is arrested again, you mean."

"So." She looked at me then in such a loving, trusting way that I forgave her coldness in keeping me from her bed. I took her in my arms.

"You'll try?"

"I'll try," I said though I knew that such a sum was impossible.

But still she kept me from her bed.

It was just now that Alessandra first proposed entering a convent. Such a thing was always possible for rich widows and sometimes possible for married couples if both agreed to it and if the dowry was pleasing to the Lord . . . and to the Mother Superior. But I could not agree to this. I told her I would give it thought and that night I hastened off to the Mercato Vecchio to ease my pain with a whore, Pellegrina, who had become my favorite. She was young and lively and knew how to meet the needs of older men.

To me our marriage was a sacred thing.

MICHELOZZO'S WEDDING WAS the occasion for another of those Medici interventions in the lives of artisans that have produced astonishing works, like Donatello's bronze David or the frescoes of Fra Angelico or the Madonnas of Filippo Lippi whom Cosimo locked in a room and refused to let out until he had made progress with his painting. These would never have existed without Cosimo's insistence. And his money.

At the wedding I noticed that my lord Cosimo was more than usually taken with Pagno di Lapo. He always made much of Pagno, greeting him with undue affection and talking with him as if he were an equal. He did not talk this way with me, though in truth I was much closer to him in my appreciation of Latin and Greek manuscripts and in my ability to reproduce them in the Italian hand he particularly favored. Nonetheless, as I say, he favored Pagno, kissing him on both cheeks and letting his hand rest on his shoulders as if he were a favored son.

"The bust of a young man," I heard him say to Donatello. "And he should wear one of my Greek medallions."

His collection of rare coins and medallions was one of the wonders of Florence and I understood from what I overheard that Donatello would begin shortly to grant Pagno a kind of immortality, recreated to the life in marble or bronze. The San Lorenzo doors were finished but not yet hung and the Inn of Santa Caterina would soon be destroyed to make way for the new Medici palace, but despite all these pressures of time and work, I proved to be right.

On the very next day I found Pagno sitting for Donatello while he turned out sketch after sketch of a young man in classical draperies looking off into an impossible future with the gaze of Saint Francis in the presence of the risen Lord. He is in truth a handsome young man, with a mass of red hair and wide gray-green eyes, but if you examine the finished bronze in profile you will see that Donatello has caught the slightly receding chin, the essential weakness of the man. Donatello disagreed with me when I pointed this out. He said that here was the classically perfect chin and he went on and on about the balance of cheekbones and the width of the eye sockets and the turn of the lips; in short he defended Pagno, in statue and in life, as the perfect man. But you can see for yourself that I was right. The statue rests on a grand chest in the main *sala* of the new Medici palace. It is bronze and, in its way, perfect.

* * *

"I HAVE ARRANGED to buy a little farm, Luca. You must take care of the paperwork for me."

This was indeed news. Donatello was now some fifty-seven years of age and had never yet shown interest in owning anything, let alone a house or a farm.

"Of course," I said. "Congratulations!" And I asked him where this little farm was located. I thought perhaps in the Mugello, near one of Cosimo's country homes or perhaps in the hills outside Florence.

"In Prato," he said.

Of course. I knew at once. It was for Agnolo.

"And will you leave Florence and live in Prato?"

"When I am too old to work, who knows where I will live."

"So the farm is for you and not, perhaps, a gift for someone else?"

"The farm is for me. It may be that in time I will make of it a gift for someone else."

So. It had come to this.

"Do you see him? In Prato?"

"I see him in Florence. And I am buying the farm against the time when I should die. When I am gone, he must have a place to live and he cannot well buy it for himself."

How could he be seeing Agnolo in Florence without my knowledge of it? Would not Agnolo be arrested if he were found in Florence? Did his exile mean nothing? I was speechless.

"He is with me even now."

"Here? In Florence?"

He nodded.

"Living with you?"

He nodded again, pleased.

"Is this not dangerous? Would you not be liable to the law if he were discovered here?"

"Who would tell?"

"The Albizzi are gone but Cosimo—my lord Cosimo—still has enemies. And what better way to strike at him than to strike at you? You could be denounced, secretly, to the Ufficiali di Notte."

"I've been denounced already. Three times. But that was years ago and it has come to nothing."

My mind reeled with this new information. That he could have been denounced three times! And I not know of it! I thought of my appearances before the Ufficiali to pay the fines for Franco Alessandro. The Night Officers were not men to antagonize. I had sacrificed all our savings in fines for Franco Alessandro but that was the least of it. These men held over you the threat of prison, not to mention torture and death. Donatello seemed not to realize this. His infatuation with Agnolo had in truth become a kind of madness.

"I'll do the paperwork," I said.

"You did not know I've been denounced three times?"

"You must be careful, Donato mio." I leaned into him and put my hand on his heart. "You should rid yourself of him." He looked away. "But if you cannot live without him, you should leave Florence. Go to Rome. Or Venice. Or Padua where they ask for you daily. But somewhere out of the reach of the Ufficiali di Notte. I know them. They will be the death of you."

He placed his hand over my hand as it rested on his heart and he fixed me with that gaze I knew so well from watching him at work.

"You are a loving friend," he said and kissed me on either cheek. I shuddered with gratitude and pleasure.

Imagine my horror then when a messenger arrived at the *bottega* with a notice that Donatello must present himself at once to the *magister* of the Ufficiali di Notte to respond to charges, unspecified and made anonymously.

1443–1453

CHAPTER 34

Donatello moved our entire *bottega* from Florence to Padua, a cause of wonder to everyone who knew him and a great disappointment to the Operai of the Duomo who concluded now that they would never see the bronze doors they had long since commissioned for the sacristy. Donatello chose Padua over Rome or Venice because of the promise of a great commission to erect the largest bronze equestrian statue in the modern world, a monument to Gattamelata, the great warrior general who had died earlier in the year. This was the official reason he offered. Michelozzo and my lord Cosimo de' Medici alone knew the real reason for our sudden removal to Padua.

The summons to appear before the Ufficiali di Notte had come as a great blow to Donatello. To be summoned and interrogated about the most intimate details of one's life was a nuisance to my Franco Alessandro and a danger to Agnolo Mattei, but to Donatello it was a disgrace and more; it was proof that he had endangered not only his beloved Agnolo but even Cosimo de' Medici himself. There was no benefit to anyone in striking out at Donatello. He was a beloved figure in Florence; his unusual fondness for his apprentices was well known and accepted; his sculpture was justification for any eccentricity. But to strike out at Cosimo—anonymously, mightily—was pure profit. The nobles who had supported the Albizzi in their time of power were now supporting Cosimo, but not all of them with equal devotion. There remained always that group of ancient wealthy families who saw Cosimo as a newcomer, a vulgar banker who exercised absolute power in the Republic by reason of his wealth and whose overthrow would be a welcome relief. And what better way to overthrow him than to undermine his moral credit by summoning his favorite sculptor and personal friend to answer charges of sodomy.

On the day of that dreadful summons the first thing Donatello did was send me running to his house to tell Agnolo to leave Florence at once. At this time Prato was under the legal sway of the Florentine Republic but it was hard to believe that the Ufficiali di Notte would pursue sodomites beyond the city limits and so Agnolo thought he would be safe in Prato. The second thing he did was send Pagno di Lapo to Michelozzo and then to my lord Cosimo with news of his summons to appear before the Ufficiali.

Michelozzo shook his head in sadness that he could do nothing, but my lord Cosimo, in his circuitous, anonymous way, took immediate action.

That night Cosimo moved against the Ufficiali di Notte. In a matter of days the charges against Donatello were dropped and the *magister* of the Night Officers sought occupation in another branch of the law. Nonetheless the Ufficiali guarded the anonymity of their sources in such a way that all of their files were protected as official and confidential. Thus the charges against Donatello remained on record to be held against him in case of any further denunciation. Cosimo could go only so far in subverting the law.

And so we began our ten-year residence in Padua, bitter weather in winter and scalding hot in summer, and the grim and endless croaking of frogs in spring.

Alessandra remained in our little house in Florence with Franco Alessandro and once again urged her petition to become a Sister of Saint Dominic. A lay Sister. A servant. Again I refused and, lacking my consent, the local Bishop refused as well.

Michelozzo began work on the destruction of the Inn of Santa Caterina and the erection of the Palazzo Medici in its place on the Via Larga. It would become the handsomest private residence in all of Florence.

Agnolo returned to carding wool in Prato, leaving us to wonder in what ways his next folly would complicate our lives.

As for us—all of us, save Caterina—we were for Padua and whatever wonders it might offer.

* * *

Bᴜᴛ ꜰᴏʀ ᴍᴇ Padua and its wonders would have to wait. We had scarcely arrived in our new city when a message came saying that my Franco Alessandro had been arrested for the fifth time. He was eighteen years and still fell under the sodomy laws for minors, but these would not protect him from a public flogging and the two-hundred-florin fine that Alessandra had been saving against. Meanwhile he was locked, shivering, in the icy cellars of the Stinche. There was nothing for it but that I go.

I arrived in Florence and found—to my astonishment—that the matter was settled. Franco had been released without a flogging and was now condemned to exile—anywhere outside the Republic of Florence—where he must remain for the rest of his life under penalty of having his right foot cut off should he return. I detected here the intervention of Cosimo and I was not altogether wrong.

Giacomo, my lord Cosimo's body servant, had been arrested *in actu* with Franco Alessandro in an alley behind the construction works for the new Medici palace. When the Ufficiali discovered whom they had arrested, they were at a loss what to do. You did not arrest the body servant of the most powerful man in the Republic and yet there he was, in prison, beside his partner in sin. They dithered. They discussed. They waited for something to happen.

And then came a message from Cosimo to the *magister* of the Ufficiali and they were both released, the boy Franco and the man Giacomo. It had been a misunderstanding. Apologies were made. There were no fines, no punishments. All the paperwork was made to disappear.

Months later we would learn that Franco Alessandro had agreed, *in segreto*, to go into voluntary exile—wherever they might send him—and to return never.

But now, in our ignorance, Alessandra and I celebrated with a great feast and much wine. I toasted her good health and happiness and promised I would pose no objection to her entering the convent. And then, though in her gratitude she offered me her bed for this one night, I politely declined and went out in search of the whore Pellegrina.

I left the next day to begin my new life in Padua.

CHAPTER 35

TWO GREAT CITIES could not have been more different than Florence and Padua. Money and the great works of artisans were the lifeblood of Florence, whereas in Padua the pursuit of knowledge was everything. Padua's great university had for centuries brought together men from all parts of the world, students and professors, for the study of civil and canon law and for the more interesting study of man and his fate: astronomy and dialectic, philosophy and grammar and rhetoric. All these young men had needs and desires and the city of Padua looked out for them.

In the past century Padua had been the home of Dante and Petrarch and Boccaccio. Giotto had frescoed the Scrovegni chapel here, a toy box for the baby Jesus. And now Donatello di Betto Bardi would bring the city everlasting fame with his great equestrian bronze of Gattamelata, the marble carvings of the miracles of Sant' Antonio, and the great high altar of the Basilica itself with its immense bronze crucifix and seven bronze saints. Thanks to Donatello, the Piazza San Antonio would become the center of a new city.

The old city was dominated by the University and the University was serviced by the Inn known as the Bo, so called for the fabled invincible Ox that once was stabled here. The Bo was a gathering place, handy to lecture halls and the nooks and crannies of the neighborhood where students shared bed and board with anyone who would have them. There were two central market squares, the Piazza della Frutta and the Piazza delle Erbe, and between them stood the immense Palazzo Ragione, the home of the law courts and a meeting place for the city council. On the top floor of the Palazzo was the vast Salone, a reception hall unequalled in size in all of Christendom. The Palazzo burned to the ground some twenty or more years before our arrival in Padua and it was immediately rebuilt, but lost in the fire were the frescoed walls of Giotto, floor to ceiling paintings of the cycles of the zodiac. The Bo, the Palazzo Ragione, and the two huge piazzas made up the public face of Padua. The private face lay deep behind the Bo, down alleys that smelled of decay, in taverns and inns that were dark and noisy even past the hours of curfew, and in those narrow, shuttered houses of pleasure with whores from all over Europe.

I was a man of forty-three years, more or less, and I had the same needs as those young men who were pursuing wisdom at the university. I sought out the private face of Padua at once.

* * *

On our second night in Padua Pagno di Lapo and I went out—there is no nice way to put it—in pursuit of whores. We had labored all day under a heavy sky that had brought on an early dusk and we were ready for the night. We were men alone, in a new city, and there was the excitement of the forbidden.

"I am not at ease with this," I said. "I have always hunted alone."

"I have never hunted at all," Pagno said. "This is new to me."

"Can it be that you have never had a woman?"

"Only Caterina," he said. "And she never more than once a week."

I was astonished. Caterina was Donatello's niece and a woman not to be trifled with. I had had her more than once and I knew she fancied Agnolo but I had never thought of her fancying Pagno, however handsome he might be.

"Is it your red hair she liked? Or are you skilled in bed?"

"I would willingly have married her," he said, "but she would not have me. She would not have any man to husband, she said, unless it be Michelozzo."

Here was no end of surprises. Caterina had stayed behind in Florence even after Donatello had left his *bottega*. She found work readily with Luca della Robbia, for she was an accomplished painter. And in Florence she would be closer to Michelozzo, though now that he had married it was hard to imagine she would entertain hope of him.

For Pagno and me hope lay just around the corner.

We had reached the Palazzo Raggione and walked on through the Piazza delle Erbe where vegetables and herbs were sold until late afternoon and where the hours that followed were given over to students and their professors and the more expensive whores. These wore the gloves and bells and high-heeled slippers that—in observance of the law—marked them out as prostitutes. There were small shops along the fringe of the market and many of these shops provided tiny rooms where prostitutes could entertain their clients. Pagno and I ducked into an alley that became a warren of small taverns and houses of pleasure and we looked into several before we were hailed by a fine, tall woman at the door of a tavern called La Procedura. She was much taken by Pagno.

"Eh, Rosso," she said softly. "You are a pretty one indeed."

Pagno left me to reply. "And you yourself," I said. "Have you a friend?"

"For you?"

"For me."

"Everybody has a friend. But Rosso is for me. My name is Stina."

Stina led us inside the tavern and up a narrow stairs. The noise from below was deafening and the tavern itself smelled of spilt wine and sweat. The students were singing an anti-clerical ballad with enthusiasm and accompanied it with much banging of tankards on table tops. Stina shook her head in disapproval and pulled aside a curtain to reveal a tiny cell with a pallet and a small table that held a bowl of water. "For cleanliness," she said, pulling Pagno in behind her. Before she closed the curtain she called out "Katya" and almost at once a hefty young prostitute appeared and without a word led me into the cell next to Stina's. She pulled the curtain, undressed me, and went through the business of washing my parts before she undressed herself and lay down on the pallet. The rest of the ceremony proceeded as you know. Katya was from Dalmatia, with fair hair and a pale coloring, and I took care to offer her the pleasures I had learned so many years ago with Maria Sabina. It was soon over and I paid her fee, with a handful of *piccioli* extra, and pulled aside the curtain. There leaning against the wall was Pagno, waiting for me, looking anxious and indeed none too satisfied. He said nothing until we were out in the street.

"It took you so long," he said.

"Speed is not the point of the game."

"No," he said, but he seemed uncertain about it.

"Do you not feel better?" I asked. "And younger?"

"I am thirty-five years," he said. "I am more than half done my life. Is it good to feel less old than you are?"

"You're very somber after such sport," I said. "Was it not good for you?"

He was silent as we continued to walk back toward the Piazza delle Erbe. The square was still alive with students, some drunk and singing, and a lovely young prostitute hailed us as we walked on in silence. I mentally marked the spot where she practiced her trade. We passed the Palazzo di Raggione and were crossing the Piazza della Frutta when Pagno paused and looked at me and said, "It is sin, finally, and no more than that."

I found myself embarrassed. I had enjoyed myself with the Dalmatian Katya and I was relaxed and refreshed and I did not want to think it a sin. Still, it was. But it was such a small sin and such a good and pleasureful thing that I could not bring myself to consider it very wrong. I would confess it during the next Easter season and I supposed Pagno would as well, but a man must get through life somehow, poor forked creature that he is, and I trusted God would allow for a little human weakness. So I was not pleased when Pagno said again, with a certain insistence, "It is sin."

Nonetheless in the months that followed we would go whoring together companionably enough, though I continued to hold him in distrust. That would change over our next ten years in Padua.

* * *

DONATELLO HAD LEFT Florence on the promise of a commission to create a bronze equestrian statue of the famous general Erasmo da Narni, whom we all know as Gattemelata, the Honeyed Cat. The Condottiere had died earlier in the year 1443 and the Venetian government—which had ruled in Padua for nearly forty years now—decreed that he should be honored in the Piazza Sant' Antonio with a monumental tomb of bronze and marble. Donatello alone should be its creator. He set to work first on the commission for a huge bronze crucifix that would hang above the main altar in the Basilica.

Our new *bottega* was established directly across from the Piazza Sant' Antonio near a little house the Operai of the Basilica had set aside for Donatello and his assistants. This little house was readied within the month and he offered Pagno and me the opportunity to move in with him. The rooms were tiny, but neither Pagno nor I objected to the narrow cells we occupied—we were grateful each to have his own room—and an elderly woman came in by day to clean and cook for us so that the living arrangements were most agreeable. It lacked only Alessandra to make it seem like home.

Early each morning we would set out for the *bottega*, a chunk of bread and a wedge of cheese in our packets, and we would make ready for the serious work of the design and execution of a huge bronze crucifix.

Donatello was determined that this Padua crucifix, five feet wide and six feet tall, would reveal the suffering, redeeming Christ and not the peasant who carved it. He was already at work on his design.

He worked well and seemed not to be yearning for Agnolo and I wondered where his old madness had gone. I wondered too if they were meeting privately. But where? And, with Agnolo in Prato, how could this be possible? Perhaps he had cast the boy aside at last. I resolved to keep a keen eye. But was there ever an eye keen enough for the duplicities of Agnolo?

Well before the *bottega* was set up and ready for the casting of a bronze Christus, there arrived a huge shipment of iron—some forty-six pounds—for the cross itself and, even before that could be packed away for later use, there came another shipment—wax, this time—for use in creating the *bozzetto* of the corpus. The Operai of the Basilica were determined to get the best from Donatello.

"They have anticipated your needs," I said.

"They have heard I'm *intricato*."

"They have heard you like to work hard."

"They think that if I have at hand all the material for the crucifix I will not easily walk away from it. They know me little."

I was unsure what he meant by this. "You have iron and wax in abundance," I said, "and you have your little house and a fine *bottega*." Still he did not respond. "We are well settled in Padua, I think."

"It is not Florence."

"Do you miss it?"

He thought for a while and said, "I miss him."

"He is well settled too."

"But in Prato."

"You will work better without him."

"If I can work at all."

But over the coming months he did work and he worked well, his longing for Agnolo caught up into his creation of a Christus that had suffered physically and in his heart as well. Love rejected. Hope betrayed. A Christus whose face is a map of disappointment and despair.

Donatello took on two new apprentices, young boys more re-markable for their strength than for their beauty. He hired three new assistants, men as experienced as Pagno and I, and he turned over to them the heavy work of casting and assembling. The chasing and polishing he reserved for himself.

In this way it was not long before the iron cross was cast and gilded. The corpus of the Christ was cast in four pieces, a miracle of detail and exquisite in finish. The torment he has suffered is evident in his face. His cheeks are sunken, his eyes hollowed, and his mouth hangs slightly open as if he has only now ceased to gasp for breath. The hairs of his beard are modeled flawlessly and the hair of his head is pulled back to reveal the strain in his neck as his head falls forward and to one side. The body of the Christ, broken though it is, remains perfect in its bones and sinews. He is naked, his private parts barely visible, a shaming to our eyes.

Donatello has caught the moment of death in the timeless act of martyrdom. Here truly is a man crucified by our sins. Brunelleschi would look upon this crucifix with wonder and admiration.

Even before the crucifix was finished, the marvel of it had spread throughout the city. Donatello was the genius of our age. There was no sculptor who could compare. He must remain forever in Padua.

The formal commission for the equestrian Gattamelata—and the money to execute it—followed fast upon news of the crucifix. Even before Donatello could give thought to this new commission—a marble tomb surmounted by a horse and rider in bronze, nearly twelve feet long and thirteen feet high—he was visited by another, even greater commission. He was to create a new high altar for the Basilica, with statues of six saints and the Virgin Mary.

Money poured in for these commissions. Our *bottega* expanded to include two shops adjacent to the Piazza Sant' Antonio. A new and enlarged foundry was created from another two shops near the expanded *bottega*. Skilled workmen were hired to do construction along with workmen who specialized in the use of wood and wax and bronze. By the feast of Epiphany 1447 there were some fourteen men employed in our *bottega*, along with one woman—Ria Scarpetti—an Amazon the size of Michelozzo who was hired for her expertise in the pouring of bronze.

All this expansion of workers and work place consumed much time and Donatello used it to conceive and sketch out designs for a new high altar with bronze and marble panels before and behind it and, surmounting the altar itself, six bronze statues of saints dear to Padua. Seated in the center would be the Blessed Virgin holding the child Jesus. These designs he executed with meticulous care so that sculptors less skilled than himself could follow his precise directions and, under his watchful eye, proceed with the creation of the altar panels first and then the statues that would surmount the altar. The finished work would appear to be from the unique hand of Donatello himself. It was as if the *bottega*—now a small army of assistants—had somehow become an extension of a single mind and heart. With no mention of Agnolo Mattei.

Overwhelmed but completely engaged in the work unfolding in his name, Donatello was not prepared for the news that came on August 14, 1447. Agnolo had once again entered his life.

CHAPTER 36

EARLY IN AUGUST Agnolo was arrested in Prato and would remain in prison there until his fate was determined: exile or death. Donatello decided therefore that I should go to Prato to learn the precise charges against him and then to Florence to seek the intervention of Cosimo de' Medici. At the last moment Donatello said that Pagno would accompany me since he might prove more persuasive with Cosimo. I was offended by this, of course. I had designed and executed the two gold manuscript caskets for either side of his private altar and I had long served as copyist for his most prized Latin scrolls and I had proved useful in transferring his gold florins to San Miniato al Monte only days before his arrest and exile. And he had told me he would not forget me. Did all this count for nothing? But Donatello pointed out that it was Pagno whom Cosimo had requested to pose for the bronze bust that now stood in his great salon and that Cosimo was ever devoted to youth and beauty. I did not point out that at thirty-five years Pagno had not been a youth for some time and that Cosimo's love of beauty was limited to bronze and paint and parchment. Instead I offered a grudging, "As you say." Thus it was with no good feeling between us that Pagno and I set out for Prato.

"That bronze bust of you counts for much with Donatello," I said. "Let us hope it counts for as much with my lord Cosimo de' Medici."

"I may yet prove of some use," Pagno replied. And with that said, and pondered, we kept the rest of our thoughts to ourselves.

* * *

WE ARRIVED IN Prato late in the morning of August 17. It was a cool day for August, with a soft blue sky and the promise of more clement weather. There was birdsong and the lowing of cattle in the fields and we found ourselves full of excitement and energy. Suddenly a good feeling sprang up between us.

As we entered the main square, the Piazza San Giovanni, we had our first sight of Donatello's pulpit on which we had both worked but which we had never seen fully assembled. It was a glorious thing, all white marble with a gold mosaic background and a bronze capital. A gigantic umbrella of holly oak spread its shadow over the pulpit and threw into relief the row of seven huge panels where singing and dancing *putti* were praising God for his mighty acts. It was at once both gigantic and airily beautiful, a perfect site for the annual display of the Virgin's sash. Pagno pointed out the *putti* he had carved and, in a moment of truthfulness, admitted how much inferior they were to Donatello's. He expected me to agree, but—as Donatello's bookkeeper and accountant—I was lost in my own thoughts about payment for the finished work. It was now 1447 and Donatello and Michelozzo had still not received their final payment of—I think I remember correctly—some seven hundred lire.

"The rich are just like us, only stingier. They don't pay their bills."

"How can you think of money when you look on something this magnificent?"

"I lack your poetic soul, Pagno. And remember, I keep the books."

And so our mood turned sour again.

✶ ✶ ✶

Pagno and I refreshed ourselves with a tankard of wine before braving the prison. A pretty serving girl lingered at our table, attracted I must admit by Pagno rather than by me, but I fixed her with a look and told her that she was very fair. Pagno seemed mindful only of what lay ahead of us at the prison.

"This is no easy task," I said, trying to put aside the sour mood.

"It's for Donatello. We owe him much."

We drank some more. The serving girl flashed me a generous smile.

"You were ever close to him. To Agnolo, I mean."

"And you were his brother." Pagno laughed a little to let me know he was joking.

"*Attenzione!*"

"He's of an age when he should have put all this behind him."

I passed up the easy joke of "behind him" and said, "He has thirty-three years now. He is the age of Jesus."

We pondered this sobering thought and had another tankard of wine.

"It's time," Pagno said. "We must look in on our brother prisoner."

We finished our wine and made ready to go but first I asked the serving girl her name and she replied, "Marguerita" with such sweetness that I knew she would let me purchase her affection for an hour or an evening. I told her I hoped I would see her again.

The prison was located just off the Piazza San Giovanni. It was a makeshift affair, a series of cells in the basement of the Palazzo Pretorio, the ancient castle that served as government offices for the Podestà. We approached the gate and explained that our desire was to speak with a prisoner. The guard at the door was unoccupied and free to make difficulties about our request.

He asked if we were the prisoner's lawyers and, since we were not, did we come with governmental authority? Were we representatives of the Podestà or the Otto di Guardia? Were we relatives of the prisoner?

"He is my brother," I said. "In a sense."

"In a sense?"

"We were raised by the same parents. I had a different father."

"So you are half-brothers?"

"In a sense."

"What was your brother's alleged crime?"

"Sodomy."

He gave a half smile at this. "Not a first charge, I think."

"There have been several charges."

"Torture perhaps. Perhaps death."

"We would like to see him."

"You can hope for exile."

"If we could see him . . . ?"

Pagno slipped a silver florin into his hand and the guard nodded, satisfied, and led us down a steep flight of stairs to the prison cells.

The air was cold and stank of sweat and urine with hardly any light to see by. There was the prison noise you would expect—fighting and cursing—but as the guard appeared leading two strangers the cells nearest us fell quiet. Our eyes adjusted to the gloom and we could make out cells full of prisoners, ten or twelve to each cell. They were starved-looking, lost behind their iron bars.

"Mattei!" the guard shouted. "Agnolo Mattei!"

There was no immediate response and so the guard said, "He is not here," and turned to lead us out.

"Agnolo!" I called out and again, "Agnolo!" One of the prisoners shouted, "He's here," and pointed to what looked like a pile of rags beneath a bench.

Agnolo got up slowly from the floor and approached the bars where we stood waiting. He clung to the iron grill for support and the other prisoners gathered around him to listen in. "Twenty minutes," the guard said and left us.

Agnolo stared at us with glassy eyes, empty. I could hardly bear to return his gaze. He was filthy, of course, and he looked near death. He was so thin that the flesh seemed to have fallen away from his body leaving only a skeleton. His eyes were sunk deep in his head and his cheekbones appeared about to poke through the flesh. I thought of my Franco Alessandro and his five arrests and I prayed that he was not again in jail.

Agnolo coughed and for the first time I felt pity for him.

"I knew you'd come," he said and, reaching through the bars, he took my hand in his. "You are a true brother."

"Are you well?" Pagno asked nervously and I looked at him as if he were mad. "I mean, have they set the charges against you? And can we help?"

"My friend," Agnolo said. "My true friend."

"The charges," I said. "What are the charges against you?"

"The charge is rape. But the boy offered himself. I paid. It was not rape."

"Was he a boy still? Was he underage?"

"He was fifteen. And willing. He gladly took money, but after his arrest he gave up my name. It was his father who claimed the act was rape."

"So do they all," one of the prisoners said, leaning on Agnolo's shoulder. "We are worth more to them in fines than what we pay to fuck them."

One-fourth of the sodomite's fine was paid to the anonymous denouncer. Everyone knew that.

"We want to get you out of here, rape or not," Pagno said. "We are going to seek powerful intervention. In Florence. You know the man. Do not mention his name here."

"Is it Cosimo?" Agnolo asked. "If it is Cosimo he will surely help me."

The prisoners looked at one another, surprised.

"Tell him I too am innocent of rape," a prisoner said.

"And I."

"And I."

"We need the name of the boy's father," I said. "Whisper it to me."

He whispered the name of Rinaldo di Bino and I had him repeat it for surety and I turned to leave. I was surprised to see Pagno lean against the bars and kiss him lightly on the lips, like a saint with a leper.

We retraced our steps down the corridor and up the stairs where the guards saw us out.

✳ ✳ ✳

Pagno thought to set off at once for Florence but I wanted to linger in Prato for the rest of the day. In truth I wanted to revisit the Tintori where the wool dyers worked at their boiling vats and I wanted to revisit the Camposino San Paolo where I had first met Maria Sabina and, yes, I wanted to revisit Marguerita, the willing serving girl from the *taverna*, and have sex with her.

"At a time like this?"

"We would be late getting to Florence if we left right now and besides Prato is my home city. I served as a Brother of Saint Francis here."

"But you want to go whoring, Brother Luca."

"I am a weak man. I confess it."

Pagno was defeated by this and said simply, "As are we all."

So we visited the cathedral and studied the outdoor pulpit again for a long time and then Pagno accompanied me on a walk through the Tintori and the Gualdimare, with a pause I did not explain at the ruined houses in the tiny Camposino San Paolo. I said an Ave there for the repose of the soul of Maria Sabina and another for the good health of my wife Alessandra. Pagno was surprised to see me mumble my prayers and make my sign of the cross because, though he did not say so, he had come to think I was without religious feeling.

"Alessandra lived here," I said. "My wife."

Pagno nodded, given over to his own thoughts.

We returned to the cathedral, and as it grew dusk we found an inn just off the Piazza San Giovanni and rented a room for the night. We sat down to a trestle table and were brought a stew of lamb and vegetables and some stout bread. We ate in silence.

"I can think only of that boy," Pagno said, and pushed aside his half-empty plate. "He looks to be dying. All bones and misery. He stinks of death."

"He is in prison. And he is thirty-three."

"He was uncommonly fair at sixteen," he said.

"I thought at that time that he was . . . special to you. You seemed always to have a smile and a good word for him and more than once I saw you giving him money."

He said nothing for a while, merely toying with the spoon in his empty bowl. "Yes, I purchased him. More than once. I was but twenty-two years of age, and curious. And as I said, he was very fair at sixteen." There came into his face the flicker of a smile.

I was astounded. Here was Pagno who was so concerned about sin when we went whoring and yet now he calmly admitted to having purchased the sad favors of a wanton boy and seemed to think it a small thing and no sin at all.

"And was that not sin?"

"Oh yes. And I knew it at the time. But it is a common sin among men our age who cannot afford to marry and whose blood is up and who do not frequent the brothels."

"But it is a better sin, and more wholesome, to fuck a woman."

He turned away from the raw edge of my language.

"It is what God intended," I said.

"God intended charity and justice, only that. But he understands our weakness, as you yourself say."

For some reason I was deeply moved by what he said—only charity and justice—and so I made light of his words. I pushed back my bowl and emptied my tankard of wine. Deliberately raw, I said, "It is time for me to get some charity and justice of my own," and I touched myself there where I had already begun to get hard.

Pagno shook his head in disgust and got up from the table.

"We leave at first light tomorrow," he said.

I set off to find Marguerita, which was quickly done for she was waiting outside the *taverna* and the evening, though brief, was highly satisfying.

The next morning at first light Pagno and I set off for Florence.

PAGNO HAD PRIVATE audience with Cosimo de' Medici while I waited in an anteroom so dim they had lit candles. When they finished talking, Cosimo escorted him out and greeted me warmly. He promised to do all that was possible, he said, but laws must be observed and must be seen to be observed. But for Donatello's sake and to honor that bronze statue in his garden he would do all he could to assure that Agnolo suffered no permanent harm.

He did not say that he would intervene in the local justice system of Prato so that in the end Agnolo would walk free—exiled but free—and ready once more to become the central burden of our lives. But it was so.

As for me, I had taken to heart Pagno's talk of charity and justice and, mindful of Alessandra's long patient love, I had decided I must sign the papers that would set her free.

"We have done well," I said. "It has been a good marriage."

"We had four sons," she said.

"And Donato Michele will be a priest."

She began to cry softly. I knew why.

"You cannot blame yourself . . ."

"I cry for the two babies," she said. "And for Franco Alessandro."

She had loved them well, all of them, I told her.

"And you," she said.

She put her hand in mine, but kept me at a little distance.

"And now that he is gone—my Franco Alessandro—I have an ill life. Only think, Luca. You will have such a busy life away in Padua, a good life, you will have Donato and Pagno and Michelozzo and . . ."

"And Agnolo," I said with a grimace. "Always Agnolo."

"I ask only that you set me free to be a nun," she said.

"It is what I want and need," she said.

"Is it so much to ask?" she said.

I looked at her with longing.

"It is God's will," she said finally and her voice was sad and bitter.

In her words I heard the words of Franco Alessandro and for a moment I knew and understood. I kissed her softly and told her that God desired charity and justice and so I would set her free. That night we slept close, touching, and I did not lay hands on her.

It was a bright, clear morning with no cloud in the sky when I said good-bye to Alessandra and left for Padua. The year was 1447.

CHAPTER 37

Cosimo de' Medici knew the true cost to Donatello of his great works and it was on his behalf that Agnolo was freed from prison.

Donatello could not work—Cosimo understood this—while Agnolo was shut up from the light, languishing in a dark cell. And so through his quiet intervention Agnolo was spared a flogging—he would not have survived it—and was sent from the Prato prison directly into exile in Padua. Donatello accepted legal responsibility for Agnolo's behavior while in the first year of exile and he welcomed him into his little house. Indeed, he assigned him my room and in great discomfort I shared my bed with Agnolo until the feast of the Epiphany on 8 January when, complaining of my restlessness and my snoring, Agnolo moved from my bed to Donatello's where he could sleep in peace. Or so he claimed.

Ever the spy, I studied Donatello with a sharp eye for changes in his behavior, but there were none that I could see. He was every day caught up in some detail of the chasing and polishing of the bronze panels and the seven statues for the altar. He seemed to take Agnolo's presence as a given, as if fate had bestowed him on us and our only task was to see that he ate and slept and put some flesh on his skeletal body. Agnolo came to us truly ill. He was so thin I could count the ribs in his chest. Now that he was clean and no longer dressed in rags, I would have expected him to look more like his old self. He was lazy, of course, and much given to lying in bed, but I could see in him unfeigned exhaustion, the way he doubled in two during his coughing spells and the way he dragged himself to the table and forced himself to eat. He ate but little. And he slept only in fits. His hair was lank and stringy and, though his tunic and stockings were clean, they were never neat. He seemed not to care any longer how he looked. At thirty-three years he appeared to be dying.

Meanwhile all around us things were happening that would come to shape our lives and we remained unknowing.

* * *

In 1447 Venice broke off its alliance with Florence when the condottiere Galleazo Maria Sforza, a friend of Cosimo de' Medici, declared himself Duke of Milan and took the throne by force. Sforza was an old enemy of Venice. The new alliance of Florence and Milan was good for the merchants of Florence but suddenly the Medici banks in Venice were forced to close and Florentine citizens were expelled from Venice and its provinces. An undeclared war existed now between the two great republics of Florence and Venice.

For more than forty years Padua had been under Venetian rule and Padua had become, by association, a Venetian city. Suddenly Padua welcomed the Albizzi, the Peruzzi, the Strozzi, and other noble families exiled by Cosimo de' Medici after his return from exile. These families, gathered together, began to realize the force of their numbers. They appealed to the Holy Roman emperor to dissolve the new union between Florence and Milan. They agitated for open war against Florence.

They would do anything in their power to destroy the Medici, even to the gradual picking away at the integrity of old friends. Even so eminent a friend as Donatello di Betto Bardi, *orafo e scharpellatore straordinario*. And sodomite.

The friend of my enemy is my enemy as well.

By 1447 our *bottega* in Padua had become a world of its own and it existed for one purpose only: to present to the city a completely new altar, with panels of bronze and marble and seven bronze statues, all complete and flawlessly finished . . . and this to be accomplished by 13 June 1448, the Feast of Sant' Antonio. It was impossible of course but it was the genius of Donatello to accomplish the impossible. Our specialized workers now included five principal assistants and at times as many as eighteen people were at work in the *bottega* and the foundry.

The rush to completion left everyone exhausted—even Ria Scarpetti, with her Amazonian strength—and it became clear that the altar itself would have to be a temporary structure. The bronze panels had been cleaned and polished and enhanced with gold, but none of the seven statues had been properly chased and Donatello was displeased to be revealing this uncompleted masterwork to the public. Nonetheless 13 June was the feast of Sant' Antonio, the day agreed upon, so in early June all the statues and the panels and the marble carvings were mounted on a provisional altar and the basilica was thrown open to the public. The effect was overwhelming to everyone except Donatello. He could see at once that the mad rush to completion had left his great design unrealized.

Now a stone framework for the altar became the focus of his attention. He hired the expert stoneworker Niccolò da Firenze and his two young assistants Meo and Pippo to replace the altar's eight wooden columns with marble ones, four of them fluted and the other four pilasters. He ordered steps for the altar in red and white marble with terracotta ornaments on the risers and he had these painted and gilded. By 13 June 1450, again the feast of Sant' Antonio, the finished statues had been mounted on the new and permanent altar and the Basilica was once more thrown open to the public. It was the wonder of the age.

The great Florentine families exiled to Padua did everything they could to encourage war between Venice and Florence. The Peruzzi, the Strozzi, and in particular the Albizzi invested what was left of their fortunes in pitting Venice against Florence, the Doge against Cosimo. Venice, however, was troubled by its ever precarious hold on trade with Constantinople and, like Naples in the south, chose to threaten war while holding on to the tenuous peace that made continued trade within Italy possible.

Meanwhile just as England longed to possess France, France began to measure its territorial ambitions in Italy. It had long desired to possess the Kingdom of Naples and now the undeclared war between Venice and Florence opened the possibility for King Charles of France to lay claim to the throne of Naples. At this moment Cosimo appealed to Charles for protection. No good could come of this.

✶ ✶ ✶

By 1450 the major work for the Basilica was behind him and the great bronze Gatamellata lay ahead. He paused to draw breath and look around him. How could so much work have been accomplished in so short a time? It should not have been possible of course and it would not have been possible to any artisan save Donatello. He was at this time sixty-four years of age, a small man of immense strength of mind and body, and though his eyesight had begun to fail a little, his hands remained strong and certain and he could carve better in this his old age than most sculptors at the peak of their powers. Also he had chosen his assistants with care and wisdom. And he was happy.

He was happy because his work had gone well and because he was surrounded by artisans he loved and respected and because at his little house off the Piazza Sant' Antonio were the men he most trusted, Pagno di Lapo and myself. There too was the great burden of his life, the other half of his soul, the unremitting source of his joy and his grief, Agnolo Mattei, once the young bronze Medici boy and now a man well advanced in the process of decay.

CHAPTER 38

From the start Agnolo complained that he could not sleep. He would lie on his back all night staring into the dark in a waking dream of horror and abandonment. These were dreams of prison in which he was made cruel sport. He was threatened with the rack and the strappado. He was put to the water torture until he could no longer breathe. He was beaten and raped. He knew he was awake but these horrors visited him nonetheless and in the morning he was sore and exhausted and, though starving, could not bring himself to eat.

During that time when I was forced to share his bed—*my* bed long before it was his—he complained that I kept him awake with my snoring, that I tossed and turned all night, that I took up too much space. To be sure, I took up more space than he since he was no more than a skeleton. We were both given respite when Donatello said, "Enough," and took him to his own room and his own bed.

Agnolo began to sleep a little and, with sleep, he managed to eat something at each meal. Over the next months he put on weight and his bones no longer seemed about to pierce the skin. He was clean and well-dressed. He coughed less. He was still very thin but he had regained some strength and talked of returning to his craft of wool-carding. Donatello urged him to stay at home and regain his strength. There would always be time for wool-carding.

* * *

Agnolo began to appear at the *bottega* late each afternoon to see how our work progressed. He was greatly intrigued by the stone-worker specialists, Niccolò da Firenze and his two comically-named assistants Meo and Pippo. Meo and Pippo were scarcely more than boys, and they responded with warmth to Agnolo's interest in them. He was known as Donatello's favorite, after all. They struck up a friendship—Meo and Pippo and Agnolo—and their common jest was who would be first to bed the giantess Ria Scarpetti. Or to scale the Alps, as they called it. Ria Scarpetti knew of this because Agnolo made a point of telling her so and in truth she found them amusing. She fell into an odd companionship with Agnolo. He possessed this incomprehensible ability to interest men and to charm women. In an earlier age, they would say he was possessed by the devil.

✳ ✳ ✳

My ROOM WAS separated from Donatello's by a thin wall. I had trouble falling asleep nights as I listened for sounds from next door. I could almost hear them breathing. And then the crickets would begin their metallic rubbing and the frogs would croak and go on croaking and I would fall asleep. Sometimes in the night I would wake up to the sound of murmured conversation, light laughter, a sigh or a groan. I listened. I strained to hear their words but I could never make out more than the edge of a word here or there, uncompromising but disturbing nonetheless. The words exchanged in bed are always true.

I had a talk with Agnolo.

"So you are sleeping once again? You get a good night's sleep?"

"Donatello does not snore. You snore."

"Nor does he take up all the bed for himself."

He looked at me as if to ask how I might know this.

"I hear you talking sometimes. In the night."

"It is the frogs you hear. We do not talk in the night."

"I've heard you."

"What do we say then?"

"I cannot make out the words. He talks softly. So do you."

"Do you think it is the sound of love? The sound of passion?"

"I say only that I hear you talking in the night."

"We do not talk in the night."

A few days later I tried again.

"Donatello has brought you back to life."

"In every sense."

I could think of nothing more to say.

✳ ✳ ✳

Some weeks later. I had not slept well during the night and I was cross throughout the morning and when I saw Agnolo that afternoon I was filled with deviltry.

"You have struck up quite a friendship with Meo and Pippo."

"They are rude young men. I like them."

"How well do you like them?"

"I've never touched them."

"But they attract you? They are comely boys."

"They are attracted to Ria. They call her the Amazon."

"They talk of scaling the Alps, I hear."

"You hear a great deal. It is only a rough joke of theirs."

"And you fancy them."

"I fancy her, but not in the way you mean. Ria and I are friends."

Two *anormali*, I thought. Two people who never fit in anywhere.

"You are alike in some ways," I said.

"Yes," he said, satisfied, as if he had put me to rout.

✳ ✳ ✳

Those were tumultuous days that led up to 13 June 1450 and the revelation of the finished altar of the Santo. Everyone rejoiced at Donatello's triumph. There was a great feast in the Piazza Sant' Antonio and during the feast Donatello was approached by the eminent Palla Strozzi, in exile from Florence, and was congratulated on the brilliance of the statues and the perfection of the bronze and marble carvings of the altar itself. He had come, he said, to make an offer on behalf of the Doge of Venice. The Doge wished a statue of John the Baptist from Donatello's own hand, freestanding, life-sized, in wood or in marble, whenever Donatello might find the time to execute it. Perhaps sometime within the next year.

"I speak for Venice," he said, "and for the Doge."

We knew then that we were seen as foreigners in Padua and we knew that this request from the Doge was in fact a command and we knew they were watching us.

"But Palla Strozzi is himself an exile," I said to Donatello when he told me of this. "Surely he has no power over us."

"Palla Strozzi is rich and important. He descends from a noble family and he is an intimate of the Albizzi," Donatello said. "He is a dangerous man. I will carve him a John the Baptist he will not soon forget."

✳ ✳ ✳

That night we all retired to our beds and, though it was after curfew, there was still no sign of Agnolo.

The next day was a cool November morning with the slightly bitter taste of fall in the air. Near dawn the last of the frogs stopped croaking and gave over to the roosters. It promised to be a fine fresh day.

I tossed back my covers, splashed my face with water from the basin, and threw on my clothes, ready for a good day's work. But first, I went outside to empty the night jar into the ditch in the garden. Coming back to my room I paused outside Donatello's room and looked in through the slightly open door. He was sitting on the side of the bed, his head in his hands. I was filled with shame for him, a man of sixty-four reduced to tears by a *bardassa* of some thirty-seven years. Or rather by the memory of that boy the man had been, bronze and bold-faced, one hand on his hip and the other on a sword, asking you to admire his naked body, asking you to touch it. I was annoyed, shamed, and I wanted to hurt him. I pushed the door open further.

"So he's not returned," I said.

"I fear for him. Greatly."

"You are well shut of him," I said. "He is ever in the way. He causes enmity between the workers. He keeps Pippo and Meo from their assigned tasks. He . . ." This was folly I knew, but it was time these things were said and as I spoke my voice grew louder. "He drains everyone's energy. He drains *your* energy. You work better without him. I . . ."

"He is my friend." He gave me a fierce look. "He is my friend."

I knew that look and usually it would have made me grovel, but this morning it merely made me angry. "*Attenzione!*" I said and lifted the night jug to him in a kind of toast and went back to my room.

I was at the *bottega* bent over my account books when Donatello arrived to begin the day. We ignored one another for as long as we could. Finally he approached my little table and asked, "Are we well set for money?"

I was all business. I flipped open the Accounts Owed and Received book and pointed to figures I knew he would not take care to understand. "Here are the moneys received for the Crucifix." I ran a finger down a long list of numbers, "and here are our payments to the subcontractors for the temporary altar and here are payments to Niccolò for the stonework on the permanent altar. He pays Meo and Pippo from his own income. And here are the statue payments, some directly to the workers, most of them—here, in this column—directly to you. The current moneys are . . ." But here he interrupted. He had heard more than he wanted to know and still I went on.

"But we are solvent? We have money available for an emergency?"

I knew he was thinking of Agnolo's fine—it would be considerable—if he had disappeared into Padua's prison. My heart softened toward him since I had faced the same emergency many times with my Franco Alessandro and I assured him we had over a hundred florins in the security box at any moment he wished.

"You are a good man, Luca," he said. "If only you were not so hard on your brother."

"He is not . . ."

"Not your brother. I know. But he is mine."

THREE DAYS WENT by and Donatello had stopped eating and sleeping. He should have been working on designs for the Gattamelata but he sat bent over his worktable, his head in his hands. None of us dared talk to him. He was inconsolable. And then on the fourth day a messenger arrived with news that Agnolo Mattei had been arrested and was being held in the Padua prison. His was not a first offense, they knew, but they had no access to records in Florence and they had only an anonymous accusation from the denunciation box and of course the testimony of the boy he was caught sodomizing. It seemed that, for some reason not clear to us, the authorities wished to make a larger case against Agnolo than they were able to. Nobody was allowed to see him. It was only out of courtesy that they informed Donatello of Agnolo's arrest.

"A courtesy," Donatello said and his voice was bitter.

I listened to him and I sympathized and I forced a sigh.

"God will be with him," I said.

"Don't be a fool," Donatello said.

AGNOLO WAS RELEASED from prison a month later. He was a ruined man, a mere sack of bones. All his vanity seemed to have disappeared. He wanted only to be quiet and, he said, to be left alone. In truth he wanted only to be cradled in the arms of Donatello.

Yes, I thought, but only wait until he is well again and see what a cruel turn he will do you.

CHAPTER 39

Donatello lost all interest in the Gattamelata. By 1451 he had completed the design for horse and rider—he had spent weeks studying the anatomy of horses—and he had made a rough sketch of the immense pedestal on which the bronze figures would stand, but now that it was time to make a cast, he turned over the work to bronze experts hired for this purpose and gave his attention solely to the John the Baptist requested by the Doge of Venice.

He was still wavering between marble and wood when good fortune brought him a huge trunk of native walnut, fine grained and with an even texture, perfect for carving the most delicate detail. He sketched Pagno di Lapo and discovered at once that Pagno was all wrong for the Baptist. Donatello's vision was a Baptist burned by the sun and bent under the burden of his message. A desert saint for whom all worldly needs had passed away, the ghost of a man made spirit by the slow disintegration of his flesh and bones. His vision was of Agnolo, not Agnolo the dying *bardassa* but an Agnolo who had been rescued from his excesses, haggard, beaten, and now at last sanctified.

It seemed clear to all of us that Agnolo was dying. His month long imprisonment had failed to finish him off only because he was released in time for Donatello to provide him a doctor's care and good food and a lengthy period of rest. Months passed and he gained back some weight and his cough became less troublesome. He rested much of the day, walking a little in the cool of evening but remaining always close to home. He was ever anxious, looking about in the piazza as if without reason and without provocation he might again be arrested and thrown behind bars. Though Pagno asked him once and I asked him repeatedly, Agnolo would not talk of his time in prison and he would not say how he came to be released.

He was eager to pose again for Donatello though he found it hard to remain in position for very long. He placed a three-legged stool on the posing platform and, with apologies and sighs of regret, he would sit on it when he could no longer stand.

"I am of little help to you," he said.

"You are fine. You are excellent," Donatello said.

I said nothing, but listened and waited for the moment when the change in Agnolo might assert itself. As it assuredly would.

Donatello had finished making sketches and as I looked them over I was astonished to see that he had caught the ghostly eyes in Agnolo's dying face in a way that transformed hunger and lust into a holy austerity. But I wondered if this miracle could survive the transfer to a block of wood. Would not Agnolo by his very nature remain simply Agnolo?

* * *

We walked together in the evening. It was May and there was always a cool breeze and the air seemed to help with his breathing. The frogs had begun to croak and the night crickets rubbed out their crackling music. Clouds scudded before a sickle moon. It seemed a time for trading confidences.

"You are posing well," I said. "Is it not a strain for you?"

"A small matter if I can be of help to Donatello."

"You are a great help. The sketches are miraculous."

"Donatello is miraculous."

This chaff was getting us nowhere.

"He has saved your life."

He said nothing.

"You are free once again. Did you fear never to be free again?"

Still he said nothing.

"You can trust me," I said. "We are almost brothers." There was a silence between us and I added, "My own son was imprisoned for . . . as you know."

"I fear for Donatello," he said.

Now, at last.

"Yes?"

"Because they wish him ill."

"They? Who are they? Do they have names?"

"The Ufficiali di Notte. The *magister* of the Ufficiali."

"The Albizzi? Palla Strozzi?"

He cast me a sharp glance. "You know of this?"

"I know they conspire against Cosimo. And what shorter route to Cosimo than through the heart of Donatello?"

"But what could be gained by ruining Donatello?" He paused to study the stones at our feet. "It makes little sense."

"But you agree that *someone* wants to ruin Donatello," I said. "By any means." I did not say, By means of you. "They are canny and we are simple workmen," I said. "Is it not so?"

"They want me to watch him," Agnolo said. "I promised nothing."

"Watch him? What did they ask? What exactly did they say?"

"They say nothing. They hint at everything. They want only that I should spy on him."

"Spying is betrayal. Spying is detestable," I said. "Judas was a spy."

"I promised nothing," he said.

I pursued this line of questioning further but without profit. He had confessed enough, however, for me to understand the grounds of his release from prison: in return for his freedom he would spy on Donatello.

But there was nothing to fear, I told myself. For many years now Donatello had had no sexual interest other than Agnolo and Agnolo would scarcely give reports against himself.

"I will keep your confidence," I said.

Wʜᴇɴ I ᴛᴏʟᴅ Pagno what I had learned, he was appalled.

"Spy on Donatello? To what end?" Pagno asked.

"To destroy Cosimo."

"Agnolo destroy Cosimo? It is too fantastic," Pagno said. "You read too much in Boccaccio."

* * *

Tʜᴇ ᴄᴀʀᴠɪɴɢ ᴘʀᴏᴄᴇᴇᴅᴇᴅ well. The walnut trunk was immense, close in grain and smooth in texture, and Donatello worked with firm control and a sure hand. He cut with the grain in strong clean strokes. He moved from chisel to chisel as if he had never left off working with wood. It was a wonder to see him carving again, perfectly, even with his imperfect eyesight.

Agnolo posed for him with a rare patience. He tired quickly and he had trouble breathing but he never complained. Nor did he object to being portrayed as ugly. Donatello had dressed him, as he imagined the Baptist would look, in a long, ragged tunic, shredded at the bottom to resemble a tattered animal skin. About his shoulders he wore a rough scarf to shield him against the night cold. His legs and feet were bare. In his raised right hand he clutched a small reed cross and in his left he held a parchment scroll. His matted hair hung in clumps. There was no trace left of that beautiful youth of the Medici boy.

John the Baptist gradually emerged from the walnut trunk while all about Donatello and Agnolo the giant equestrian statue was coming to life as experts in bronze created a giant *bozzetto* from Donatello's designs. Now and then he left off the Baptist to give instructions on the rough casts for the horse and rider, but his first concern remained his wooden statue of the Baptist.

In this year, 1451, tensions between Venice and Florence grew worse and as a result we Florentines were daily less welcome in Padua. Venice closed Cosimo's banks. Cosimo opened new ones in Milan. Venice ended all trade with Florence. Milan took up the trade that Venice left off. Threatened by the Holy Roman emperor, Cosimo decided he had no choice but to request the aid of the king of France, the ancient enemy of the emperor.

My enemy's enemy is my friend.

Cosimo sent ambassadors to France and won a guarantee of trade between the Republic of Florence and the kingdom of France, conceding only that Florence would remain neutral should France some day decide to pursue its claim to the kingdom of Naples. But in the year 1452 that is exactly what France did and the king of Naples marched north against Florence to punish Cosimo for his pact with France. The Neapolitan army swept everything before it as the soldiery penetrated the countryside and harried the outlying villages, plundering and looting. All of Florence trembled under the imminent attack.

Cosimo de' Medici, an old man of sixty-four, took to his bed, broken.

And then when all hope seemed lost, the ferocious French army appeared on the northern borders hastening south to defend the Florentine republic. The Neapolitan army fell into retreat as the citizens of Florence drew a deep breath and offered prayers of gratitude in all of its many churches. For the moment Florence was saved. Cosimo left the city for his fortified villa in the Mugello.

✳ ✳ ✳

Donatello's John the Baptist possessed a soft silken glow before he painted it in brown and gold. In its silken state the statue was ethereal: here was a man no longer of this world. But painted, it became something new, unlike anything Donatello had yet done, unlike anything any of us had seen. At first glance it was supremely ugly: the portrait of a dying man whose flesh was desiccated and whose limbs were mere bone. Sunken eyes. Gaunt cheeks. What in Agnolo Mattei was the wasting of a human being became in John the Baptist the triumph of the spirit over flesh. In him humanity approached the awesome nature of divinity. Ugliness became a new kind of beauty. Weakness became a source of perfection. His statue was an act of faith: Donatello had revealed in it what happens when you draw too close to God.

Yet he did not surrender it to Palla Strozzi or to Venice. He kept it locked in his private chamber, unwilling or unable to let it go.

* * *

DONATELLO NOW DISCOVERED that the Gattamelata was well advanced under the care of Pagno di Lapo and the bronze experts he had hired. It was still able, however, to receive the impress of his own hands. He sculpted a new head for Gattamelata—in a rage he had taken a hammer to the earlier head because it lacked nobility—and he made corrections in the arch of his back and the thrust of his legs and the position of the lance. He took great care too that the front left leg of the horse balanced perfectly on the canon ball beneath it. And then, finally, he turned over the many finished pieces to the care of Andrea del Caldiere who had cast the bronzes for the high altar of the Basilica.

At the same time the immense pedestal was being completed, with its mourning angels and its winged *putti* and the two great marble doors that made it both a monument and a tomb. Donatello was eager to finish the work on schedule and with a perfection worthy of the statues of the high altar. And he was eager to make amends for the time lavished on John the Baptist.

"I AM NO longer so ugly. Say I am not."

"You are transformed. You are made a saint," I said.

"In the statue, you mean."

Donatello had brought the statue of John the Baptist from his locked chamber to examine it once more in the light of day. It stood in the great room of the *bottega* where it had been admired all through the long May afternoon.

Agnolo was contemplating the finished statue with something less than satisfaction. In the year since its completion he had indeed put on weight. He looked more his old self and he had taken on some of his old restlessness. I knew where this would lead.

"You will not go night prowling once again."

"Never. I will die before I go back to prison."

"Well done."

"I have such nightmares," Agnolo said. "No young boy is worth it."

I thought of Franco Alessandro somewhere in Venice in exile. I could not look at Agnolo without thinking of my lost son. I offered each day a small prayer that God would be merciful to him and help him change his ways, though I understood that Franco's ways were not his own, that somehow he could not help himself, that he was fated to be what he was. And which of us escapes our fate?

"Yet you remain restless," I said.

"It is as if I cannot help it. As if I were possessed by the need . . ."

"The need to fuck?"

"The need to love."

"You are a sad creature," I said.

"But I will never suffer prison again," he said.

I did not hate him then. He too was bound by fate.

Is one's fate the same thing as God's will? I wonder about this even today.

IN LESS THAN a year—in 1453—Florence would again face the like-lihood of disaster, this time from the mercenary armies of Venice, and once again it would be God's strange interventions that would save the Republic. In June of that year Constantinople would fall to the Turks and his holiness Pope Nicholas V would call upon all of Christendom—even Venice and Florence—to unite against the Muslim enemy. It was a fine excuse for peace and the renewal of trade. Let us unite to crush the Turks. My enemy's enemy is my friend.

✳ ✳ ✳

IN SEPTEMBER 1453 Gattamelata was mounted on its pedestal and all Padua came to marvel at it.

Donatello's work in Padua was complete.

Mine, alas, was not.

CHAPTER 40

ON 13 JUNE 1453 the Operai of Padua made a great feast to celebrate the completion of the monument to Gattamelata. In truth it would be some months before we packed away all our tools but it was not too early to celebrate Donatello's great accomplishments. An old man of sixty-seven years had achieved what many men together could not have: a new high altar for the Santo, seven statues flawlessly executed in bronze, a crucifix that would be the envy of Brunelleschi, and the largest bronze equestrian statue in the modern world. And all of it so praised that Donatello said he longed to return to Florence where he could hear some honest criticism.

The wine flowed freely long past nightfall and even after all the remaining food had been cleared away. I was light-headed though not really drunk. But Pagno was drunk and in a great sadness at the thought that he was moving toward old age and was still un-married. We decided we should gladden ourselves by visiting the houses of pleasure in the ancient parts of the city. In a feeling of good fellowship we strolled arm in arm through the Piazza delle Erbe with all the expensive whores in their gloves and bells and high-heeled shoes until at last we penetrated the alleys down be-hind the Bo.

We were searching out our old favorites Stina and Katya. Stina was free and delighted to see her Rosso after so long a time but Katya was employed and so I satisfied myself with a new girl from Africa. She was lovely and untrained but we got on well and for the next hour I gave small thought to the curfew or to my account books or to my son Franco Alessandro who, for some reason, always came to mind when I was with a whore. Pagno was waiting for me—he was ever quick with his whores—and we walked back together arm in arm.

We were passing a tavern called the Porco—a haunt of sodomites—when something caught my eye. It was a gold tunic over blue and lilac parti-colored stockings dissolving rapidly into the shadows. Agnolo had been wearing just such a costume at the feast this night and now here he was, dressed like a peacock with his hair neatly done, and at his side a young boy of no more than fourteen. Pagno was given over to singing a rude drinking song and had not caught sight of Agnolo so I did not point him out. And yet I wondered, is this a trap? Has this boy been chosen to seduce Agnolo and then betray him? As a path to Donatello? It was too fantastic to consider reasonably.

"Did you see Agnolo just now, passing behind the Porco?"

Pagno laughed, drunk. "Agnolo is home with Donatello."

"I saw him just now with a young boy."

"He is too old for boys. He should be married. So should we all be married, but Caterina is taken and Ria Scarpetti is an Amazon. You, Luca, you have a wonderful wife. If she enters a convent I will marry her." He thought about that for a moment and then corrected himself. "If you are dead, I mean, then I will marry her. If she will have me." He was drunk and happy.

So I could expect no sensible response from Pagno.

"He was wrong to spoil Franco Alessandro," Pagno said. "I told him I could never forgive him that. It was bad. Bad."

"What are you saying? He spoiled my Franco Alessandro? But when? But how?"

"How? There is only one way, my brother. From behind."

The blood froze in my brain and I felt my left arm begin to tremble and I could barely speak. But I must hold off the fit until I learned the truth.

"When Franco was but twelve, I think. Franco was his first boy, he told me, but it may be he was jesting. Or intended only to shock."

I grasped him by the arm and stopped him where we stood before the Palazzo Raggione. "I'll kill him for this," I said, "if it is true."

"I thought you knew, Luca. It is not as if he raped the boy. The boy was willing. Surely you know that."

I sputtered in anger. No words came to me.

"Still it must be hard to hear your own son spoken of this way. You must forgive me, please, you are my own true brother and it is drink that has so loosened my tongue. Say you will forgive me. Say it."

"It is Agnolo I cannot forgive. I always blamed him for the death of my two youngest. I could not have guessed this other thing."

"It is all poison. All fucking is poison. Say you forgive me. Say it again."

The pain in my head began to lessen and the shaking of my arm had stopped. The brain fit passed as suddenly as it had come on. I felt nauseous of a sudden and I turned to the gutter and vomited up a great quantity of wine. I was calmer now because, awful as it is to think on it, I knew it was true that my pure and beautiful young Franco— even at twelve years—was more than willing, he was eager. Why is he made so? Our God is a mysterious God.

"I forgive you," I said, and I meant both God and Pagno.

"And I forgive you," Pagno said, still drunk and happy.

"Perhaps he will die and we will be free of him at last," I said.

I should have known then that we would never be free of him.

* * *

T HE NEXT MORNING I was quick to notice that Donatello had slept alone. There was no sign of Agnolo. Toward evening I found myself alone with Donatello in the sculpting area of the *bottega* and, as casually as I might, I asked him if he had seen Agnolo this day. He gave me a sharp look and said nothing. He went back to his carving, a *tondo* of the Virgin and Child in white marble.

"I saw him," I said. "Late last night outside the Porco."

"Do you frequent the Porco now?"

I chose to ignore his meaning and said. "It is more than dangerous for Agnolo to be found with a boy, even a willing boy."

"I am an old man. I have some sixty-seven years. Do you suppose my heart stirs in anger at the thought of him with someone else?" He threw down the small-toothed chisel he held in his hand. "Do you think I am such a fool!"

"No, of course not. I . . ."

"Well, I am. My blood no longer heats like yours, like his, and my *cazzo* stays soft even at the touch of him, but I ache for him still. I am an old man, covered in shame. Let me know my shame in privacy, at last."

I left him with his Virgin and Child. In privacy.

Agnolo was gone for two days and then I heard through Pagno that he had reappeared in the *bottega*. It was late in the afternoon of the second day and I lay abed in Donatello's small house, recovering from my brain fit and seeking the calm and cool of my tiny cell. Pagno appeared at my door, cautious.

"Are you all right? Is your brain still under siege?"

"I am as cool as God's justice," I said.

"A frightening thought," Pagno said. "Are you cool enough to meet with him? He has something he wants to say to you."

"About what?"

"He wants to say it to you, not me. He looks very penitent."

"If it is about Franco Alessandro, I will kill him."

"I will go with you. You can kill us both." He left my room and went next door to Donatello while I dressed.

Donatello was lying down on his bed resting and Pagno leaned in at his door. They fell silent as I came from my room and joined them.

"Agnolo is back," I said and Donatello nodded.

"He wants to see me. He wants to tell me something. So Pagno says."

Pagno put his hand on my shoulder and squeezed it gently. "You are a good man," he said. "I will meet you at the *bottega*."

I was suddenly furious and turned on Donatello. "What is this 'good man' business? Am I to be put upon again? Am I once more to play the fool between you and Agnolo?" I did nothing to conceal my anger. It is time he knew, I thought. It is time he came to his senses. "He plays *you* for the fool," I said. He spies on you for them! For the Ufficiali! Here in your own house!"

"Luca *mio*," he said with that soft voice that spoke of understanding and concern. "You must try to understand. You have had so much in life and he has nothing. He has only ever had my love. Do not begrudge him."

"Can you not rid yourself of him?" I was near tears. "Even now can you not make him go?"

"I am tethered to him like a goat at the stake. But I am all he has."

"You are a great artisan. You have created . . ." Tears pricked at my eyes.

"I have created nothing. It is all straw. The heart alone survives."

I wept then as my sense of betrayal overflowed in tears. He got up and poured me a cup of wine.

"Drink this," and after I calmed down he said, as if he were merely thinking aloud, "We love where we must, not where we choose."

✳ ✳ ✳

IT WAS A cool evening for June and the frogs had not yet begun their croaking when I arrived at the *bottega*. A thorn bush grew near the *bottega* door and bluebells poked in from behind it and a soft breeze moved the flowers back and forth. It was the start of a new and gentle season. I sighed for all the fallen things in my life as I raised my hand to knock at the door.

Pagno opened to me with his hopeful, "Come in, come in," and I saw that he had been in conversation with Agnolo when I arrived. No one else was there. Pagno excused himself and went out back to the privy. There was nothing for it but to engage with Agnolo.

"You're out of prison," I said. "It was a short stay this time."

"Any stay in prison is long. Too long."

"But you were gone a single night."

"A single night of—as they call it—interrogation."

"Did they torture you?"

He placed his hand on his privy parts and nodded.

"But you are well. And free."

He nodded once again.

"Can it be true that you played the man with my son?"

He was not surprised I knew this. "It was not what you think, Luca."

"He was but twelve years old. And you had him in that way?"

"It is true, but only that once. And he was willing."

A picture flared up in my brain then: Franco Alessandro at twelve years of age with Agnolo working him from behind, thrusting hard and harder, again and again and again. My mind clouded and I lost balance for a moment and when I came back to myself I realized Agnolo had been saying, "I pray you for pardon," over and again. I steadied myself and sat down at Donatello's work table. We were silent then. There was a great abiding pain in my head.

It grew dark and Agnolo lit the torch that stood by the table. The flame flickered and caught and there was the sudden smell of burnt reeds. The pain grew stronger. I lowered my head to the surface of the table and felt against my face the chisels Donatello had been using for the Virgin and Child. Some sliver of an idea lodged in my brain, but I shook it away and said, "You are a great corrupter of the young, Agnolo."

"For which I beg pardon . . . of you and of God." He was silent then and I rested, my eyes shut against the sight of him.

"It is a greater wrong they ask of me now," he said. I was silent, waiting.

"They ask that I embarrass Donatello."

I opened my eyes and gave him a hard look.

"It is why they let me free. It is the condition on which I stay from prison. It is this or life behind bars. And torture. And death. I cannot. I cannot."

After a long while I asked, "And how are you to embarrass Donatello?"

"It is nothing. It would come to nothing. The whole world loves Donatello. They wish only to get at Cosimo through him."

"Who wishes it? Who are *they*?"

"The Albizzi of course."

"Working through the Ufficiali?"

"Of course."

"And they ask of you exactly what?"

"It is a small thing. That as I sleep with him they arrest us both for sodomy. He would be accused but he would be fined only and let go free. And I would go free. But the scandal would be public and a great hurt to the Medici."

"They would do so much for so little? For a scandal?"

"They believe that such scandals will topple the Medici before too long."

"And you would do this? Be taken in his bed?"

"Tonight. At the fourth hour after curfew."

"Like Judas."

"It is arranged."

"And you tell me this, why?"

"That you may know I do him no permanent wrong. That you understand and forgive me . . . as a brother."

"As a brother."

"Because I know that you alone have loved me . . ."

That sliver in my brain lodged deep and I felt a tingling in my leg that I recognized from old. My foot began to tap tap tap of its own accord and a wet gray mist clouded my vision. I could not catch my breath. I made as if to rise but blood rushed to my head and I fell back in my chair. I tried to cry out but no sound came. And then the pain exploded in my head and I set up such a shout as could be heard throughout all of Padua. It was a roar, wordless, the cry of a beast without tongue, and even before the sound had ceased I snatched up one of Donatello's pitching tools—long and sharpened to a point—and, rising from the table, I lunged at the stuttering Agnolo and drove it in his throat, his chest, his heart until the blood gurgled from his mouth and I stood above him, breathless both of us, the chisel clutched to my bloody breast.

Pagno was there of a sudden, pressing me back against the table, hushing me, calming me. Quickly, deftly, he took another pitching tool and I shrunk away as he cut me with it on the neck and placed the tool in Agnolo's dead hand. He turned to me and said, "He attacked you first. You were defending yourself."

And then the pain in my head overcame all my senses and my left arm fluttered uselessly and my leg gave way and, glad of the oblivion, I fell to the floor beside the body of Agnolo Mattei, brother to no one any longer.

1467

CHAPTER 41

For TWELVE YEARS now I have been held prisoner in the monastery of Santa Croce. In truth I am a prisoner in name only. I am allowed, if I wish, to follow the daily schedule of the Frati Minori. I wear the simple gray gown of the Franciscan novice. I make morning meditation and attend daily mass and sing as many of the liturgical hours as please me. I can gaze upon Donatello's Christ crucified—the one Brunelleschi called a peasant—and I can marvel at the frescoes of Giotto celebrating the life and miracles of Saint Francis. In the morning and evening I walk in the monastery cloisters. I am living the life I would have lived had I never met Maria Sabina and discovered the joys of sexual congress. This is a pleasant incarceration, the only penalty being that I know I am not free. But which of us is free in this life?

My oldest son, Donato Michele, is the Father Superior of the monastery and he is my jailer, a kind, good man without imagination and without malice. He sees me for the murderer I am and the brain-wrecked husk of a man I have become. I believe he loves me and feels sad for my imprisonment, but he has given his heart to God and there is little human love left in him. Mine is a good life, quiet, harmless, silent as the grave that awaits me.

After the murder of Agnolo I thought to find that grave in Padua. I was taken at once to the *stinche* where for six months I awaited trial. The *stinche* is a true prison where brutalized men—some fresh from the rack, some yet unbroken—feed on hatred and anger and guilt till they cease to be men and are merely vessels for pain. I was spared this. My brain was yet addled from the seizure and my left side remained for a time in paralysis, and so I was allowed a cot and a night jar of my own. I was fed on bread and gruel and given two cups of water each day, but the filth and the stench of the prison made me long for death. Nonetheless, as these things will happen, I survived. My strength returned and my brain-fog cleared and I could move about again and even walk. I was able to stand during the long hours of my trial.

I was sentenced to life imprisonment. I had spent six months in the filthy *stinche* before my trial and I spent a year there following it. Before my trial I survived on hope that Pagno di Lapo would continue to perjure himself and swear that Agnolo had struck first, that I had acted in self-defense. He was true to his word, lying boldly before the court, and so my life was spared. Cosimo de' Medici, who had promised he would not forget me, remembered me a year later when the political winds had turned and he was able to have my sentence in Padua commuted to Florence and a lifetime in prison commuted to a lifetime with the Frati Minori of Santa Croce.

And so the death of Agnolo Mattei became for me only a painful memory. For Donatello, however, it was catastrophe. He lapsed into a kind of trance, as if life was too much to bear and only death would satisfy him. It was not like early times when Agnolo would leave him for a passing soldier, nor like later times when Agnolo fled to another city or, worse still, disappeared into prison on some dark night. This was a different kind of trance. Donatello was unable to eat or drink or work. He had no interest in marble or bronze. He prayed each day for a quick death. Michelozzo called for medical help and saw that Donatello was well bled and thoroughly purged but still he did not return to his old self. And then Michelozzo turned to a Doctor Chellini who was famed for his skill at relieving the burdened soul. This doctor gave Donatello herbs and potions and looked into his mind to see why he preferred death to life. He found there only gloom and lost love and anger and so he prescribed work. He commissioned for himself a *tondo* of the Virgin and Child, in bronze, to be executed within the year. And thus he brought Donatello back to life.

In little more than a year Donatello presented him the *tondo* as a gift and with that he returned to his old self and at once set to work. He sculpted—again in wood—his Mary Magdalene in penitence. She is gaunt and terrifying, wasted by fasting and abstinence, a woman who has loved much and whom much has been forgiven. But her face and body are the face and body of Agnolo Mattei. Donatello lost himself in work. He sculpted then the great Judith and Holofernes, in bronze and gilt, and there too you see the face of Judith is the face of Agnolo . . . and Holofernes is Donatello himself.

He would never recover from the life and death of Agnolo and he would never lay eyes on me again.

Nor did Pagno di Lapo. Nor did my wife Alessandra. Only Michelozzo was willing to look again upon me. Pagno, having lied at my trial and thus saved my life, left Padua for Florence and within the year left Florence for Bologna. He wished me well. He sent me a note upon my transfer from the *stinche* of Padua to the monastery of Santa Croce. He said he would pray for me and asked my prayers for himself. He was my true friend—who could have guessed it?—but I fear his compassion is more than human and in the end will prove the death of him.

Alessandra petitioned entry to the convent and, with her dowry of forty gold florins, the price of a slave girl, she was admitted to the Dominican nunnery at Santa Maria Novella where she prays for me. She became Sister Adriana, O.P., a lay sister, allowed to live the spiritual life of the convent and to perform the work duties of a layperson: washing floors, cooking meals, spinning wool. This she saw as the will of God. I think of her often as I lean away from my writing, my eyes tired and my hand stiff. I call up her dear face and body—the young Alessandra when I first knew her—and I pleasure myself as in the old days, but not often and always with a sigh of regret. Sex is not for old men. We are tethered between life and death and sex is unseemly. But then life itself is unseemly and, old or young, we let it pass from us with difficulty and with regret.

Michelozzo alone remains a constant in my life. His eight children—four boys and four girls—are a joy to him. He has designed a new cloister for the Frati Minori of Santa Croce and I see him daily as he executes his plans. It is Michelozzo who by night stole me from my prison here and took me—in a dark cloak, a midnight monk—through the streets to the church of San Lorenzo that I might visit Donatello's tomb. But I get ahead of myself.

I have been here twelve years, writing, copying. While he lived it was the will of Cosimo that I transcribe manuscripts for him and he arranged that Michelozzo bring me the originals and take away the finished copies. At his death, the care of his business and in particular the care of his library was taken up by his son Piero, called *Il Gottoso* for his gouty feet. I copy for him as once I copied for Cosimo. My final brain seizure left my body in large part a wreck. In truth my left side is nearly useless, my hand flopping about of its own accord, but my other side is dependable with a good right hand that is sturdy with a quill and parchment. Indeed my script has grown more fluid and more elegant with the passage of time and I have moved on from Latin texts to the rarer and more complicated Greeks: Plato and *sequaces ejus*, I know them all. In the matter of transcription I have more than satisfied the Medici and it is pleasing to know that many of the rare manuscripts in Cosimo's vast new library have been copied by my hand.

Cosimo died in 1464 and at his great funeral procession—the entire city was in mourning or pretended to be—the Signoria proclaimed him *Pater Patriae* . . . in shame for having sent him into exile and in acknowledgment that he had been friend to philosophers and poets, patron of sculptors and painters and architects, and founder of the greatest library since the fire at Alexandria. He had sponsored the work of Ghiberti and Brunelleschi and Michelozzo, of Fra Angelico and Filippo Lippi and Verochhio, and above all Donatello. He had loved him faithfully to the end and at his death he directed that Donatello be buried in San Lorenzo in a crypt next to his own so that he could be near his friend in death as he had been in life. Piero di Cosimo de' Medici has seen to that.

After Donatello's death in 1466, Piero arranged that all the documents of the *bottega*—notes, sketches, commissions, records of payments made and payments owed—should be delivered to me here in Santa Croce so that I might create a record of the man himself. These documents, along with the many I myself have secreted away, I have arranged in sequence that the reader might know what work Donato did and when he did it and where it rests today.

As to Donatello himself, who could ever recreate him to the life? The facts, yes, I have those in writing. And the documents that date his commissions and record his payments and list his triumphs, but what of the man himself? His passion, his devotion to work, his great rollicking laughter, his kindness, his cruelty, his irreverence, his disdain for the great and the proud, his humble nature and his overarching pride, his sudden rage, his love of children, his patience with them and his impatience with his patrons, his blind fear of failure and his conviction that he could do anything he tried, his loyalty, his generosity of spirit and of mind: Who can capture this? I cannot write his life and so I have written my own and considered his only at a glance, a life caught from the corner of my watchful eye. I asked him once what he thought was Ghiberti's most significant accomplishment and he responded, instantly, "Selling that useless farm land in Lepricino." And when he looked upon Brunelleschi's crucifix, he said, "It is for you to sculpt the true Christ; I am the sculptor of peasants." And in this comment I hear two Donatello's: the humble giver of praise and the other, the confident sculptor who knows that the peasant in Christ is in truth our redemption. How do you capture such a spirit?

Donatello died in his little house on the Via del Cocomero and ascended to his Maker on 13 December 1466. He was perhaps eighty years of age.

He never recovered from Agnolo's death and he never forgave me for causing it. He recovered his health, however, and though his eyesight continued to fail, he went on sculpting—in Siena, in Florence— and his last great works, I am told, are the bronze reliefs of the Passion, Death, and Resurrection of Christ for the pulpit of San Lorenzo. They are rough-hewn bronzes, left unfinished at his death, but as powerful and poignant as anything he ever sculpted. So Michelozzo says. I have not seen them.

Donatello was buried with a royal funeral. Some two thousand Florentines filled the streets for his funeral procession. There were prayers and masses and praise for his completed works, and the feeling that perhaps he had not been rightly appreciated, that with the Medici boy he had changed the shape and nature of sculpture forever, that mere beauty would never again be enough.

How did he go to meet his Lord Jesus? With humility, I think, and with pride for work well done.

And how will I meet my Lord? As a murderer, as a penitent, as a spy. I still cannot imagine he will damn me. I will be one of those ragged street urchins he invites to the banquet at the eleventh hour. And I will eat and drink with him and rejoice that he is merciful.

I had always thought the Black Pest would carry me off but I have come to think—within these celestial prison walls—that it will be a fatal lightning bolt in the brain that will do for me. The brain will crack finally, and the heart as well, and then all will be quiet, everlastingly. And will I at the end remember Agnolo? I think at last I bear him no ill will. I wish to repent invoking his damnation. He was destined to be the life and death of Donatello and who am I to come between that great man and his fate? Perhaps Agnolo too will be at that final feast. If a man loves much . . . And yet . . .

★ ★ ★

Post-scriptum

In the year of our Lord 1467 on the thirteenth day of December Luca di Matteo passed to his eternal reward, taken as he sat writing of the life and works of Donato di Betto Bardi. He dwelt as a prisoner for twelve years in this monastery of Santa Croce and it is a sad and great hurt to record that he died in disgrace, impenitent, and with small remorse for his sins. It is to be hoped that he loved much for it is certain there is much to be forgiven.

May God have mercy on his soul.

Donato Michele di Matteo, OFM

Author's Note

On my first visit to Florence I had the exhilarating experience of seeing Michelangelo's David at the Accademia and later that same day seeing Donatello's David in the Bargello. Michelangelo's deeply moved me but Donatello's was a revelation. It was naked in every sense and seemed to me personal, erotic, a testament to the sculptor's sexual obsession for the teenaged boy he had created. Someone, I thought, should write a novel about it.

I spent years reading in a general way about early Renaissance art, politics and religion, and during those years revisited Florence many times, always with a long stop at the Bargello. In 2006 the John Simon Guggenheim Memorial Foundation awarded me a generous grant that allowed me to spend an extended period in Italy doing research. Research aside, *THE MEDICI BOY* is pure invention, whose purpose it is to entertain, provoke, and disturb. The statue of David is its own narrative.

I want to thank the Guggenheim Foundation and especially Edward Hirsch and André Bernard. And for their generous critical support: Eavan Boland, Edie Wilkie Edwards, Nancy H. Packer, and Arnold Rampersad. And for all those years of faith and patience: my agent, Peter Matson.

A Brief Bibliography

FOR READERS WHO want to know the true history of this amazing period of Renaissance Florence I offer this small list of works to which I've been most indebted in writing *The Medici Boy*.

Bassett, Stephen. *Death in Towns: Urban Response to the Dying and the Dead.* Leicester University Press.

Bennett, Bonnie A. and David G. Wilkins. *Donatello.* Oxford: Phaidon.

Brucker, Gene A. *Renaissance Florence.* University of California Press.

Brucker, Gene A., ed. *The Society of Renaissance Florence: A Documentary Study.* University of Toronto Press.

Cagliotti, Francesco. *Donatello e i Medici, storia del David e della Giuditta.* L. S. Olschki. Studi, 14.

Cennini, Cennino d'Andrea. *The Craftsman's Handbook (Il Libro dell' Arte).* Dover Publications.

Chapman, Hugo. *Padua in the 1450's.* British Museum Press.

Cohn, Samuel Kline. *The cult of Remembrance and the Black Death: Six Renaissance Cities in Central Italy.* Johns Hopkins Press.

Crum, Roger J. and John T. Paoletti. *Renaissance Florence: A social history.* Cambridge University Press.

Duby, G. *A History of Private Life.* Harvard University Press.

Ewart, K. Dorothea. *Cosimo De' Medici.* Cosimo Classics.

Father Cuthbert. *The Romanticism of Saint Francis.* Longmans, Green.

Gilbert, Creighon E. *Italian Art, 1400–1500: Sources and Documents.* Northwestern University Press.

Glasser, H. *Artists' Contracts of the Early Renaissance*. Garland Press.

Greenhaigh, Michael. *Donatello and His Sources*. Duckworth.

Hartt, F. *Donatello: Prophet of Modern Vision*. Abrams.

Hibbert, Christopher. *The Rise and Fall of the House of Medici*. Penguin.

Hoffman, Malvina. *Sculpture Inside and Out*. Bonanza Books.

Janson, H. W. *The Sculpture of Donatello*. Princeton University Press.

Lightbown, R. W. *Donatello and Michelozzo*. Harvey Miller Publishers.

McBrien, Richard P. *Lives of the Popes*. HarperSanFrancisco

Mills, John W. *The Encyclopedia of Sculpture Technique*. B. T. Batsford.

Najemy, John M. *A History of Florence, 1200–1575*. Blackwell Publishing.

Newman, Paul. *Daily Life in the Middle Ages*. McFarland.

Origo, Iris. *The Merchant of Prato: Daily Life in a Medieval Italian City*. Penguin.

Parks, Tim. *Medici Money: Banking, Metaphysics, and Art in Fifteenth Century Florence*. Norton.

Plumb, J. H. *The Italian Renaissance*. Houghton Mifflin

Poeschke, Joachim. *Donatello and His World: Sculpture of the Italian Renaissance*. H. N. Abrams.

Pope-Hennessy, Sir John. *Donatello: Sculptor*. Abbeville Press.

Rich, Jack C. *The Materials and Methods of Sculpture*. Oxford University Press.

Rocke, Michael. *Forbidden Friendships: Homosexuality and Male Culture in Renaissance Florence*. Oxford University Press.

Rosenauer, Artur. *Donatello*. Electa.

Singman, Jeffrey. *Daily Life in Medieval Europe, 1476–1492*. Greenwood Press.

Strathern, Paul. *The Medici: Godfathers of the Renaissance*. Vintage Books.

Turner, A. Richard. *Renaissance Florence: The Invention of a New Art*. Abrams.

Vasari, Giorgio. *The Lives of the Artists*. Oxford University Press.

Waley, Daniel Philip. *Later Medieval Europe, 1250–1520*. Longman.

Walker, Paul Robert. *The Feud That Sparked the Renaissance: How Brunelleschi and Ghiberti Changed the Art World*. William Morrow.

Wirtz, Rolf. *Donatello, 1386–1466*. Könemann.

Ziegler, Philip. *The Black Death*. Harper and Row.

About the Author

John L'Heureux is the author of eighteen books of poetry and fiction. His stories have appeared in *The Atlantic Monthly, Esquire, Harper's, The New Yorker*, and in Best American Stories and Prize Stories: The O. Henry Awards. Since 1973, he has taught fiction writing, the short story, and dramatic literature at Stanford University. His recent publications include a collection of stories, *Comedians*, and the novels, *The Handmaid of Desire* (1996), *Having Everything* (1999), and *The Miracle* (2002).

Photo by Dagmar Logie

An Afterword

"In the courtyard of the Palazzo Vecchio there is a life-size bronze David who has cut off the head of Goliath and places his raised foot on it; in his right hand he holds a sword. This figure is so natural in its lifelike pose and its rendering of the soft texture of flesh that it seems incredible to artists that it was not formed from the mold of an actual body. This statue once stood in the courtyard of the Medici Palace." Giorgio Vasari, *Lives of the Most Excellent Painters, Sculptors, and Architects*, 1550.

The Medici Boy relies for its fictional characters on a fairly long list of historical figures and for its events on several important moments in the history of Florence. For information about these people and events I have depended on a great many historical and literary sources to which I am much indebted. The facts are theirs; the errors are mine.

Here are some thumbnail biographies of a few real people who appear in this novel.

Brunelleschi. (1377–1446) Filippo Brunelleschi was one of the foremost architects and engineers of the Italian Renaissance. He designed and executed the dome of the Florence Cathedral. He had a lifelong friendship with Donatello and a lifelong feud with Ghiberti.

Cennino Cennini. (1370–1440) Cennino d'Andrea Cennini—a student of Gaddi—composed *Il libro dell'arte*, an early how-to book on the techniques and ambitions of late medieval art. *The Craftsman's Handbook* is still in print.

Cosimo de' Medici. (1389–1464) Cosimo di Giovanni degli Medici, founder of the Medici dynasty, was first of the de facto rulers of Florence during the Italian Renaissance. His vast new wealth derived from his banking business and by the 1430s he came to be seen as a threat to the old wealth of the Strozzi and the degli Albizzi. He is the archetypal patron of painters, sculptors, architects of the early Renaissance.

Donatello. (1386–1466) Donato di Niccolò di Betto Bardi—goldsmith, artist, sculptor—carved the way from Gothic classicism into early Renaissance modes of realism and human emotion. His nude David, the first freestanding bronze in a thousand years, is sometimes said to have altered the history of Renaissance sculpture.

Ghiberti. (1378–1455) Lorenzo di Bartolo, later called Ghiberti, trained as a goldsmith and at age twenty-three defeated della Quercia and Brunelleschi in a contest to create the monumental bronze doors of the Cathedral Baptistry. Brunelleschi never forgave him.

Michelozzo. (1396–1472) Michelozzo di Bartolomeo Michelozzi. Intimate friend and sometime partner of Donatello, he was a goldsmith, sculptor, and architect. He followed Cosimo into his Venice exile in 1433 and designed and built the library of San Giorgio as Cosimo's gift of thanks to his hosts. Michelozzo designed the Palazzo Medici-Riccardi and rebuilt the Convent of San Marco. He married at age forty-five and fathered eight children.

Pagno di Lapo Portigiani (1408–1470) worked as an assistant in the *bottega* of Donatello and later became a minor decorative sculptor in Bologna. His one undisputed work is the marble relief of the Madonna and Child in the Museo del Duomo in Florence.

Piero di Jacopo, a coppersmith from Bologna, was found guilty of sodomizing and committing violence upon a ten-year-old boy. He was burned at the stake in the district of Santa Croce on October 1, 1429.

Rinaldo degli Albizzi (1370–1442) belonged to the Florentine nobility. With assistance from Palla Strozzi, he waged a lifelong conspiracy against Cosimo de' Medici, whom he saw as an upstart and potential dictator. He sought Cosimo's death but managed to get only his exile. Cosimo, upon his return from exile, dealt softly but swiftly with the Albizzi conspirators.

Alberti, della Robbia, della Quercia, Fra Angelico, Filippo Lippi, Masaccio, Uccello, contemporaries and friends of Donatello, were among the principal artists of the Italian Renaissance. They appear only nominally in *The Medici Boy*.